Emergence

Nick M. Lloyd

Dear Alex
Good luck in parenthood
hope you enjoy it!
& the book
Nick

First Edition

Published in 2014

Copyright © 2014 by Nick M Lloyd
www.nickmlloyd.com

Art Work by Jay Aylmer at The Potting Shed Design
www.thepottingsheddesign.com

ISBN: 978-0-9930779-0-6 (Paperback)

To those for whom fear and wonder come hand in hand… be brave.

ACKNOWLEDGEMENTS

Above all others has been my wife, Therese. She has been my emotional foundation; without her good humour and encouragement this book would never have been finished.

Secondly, my kids, who have been simply amazing, wonderfully supportive, and accepting of my quirks.

Not far behind, and in no particular order, a heartfelt thanks to the following:
James (elf), Gus (reader), David (blockade runner), Sally (tough love), Phill (geek), Willis (cuz), Mum (dearly loved), Dad (dearly missed), Jay (boy-wonder), Ems (blurber), Tony R (counsellor), Faye (agent), Bruce (professor), Guido (eWiz), Jindy (writer), Fergus (information crystalliser), Andy M (playwright & coach), Paul (open-handed), Krishen (friendly pedant), and Mark F (coach).

I have been very well supported.

PROLOGUE

February 1965

Escape was the only thing on Bill's mind as he ran through the dark backstreets. Police sirens were closing in. He'd not seen an actual police car yet, but it was just a matter of time.

Can't stop.

His legs ached as he pushed himself onwards. He turned another corner fast. And fell, losing his footing on the wet pavement. Pain shot up through his hip as it took the brunt of his fall. At that moment, the headlights of a police car swept around the corner behind him. Gritting his teeth, he scrambled through a hedge into the garden beyond, branches ripping into the skin on his face and hands.

Bill crouched down, stock-still, willing them not to see him. The police car flashed past without slowing. Recovery was quick; he took a few deep breaths and started to run.

Have to warn Tom.

He knew physically getting to Oxford would be beyond him; there were simply too many people chasing him, but a phone call might be possible. Taking a quick look around, he recognised a side road that led up to Hampstead Heath. He had friends close by who would help.

In almost total darkness, his hip pain gone, Bill powered up the hill towards the heath. As he reached the entrance, he forced himself to slow down. He peered into the gloom of the heath. Perhaps he had a chance in there. He looked back down the road; there were no more vehicles yet.

About to move off, he froze at the unmistakeable sound of a gun being cocked. A rough voice came out of the darkness.

'Stop there and you won't get hurt.'

Dread overcame him. His legs, so strong when running, went weak. It was all he could do to simply stand upright. A shape appeared - one of the soldiers from the laboratory - with a revolver pointing directly at Bill's face. Neither the revolver nor the voice wavered.

'Okay, Bill, face down on the ground while we wait.'

He felt sick. *Can't go back.*

The soldier turned on the radio on his belt; it crackled.

Bill considered his position. Could he escape into the darkness? But the revolver pointed directly at him drained his hope.

'I said lie down.'

Suddenly, the radio crackling loudly, a fragment of conversation. '… closing in …'

Although distorted, Bill recognised the voice, his nausea got worse. It was the psychotic programme director. A wave of hopelessness washed over Bill, and he lay down on his front. Now the pain from his hip, and his bloodied face and hands, made itself known. He was shaking badly.

They'll do the experiments again.

Lying face down on the ground, Bill remembered the electric shocks and involuntarily retched up. He wiped the vomit away from his mouth.

A few moments later, he realised the radio was still crackling and the soldier hadn't spoken yet. He looked up, just as the soldier collapsed to the ground with a thud.

There'd been no gun shot and nobody else was around. *What just happened?* A flash of headlights. A few hundred metres away a car was coming up the hill. Adrenaline surged through him. Fear pushing him onwards, Bill jumped up and stumbled deeper into the woods.

Once amongst the trees his strength began to build, and soon he was moving fluidly. He headed across the heath. Friends in Highgate would have a phone he could use to warn his son. Behind him, there were some muffled explosions, and more police sirens. But, as he moved steadily eastward, the sounds of pursuit faded away.

This deep, amongst the trees, it was pitch black. Bill slowed his pace to a jog, listening carefully and looking around for lights. He picked his way through the trees for a few minutes. A dull glow grew ahead of him; he could see the streetlights of Highgate up ahead – a glimmer of hope. He just had to cross the final field.

With the end in sight, Bill quickened his pace. Escape. He'd be out of the country before they could stop him. Then revenge. Suddenly there was stinging pain in his leg. He reached down instinctively to rub it. *A bee?* His leg went momentarily numb, and collapsed under him. Bill fell.

Got to warn Tom.

Again, his strength returned quickly. He got up. But almost immediately upon getting back his feet, another sting hit him in the small of his back. He stumbled; he could tolerate that one. He staggered on. Then there was a muffled shriek close behind him and a pain bloomed in his skull; he fell. Heavy footsteps were closing in as Bill struggled to remain conscious. *What?* Disorientated, Bill pushed himself to his knees. *Have to get away.*

Footsteps were very close now, and a new background noise – a mechanical humming. Still on his knees, Bill half-turned and watched with mounting terror as a shape loomed out of the darkness.

In the gloom, a hand with six fingers reached down towards him; the hand was large, very large. His eyes lingered on it for a few seconds, then his attention was drawn to the muscled forearm disappearing into a heavy sleeve. Horrified, but unable to look away, his gaze continued up the arm to a chest the width of two normal humans; and then the creature's head: green, enormous eyes and carnivorous teeth.

Bill tried to scream, but the sound wouldn't come. Terror froze him as the creature took a firm hold of his coat and effortlessly lifted him into the air.

At first light the next day, the hunt for Bill continued. Police with dogs were drafted in, but they hunted in vain. No trace of Bill was found. He'd disappeared, along with the soldier who had been patrolling the southwest side of Hampstead Heath.

CHAPTER 1

<u>*October 2015*</u>

Jack Bullage felt slightly nervous as he walked through the restaurant. Looking around, he could see people crammed around wooden tables laden with steaks, red wine and heavy looking cutlery. The waitresses, with good-natured smiles, ran around and took orders against the clamour of bar-room bustle. Jack looked back towards the door; his two business partners were following. *They look relaxed – good.*

A squeeze on Jack's hand brought him back to the present. In fact, he had three of the firm's directors with him tonight.

Sarah smiled at him and, leaning in close, whispered in his ear, 'It's all fine, love.'

'The next few weeks are going to be critical...'

'It's fine. They love you... and your plan.'

As they sat down, the waitress brought their drinks through from the bar. Jack reached for the bottled water on the table. 'Welcome, gentlemen, and Sarah. This is mostly just a social visit to the infamous Spatchcock Saloon, but if you have any concerns about the deal then speak out.'

One of the guests murmured, 'Don't worry Jack, we're on board.'

Jack let out a quiet sigh of relief. *That's it?*

Under the table, Sarah gave Jack's hand another squeeze and when he met her eyes, she smiled broadly. 'So, Jack – what are you having?'

Jack perused the menus, then winked at Sarah.

Sarah arched an eyebrow but remained silent.

After a few minutes, the waitress returned. Jack waited for the others to order, in each case making a supportive remark on their choice. Then he leant forward. 'Would you be prepared to arrange a fight between your two biggest lobsters and then cook the winner?'

The waitress laughed. 'So you want a big lobster?'

Jack put on his mock hurt expression. 'Have you heard it before?'

'I don't hear it every day.'

'Well, I don't come here every day.' Jack laughed, and the waitress disappeared. He raised a glass to his other dining companions. 'A toast to our dynamite CFO, Sarah Jukes.'

Glasses were raised. Sarah leant over to Jack and whispered in his ear. 'In polite company I'd probably prefer you referred to me as dynamic rather than dynamite.'

Jack turned and gave Sarah a quick kiss on the cheek, noticing out of the corner of his eye the other two discreetly looking away. Sarah mocked a scandalised face.

With the tacit agreement to the deal from the two directors secured, Jack felt very relaxed. He regaled the table with stories, rumours and lies, until the waitress politely told them their table was promised to a late sitting. Sarah flashed out the company Amex Platinum; then they all made their way, a little unsteadily, into the car park.

The stretched executive BMW was waiting. As they approached the car, the chauffeur jumped out and opened the doors. Jack organised the seating and then climbed into the back, between Sarah and one of the others.

Sarah made a fuss of adjusting her seatbelt before cuddling into Jack. 'You're a bit skinny, but I'll make do.'

Before settling back in his seat, Jack passed his iPod to the chauffeur. 'The Relax Jack playlist please, and we must be home before the last track finishes.'

Moments later, the soporific music drifted around the car's warm interior and Jack smiled contently. Sarah opened her eyes for a split second and ran her hand through his hair. Jack returned the favour, caressing her cheek. Sarah mumbled something affectionate but unintelligible, and snuggled closer into his chest. Jack started to reach for his seatbelt, but with Sarah mostly asleep, almost on top of him, he decided against disturbing her; he left it off.

The rain began to fall as the car moved out of Woodstock. Jack closed his eyes and thought back over the past week. It had been a good week: business was booming, Sarah was loving. The patter of the rain on the roof of the car gave Jack an even more tranquil feeling and he started to doze off.

Approaching the M40, the weather was deteriorating, very heavy rain was reducing the visibility, and on the entry ramp the BMW slowed to make way for a heavy truck struggling for control in the high winds. Cocooned within the backseat, and with his eyes closed, Jack noticed the slowing. 'Home before the last track …'

The BMW gunned forward and joined the outside lane, heading for London.

Jack continued to drift in and out of sleep. He felt the warmth of Sarah pressed in close. The car was going smoothly at 90 miles an hour and, to Jack, it did feel good to be alive. *Board approval and 100 million … Tonight just me and Sarah.* He opened his eyes to look at Sarah. She was sleeping deeply.

A little while later Jack drifted out of his doze again. The rain was hammering down and he could see signs for the M25 indistinctly in the distance. He could see the instrument panel – 90, maybe it was a little fast for these conditions. *I suppose I did tell him to get us home quickly.* Jack considered saying something, but the chauffeur was a professional and Jack drifted back to sleep.

ய

'Brace! Brace! Brace!' screamed the chauffeur.

Jack's eyes came open in an instant. About 60 metres away in the road ahead, he could see a fiery inferno, and they were rushing inexorably towards it. The tyres screeched as the brakes locked up, but the car did not seem to be slowing. Time, however, was, and Jack watched in horror as the scene unfolded.

The line of fire contained a mass of burning vehicles; they slid towards it, 40 metres away, then 30 metres, then 20. Jack looked left and right; no one else in the car seemed to be moving. The driver's face was locked in a rictus of fear. The car continued towards the fire's embrace. Jack felt as though he was being force-fed into the mouth of hell. He could feel the enormous heat on his face, smell the burning hair. Then hell swallowed him and there was a noise like an enormous rushing waterfall; then pure silence.

This was not a calm silence for Jack. In utter terror, he drifted towards the windscreen. He turned as he was pulled away from Sarah, still attached to her seatbelt, and still asleep! *I'm going to die.* Looking forwards again, the windscreen was a little closer and he could see a spider web of cracks covering it. The silence was absolute as he closed in on it; his arms raised to his head. The windscreen exploded in slow motion, Jack couldn't tell if he had broken the windscreen or not; there was still no pain. He looked around; he was outside amongst the flames. He saw the roof of another car as he passed over the top of it. A few metres away, a ruined car contained two inert bodies broken and charred. Then Jack felt movement and motion speed up, and he burst out of the smoke and flames. The tarmac of the motorway was coming up fast. He blinked.

Opening his eyes, Jack looked at his feet, his legs, his body, his arms … all intact. His heavy overcoat was a little scuffed up, but otherwise he was unharmed and standing. He turned back to the raging fire. *Sarah!* His senses, more than just coming back to normal, were being assaulted: the smell of burning rubber, the screech of steel being shredded. Jack saw burning bodies, flying bodies, all of them dead bodies. He fought to keep control. *Sarah!*

Jack ran towards the inferno, *I have to get back in.* But the heat stopped him twenty metres away. 'Sarah!' He covered his face with his heavy coat and edged forward, he could smell his hair smouldering; the heat was unbearable. He screamed over the noise of the roaring flames. 'Sarah!'

A man came up behind him and pulled him back. 'There's nothing alive in there, buddy. Don't throw your life away.'

'Sarah's in there.' Jack slumped down on the motorway. 'My rock …'

A woman came up and comforted him. 'It'll be all right.'

Jack looked up at her. 'One moment I was holding her in my arms, the next moment I'm here and she's not.'

Soon a crowd was gathering at the perimeter of the dead zone.

CHAPTER 2

At the same time as Jack Bullage was leaving the restaurant, Louise Harding was exiting the tube. Once outside, she put on her small rucksack, and walked up the road heading home.

After only a few minutes, she mumbled a curse, turned around, and walked faster back to the high street. Her curses increased as the first drops of rain fell. Powering onwards, she was oblivious to the raised eyebrows as she swept past the other pavement users going too slowly for her tastes.

By the time she'd arrived at the local shop, the rain had matted her hair across her face. She picked up a few necessities and took them to the counter. 'Evening, Mr Singh.'

'Another late night at the office?' Mr Singh started to process the contents of her basket. 'How's my mate Jeff doing?'

'He's fine, as always. I suspect he's probably curled up on the sofa watching a movie.' Louise ran her hands through her hair. 'Yep, another late night at the office.'

Mr Singh picked up a few bars of chocolate from her basket. 'This helps.'

'They're not all for me. I use them to bribe Jeff.'

Mr Singh chuckled and Louise left with a smile which quickly turned back into a frown; the rain seemed to have settled in over Kilburn for the night.

Arriving back home, on Exeter Road, Louise had a quick look up and down the street before entering. Once inside, she pottered in the kitchen for a minute before slumping down on a chair.

Moments later Jeff came down the stairs with a towel wrapped around his waist, and another around his shoulders; he was using a third towel to dry his hair. Louise looked appraisingly. 'Got enough towels there?'

Jeff raised his eyes in apparent mock surprise and gave her a kiss. 'Do you know where there are any more?'

Ignoring him, Louise fetched herself a glass of wine. 'I've been subjected to just general drudgery today. Nothing unusual. A new corporate malpractice investigation.'

Jeff smiled. 'They still let you do those?'

Louise frowned but a ping from the microwave interrupted her train of thought. She retrieved her dinner, took out her laptop and booted it up while wolfing down the food.

Jeff dug around in the shopping bags, located the chocolate and retreated to the sofa. Jeff's phone buzzed – an incoming text. 'Mike says he fancies a pre-closing time drink.'

'My new case has nothing to do with Jack Bullage.' Louise scanned her anonymous email accounts for a few seconds. '… yeah, sure, we can meet Mike for a quick one.'

'Don't the terms of your restraining order even forbid you to use Bullage's name?'

'You want to go there? Criminal malpractice, fraud, and the toughest lawyers money can buy. What chance did I have?' Louise waved her empty wine glass.

Jeff got up from the sofa, collected the wine bottle and refilled Louise's glass. 'I had to cover the first year's lectures today, and I'm falling behind on my research.'

'The precious research you dropped for two months during the Olympics?' Looking over, Louise saw Jeff's shoulders sag.

'It's not a competition.'

Louise smiled to herself. *Well, not a close one anyway.*

For the next thirty minutes Louise furiously clicked her mouse, skimming between web-sites, checking facts and figures, trying to correlate it to her own information. She interspersed her hammering with the odd shouted expletive or gruesome fact. Jeff responded with non-specific grunting sounds Louise took for affirmation and encouragement. She typed up information gleaned for the next day's newspaper report.

'Come on, let's meet Mike.' Climbing off the sofa, Jeff wandered over to the kitchen table and started fiddling with his iPad. 'Check out Twitter – a massive pile up on the M40.'

'No time for voyeurism or schadenfreude.' Louise continued bashing through her keyboard two fingers at a time.

'But it's news! And you're a news… person.'

Louise looked up. 'There are loads of crashes every day. It's statistics, and normal, and sad, but unless it was the Queen driving with Michael Jackson's body strapped on the roof, it's not news.'

'You mean, it's not your news.' Jeff shot a cheeky smile at her.

Louise put her laptop onto standby and stood up. 'So let's go.'

Louise and Jeff found Mike in his usual seat, in his usual pub, The Three Kings, nursing an almost empty glass of red wine. Mike stood up as they approached, nodding towards them. 'Harding, Junior and Senior.'

After giving the seat a brush with the back of her hand, Louise sat down. 'Just a quick one, Mike, I've got an early start tomorrow.' She looked around. 'Is this the only pub in North London that hasn't been gentrified?'

Jeff disappeared to get drinks.

Mike shrugged, but appeared to be looking lovingly at the crushed red-velvet curtains and nicotine stained wall paper.

'Seriously Mike, the smoking ban was almost ten years ago. Couldn't they give the place a lick of paint?'

'No money, I'm afraid, they don't generate sufficient margin on the price differential between retail and wholesale.'

Louise raised an eyebrow.

'Their drinks are too cheap.'

Louise snorted and took a look at Mike's papers spread across the table. As usual there was a heady mix of deeply technical science and 'red top' news drivel. She sifted through the pile, raising eyebrows at various pieces. *Well, he won't be happy until he's shocked me.* 'So what's today's topic?'

Mike looked innocent, straightened his glasses and picked up a piece of paper. 'Atheism?'

Sighing theatrically, Louise crossed her arms. 'And?'

'Well … I have been arguing with a bunch of atheists today. Laying down the ecclesiastical law ...'

'Drinks!' Jeff arrived with the drinks, distributing them quickly.

Mike continued. 'So, as I was saying, I was on Recursive Genius …'

Louise interrupted. 'Your group of like-minded navel gazers, we know it, quicker…'

'Yes, anyway… these atheists said they had souls.' Mike raised his eyebrows. 'Well, really! I said that they couldn't have it both ways and that by taking the intellectually moral high ground of atheism they had given up the right to have a soul.'

Jeff joined in. 'Buddhists?'

'Nope, these people were genuine card-carrying nihilists; albeit they were adamant they had souls.'

'And how did you insult them?' asked Louise.

'Who says I insulted them?'

Louise looked over the top of her win glass. 'You always do.'

'I may have said they were being greedy.'

'Quite soft by your standards. And the fact that you're an atheist yourself?'

Mike chuckled. 'I joined the atheists in the 60s because someone promised me that lack of eternal judgement drove disgraceful promiscuity… you see, atheism is only intellectually the moral high ground.'

'And how did that work out for you?'

'I didn't galvanise any followers.' Mike smirked.

What? Louise raised an eyebrow to Jeff, who shrugged. Then she picked up a particularly disreputable red top newspaper and flicked through it for 10 seconds before throwing it down in disgust. She noticed Mike and Jeff share a look, and thought that Mike mouthed something to Jeff. It was bound to be puerile, so she shook her head and stood up. 'Home time, Jeff.'

And they left.

The next day, a gentle but persistent elbow roused Jeff from his sleep. He opened his eyes and rolled over to see Louise sitting up in bed typing away on her laptop. Leaning over he gave her kiss. 'Morning, love.'

Louise smiled. 'That crash was a bit interesting, the blogosphere is flooded. It was a massive pile up.'

I knew it was news. Jeff took a few deep breaths and collected himself. He'd have to go into the university today, but not quite yet. He watched from the bed as Louise got dressed at breakneck speed. Then he followed her down the stairs as she ran to the front door, stopping only to pick up her personal laptop.

Once Louise had definitely left – it was not unusual for her to barrel back into the house, within minutes of leaving, to collect forgotten items – Jeff started his day at his own pace. He went back to bed.

Jeff would describe his usual morning pace as measured; although, in a court of law, he might have been forced to admit it was closer to meandering. When he next opened his eyes and peeped at the bedside clock, it showed 10am. This important milestone triggered a quick standard snooze; then, after a tiny bit of further pillow-based cogitation, he finally got up. It was 10:45am and, six miles away, Louise had just completed drafting her second article of the day.

He didn't need to be at the University until lunchtime so Jeff surfed the web for five minutes, then drifted out into the back garden to have a quick chat, and a smoke, with his neighbour, Mrs Saunders. He looked at the clear blue sky and took a deep breath of the cold, crisp air. *Smoking in the open air must technically be a little healthier ... even if it's not statistically meaningful in the long run.*

Mrs Saunders was pottering around her garden. Jeff wasn't completely sure he approved of bright red lipstick and double-denim on a lady in her late fifties, but he admired her zest. Mrs Saunders noticed Jeff had arrived and walked over to the low garden fence. 'No school for you today, Jeff, darling?'

'I'm going in later.'

Mrs Saunders leant on the fence. 'How's the tenacious Louise? Any more brutal attacks? Any more restraining orders?'

Jeff smiled. 'Fine, no and no. How's your gardening?'

Mrs Saunders looked back over her shoulder at her garden. 'Oh, just the usual pruning; preparing them for the winter – nothing much going on.'

Gazing around the garden, Jeff lit up his cigarette, and then, after receiving a meaningful look from Mrs Saunders, lit another one and passed it over.

Smiling, Mrs Saunders took the cigarette. 'Plans for the weekend?'

'Possibly a pub quiz on Sunday with the quiz maestro. There's one in Surbiton Mike loves.'

Mrs Saunders took a drag and held the smoke in for a good few seconds – really savouring it – before exhaling. 'Is it the one starting at midnight?'

'Yep. But Mike has a good friend down there, so it's worth the trip.'

'Did you hear about the M40 crash?'

'Yeh, it seemed like Armageddon, lots of burnt-out cars.' Jeff screwed up his face. 'Lots of bodies too. But there is talk of a survivor.'

Mrs Saunders held Jeff's eye for a few seconds. 'I heard the same thing, but they say he lost his wife.'

'Well… every cloud…' Jeff gave a cheeky smile.

Mrs Saunders was not amused. 'Jeffrey Harding!'

'Only joking… sorry.'

'Thank you for the cigarette Jeff, and for the nice feeling of moral superiority I will nurture for most of the day.' Mrs Saunders nodded, turned her back on Jeff and started fiddling intently with one of her flower beds.

Back in the house, Jeff checked his email. There were precious few of note and he decided he wasn't needed at the university quite yet. He rattled off a few quick replies to the marginally more important ones, then reclined on the sofa and wasted a few hours wonderfully immersed in his latest science fiction novel.

CHAPTER 3

A Gadium spaceship sat in orbit, a few thousand kilometres above Europe. The size of a small town, but even from up close it was hard to see. Its black surface shimmered along the conical shape, defining uncertain boundaries.

Commander Aytch marched smartly along inside the ship on his review of the critical systems. He moved purposefully through the corridors, skipping slightly to account for the ship-generated gravity, which was marginally less strong than his over-muscled biology would have preferred. As he passed through the various doorways, he stooped a little to get through some of them. The ship was enormous on the outside, but the space was taken up by the propulsion, stasis and communication systems. There was limited working space inside.

A few moments later he reached his final item to check, a heavy set of doors currently shut tight. He punched in the code, the doors slid open, and he entered the stasis room. Meticulously, Aytch inspected the main control panel. There were no critical biological life signs to be checked – time, within the tubes, was stopped – but the technical data on the stasis fields had to be checked carefully. There was one minor aberration. The Spectrawarp gravity wells were stable, with gravitational fields steady, but the space-time sheer readings for Commander Justio's tube were only just within acceptable limits. Aytch made a record on his communications tablet and logged a new risk alert.

Aytch moved over to make a physical inspection of the actual tubes: three were empty and two were occupied. He checked on the inhabited tubes; the two humans looked fine; at least they looked fine for people frozen in time. He gave the empty stasis tubes a more thorough inspection. They all looked in good shape physically, no obvious malfunction or deterioration of the electronics. Ready for use, although the mission schedule didn't have him assigned for a break in the next five years.

Aytch returned to the crew room which, unlike the rest of the ship, was spacious enough for two male Gadiums to work side by side in comfort. Commander Justio was sitting on the central bench, his concentration immersed in his own communications tablet. Aytch tried to catch Justio's eye but, regrettably, failed.

Might as well complete the checks in here.

Everything was in good shape, although one of the two flight-chairs used for high gravitational manoeuvres had a small gyroscope malfunction.

Aytch walked over to where Justio was sitting. 'Commander Justio. I've completed the standard checks. The regulations require your input on the two minor issues outstanding.'

Justio didn't physically acknowledge Aytch's arrival. He seemed to be engrossed in alternately fiddling with a console lying across his lap, and staring at the data on the walls. Aytch stood still, waiting.

After a few moments, Justio looked up. 'All clear, did you say?'

'There are two minor issues, the regulations require you to acknowledge.' Aytch looked around the room quickly.

Justio reached out for Aytch's communications tablet then, after quickly reviewing the items, rolled his eyes and stood. 'I can fix that gyroscope now.'

'It needs to be done.'

Standing up, Justio whispered under his breath. 'We don't need it for about 500 years.'

Aytch pretended not to hear.

Justio limped over to the flight chair, removed a panel and started working on it.

Aktch shuffled over to stand behind him, craning to observe the maintenance activity.

Justio turned. 'Are you learning or marking me?'

'Four eyes validation required for critical system parts, even if the fixes are minor.'

A few moments later Justio put the panel back. 'All done. Now… back to my real work.' He flicked through a few screens on his communication console. 'I've refined some search parameters to allow for new data sources on Earth… social media and loyalty cards.' He moved slowly back to the central bench, again his right leg not quite supporting his weight effectively. 'It should help us correlate more data. But things are quiet at the moment, I may take a stasis break in a few months.'

Aytch looked at Justio's right leg. *Why doesn't he get it fixed?* Picking up his own communication console, Aytch sat on the bench facing a blank wall. 'I have Level Five exams soon. Lots to do: case studies, error examples, lessons learned.'

'Who'd believe a million years of operational missions could generate so much data?' Justio raised an eyebrow. 'Level Four is plenty enough qualification.'

A paragraph of text was displayed on the wall, Aytch looked up at it. 'Professor Harkin's critique on the Trogian Event. Do you mind if I turn on the audio narration? Studies show we retain more if we read and listen simultaneously.'

Justio shrugged. 'As long as you don't mind the occasional sighs of derision as the pomposity levels breach my defences... actually Harkin's okay.'

A computer-generated narration voice read out the text.

Chapter 3.2.D – Trogian Event
Professor Harkin Commentary

'The Trogian Event was a relatively recent inflection point in the collective attitude of the general populace of Gadium. Post the event there has been a significant revival in non-interventionist thinking and open criticism of the traditional precedent. It is no longer utterly unthinkable (or borderline heretical) to suggest the Gadium society should stop shepherding unemerged civilisations towards a Full Emergence. The Trogian Event is universally accepted to have been a catastrophe, particularly for the people of Trogia, and some genuine lessons must be taken by the other Gadium missions who are currently on station around an unemerged civilisation.'

Aytch turned to Justio. 'How did the process allow for those decisions to be made?'

'There were two commanders; one of them came up with the idea and the other one agreed.'

'I don't understand *why*. The process should stop them. Did they both go mad?'

'The mission commanders tried to unnaturally accelerate the Emergence. Probably they were under pressure to get a good news story.' Justio spoke clearly at the wall. 'Detailed timeline please.'

A new screen of text was projected up and the narration continued.

Chapter3.2.B – Trogian Event
Summary Timeline

1. *Trogia was host to a strong industrial-based sentient species*
2. *The species was free from energy and food deprivation*
3. *There were indications of a prevalence of Beta to Alpha transitions*
4. *One Trogian species member was found to be a Triple Alpha*
5. *The Triple Alpha was taken off Trogia into stasis*
6. *The wider species Emergence continued, more Beta to Alpha transitions*
7. *However, Emergence stalled at just under 1% of the population*

Freezing the narration, Aytch turned to Justio. 'It just stuck at 1%?'

'Yes, a Partial; it happens.'

Aytch was concerned. 'And they were sure it wasn't just another Triple Alpha stopping the transitions?'

'You have to assume they looked. Triples are pretty easy to spot.'

'I would prefer to have nothing happen than to preside over a Partial Emergence.' *I've seen the personnel records of the Gadium Emergence Committee – no Partial Emergences there.*

Justio spread his arms wide and looked up to the ceiling. 'If it comes to Partial Emergence, your job… our job… is to limit damages. Come on, play the rest of this review so we can see exactly how it isn't supposed to be done.'

Chapter3.2.B – Trogian Event
Summary Timeline (Continued)

8. *Against all historical precedent the Gadium team on-site at Trogia tried to intervene to increase Beta to Alpha transitions, including revealing themselves to the Trogian governments*
9. *The Gadium team failed to proliferate the Alpha Emergence of the general population*

and failed to secure the trust of the Trogia
population
10. *Trogian nations learnt how to convert Alphas*
    to Triple Alpha and did so – causing massive
    power imbalances
11. *The Gadium team ended up trying to police a*
    planet at war with itself
12. *The planet is currently under transmission*
    suppression – an enforced fallow period

Aytch stood up and starting pacing around the crew room. 'What were the Gadium commanders thinking? The disgrace of it.'

Justio frowned. 'How about a thought for the poor Trogians? An enforced fallow period – not good for them, not good at all.'

CHAPTER 4

On Saturday afternoon, the Daily Record offices buzzed with people preparing for the Sunday edition. Louise arrived and made a beeline for her desk. Walking across the main floor, she passed her colleagues, collecting cold shoulders mingled with a few warm greetings.

As she sat down at her desk, Karen, one of the good guys, walked over. 'Busy today?'

'Nah, just tidying. I'll be out in an hour.'

'An hour? I'll believe it when I see it.'

'Mike's coming for dinner.' Louise smiled, turned back to her computer, and started bashing away.

Karen walked away. 'Laters!'

For about thirty minutes, Louise mooched around the internet. She actually had very little to do, mostly she was getting out of the house to allow Jeff his creative cooking space. Something exotic had been promised for the three of them.

A stage whisper interrupted her thought pattern. 'Louise!'

Louise turned to see Harry Jones leaning out of his office and beckoning to her. Louise nodded an acknowledgement and walked towards his office, trying to ignore the looks of sympathy that followed her.

As usual, Louise had a good look around the walls of Harry's office. They were adorned with framed newspaper clippings from the previous forty years. Harry had won the Daily Record, and himself, a number of prestigious national awards.

Once Louise had stopped looking round, Harry caught her eye and held it for a few seconds. 'Don't worry, your time will come, the slip-up wasn't fatal.' Harry made a show of looking around the walls himself. 'The reason I sit you just outside my office isn't to keep an eye on my reckless apprentice, it's to copy over the shoulder of my star reporter.'

Louise smiled and, forcing her shoulders to relax, sat on the sofa. 'So what's up?'

'I wanted you to hear it from me, but you are not allowed to act on this information. However …' Harry left a long pause. 'Jack Bullage … Jack the bastard … Jack the business man.'

'What about him?'

'I have a new title for him ... Jack the M40 motorway miracle man!'

Louise was speechless for a few seconds, then less so. 'Fuck a duck!' For the next few moments Louise unloaded her full repertoire of expletives, getting more and more gratuitous and graphic as she went.

Harry held up his hand and Louise listened while he gave her the basics on the M40 crash.

'Give me the story, please!'

'No chance. This is just news cycle filler. Get on with one of your investigative pieces. Anyway, Jack is totally off your menu. Forever. You are *not* to investigate, it was part of the settlement agreement. I brought you in here to remind you of the considerable expense of the court case.'

Louise nodded demurely, made the right sounds and went back to her desk. She immediately started searching the internet for references to Jack Bullage and the M40 crash. She didn't stop surfing until late afternoon when Karen mouthed 'one hour' at her. Louise jumped up. 'Jeff!'

At 6pm, while Jeff stood by the cooker quietly stirring the contents of various saucepans, there was a loud bang. Louise crashed at full steam into the house. She marched into the kitchen, opened the fridge, took out the red wine and sloshed down a large glass before turning to Jeff. 'One word. Well, two words. Jack Bullage. Okay, more words. You'll never guess what. You will never flipping guess what.'

Jeff waited, and then, after what seemed like an appropriate pause. 'You're marrying him?'

'Jack Bullage is the M40 miracle survivor.' She gave Jeff a quick kiss, then turned and rushed up the stairs.

Unperturbed, Jeff internalised the information. *Another day living on the knife-edge.*

Upstairs, Louise took her laptop out and jumped on to the bed. By the time she had stopped bouncing she was typing furiously, with her shoes, socks and jumper strewn on the floor. At some stage she heard Jeff shout up the stairs. 'Louise, are you ready?'

'Nearly!' Louise called out, although she had not moved from her laptop for the past 45 minutes. She continued to scoot around various chat boards frequented by the internet's more conspiracy-imprintable participants. Her mind raced through a number of angles. *Maybe Jack Bullage has fixed this crash to get a sympathy vote?*

After a further 30 minutes of looking, she faced a lack of even tenuous circumstantial evidence. Even though the crash was almost 48 hours old, there was not even a sniff of Jack Bullage being a criminal mastermind. Louise rubbed her temples and wondered if, perhaps, she was getting carried away. She couldn't really believe the whole thing would have been staged or faked, considering the destruction involved. Anyway, the court cases had been completed and Jack had been found innocent of everything. Louise dragged herself away from the screen, concluding this weasel had simply been lucky and survived a genuine crash. She called up some of the pictures of the carnage. *But how did he escape with just a few scratches?*

Louise jumped at a sudden noise directly behind her.

'You haven't moved for the last two hours.' Jeff had clearly sneaked up the stairs to observe the veracity of Louise's *ready* statement and found it wanting, by a significant margin. 'And, with my poor cooking, I am facing the real possibility of poisoning you and my best friend.'

'I thought *I* was your best friend.'

'Of course you are.' Jeff paused and blew Louise a kiss. 'Except for Mike, obviously.'

Louise stuck out her tongue, smiled, got up, and put on her socks and jumper. 'Okay, let's go and host Mike for a Jeff mega curry.'

As Louise followed Jeff down the stairs he turned back. 'And… no chat tonight indicating you'd have preferred it if Jack had fried. Yeah?'

'Yeah, yeah. Karma. I get it.'

Louise settled herself at the kitchen table and flicked through a magazine. Jeff continued to potter around by the oven, stirring, tasting, seasoning.

Jeff looked at his watch. 'Mike's late.'

Not long after, the doorbell rang. Louise stayed seated while Jeff went down the hallway and greeted Mike at the door. She watched Mike come in, his eyes flicking to the usual corridor mess, which she knew he secretly yearned to tidy. Mike was a tidier, not a cleaner, but a tidier.

She half listened to his explanation, to Jeff, of his tardiness. '… cut myself shaving, came out like a Harkonnen Heart Plug… took ages… considered A&E.'

Moments later Mike came through to the kitchen wearing his usual faded jeans and corduroy jacket with leather elbow patches. As usual, he looked like the archetypal absent-minded professor with messy hair, glasses and a shirt which seemed to have been cleaned by hoping that simply not wearing it for a few days made a difference. Mike hugged Louise amiably, and sat down at the kitchen table.

Jeff took a beer bottle for himself and passed one to Mike.

Mike got up, collected a glass from the cupboard, and filled it before taking a sip. 'So, what's going on in the Harding household?'

Louise couldn't see where he'd cut himself shaving. *Drama queen.*

Jeff replied. 'We're having a dinner party for some of the neighbourhood's greatest minds to ponder the vastness of space and the wonders of the universe.'

Mike's eyes narrowed slightly. 'Yes?'

'So, you'd better finish your drink and leave before they get here!'

Mike gave a little salute of acknowledgement. 'We all know you're one of the world's great intellectuals, Jeff, and I'm pretty sure you are academically correct almost 90 per cent of the time.'

Louise took the bait. 'And?'

Mike removed his glasses and cleaned them. He took his time. Then he wagged a finger at Louise. 'Not *and*, it's *but*… and the but is… for the ten per cent of the time Jeff happens to be incorrect, that's exactly when he's at his most convinced he's actually one hundred per cent correct.'

Jeff threw a mock punch at Mike. 'Boom boom!'

Mike put his glasses back on. 'So how're things going for you at NLUST? Is the place still standing?'

'The department's ticking along; Sophie's keeping it running nicely.'

'And she's treating you okay? Not too much of a blow to your masculinity deferring to a woman?'

'Are you still kidding? She's joined a long queue of women I defer to.' Jeff took another beer from the fridge.

Mike turned towards Louise. 'How's things with you?'

'I've got news.' Louise gave Mike a quick summary of the Jack Bullage situation.

'Miracle survivor. Nice job. Particularly nice if you're in a situation where you need it…' Mike drew breath to expound on the subject, but was interrupted.

'Okay, food's ready.' Jeff served the curry and they started to eat. A few moments later, Jeff looked up with a grin. 'I saw something in the news related to Bullage. All those wrecks with no chance of functioning again… but enough about the old peoples' home, let's talk about the crash.'

Louise snorted. 'He escaped all the legal charges and now he escapes a massive car crash.'

Jeff waved his beer bottle around. 'He also escaped a death missile.'

Louise gave Jeff a long, flat stare.

Jeff continued. 'But where's the story? An evil man walked away from a crash, so what? Good things happen to bad people all the time. Did Jack do something actively miraculous?'

'He's quoted as saying he was dozing in the rear passenger seat when the crash happened. He wasn't wearing a seatbelt and just got catapulted out.'

Mike leant forward. 'Any other witnesses?'

Louise shrugged. 'Plenty of people remember seeing him on the side of the motorway. No-one saw how he got there. A few said he was trying to get back into the burning wreckage to help the other passengers. Fat chance!'

Wagging a finger, Jeff reminded Louise of her promise. 'Karma down.'

Louise wagged a different finger back, with only the most transitory hint of a smile to soften the image. 'Don't worry, I'm under orders from Harry, I can't investigate.'

In an apparent attempt to break the mounting tension, Mike caught Louise's eye and theatrically spooned more curry onto his plate. 'Korma down?'

Without waiting for Mike to finish his second helping of curry, Louise helped herself to ice cream. 'Okay. So, Mike, what are you up to at the moment?'

'Enjoying semi-retirement. A tiny bit of advisory work for the university; just corporate sponsorship stuff. The Dean likes to wheel me out as a stereotypical academic.' Mike paused and turned to give Jeff a meaningful look. 'Waiting for research papers to review...'

Jeff didn't meet Mike's eye. 'I thought we'd agreed you reading my work may be detrimental to our friendship? Anyway, I don't need your review. The paper is coming along just fine.'

There was a brief silence and then Jeff spoke again. 'I'm still waiting for you to invite me to that tennis match.'

Louise whispered under her breath. 'Handbags!' But neither Mike nor Jeff gave any sign they had heard.

'Well, I'm also spending time reading, walking, writing and looking for love.'

Louise reached out and patted Mike's arm. 'Any sign of a meaningful relationship?'

'No, I am particularly singular at the moment. I could do with a bit of Bullage's luck.'

'Sorry to hear it, Mike...' Louise paused for a moment, her attention focused on her spoon. 'I suppose it *was* just luck for Bullage.'

Mike clicked his fingers. 'We were talking about me!'

Shaking her head clear, Louise continued. 'There's no great alternative, I mean he could have staged the crash to appear he'd been in it.'

Jeff groaned. 'He'd hardly murder twelve people just to get a little sympathy. Anyway the court case is over.'

'There'll be more, mark my words.'

'Okay, okay, if you're both obsessed with not talking about my love life.' Mike theatrically waved his hands in the air. 'It could be Jack has super-powers, or he did stage the crash for sympathy. But what's most likely is Thursday was just a good day for him. There were probably 10,000 serious crashes around the world that day; he was one of the lucky survivors.'

Louise's attention drifted again, then she looked at them both in turn. 'There's the word *luck* again. Could Jack Bullage be somehow, genuinely, intrinsically lucky? It would explain how he escaped the court case.'

Pointing through the open door at the bookcase in the corner of the living room, Jeff replied. 'There are a few sci-fi novels based on luck being intrinsic and wired into our DNA. But they're novels, just fiction.'

Mike concurred. 'Scientific theory doesn't allow for any sort of intrinsic luck.'

Jeff leant forward. 'Yeah, the whole point of luck is it is *chaotic*. If a favourable outcome were repeatable through skill then it wouldn't be chance.'

'Semantics, Jeff! The word you want is random, not chaotic. If it were chaotic then it, logically, would be predictable, and so repeated favourable outcomes could be obtained through exceptional skill or highly detailed planning.'

Louise stepped in. 'Guys… get to the point.'

Mike shrugged. 'The point hasn't changed. If something is random, like the lottery then, semantically, you're lucky to win it once. You've got a favourable outcome to a random event … But no single person wins it week after week… no one is sustainably lucky.'

Jeff looked at Mike momentarily and then back to Louise. 'So we're pretty sure it is impossible to get lots of repeated lucky outcomes across lots of *random* events.'

Mike looked sharply at Jeff. 'Pretty sure? No… Semantically, we're absolutely certain. There cannot be any such thing as predictable repeated favourable outcomes to purely random events, because *semantically* if something is random then it's really random. So since *luck* is just the way of describing the favourable outcome of a single random event, then…'

'Mike! No going postal!' Louise was waving her spoon at him. 'Semantics aside and simple sentences, please; if we can't understand you, you may as well keep quiet.'

Mike smiled and spread his hands wide. 'Sorry, I've no idea what could specifically cause Jack to survive the crash, other than random dumb luck.' Mike paused. 'But we must also accept the possible existence of a situation which, to us, looks random because we have insufficient data to show other factors in action… hidden variables… either because we have no concept of them, or, alternatively, we simply haven't considered them.'

Louise walked back over to the kitchen table. 'So it could be that certain people are more likely to survive a crash or trauma than others.'

'Of course, some people are more likely to survive a crash than others. If we had all the data on car crashes across the whole world, we would definitely see survival correlation factors: age, fitness, seatbelts… lots of things.' Mike paused. 'And, without wanting to complicate matters unduly, let's not forget there are also some people who are young, fit and wearing seatbelts but die from very small and innocuous crashes. The other side of the coin.'

Louise puffed up her cheeks and blew out. 'Unlucky people?' Mike grimaced and Louise continued. 'Okay, forgetting the L word, could it be that Jack is special in some way that makes him a survivor?'

'Sure, there could be something particular about him, to make him more likely to survive car accidents, or perhaps thrown bricks.' Mike studied his glass for a while, thinking carefully. 'But it would probably be a completely different something from the one that would make him more likely to receive a favourable ruling in a court case.'

Conversation moved on to office politics at the university; Jeff was still worried about budgets though, as Louise noted, not so worried as to make daily attendance an absolute priority.

Just after midnight the party broke up and Mike left the house.

As Jeff lay gently snoring, Louise reviewed the evening's conversation. Her mind kept returning to lucky survivors. Mike had said no-one was sustainably lucky. *Was he sure? Could there be individual survivors of multiple accidents? It couldn't hurt to have a little look. Or at least some correlation between survivors of single events.*

CHAPTER 5

Back in the crew room of the Gadium ship, the Professor Harkin summary on the Trogian Event remained projected on to one of the grey walls, filling 10 square metres of wall space with text and data.

Aytch paced around the room with his communications tablet in one hand, studying his notes, and making more. 'Trogia was stuck in a Partial Emergence. Beta to Alpha transitions had stopped. The Gadium mission commanders tried to artificially boost the transition rates.' He shook his head, bewildered. 'Why?'

Justio looked up. 'Desperation. Bravery. Ignorance. Take your pick. They obviously genuinely thought they could succeed. But there's no historical precedent. Trogia was stable.'

'Stable? Wouldn't stalled be more appropriate?'

'No, they were stable: 1% Alphas, 99% Betas, and no more transitions.' Justio sighed. 'Well maybe stable is not the word. Once the Trogians learned…' Justio trailed off and left a silence.

Aytch looked for a few moments at Justio, wondering if he was going to pick up again, but Justio remained silent. 'I imagine that day-to-day there were no real differences.'

Justio struggled for a few moments with his walking stick and stood up. 'None at all. No one had a clue whether they were an Alpha or a Beta.'

As Justio walked passed Aytch he stumbled. Reflexively, Aytch reached out to steady him. *Small and crippled. Tough start.*

But Justio steadied himself quickly and brushed away Aytch's help with a grumbled, 'I'm fine.'

Slightly put out by the rejection, Aytch looked back at the screens. He felt his anger growing; those Gadium commanders had been a disgrace to their positions. 'Until we interfered, and the Gadium commanders tried to kick-start the transitions.'

'But their plans were so intrusive they needed the tacit agreement of a few of the Trogian governments. The selected governments were promised longevity, physical resilience and enhanced reactions for their own populations. It's not surprising they were tempted.' Justio walked around the crew room, working flexibility into his damaged leg. 'But we… they… couldn't deliver on the promises, it didn't work. The processes were tweaked, making them more and more dangerous until fatalities became an issue.'

Aytch remained silent for a moment, taking it in, Justio had seen these types of things all before. But, operationally, it was new to Aytch – up until now he'd only had the theory. 'Am I right in thinking that the wars only started after the Trogians found out about Triple Alphas?'

'While only a few Trogians knew about Beta to Alpha transitioning there was no problem. But then there was an incident in which an existent Alpha was converted into a Triple, and this Triple became very noticeable, very quickly. The Gadiums tried to cover it up, but failed.' Justio walked back to the central bench and sat down. 'Once the particular Trogian government saw the power of their very own Triple Alpha the outcome was inevitable. All made worse by the rumours that aliens were supporting various factions more than others.'

Aytch nodded. 'Then all the Trogian governments started trying to produce Triple Alphas.' He took a few more notes.

'Gadium couldn't stop them, not short of an actual attack, which would have been pretty poor first-contact diplomacy.' Justio sighed. 'So the governments with Triples started exerting their will.' Justio stretched out his leg. 'The usual stuff, probability-based attacks on technology systems: code breaking, denial of service, faked messages, etc. It was easy while the *Haves* were simply bullying the *Have Nots*. Then one country got greedier and made a significant attack on another Triple enabled country. They dropped their own Triple Alpha commandos into the rival government command centre with orders to kill the government and military officials.'

Walking over to the nutrition dispenser, Aytch pulled out an energy tube. He unclipped one end, put it in his mouth and inhaled deeply. The chemical compounds flooded Aytch's lungs and were quickly absorbed into his blood stream. 'Traitors. Why didn't the GEC intercede?'

'The GEC were over twenty light years away, sitting in their committee room on Gadium. They only knew what they were told by the commanders who were in orbit around Trogia.'

Aytch looked around the walls of data. 'Thank you for your insight, commander.'

Justio nodded an acknowledgement and turned back to his own work.

Aytch returned to his own reading, but Justio broke the silence. 'They were traitors, but they may not have been completely out of control. I heard a rumour once of a case where a Gadium team did create a Triple from a normal Alpha using standard conditioning.' Justio paused. 'They kept the Triple on-planet for a year and then took it off-planet. The claim was it re-boosted the Beta to Alpha transition rates.'

'Do you believe it?'

'It was many hundreds of thousands of years ago. And there's no proof and no underlying scientific explanation. Most people reject the example as an error in measurement. I've not heard it repeated in the last few thousand years… definitely don't mention it in your exams.'

Aytch turned back to his own work.

Again the silence was broken by Justio. 'Another thing to be mindful of, but not to mention in the exams, is that the meddling probably condemned billions of Trogians to an early grave; not just the war, but the inevitable delay to Full Emergence as we cleaned up.'

CHAPTER 6

All quiet currently. Just over a thousand light years away, Commander Jenkins, of the Gadium Emergence Committee (GEC), sat in his office and reviewed the latest real-time message back from Earth, courtesy of the QET communications grid. Jenkins recalled that, fifty years previously, there had been some furious activity on Earth, but it had not developed into a Full Emergence.

An alarm on his desk chimed quietly. Jenkins reached over and switched it off. Bringing his hand back, his gaze flicked across the desk and lingered on the hologram of his daughter, the only truly personal ornament in his entire office. *Cleaning up Trogia.*

There was a polite cough from the doorway, Jenkins' adjunct had entered the room. 'Sir, the Gadium Emergence Committee meeting will be commencing soon. Shall I call you an escort?'

'I'll walk.' Commander Jenkins stood up briskly. *Another long meeting of sideways glances, hand-wringing and indecision.* He picked up his jet black jacket and put it on. With his various medals gleaming across his chest, he left the room shaking his head.

As usual, the GEC meeting was being held in the main government buildings in the centre of Gadium City. It took Jenkins a brisk ten minute walk to get there. Once inside, he made a quick detour to the Military Intelligence offices. There were a few people in the reception and he put his head inside. 'Good afternoon, gentlemen. Status?'

One of the officers noticed Commander Jenkins, and threw himself to attention. 'Sir! Currently 95 missions active: 33 in transit outward and 62 on-station. There are also 22 missions in transit inward back to Gadium. Of our 62 active missions, we have 12 Full Emergences under control, and 5 other planets with early signs.'

Jenkins smiled. 'I really just meant… How are *you* all doing?'

'Fine sir! Thank you for asking sir.'

With a friendly nod, Jenkins walked on. He was sure he hadn't been so regimented when he had been the head of Military Intelligence. *I should have asked to speak to someone about the latest on Rolumpus. Secession risks. They've been making noises about quarantine zones and use of AI for a while now.*

A few moments later, Jenkins arrived at the Gadium Emergence Committee meeting. It had not quite started yet. There were a few Gadium members dressed in black military uniforms, the rest wearing the more common cream citizen robes. Taking his seat at the conference table, he studied the members.

As he was sweeping his gaze around the table, his eyes locked with the Deputy Chairman sitting opposite. The Deputy was close to being the eldest member of the Gadium government, and was certainly one of the most respected. Jenkins nodded his head in silent greeting and got an almost imperceptible nod back. The Deputy looked unusually sour today; every few moments he turned and whispered commands to one of the four lackeys who stood in readiness behind him.

The rest of the table held the remaining 30 or so active members of the GEC. The rules were clear; to have a voice on the council you had to be physically present. Jenkins continued to look around. There were very few gaps at the table, except in the most important places.

For a few minutes the background of conversations continued to bubble, then there was a loud knock and a junior council member held the doors open. Jenkins watched as the Chairwoman and Commander Sharnia walked in slowly, their heads close to touching, whispering to each other as they made their way to their places. He heard the jingle of Sharnia's medals tightly packed on to her full military dress uniform, as she passed behind his seat.

Jenkins could feel her stare on the back of his head, but he kept looking straight ahead, not daring to turn and meet it. There were some games of nerve you didn't play unless you played them for real.

The Chairwoman sat at her place, and without looking up, read from the agenda. 'Item 1, mission summary, please.'

A junior minister, at the far end of the table from Jenkins, directed his answer to the Chairwoman. 'Lady Chairwoman, the 64 open missions are mostly quiet in the pre-Emergence stage.'

From across the full length of the 20 metre long table, Jenkins interrupted. 'I thought there were 62 open missions.'

The junior minister turned towards Jenkins and slightly shook his head. 'The latest report did show 62 sir. However, it was a manual entry operator keying error. We're definitely at 64 sir.'

Jenkins shook his head. 'Poor data? I accept that we don't want to risk over-reliance on computers, but...'

The Chairwoman looked up and interrupted. 'Commander Jenkins. We all live with the restrictions on computational activity. If the only issue we get is the occasional piece of incorrect data then the price is cheap.'

Jenkins acknowledged the point with a slight nod. *I'm sure we could improve our data analysis without accidentally creating artificial intelligence.*

The Chairwoman turned back towards the junior minister. 'Please continue. Are there any planets we think are close?'

The junior minister consulted his notes. 'We have four looking warm, with potential Emergences underway.'

Jenkins could not help himself. 'I have heard there were five, and the truth …'

The Chairwoman cut across him. 'Commander Jenkins, *the truth* is whatever we report in this meeting. Don't quibble over plus or minus one unit.'

Sharnia leant over and whispered into the Chairwoman's ear. She nodded, then looked back at Jenkins.

Jenkins held out his hands palms outwards in supplication, then he looked around the room, briefly locking eyes with the Deputy Chairman. The Deputy gave a small smile. Jenkins sat back in his seat, wondering why he always came to these things with such high expectations.

The Chairwoman looked up, straight ahead. 'Mr Deputy Chairman, if you would give your updates please.'

The Deputy Chairman stood, paused and looked around the table. 'Our mission team is closing in on the Vantch system. The remaining journey time is something of an unknown, but they have recently reported passive receipt of electromagnetic emissions from Vantch indicating significant ongoing conflicts. We need authority to order the incoming Gadium mission to increase its velocity.'

A moment passed while the Chairwoman considered the situation. She had a short whispered exchange with Sharnia, then turned her attention back to the Deputy, who was waiting with ill-concealed impatience. 'As I understand, you want us to authorise the Gadium mission to increase velocity to 0.98c? With all the associated risks of getting close to light speed?'

Jenkins watched Sharnia out of the corner of his eye, she was sitting with barely concealed tension. *What's her view?*

After a short pause, the Deputy replied. 'Yes, Madam Chairwoman. They're currently at standard operational speeds, but we have to get on-station as soon as possible. They may be slipping into a Full Emergence without any support.'

A murmur from somewhere around the table sounded like 'good luck to them'.

Sharnia leapt to her feet, towering over the table. She growled. 'Treason!' She stood stock still while sweeping her gaze across the members of the council. 'Let me remind you all membership of the GF is still currently illegal as well as eternally immoral.'

The Deputy had not yet seated himself when Sharnia stood up, but even from across the table she loomed over him. She was a good metre taller, and well over twice his weight (as were all females of the Gadium species). Their eyes locked, and it was Sharnia who nodded her head slightly and sat down.

The Deputy stood for a few moments and then sat down too.

The Chairwoman turned to Jenkins. 'Commander Jenkins, can you give us a military assessment?'

Jenkins stood. 'A 20% increase in velocity would be meaningful. All the intelligence so far has been gathered from passive scanning of Vantch, but we've only been signalling ahead for the last fifteen years. The quicker we get the first return signals the better.'

The Chairwoman nodded slowly. 'And how far are we away now?'

'The latest estimates are that we are just over a year away.'

'But?'

'There is some uncertainty; however, the commanders on the Vantch Mission believe they are about one year away.'

Jenkins noticed a quiet, but noticeable, grumble around the table. The uncertainty was a cause for concern. He sat back down.

The Chairwoman held up a hand and the grumbling stilled immediately. 'All of us here are very aware of our custodial obligations.' Slowly she scanned every face at the table, looking into their eyes in turn. 'These new civilisations need our stewardship, and particularly our guidance, in their development of new capabilities. Are there any votes against authorising the velocity increases?'

No concerns were raised.

The Chairwoman nodded to the Deputy. 'Passed.'

Sharnia leant over again and whispered into the Chairwoman's ear. This time, Jenkins noticed the Chairwoman give a look of slight disapproval.

A waiting silence settled on the room.

'Now a related matter.' The Chairwoman stood up. 'I am aware that some of you here have sympathies with the GF. Let me remind you, they are an illegal organisation and their mantra of non-intercession runs counter to our creed. You will not support them.' She paused. 'Secondly, we are coming up to a pivotal point for the Gadium civilisation. You are all aware that more and more star systems under our protection are wondering if perhaps they would benefit from a little more freedom. Let's be honest with ourselves; individually they would benefit from some loosening of our rules, but collectively it cannot be allowed.'

As he looked around the table, Jenkins noticed a few faces not wholly sympathetic to the last rallying call from the Chairwoman. But there was a general murmur of assent, and he sat quietly while the rest of the meeting continued with negligibly interesting reports.

After a few hours of general discussion, the committee filed out, but not before Sharnia addressed the meeting herself.

As she stood, her bulky muscles and savage scars dominated the room. 'Let me be perfectly clear, I will not allow the GF to whisper lies about the so-called freedoms we withhold from our territories. The GF are pushing for us to withdraw from certain star systems – Never. The GF are pushing for us to provide all technologies to our dependencies – Never. The GF are looking for political legitimacy to retrench the Gadium civilisation – Never. We have a duty to the galaxy, and we will execute on our duty to the fullest of our abilities.'

Once outside the meeting room, Jenkins found the Deputy waiting for him. 'Commander Jenkins, please walk with me.'

Jenkins fell into step with the Deputy, with the Deputy's retinue trailing behind at a respectful distance.

After they'd walked down a little way down the corridor, the Deputy turned to Jenkins. 'You will be pleased when the Trogian interim review gets back, I assume?'

Katrina. 'Yes, Mr Deputy, very much so. It's been hard to be away from my daughter: stasis holidays, personal diaries and QET messaging help, but it's still hard.'

They stood in silence for a few moments. Commander Jenkins knew the Deputy's own son had taken a deep space mission some years earlier and was basically gone forever – at least 8,000 years. Although the Deputy would very likely still be alive on his son's return, emotionally they would be nigh-on strangers. What was even more saddening was the Deputy's son had also taken his wife and children. Jenkins supposed this had broken the Deputy's heart. 'We take too much on ourselves.'

'Yes, we do... But it's our calling. We do what we must. Endure what we must. Give up what we have to.' Then he looked directly into Jenkins' eyes. 'However, I fear that, on Vantch, the late arrival of the Gadium mission will be very much short of the mark. It's almost impossible to safely shepherd civilisations through an Emergence once a major conflict has taken hold.'

For a split second, Jenkins thought there was a hint of a smile creeping into the corners of the Deputy's mouth. 'I agree, sir, Vantch is most likely beyond saving.'

'And Earth?'

'We have an experienced commander. Justio has over 30 missions to his name.'

The Deputy raised his eyebrows. 'Is he older than me?'

'Not quite, sir. He's done a lot of deep space missions but biologically he is closer to 9,000. Anyway... he has our interests at heart. His co-commander, Aytch, can be trusted to do things by the book.' Jenkins looked back towards the meeting room. Sharnia was emerging with the Chairwoman.

The Deputy followed his gaze. 'They're both very worried about the GF. Rightly too. I've heard they're launching a major push.'

Gadium First. Jenkins scrutinised the Deputy's face, but the Deputy looked away.

The silence dragged on, then the Deputy turned back to Jenkins. 'Perhaps we can complete the conversation in the next few weeks, if you can make it to my favourite restaurant.'

Jenkins nodded and mumbled an acceptance; the Deputy moved off with the cadre of Gadium bureaucrats waiting to accompany him back to his office suite.

Jenkins stood for a moment, watching the retreating back of the Deputy, now lost in his own thoughts; the Gadium Republic had made galactic peace and prosperity a key tenet of their constitution and, admirable as it was, this put a large strain on the actual citizens of Gadium. Fundamentally, the whole planet seemed to spend most of their extended lives on either covert observation, active intervention or long-term bureaucratic missions. A hundred billion stars in the galaxy, of which about 30 million actually fell within Gadium's operational range. Almost a thousand planets with either emerged or pre-emerged sentient species were being nurtured or administrated. *So much effort and sacrifice; for what?*

A low voice cut through his reflections. 'Commander Jenkins.'

Jenkins turned round. Sharnia stalked towards him, her reptilian face a mash up of age-earned wrinkles and valour-earned battle scars. As she got close, Jenkins fought the urge to step backwards. Looming over him, she was all muscle, scars and menace.

He nodded a respectful greeting. 'Commander Sharnia.'

She flicked her eyes towards the retreating back of the Deputy. 'So how is our Deputy?'

Jenkins tried to hold Sharnia's gaze but the genetics of over ten million years of subservience could not be undone by his will alone; his gaze drifted to the floor. 'Just the usual; missions, statistics, operational choices.'

'Any mention of Earth?'

Jenkins looked up briefly. 'Not specifically… why?'

'Don't insult my intelligence, Jenkins. You know perfectly well Aytch is a grandson of mine.'

He forced a smile. 'Earth is going fine. You know as much as I do, it's all on track.'

The smile Sharnia returned was all teeth and didn't get close to her eyes. 'As it should be.' She let her gaze drift down the length of Jenkins' body and back again to his face. 'As it should be.' Then she turned on her heels and marched away.

Jenkins let out a breath, not realising quite how long he'd been holding it for. He closed his eyes and took a few calming breaths. She was always unnerving; there was so much blood on her hands only a fool would underestimate her. Jenkins shook himself back to the present. He had work to do.

CHAPTER 7

Aytch stood in the middle of the crew room with various bits of Earth data projected on to pretty much every wall of the crew room. Many graphs, tables and statistics were overlaid on top of each other like the pieces of a giant jigsaw waiting to be connected.

Justio entered and looked at the main display for a few moments. 'Interesting items?'

'Aggregate accidental death rates still steady at three million per year.'

'Not dipping at all?'

'The actual number has been reducing in some areas; but once we allow for safety improvements and the like, there is no statistical significance. We're most likely still in the range of 0.1% Alphas.'

Justio took a nutrition energy tube, his face grimacing slightly as he inhaled. 'Sounds about right.'

'It's not really moved since we got here, since we took Bill Jones. I'm worried we're stuck in a perpetual Partial Emergence.'

Shaking his head, Justio walked over and sat down. 'It's only been 50 years. If you're getting impatient then take a stasis break. I can watch the ship for a few years, wake you up if things get interesting.'

'My expectations are probably too high, but we were unlucky taking Bill Jones didn't herald more.'

Justio frowned. 'We were incredibly *lucky not* to get a Full Emergence when we took Bill Jones. I'm actually ashamed I championed the original decision. It would have been carnage, their civilisation was not emotionally or intellectually ready.'

Aytch paused. 'You're probably right.' He turned back to the screens, his eyes focusing on a number of Earth news feeds. 'They don't seem any more mature now.'

Justio nodded and looked around at the data covering all the walls. 'Is this general revision or a specific investigation?'

Aytch showed his communications tablet to Justio. 'I'm just creating some new correlation programmes. The computer can't handle the logic so I have to do the manual logic linking.'

Bringing up some additional screens, Aytch showed maps on Earth pinpointing where Gadium had their data interceptors located. There were thousands sequestered across the globe. Some were simply pieces of software hidden within the operating systems of strategically selected computers, while others were actual miniature robots physically recording sounds and pictures from key locations.

Justio chuckled. 'This monitoring is so much easier now they've got up to speed with personal mobile communications and the internet. I'm glad we gave them a nudge there.' He walked towards the doorway, then turned, and with exaggerated solemnity poked a finger towards Aytch. 'And their 256 bit encryption keeps everything they say completely secure.'

'Which reminds me, I haven't checked in recently on the US AI programme. Have you?'

Justio nodded. 'I checked a few weeks ago. They're making progress, but nothing to give us any worries. When their Emergence comes they'll have to give up the AI programmes as part of their treaty with us. We'll ensure there's no Skynet issues for us.' He paused. 'I'm just going to check on the QET grid – we've got a status report to send.' At the doorway he turned. 'I'll be back.'

Aytch looked up and saw Justio looking at him expectantly. 'Don't forget your cultural assimilation lessons, Aytch.'

Once Justio had left, Aytch turned his attention back to the maps on the largest wall. As usual, he was a little worried about the relatively large number of red shaded areas representing locations where they struggled to get real-time signals from either Gadium assets or subverted Earth assets. The main issue remained their lack of ability to process vast quantities of data.

Pulling up some statistical analysis on a range of reported accidents, Aytch accessed hospital records and, running correlations with police records, looked for survival patterns. Dangerous accidents tended to be a rich area for locating individuals who were potentially Alphas – the fear generated within an accident triggered a survival instinct. The numbers seemed to be a little skewed from the expected. Possibly there was a general increase in crash survival, nothing statistically significant yet.

Aytch instructed the computer to open up a communications application. There were two options, (Option A) instantaneous QET communications to Gadium planet, and (Option B) tight-beam signalling, which would take 1,200 years. Aytch dictated an instantaneous QET message first. 'All is well.' The computer used a conversion matrix to strip the message down to a single character and then stored it.

For a few moments Aytch considered his position; he wasn't sure if he should waste his allocation of QET communications; after all, his wife was safe on Gadium – frozen in time in a stasis pod. It would be at least fifty more years until she was brought out for her next periodic medical check regarding energy state mutation. But these long distance relationships were so complicated and Aytch had seen a few of his friend's relationships go sour, so he felt a time-stamped message showing he was thinking of her would help. *This will almost definitely come up in my exams. Relationship pressures of long distance travel.* Aytch decided to check up.

'Computer, please bring up my next revision section on Family Unit.'

The text appeared with an accompanying narration.

Chapter 6.3.A – Family Unit & Stasis Controls Overview

The social upheaval generated by relationships skewed by stasis is controlled by tightly enforced legislation to protect all parties from emotional imbalance. The basic rules are as follows:

1. **No Gadium citizen may have any contact at all with any descendants more than 3 generations distant; the ancestor must enforce this even if they are (due to stasis) biologically younger than their descendants**
2. **No Gadium child may be placed in stasis before their 12th year; No parent may enter stasis if children are younger than 12 years old**
3. **Any Gadium citizen entering a deep space trip (defined as > 7,000 light years) must renounce all relationships or take those parties with them. It is not sufficient for the parties to commit to long-term stasis**
4. **Any Gadium citizen who shows more than 20% degradation in their cellular function is restricted to the home system**
5. **No Gadium female may give birth whilst on a mission of any type, or whilst their partner is on a mission of any type, unless the partner has renounced parental status**

As the narration stopped Aytch heard a sound behind him and turned. Justio was standing in the doorway looking at the rules with a grim expression etched on to his face.

After a moment of thought, Aytch spoke. 'I was 25 when my father went away on a 30 year round trip. It was a critical treaty review and he agreed with my mother we wouldn't go into full-time stasis. When he returned, he'd been in stasis for most of his trip so we were fresh in his memory. My mother, brother and I had lived through over 10,000 full days continuously without him, almost no stasis. It was difficult for a while.'

Justio just grunted and tapped away at his communications tablet. 'The QET grid is down to 40 per cent; clearly we used up a lot of entangled pairs in the early days. But we've also had a fair amount of entropic decoupling. We need to enforce more stringent usage controls.'

'I just requested your authorisation for a QET message to my wife. I'll cancel it; we can't risk losing QET contact with Gadium.'

'How many characters?'

'One.'

Justio shook his head slightly and turned to the screens. 'Commander Aytch - QET message approved.' Justio turned back to Aytch. 'So what happened with your father?'

'We patched it up, but there were scars for a while.' Aytch pointed at the section of the wall displaying the manual entry on Family Unit. 'I can't quite see why we legislate, it seems like common sense.'

Justio was a silent for a while, then limped into the middle of the crew room and sat down. 'Do you think it's common sense not to love your family?'

Too late, Aytch remembered Justio's expression from a few moments before, and reading the pre-mission reports detailing Justio's complicated family history. 'I suppose it can get difficult.'

Justio fixed Aytch with a cold stare. 'So do we need legislation or not?'

'I apologise. I know your situation was complicated.'

'You don't know everything about my situation.' Justio paused for a moment and then continued. 'If I could travel back in time to the point I accepted my original deep space mission, not all the money in the universe would get me on to the ship.'

Aytch took stock. He'd been told by Sharnia to find opportunities to talk to Justio as an equal, but Aytch had never discussed this with Justio before. He'd avoided the subject studiously for many years – embarrassed to accidentally highlight a deficiency. 'Why didn't your wife and children go into stasis?' He looked at the floor.

Justio let out a long breath and spoke slowly, pushing each word out. 'It was my duty to take the mission. I was the best qualified. She promised to go into stasis and take my 12-year-old twins as well. We'd been waiting for the twins to reach that magic birthday. The whole mission had been waiting for it.'

Aytch looked up and when he met Justio's eye, Justio continued. 'For the six months leading up to the trip, I played with my kids for ages every day. I knew they would be frozen in time until my return, but I was storing memories to cherish during the one thousand days I would be awake... I was to be away for fifteen thousand years.'

Another pause stretched, then Justio spoke again, his voice sounding increasingly hoarse. 'After I left, my wife decided to stay out of stasis up to the end of the year to finish off a project she was on. So the kids kept her company. Then, after few months, she extended, and by that time, I was on an unstoppable ticket for a fifteen-thousand-year round trip.'

The silence stretched on. Justio seemed to be blinking back tears. Then he spoke in little more than a whisper. 'I shouldn't have left. My children and my grandchildren all lived happy fulfilled lives on Gadium. They grew up, lived, loved and died. I've read their diaries. They were happy, but they did it all without me. I was dead to them.'

Aytch remained silent.

Justio turned away from Aytch. 'Perhaps you can turn off the caring in some circumstances. Emotionally cut your great grandchildren or grandchildren loose. But your kids... not so easy. I never found a way to turn it off. You hold them, feed them, clean them, clothe them, comfort them and teach them. Your love is selfless and limitless – as much as you can give. And yet, somehow, you get it back double strength. Love mainlined.'

Aytch remained silent. Justio paused and continued.

'And it's good. Their love is amazing; it's fulfilling, it's all you need, and at the same time it's the barest minimum you feel you could possibly survive on.' Justio shuffled from foot to foot, looking downwards. 'I never tried to find that level of happiness again. Just threw myself into mission after mission. But I don't forget the loss.'

Justio turned and left the room.

CHAPTER 8

Louise woke up at 5am on Sunday morning. For a few minutes she lay awake staring at the ceiling. *Just another quick look... then back to bed.*

Quietly she climbed out of bed and walked down to the kitchen table, where her laptop sat, still warm from the previous night. After logging on, Louise started browsing the internet, again looking for evidence as to whether Jack may have staged the whole crash. Of course there was no evidence, she chided herself, but she kept looking.

Louise looked up at the clock – 9am. She stood up and walked towards the stairs. *Other miracle survivors?*

Switching on the kettle, Louise returned to her laptop.

Just before lunchtime, there was a noise upstairs and a few moments later Jeff entered the kitchen. 'How long have you been up?'

'Not so long.'

'Your side of the bed is stone cold.'

Louise shrugged and returned her concentration to her computer. 'I did a little sniffing around Jack Bullage; but I'm over it.'

On Monday morning Louise decided to do a little more investigation, but agreed with herself it would be in a more measured way. She got up at 6am and continued to look for miracle survivors and any background to their situations.

At 8am Jeff wandered into the kitchen. 'Did you even come to bed last night?'

'Of course, I'm just doing a bit of research. So how did the pub quiz go with Mike last night?'

Jeff helped himself to breakfast cereal and sat down. 'We came second, behind some ginger moron who seemed to know the name of every beer in the south east.' Jeff nodded towards the laptop. 'Are you sure about this? You've been told to stay away.'

'I'm not really looking into Bullage. I'm just researching miracle survivor stories.'

'Why?'

'Just to get it off my plate. So I can sleep tonight.'

'And have you found anything?'

'There are some conspiracy forums talking about miracle survivors from multiple events.'

'Like what?'

'Like… well, I don't want to talk about it until I've validated some of it.'

Jeff looked pained. 'Come on… I always help you with the conspiracy stuff, you know… scientific rigour.'

Louise looked intently at Jeff for a few moments and then sighed. 'Okay, well, I found a few sites postulating that some people are intrinsically lucky. I know you don't like the word lucky but Bullage survived the M40 crash; 12 other people didn't.'

'So you are investigating Bullage. Don't do it. Anything you say will be taken out of context.'

Louise stared. 'I'm *not* investigating Bullage. It's about miracle survivors.'

'Okay then, miracle survivals. What are your search criteria? You don't want to look into every accident there's ever been.'

Louise forced herself to relax her shoulders. 'Suggestions?'

'Perhaps you could use the Bullage crash as a template. How about only looking into crashes with one survivor and at least four deaths?'

'They'll be rare.'

Jeff smiled. 'Miracles don't come easy.'

Later that day in the Daily Record offices, with her real work done, Louise turned her attention to the online newspaper archives. She started by looking into reports from the previous 10 years where survivors had seemed to defy the odds. Mostly it was car crashes, but she also found a few building collapses.

As she browsed through the materials, the data was almost overwhelming. Louise rubbed her temples as the articles seemed to merge into one. There were so many crashes with multiple deaths and multiple survivals, but accidents with at least four deaths and *only one* survivor were rare.

Louise searched across news archives and internet sites to build a picture of each accident. In particular, searching for any personal testament of either the survivor or eye witnesses, trying to identify any themes.

In the evening, Louise continued her searching, and the next day, and the next. She hunted early mornings; snippets during work; evenings and late into the nights.

Her search went on unrelentingly.

ЦЏ

By Thursday evening Louise had a good enough picture to discuss possible conclusions with Jeff. She sat at the kitchen table nursing half a glass of red wine. 'There's no smoking gun. Nothing obvious. And no reported run of survivals for a single individual.'

Jeff acknowledged this with raised eyebrows. 'Nothing at all?'

'There was one guy who survived a crash and then his ambulance was hit by a bus on their way to the hospital, but he died in the second crash. And another guy with cancer who'd been given 24hrs to live by doctors on five separate occasions in two years.'

Jeff shrugged. 'The cancer example won't be unique.'

'And there were building collapses and bomb explosions.' Louise drained her glass. 'But it was mostly car crashes, there's a lot of them … one million deaths per year on the roads!'

Jeff looked surprised. 'Any linking factors?'

'For the deaths, yes: speeding, drinking and lack of seatbelts.' Louise paused. 'But in terms of the survivors, mostly the usual crap… I thought I was going to die… or… my life flashed before my eyes… or… time seemed to slow.' Louise took a sip of wine. 'There were a few other leads though; firstly, a number of crash survivors had testimonies indicating they'd been half-asleep at the instance of the crash.

Not unusual I guess, but it resonated with me because Bullage actually said something similar yesterday.'

Jeff looked at the book shelf. 'I'm sure I read a novel once implying half-asleep people are floppier and so tend to bounce rather than break.'

'Good that your primary source of facts is your fiction collection. But it does make sense. But fully asleep people are floppy as well, and I didn't find any notable correlation with fully asleep people surviving.'

Jeff remained silent while Louise collated her thoughts. 'There was a weird, and I mean very weird, reference.'

Jeff looked expectantly at Louise. 'Yes?'

'I found an internet chat board talking about miracle survivors and on a few occasions there was a reference to hedgehogs. I assumed it was road safety but then I found a hedgehog reference related to a collapsing stadium in South America.'

'Weird.'

'Yeah, and when I searched down hedgehogs and accidents, the internet returns were all about road safety. Nothing strange at all. Although, I got one strange bit … it seemed to be a military reference. I've got more to check up there.'

'What about the internet chat boards, anything from the user names?'

'There were two names dominating the boards: Adamo34 and Xeeta55. But I didn't manage to find anything more out. Will you see if you can find anything?'

'Sure, I'll try later to see what I can find out about them. Did you look into any testimonies from Jack Bullage?'

Louise grimaced. 'There have been a few pieces, nothing comprehensive. I just managed to stomach the internet report saying he felt blessed but personally remembered nothing of the crash.' Louise paused to refill her glass then continued. 'It also said a few eye witnesses had basically seen Bullage thrown out of the car, then, after he had landed in a heap, he had stood up straight away and seemed physically fine, just a little shaken.'

'He's out of hospital now, though?'

Louise nodded.

Jack Bullage did not feel lucky, he felt ashamed. Sitting on his sofa in the dark with the curtains drawn he sipped from his small whisky bottle. He'd been home for only 48hrs but had already had three visits from stress counsellors, one from the NHS and the other two sent by the Glowview Corporation. *Probably just trying to limit their liability. It was a business dinner.*

The doctors had kept him in hospital for a few days while trying to determine if he had any meaningful injuries. He'd complained of headaches and a fuzzy sense of detachment, but the medical tests had been a farce. The MRI scanner broke down while he was inside and the ECG packed up mid test.

As the tests wore on, and no internal damage was found, Jack had decided he'd be better off at home. He'd discharged himself.

Now he was at home. And he didn't feel better off at all. He felt just as distraught, only now he was alone as well. At least the press reporters had been reasonably considerate, they'd spent a few days trying to make a story out of the 'Miracle Survivor' but got nowhere. Partly because Jack refused to say more than the barest minimum, and partly because there was nothing much to report. The media circus was already ramping down.

He chuckled ruefully to himself. Although it wasn't nice to be the subject of the press's attention, it was much nicer now than before – during the reign of Louise Harding. Then, he'd been afraid to leave the house.

CHAPTER 9

Back in his cabin, Aytch reflected on Justio's comments while browsing his own family correspondence. The few real-time QET messages were augmented by a vast array of video logs he'd brought on the mission – storage was cheap, bandwidth was very expensive. *I'll check my QET First.*

His most recent QET message had come from his eminent grandmother, Commander Sharnia, a few weeks previously. The message had been short and devoid of sentimentality.

> **Work hard. Stay sharp. Practise exams. Earn promotion. Serve Gadium.**

Aytch turned back to his revision. Much of what Justio had said was not completely new. Neither was it particularly unusual in Gadium life. The prevalence of time stasis made family matters complicated. *Stasis and time dilation!* There was always a trick question in the exams on the effects of relativistic time dilation; basically at normal operational speeds of 0.8c the effect was minimal compared to the use of stasis tubes.

The exams also put significant importance on the internalisation and acceptance of lessons from Gadium case studies. The mantra ran: Measure and Learn, Measure and Learn, Measure and Learn. With this in mind, Aytch looked up the most pertinent case study related to Family Unit Controls.

Chapter 6.3.B – Voight-Reiss Case Study

1. *Jackson Voight returned from a series of very deep space missions almost 50,000 elapsed years after he had left Gadium*
2. *His biological age (through use of stasis) was only around 7,000 years old*
3. *He rejoined his extended family and was initially welcomed*
4. *He assumed he would be the family patriarch due to the fact that the family lived off the fortune he'd left behind*
5. *The family members were, on average, five generations separated from Voight and felt entitled to the money they had inherited in his absence*
6. *There were insufficient emotional links to bridge the gaps and within five years there had been multiple assaults; Finally Voight was murdered by his descendants*
7. *Their claim of self-defence was not upheld in court*

Chapter 6.3.D – Voight-Reiss Case Study
Professor Harkin Commentary

'Poor deluded bastard.'

Aytch wondered how Justio felt about the Voight-Reiss legislation, but resolved not to ask Justio about it until a few days had passed. Instead, he quickly wrote up his notes and, closing his revision, reviewed the Earth network.

Most surveillance activity was statistical analysis to understand the political stability, population attitude towards aliens and, most critically, the proportion of Alpha individuals and the transition rates of Betas to Alphas. This was 99 per cent of his job, and he was glad to do it. Which was doubly good for the mission as Justio tended to avoid it, saying that transition data was so hard to estimate accurately it was not worth doing. Aytch shrugged and reviewed the network, which included technical infiltration of most intelligence and military agencies around the globe. Aytch smiled, remembering his original mission briefing. *Purely for observational purposes.* Political and social intervention was forbidden – except for purposes of controlling an Emergence.

The activity that Justio did seem more enthusiastic about was the identification and processing of randomly occurring Triple Alphas in the run up to Full Emergence. It was critical to identify individuals who showed signs of being a Triple Alpha: increased physical resilience, unreasonable levels of luck, and chaotic interactions with technology. But there'd been very few of those in the previous 50 years – nothing since Bill Jones.

Aytch performed a quick sweep of surveillance assets in place with the UK's Ministry of Defence. In particular, he checked the sub-department known as G60. There were no recent alerts of any consequence.

He returned to the crew room.

Aytch arrived in the crew room to see Justio sitting on the central bench. Not wanting to disturb him, Aytch went to his own seat and continued reviewing the Earth data sources.

As he reviewed his materials, Aytch saw a few new screens open up on the main crew room wall. Justio was browsing Gadium Manual entries on Triple Alphas. This was unusual. Aytch turned. 'Are you considering taking exams?'

Justio chuckled. 'No. I just wanted to check on a few case studies related to Triples, and the easiest way is to root through the manual.'

'You don't think there are any Triple Alphas on Earth? It would explain the lack of obvious Alpha increases.'

Justio frowned. 'You can never be sure, but we'd notice a Triple.'

Aytch watched as Justio used the Triple Alpha summary to find a few case studies of places he'd never even heard of. 'Please don't close the summary yet, I'll take a look once I've finished with Voight-Reiss.'

Aytch saw Justio's jaw tense. *Shouldn't have mentioned it again.* 'I …'

Justio cut him off. 'Everyone needs connectivity. Voight had lost his children and grandchildren, he was just trying to hold on. Just trying to keep whole.'

Aytch remained quiet.

Justio stood up, activated the narration, and hobbled towards the door. 'I'll leave you with the summary. I'll review my case studies later.'

The text was displayed on the wall. The narration started as Justio reached the door, and he stopped, took a deep breath and simply stood in the doorway.

Chapter 9.4.A – Triple Alphas Overview

1. Individuals who are Triple Alphas will show significant ability to alter probability functions around themselves, consciously and subconsciously
2. Alphas (Single Alphas) require life-threatening situations to alter probability functions; only their subconscious has the ability to do this
3. Triple Alphas will have significant natural longevity; enhanced physical attributes (e.g. strength, speed of recovery)
4. Conversion of Alphas to Triple Alphas is a mechanical conditioning process
5. Spontaneous conversion Alpha to Triple

> *Alphas is possible but very rare*
> 6. *Any single Triple Alpha individual of the host*
>   *species on a planet suppresses all other Beta to*
>   *Alpha transitions*

Aytch frowned. It was all so simple when written in this way, but the practicalities were many and complex. 'Should we have expected a Full Emergence when we removed Bill Jones?'

Standing at the doorway Justio was impassive. 'Yes. No. Maybe… Look, Aytch, in this business, you get what you get. We'd just arrived, we acted on a hunch. Alpha rates seemed to have been moving in the run up to Bill's transition.'

'I am concerned that Earth is stuck in a Partial Emergence.' He paused. 'But I'm also worried that a Full Emergence occurs and we fail to manage it correctly.'

Justio took a step back into the room and pointed at the screens. 'That's the benefit of all this experience. We'll react when things start to happen. We won't worry about what could happen.' He paused. 'Well, I won't worry. I suspect you'll worry irrespective of what I say.'

Aytch turned his attention back to the screens. 'At least Bill Jones was compliant once he understood his position.'

'We've plenty of ways of dealing with Despots as well. Bring them on.'

This time Justio did leave the room and Aytch was alone. The summary screen was still up and it offered him little reassurance. The minimum bar for acceptance in his family was a full and successful Emergence on Earth. Everything else was a sliding scale of failure, with an alien aware Despot breach at the bottom. *Will I preside over a new Dark Age for Earth?*

CHAPTER 10

'Come on!' Louise called up the stairs on Sunday morning. 'We're meeting Mike in an hour and I'm meeting my sister later.'

There were no signs of activity from the bedroom. 'Jeff! Shift yourself!'

A plaintive cry came down the stairs. 'I'm tired!'

Louise turned back to the kitchen, biting back the expletives naturally forming in her head. *He worked late on Friday, but* ... 'I'm not rising to it, Jeff. You had all of yesterday to recover. We agreed 10am.'

A few moments later Jeff plodded down the stairs. 'It's only 9.50.'

'10am means nine-fifty.'

Louise, with Jeff still grumbling, climbed into her beaten-up old car and they headed out of London in search of some fresh air and a good old-fashioned country pub.

Jeff settled down in the passenger seat. 'It'll be nice to waste an afternoon with the supplements and a beer.'

Louise sighed. *Waste* was not in her vocabulary, she'd been working hard all Saturday and thoroughly wanted to get analysing her findings with Mike and Jeff.

Jeff started to doze off.

No way. 'Jeff, give me directions to the Dog and Pheasant. We're supposed to be there at noon. Stop sleeping!'

Jeff opened an eye. 'Stay on this road for the next hour and then ask me again. By the way, I love your company…

I'm only dozing off to give myself a better chance of surviving a crash!'

Louise didn't deign to answer.

On arrival at the pub, Louise nodded approvingly – it looked very acceptable: brick walls, thatched roof, and ivy climbing around a smoking chimney. She pulled into the large gravel car park and manoeuvred between a couple of much nicer cars before leaving Jeff for a smoke and going inside.

The internal décor matched the exterior; smart but comfortable. With a polite nod to the barman, Louise walked past the bar, scanning for Mike. She found him sitting near to the open fire, wearing his Sunday best: sports jacket, *clean* shirt and pressed chinos. 'Hey there, you expecting polite company?'

Mike looked up from his newspaper. 'Felicitations, Mrs Harding. Where's Jeff? Did *you* finally crack?'

Louise looked around as she sat down – the pub was a significant improvement on their local. She smiled. 'Nice choice.'

Mike smiled broadly. 'My sort of place, when I can afford it, every starter costs 10 pounds and comes with a dollop of Foie Gras.'

Louise arched an eyebrow.

'I'm joking, I'll have the quinoa and tofu.'

'He's puffing in the car park. He'll be in shortly.' Louise took out her notepad.

A few minutes later Jeff joined them.

Mike started to stand. 'Drinks?'

'You've already got one. I'll get them.' Jeff did an about turn and walked over to the bar.

As Jeff walked over to the bar, Louise followed his movements and took in some of the clientele. *And the requisite smart crowd.* Her eyes locked with a glamorous lady across the room.

There was a cough. 'I said… what did you find out?'

Louise became aware that Mike had been speaking. She turned to Mike. 'Sorry, Mike, what was that you said?'

Mike paused, his eyes searching out the focus of her recent interest. He nodded approvingly. 'Probably more my type than yours.'

'Well, you're the promiscuous atheist, maybe you should speak to her.'

Mike looked down at his clothes and made a show of tidying his hair. 'I fear that quarry is too exclusive for my meagre facilities.'

'Or are you seeking to protect your immortal soul?'

'If I have one at all… I'd be a fool not to protect it. But it's in no danger… hopefully I'll be judged by my actions, not my thoughts.'

'Or, indeed, your fantasies.' Louise raised an eyebrow at Mike and was rewarded with a smile.

'Well…'

Louise wasn't finished. 'You wouldn't know what to do anyway!'

Mike remained silent. He returned his attention to the newspaper.

'Sorry Mike, did I go too far?' Louise looked over to the bar. Jeff was chatting with effortless charisma to the barwoman. Not flirting – well, not much – just enough to make the connection. He turned and flashed a smile back at Louise, and a cosy warmth flushed through her. 'Well, Mike, if you don't ask you don't get, I should know. I asked, and I got.'

Mike smiled. 'As I remember, you decided and you took.'

Returning with the drinks, Jeff sat down. 'Did I miss anything?'

'Just Louise dispensing some universal truths.' Mike smiled at Louise in a friendly way.

'Okay, so I've done a few checks.' Louise selected a page in her notebook. 'Bullage didn't engineer a crash to garner sympathy. He was just lucky.'

Mike clapped his hands together. 'Excellent, so roast beef lunch and a snooze. We're done.'

'No, we're not done, Michael. I found other things… of interest.'

Jeff shook his head slightly. 'He wasn't really lucky. He lost his long-term girlfriend and probably suffered severe mental trauma.'

Louise scowled. 'Keep up, Jeff.'

'Please elucidate, then.' Mike looked expectant.

'I found conspiracy websites saying there is something genuinely special about certain miraculous survivors.'

Mike nodded taking it in. 'Nothing specifically linking to Jack?'

'Nothing specific.' Louise paused. 'But I found some references to subconscious luckiness; an implication that some people can control their own destiny in random situations.'

'But was there a smoking gun?' Mike looked thoughtful. 'Semantics aside, what I said last week still holds. There's a basic premise of science protecting the future from being absolutely deterministic. So no-one can know what will happen in a truly random event…'

'Chaos Theory?'

Mike shook his head. 'Close, but no. Chaos Theory states that it's really difficult to model the future state of a complex system. Small changes in initial conditions create massive changes in the end state.' Mike paused and took a sip of his beer. 'What I'm talking about is the Uncertainty Principle, which says fundamentally you can't know everything, because measuring one bit of a system will alter another bit of the system.'

Louise waited a few moments. 'Jeff did mention something about it last night.'

Jeff grinned. 'We have pretty racy pillow talk.'

Louise shook her head. 'But back to my original question; if someone could have, say, conscious control over their luck, what could it look like?'

For a moment, Mike thought. 'Let's say you had a guy who could always choose the winning lottery numbers. Off the top of my head, there are three possibilities.'

Mike held up three fingers to mark them off. 'One. He can travel into the future, see the result and then travel back in time.' Mike tucked a finger away. 'Two. He can see into the future, see the results before they happen in his time.' Mike pointed directly at Louise with the remaining finger. 'Three. He can influence which winning numbers are chosen.'

Mike looked around, then returning his attention to Louise, continued. 'They're all counter to any science I know, it's paranormal territory, but we're in the game of pushing the boundaries of credibility. Do you have any clues as to what your internet theorists are thinking?'

'Nothing related to those options. But I found a few conspiracy websites talking about miracle survivors and making references to hedgehogs. There were a couple of repeated user names across multiple chat rooms.'

Mike raised his eyebrows. 'Who are they?'

Louise replied. 'The user names are Adamo34 and Xeeta55.'

Jeff shook his head. 'There's no trace of them anywhere else either, just these particular chat boards. And we couldn't find any links between the user names either.'

'No links, my friend? None at all?' He paused. 'Nothing except for the fact 34 and 55 are both Fibonacci numbers.' Jeff looked sheepish and Mike scribbled on his napkin in silence for a few moments and then continued. 'Adamo and Xeeta are cyphers for the numbers 34 and 55 using a standard Caesar shift.'

Louise chuckled. 'You're the man, Mike! Another lead to chase down. Fibonacci!' Louise turned to Jeff and raised her eyebrows.

Jeff gave an amiable half-hearted huff. 'So what's Fibonacci then Louise?'

Louise fixed Jeff with a stare. 'Special nerd numbers making pretty spiral patterns and running our world.' Louise paused. 'And you get them by adding previous two numbers together: zero, one, one, two, three, five, eight, thirteen, and then twenty-one.' Louise stuck out her tongue at Jeff who stared intently at his glass.

Mike smiled. 'It's still all conjecture, but there's a link - Fibonacci and a prickly hedgehog. So, we're not the first ones to wonder whether there may be something special about *certain* people in *certain* situations ... but just because people have looked doesn't mean there's anything there.'

As their food arrived, Louise fiddled with her phone. 'I do have a few hits with Fibonacci and Hedgehog, but my phone can't handle the web pages. I'll wait until I get home. Eat up, Jeff.'

Jeff made exaggerated movements of food chewing.

Mike turned towards Louise. 'Are you sure you want to progress this? Isn't this just more unhealthy attention to Jack Bullage?'

Jeff rolled his eyes.

Louise shrugged. 'Seriously, Mike, this is just my reporter's instincts, it's not personal. It may be paranormal, but I'd prefer science.' She stood.

Mike looked unconvinced. 'Well, subatomic science, the world of quantum mechanics, does allow for pretty weird behaviours. But at the aggregate level… I don't think so.'

Jeff chipped in. 'Some mathematical solutions predict parallel universes and alternative dimensions, but there's no observational evidence.'

'But, Louise, what about the Record?'

'I'll have to keep Harry on side.' Louise collected her hat, gloves, scarf and coat, and signalled to Jeff they needed to make tracks. She was already planning her next bit of investigation. *Can I link hedgehogs to Fibonacci… and where will it lead?*

Jeff spent most of the drive home begging Louise to slow down. After one particularly desperate bout of pleading Louise turned to Jeff with a smile. 'Let's assume in a parallel universe out there, I did slow down, but not here.'

Back home, Louise made some tea, changed into her comfy clothes and logged on at the kitchen table. Jeff came in a few minutes later, after a much needed puff of unhealthy air in the garden. He gave Louise a quick kiss and took himself through to the sitting room and turned on the television.

Louise started to search the internet, using the names of the crash survivors, the word *hedgehog*, and the word *Fibonacci*. Just as before, the comments from Adamo34 and Xeeta55 came up. Louise gave Jeff a running update. 'There's an old message here posted by Adamo34, it says *you and the hedgehog* and another old one from Xeeta55 says *hedgehog luck*.'

Jeff called back from the sitting room. 'Is there anything else?'

'I'm looking now using the word Fibonacci.' Louise typed away vigorously. 'Hold on… a link to web-site about a military programme called Project Hedgehog – Gotcha!'

Jeff came through from the sitting room and looked over Louise's shoulder. 'Ah, yeah, you've got it! The US government have been breeding hedgehogs and using them as spies, with miniature cameras secreted in between their prickles. This is the lead we've been waiting looking. I'll go to the police station and report Mrs Tiggy-Winkle.'

Louise threw her elbow backwards, but Jeff evaded it and returned to the sofa in the sitting room. Louise grimaced. 'Okay, a false alarm, but I think there is something here. There are comments by a person with the username called *FibonacciEddie*.'

Louise was silent for a quite a long while as she scanned the web for more posts by *FibonacciEddie*. After a few hours a general theme emerged. 'Jeff, I've got something. This guy has a few posts related to a thing he calls Project Hedgehog, capital *p* and capital *h*.'

Jeff came back into the kitchen and looked over Louise's shoulder.

'It says 1960s and the UK Ministry of Defence.'

The telephone rang and Louise got up to answer. It was her sister asking Louise why she was not at the cinema as agreed. Louise swore to herself and rushed for the door.

CHAPTER 11

When Louise arrived at her desk at the Daily Record on Monday morning, the cleaners were still vacuuming. She'd left Jeff fast asleep, although he had been murmuring about a meeting he had with the faculty head later in the day.

She powered through her inbox, stopping occasionally to say hello to colleagues as the office slowly filled up. At 7.30, Karen came in and went to her place on the politics desk. *A comrade.* Louise ran over. 'Karen, really weird one, do you have any record of historic MOD secret projects?'

'Slightly too broad, we have National Archives materials; what are the specifics?'

'Project Hedgehog.'

'Never heard of it. When did it run?'

'Not sure, 1960s?'

Karen typed away. 'You're in a little luck but not much. In 2010, there was a release of a list of top secret project names, but zero details about what they did. There was a Project Hedgehog in the 1960s. I have nothing more, sorry. Did you ask the Military Zak?' She nodded towards the opposite end of the office.

'Military Zak is part of my non-supporters club.'

'There's no such thing, Louise. You're doing this to yourself.'

I don't think so.

'Maybe… anyway, thanks.' Louise shrugged and ran back to her desk.

Not long after eight, Harry Jones stopped by Louise's desk. 'Could you please join me in my office for a few minutes?'

Louise followed Harry to his office. 'So what's up, Louise Lane?'

'Louise *Harding*, thank you very much. And if you'd met my husband you would know your metaphor doesn't stretch very far.'

'I have met your husband, at the newspaper pub quiz a few years ago. I also remember your competitive instinct forced you to bring that *quizzard*.' Harry smiled.

'Ah yes, Mike... So what's new, Harry?'

Harry puffed out his cheeks and leant back. 'Not too much. Just reminding you not to investigate Jack Bullage.'

'Why do you think I would?'

'Other than my in-depth judgement of your character based on seven years of close observation and mentoring?'

Fair point. Louise smiled to herself. 'Yes... other than that?'

'One of the tabloids is running a piece tomorrow on Jack Bullage's post-crash medical examination. They claim doctors couldn't find a scratch on him.' Harry paused. 'And they may add some sensationalist stuff about medical machines going haywire.'

Harry passed over a rough copy. There was a picture of Bullage attempting to look innocent and contrite. Louise studied the image. *Twat.* The words were not much better, sensationalist and vacuous.

But there was something in the story that, perhaps, she wanted to believe. Did she want to believe that Jack was special? Louise shook her head and passed the paper back to Harry. 'Pretty weird, but I won't let it distract me.'

'Good. Our rival newspapers had a field day on your little incident with Bullage. We stood by you, quite rightly, but you are not to touch him.'

The warning was over and Louise stood. 'Clearly understood. What else have you got on?'

Harry stood as well. 'I have to get on with my number one priority for this week, which is the most recent discussions about the Scottish parliament demanding the removal of all nuclear weapons from Scottish soil. They're flexing their muscles and we have a contact at the MOD with General Crowley who has some pretty firm, and totally unprintable, views on impact to the UK's nuclear deterrent.'

'I'll do the interview Harry. I realise I usually do investigative pieces, but my reporting skills would benefit from doing some domestic policy work.'

Harry face brightened. 'I love your enthusiasm. That is to say, when it isn't causing you to have restraining orders imposed.'

Louise smiled. 'It doesn't happen every time.'

'Noted. Okay then Ms Lane – spend a little time with Karen on the politics desk to get the angles we want to explore. It probably won't come as a shock to you we want to play the angle it would be a terrible thing for the UK, including Scotland.'

Harry reached out and gently took Louise by the arm. 'We don't want anything interesting in this report. We have given General Crowley a nod and a wink that it will basically be a puff piece for him.'

Louise acknowledged Harry with a smile and a nod, and then she walked quickly back to her desk. *First off Project Hedgehog, and maybe just a little look at Jack Bullage.*

Louise logged on to the Daily Record news archive and typed in various search options to see if they had any record of Project Hedgehog from the 1960s. The only information returned was to confirm what Karen had said. There was a Project Hedgehog in the 1960s. However, there was no accompanying information. Louise got herself a coffee and went over to Karen to get briefed on the impact on the UK's nuclear deterrent if the Scottish parliament were to get their way.

Later in the morning, Louise called Jeff's mobile, but it switched straight to voicemail. So, on a not so uneducated whim, she called on the home landline.

The phone was answered. 'Hello?'

Louise rolled her eyes (only for the benefit of herself). 'So, Jeff, slow start today?'

'My lectures were cancelled and so I thought I would get some critical research done at home.'

'And the meeting with the faculty head? No, don't bother... Okay, so what have you found out about Project Hedgehog?'

There was silence.

'Okay, so what have you found out about Jack Bullage?'

There was silence.

'Okay, then. I will be home at 7ish. Love you.'

Louise massaged her temples with her fingertips. Well, let's see how I can get General Crowley to help me out.

CHAPTER 12

On the Gadium mission ship, a warning message flashed across the living quarters.

```
Potential Alpha Identification
Cross Reference Qualification Required
```

Aytch hurried from his cabin to the crew room. 'Commander, it looks like your intuition was right. That was very valuable.'

Justio looked up from his work. 'I appreciate the gesture but there's no need to perform for the voice recorders.' Justio paused while he worked on his tablet for a few moments. 'Note the word *potential* before you get all worked up.'

The information was displayed on the wall.

```
England (London) - 15th October 2015 22:05 GMT
Automotive crash involving multiple vehicles
One 4 vehicle group contained 12 fatalities
and 1 lone survivor
Survivor name is Jack Bullage (10th May 1971)
Two other recorded incidents for Jack Bullage
10051971
```

Justio continued to type and read. 'No video footage of the actual accident. However, the computer seems to have correlated two other events for the same individual.'

Justio continued to search through the background data the computer had used to raise the alert. 'Jack Bullage has another news story with a tag line *miracle escape* from 2010 and a separate item with the tag *narrowly avoided death* from 2011.'

'Do we have the background for these other events?'

Justio sat down slowly onto the central bench. 'I will take a look; we're bound to find something.'

Aytch took his own communications tablet and started accessing the historical records. 'If he's really had three near death escapes then there's a chance he may have spontaneously converted to a Triple Alpha.'

Justio looked unconvinced. 'A very slim chance, but possible... given that he may have been involved in three separate escapes. This could indicate a higher proportion of Alphas than we thought.' Justio paused, apparently finished, but then added a post script. 'A spontaneous conversion to Triple Alpha would be serious, but quite easy to validate and take control.'

Aytch called up the sections of the Gadium manual to check Alpha population probability projections and Triple Alpha conversions. 'If we find a Triple Alpha then we may have to decide quickly about intervention.'

'If he's a Triple then we'll intervene.' Justio looked directly at Aytch. 'What's your current view on preferred intervention?'

It was not often that Justio asked his opinion straight out in this way. Aytch looked around the room quickly. *They're recording.* He took a few deep breaths. This is exactly the type conversation that would be replayed when they returned home. *First contact intuition.* 'My preference is to rehouse him on Earth and stall the Emergence.'

Justio nodded and appeared to make a note on his communications tablet. 'The alternative is we take him out and trigger the Full Emergence.' Justio paused. 'You could get a field promotion if we manage it smoothly.'

Aytch's eyes widened for a brief second. 'I don't think Earth's ready. Standing orders are safety first.'

Justio nodded. 'Firstly, I will dig into the data of the other two events to ascertain if they really were life threatening escapes. Secondly, surveillance for Jack Bullage. Finally, we should start planning for some type of action in the case Jack Bullage is a Triple. As you say – safety first – we cannot risk a Despot situation.'

'I'm going to review some relevant materials on interventions.' Aytch stood up.

'Sit down, Commander. We'll do this together. Put it up.' Justio pointed at the wall.

Aytch engaged the computer.

Chapter 2.3.A – Emergence Pitfalls
Overview

Once a Full Emergence is underway (10 - 20%
Population are Alphas) then stalling back into a
Partial Emergence is very unlikely. The key jobs of
the Gadium mission are: to remove any randomly
occurring Triple Alphas, to stop major conflicts,
and to prepare communications. Noting actual
communications cannot occur until the 99%
threshold is passed. It is critical Gadium presence
remains a secret.
Once a Full Emergence is achieved (>99%
Populations are Alphas) then Gadium must engage
with the host population to initiate the
conversions.

The main risks to Gadium intervention are:

1. *Local oppressive regime does not engage with*
   Gadium; typically this will be a regime with
   access to Triple Alphas
2. *Conscious inequality conflict where major*
   sections of the populations feel unfairly
   treated; known as 'Grapes and Peanuts'
3. *Loss of reason from the host population due to*
   inability to grasp the situation, or (more
   seriously) with links to the Parallels doctrine

Once the narration had completed Justio turned to Aytch. 'At the moment it's all about Triple Alpha suppression.'

'Which one of the risks is the worst?'

'Any hint of us aliens before the 99% limit is reached usually spells disaster for the host civilisation. The Gadium process demands a quarantine. Generally, a hundred generations, suppressing Beta to Alpha transitions by doping a few Triples into their population.'

Aytch thought for a while. Anonymity was very much under their control. That risk was not a big one. 'It doesn't feel too serious, we just put them on hold.'

Justio looked Aytch in the eye, holding his gaze for a good few seconds. 'Billions of them die an early death. Billions who would have flourished if they had converted to Triple Alphas.'

'Understood, but what about actual peer to peer conflict within the host civilisation?'

'Once the majority have converted to Triples, the third one can get pretty bad. Any population that doesn't have a constant consistent view of the Triple powers in terms of SISR is susceptible to severe wanton destruction.'

Aytch thought about it for a while. The powers he got when he was converted during his juvenile years to a fully-fledged Triple Alpha were pretty amazing. But the Gadium society did not understand the underlying science; there was only one legal interpretation SISR – Single Instance State Reduction. The alternative was *The Parallels*. The Parallels had been declared an anathema and denounced by the GEC over eight hundred thousand years earlier. Any teaching that gave credibility to The Parallels was punishable by death.

Aytch turned his attention back to his communications tablet. 'Okay, so for now we'll just investigate Jack Bullage. Then, we watch and wait to see if Alpha rates increase.'

'Just standard procedure.'

Aytch nodded. 'Okay, let's send in the mini-bots. Agreed?'

Aytch paused while Justio was unresponsive.

'I acknowledge the computer flagged it as a potential Alpha event, but I believe we now consider it a potential Triple Alpha event. So we need formally logged approvals.'

Justio sighed. 'Surveillance agreed.'

'Okay, for Jack Bullage – let's send Jeremy Benedict. Hold on, I'll bring up the records.' Aytch typed for a few moments and a new screen displayed on the wall. 'We've got about 30 mini-bots either on Jeremy Benedict or at his offices.'

Justio brought up a map of the south east of the UK. The map showed where all the active mini-bots were located. There were well over three hundred little pinpoints of red denoting active mini-bot surveillance. 'Let's send him on another infidelity stakeout.'

Aytch loaded up the details of a company Gadium had set up called Merrily Associates. Jeremy Benedict believed it was a legal company specialising in divorce proceedings. They used Jeremy for observation of cheating wives or husbands, they paid online, on time and full rates. Jeremy had unknowingly delivered Gadium mini-bots all over the UK: embassies, army bases and nightclubs. The very small size of the mini-bots made them susceptible to vagaries of the weather so any long distance travel was done by unknowing couriers.

Justio wrote and dispatched the email to Jeremy.

Dear Jeremy,
Slightly strange one for you this time. I need you to investigate a very sensitive subject. I rely on your ingenuity and on your absolute discretion. I have a client who is very keen to understand the extra-marital activity of Jack Bullage. He has recently escaped a serious car crash and he is actually unmarried

himself; but we have reason to believe he has
been seeing people who are married.
At this moment please just build up a set of
background information of what he has been
doing over the last few months.
As before, we will pay you a retainer of £50
per day and then an additional £25 per hour
for all relevant activity related to
investigating Mr Bullage. We are particularly
interested to understand the nature and cause
of the car crash he was in; although we don't
think there was any foul play we would like to
rule it out.
All results can be sent to this email address.
Signed
Merrily Associates

Justio looked at Aytch. 'Done.'

'I just want to avoid Trogia-like mistakes.'

Justio's eyes widened and smiled. 'Setting the bar that high, eh?'

'Although I suppose we'll get the right result on Trogia ultimately.'

The smile quickly left Justio's face. 'Our mistake condemned many Trogians.'

Aytch nodded and busied himself checking that the Jeremy Benedict email had launched correctly; then he went back to his cabin.

Alone in the crew room, Justio chuckled to himself as the details of Jack Bullage's previous miracle escapes were fed back to him by the ship's hopelessly underequipped computer system. The first escape was a court-room escape in which he had been found not guilty of something insignificant. The second escape was when a disgruntled journalist had thrown a brick at him. *Repression of AI has given us data matching not much better than random.*

For a moment Justio considered speaking to Aytch and calling off the surveillance. But, after a few moments of thought, he decided against aborting the mission. *Bullage did escape a serious crash, and I want to get moving anyway.*

Back in his cabin, Aytch was happy with his participation in the day's discussions. The previous interesting activity on Earth had been many years before, and Justio had taken all of the decisions pretty much unilaterally. This time Aytch was confident he would make an equal contribution. It was important, too, the ship's logs would be scrutinised in any promotion review, and he had to be seen to be taking an equal role – or even driving the Gadium agenda.

Aytch turned back to his revision programme. A few things had come up he really needed to take a deeper look at. The prospect of Jack Bullage being a Triple Alpha (unlikely but possible) prompted him to look at the role of Aware Triple Alphas in Non-Emerged Civilisations a.k.a. 'The Despots'.

Aytch triggered the communications tablet to show the relevant sections.

Chapter 8.1.A – Despot Breach Overview

There is little risk of a Despot situation starting once a civilisation has Fully Emerged, for two reasons: Firstly, a Fully Emerged species contains almost all Alpha individuals, who benefit from a level of subconscious protection – so the threat from a Triple Alpha is lessened. Secondly, after Full Emergence (when everyone is at least an Alpha) there will be many multiples of Triple Alpha individuals – the early adopters. With multiple factions all having access to Triple Alpha individuals the relative power of any one individual is severely limited.

However, within a Partial Emergence (or in the ramp up to a Full Emergence), with relatively fewer Alpha individuals (~1%), any Triple Alpha individual will be less likely to face significant numbers of other Triple Alphas, particularly given:

1. *The onsite Gadium mission will not support (and must try to suppress knowledge of) Alpha to Triple Alpha conversion until the whole population is in an Alpha state*
2. *The simple existence of any Triple Alpha individual will stop additional Alphas naturally transitioning from the Beta population (so the population of Alphas from which another Triple Alpha could convert will not be increasing)*

So, a self-aware Triple Alpha in a Partial Emergence will have unprecedented control over the host population.

Aytch knew all of this and it worried him. Before he'd left on the mission, Sharnia had drummed it home to him with her fists, Despot Breaches were to be avoided at all costs. '*You end up having to kill almost all of them,*' she had said. Aytch wasn't sure which *all* she meant, and he hadn't asked for clarification at the time. He turned back to the narration.

Chapter 8.1.D – Despot Breaches
Professor Harkin Commentary

Partial Emergence Despot situations are uncomfortable because removing the self-aware Triple Alpha is difficult and generally forces the Gadium mission to come into open conflict with the host species ruling party, which in turn brings the issues of alien awareness.'

Aytch lay back on his bunk and decided to enter a two-hour meditative regeneration trance. This was standard procedure on a weekly basis to give the conscious and subconscious parts of the mind some uninterrupted healing time. He wanted to be at the top of his game once the specific surveillance from Earth started giving results.

CHAPTER 13

Late on Wednesday evening, Louise crashed through her front door in a jumble of concurrent activities, planned out on her walk back from the tube: shoes off, keys down, laptop out and booting up.

'Hi, Jeff!'

A voice came from the kitchen. 'Hey, love! How's it going?'

Entering the sitting room, Louise replied over her shoulder. 'I've found a few more accident survivors. Some of these new ones had really special escapes.'

'More than just special because they survived the accidents?' Jeff walked into the room. 'Should we try to survive a bunch of accidents and then ask ourselves if we feel special?'

'I had a thought on the way back from the tube.' Louise looked at Jeff. 'Could we set up some experiments to test luck?'

'Looking for what exactly?'

'Luckiness!'

'Can you be a bit more specific? Clearly we can't do car accident survival.'

'You're the scientist, Jeff.'

Jeff stood resolute for a few moments then wilted under Louise's stare. 'Look, Mike's coming for coffee tomorrow morning. I'll discuss it with him.'

Louise walked over and gave Jeff a kiss on the cheek. 'Don't either of you ever actually go to work?'

Jeff replied with mock solemnity. 'The academic life is not work Louise. It's a calling… and a burden.'

'Bollocks.'

At 8am on Thursday the phone rang. Louise had already left, so Jeff answered. 'Hi, Mike, how's it going?'

'I'm a few minutes away. Just warning you to give you time to get dressed.'

'I'm ready now, Mike.'

'I know that … but are you dressed?'

A few moments later, Jeff welcomed Mike into the house with a cup of coffee. They walked into the living room where a new flat-packed coffee table stood half constructed with the cardboard box lying close by.

Mike looked at the coffee table, then back to Jeff. Then he put his coffee cup down, took off his jacket and picked up an Allen key. 'Someone been on the North Circular recently?'

Jeff stooped down and pulled away wrapping from the various piece of coffee table that hadn't found a purpose yet. 'She wonders if we could do some tests. But I've no idea what we could do.'

'So she's serious?'

'Is she ever not? She's not going to drop it.'

Mike attached a leg to the table and tightened. Jeff passed him the various pieces required by the instructions. 'I suspect it's a surrogate for the pent-up frustration triggered by her nemesis.'

Jeff remained silent.

'Is there any possible way we could get unusual results from a luck experiment?' Mike attached the fourth leg. 'Perhaps …'

'Well, she's at the MOD tomorrow, so we can wait to see what she gets.'

The table did not take much longer to finish. Mike collected all the wrappings and Jeff, picking up the coffee cups, followed him through to the kitchen where Mike filled up a recycling bag. They sat at the kitchen table.

After a few moments of silence, Jeff spoke. 'What do you think?'

Mike looked at his watch. 'I have a fundraising meeting in an hour, and I have to prepare for it.' He paused. 'I'm pretty open to the unknown, but if Louise progresses this we'll really need to suspend our disbelief.'

'Don't I know it!'

'Semantics aside, the existence of *focusable* luck – the ability to effect apparently random scenarios – is almost certain not to exist.'

Jeff could see the wheels whirring behind Mike's eyes. Was there something more? There was. Jeff waited expectantly for Mike to continue.

'But you see, Jeff, the likelihood of the actual existence of *focusable* luck is significantly higher than the likelihood of us being able to prove its existence using current scientific understanding.' Mike paused. 'You know – the stuff what we know.'

Jeff sat at the kitchen table for a few moments thinking his way through this latest statement. Not the goldmine he'd hoped for.

'But, as we discussed in the pub, there are some very disturbing philosophical issues brought up in quantum mechanics. So we could have a look there, if only to help design an experiment.'

Mike left for his fundraiser and Jeff returned to the living room to try out the new coffee table. It supported his feet beautifully as the morning television guided him through the breakdown of modern society.

뽀

Much later, Jeff made his way to the university. Once there, he went to the science common room and started jotting out a few notes on the key tenets of the strange behaviours in quantum mechanics. *Many-Worlds… Copenhagen.* After a while he stopped, exhausted, Mike was right. Given their current knowledge, a proof was impossible.

As Jeff was finishing off, a few researchers wandered in. One of them spied Jeff in the corner and made his way over. 'Hey Jeff, how's the world of metallic materials? Still a conducive subject?'

Jeff groaned inwardly, both at the pun and the reminder. His subject was under severe funding pressure. The world had moved on from metals; his colleagues in ceramic material science were getting larger research budgets, while he laboured on with much less. 'Yes, we're still plodding away.'

The researcher nodded in sympathy. 'We're struggling to get any money for our quantum computing but the organic computing research is getting a trickle. Just enough to keep us going.'

'Where's the big money going?'

'The guys across the hall get most of the cash for their neuroscience work. But I can't be too upset, it's linked to genuine medical research.'

Jeff murmured an empathetic response and the researcher wandered away. Jeff swore under his breath, redoubled his efforts on his planning, and sent a quick text to Louise to wish her *good luck* for the upcoming interview at the MOD.

Not that she needed luck. She was a great reporter, and well respected at the Daily Record, even if she didn't see it.

CHAPTER 14

Early Friday morning, Louise arrived at the Ministry of Defence to conduct the interview with General Crowley. After being held waiting for around twenty minutes, Louise was ushered into the General's office. The General looked up at her over his glasses, and put his papers aside as she sat down. 'Ah, Mrs Harding, thank you for making time for me.'

Louise nodded deferentially and made herself look as demure as possible. 'Thank you, General Crowley, for making time for me.'

'So, you are here, hopefully, to discuss the impact to the UK in the case where Scotland gains a legal remit to remove the UK's nuclear weapons?'

'Yes, General, I've had some initial briefings from our military correspondent at the Daily Record, but I'm here to get some comments, off the record of course, to weave into the piece I'm writing.'

'Good. That's what I agreed with Sir Stephen.'

Louise nodded. 'Yes, his instructions were clear. Albeit I got them second-hand from one of his assistants.'

The General smiled affably. 'The gist is: it will be very expensive to move the weapons, the Scots currently get the benefit of the security, and they have the largest expanses of unpopulated areas.' The General paused while Louise made notes. 'Frankly, they get a lot of jobs from the bases also.'

The meeting went on with Louise asking a few gentle probing questions, allowing the General to expand on the complexities. It was clear to Louise the MOD would not make it easy, irrespective of the democratic rights of the indigenous Scottish people.

Once the initial discussions trailed off, Louise played back the major themes, and the General nodded appreciatively. He relaxed visibly when it was clear the Daily Record was going to produce a piece of reporting which was very sympathetic towards the British Armed Forces.

'Thank you, Mrs Harding. As you know, the army has a very good position in the nation's heart at the moment and we want to capitalise on this.'

'General, I understand your position, and the position of Her Majesty's Armed Forces. I'm very pleased to see we are in total accord.'

Looking downwards, the General started shuffling his papers on the desk. The meeting was over. Louise leant forward. 'It's a shame the recent extra empathy feeding the army's standing in the nation's heart must be paid for with the blood of your soldiers.'

General Crowley looked up at Louise and held her gaze for a few moments. Louise instinctively held eye contact, and then, catching herself, looked away abruptly. The General put the papers down and spoke quietly. 'I know. I know… Every car passing through Wooten or Brize enhances our influence. Machiavelli would be proud.'

A silence began to stretch.

The General unexpectedly stiffened up and leant forward. 'Totally off the record. Obviously, full Scottish devolution is off the menu for a while, but we have a back-up plan for that eventuality.'

Louise's interest was piqued. 'I suppose you will have to dismantle the military bases in Scotland. Turn the real estate into hotels?'

The General motioned Louise to lean forward some more, and tapped his nose. 'No, the day after full devolution, we... invade!'

Then the General threw his head back and laughed. Louise joined in. The General passed a piece of paper to Louise. Louise gave it a quick scan; it held a few direct anonymous quotes for Louise to feed into her piece.

As she started to get up from her chair, Louise paused. 'I know what I'm about to ask is highly irregular, but I have a personal request.'

'Go on, but I can't promise anything.'

Louise spun her story. 'My mother's best friend is dying. This best friend, Elsa, is very proud of her older brother, who in the 1960s was a member of the Armed Forces, the Welsh Guards. He saw action in a few places before coming back to England to take up an administrative post.' Louise paused. 'He died in 1964 and Elsa was never told why or how. The official line was he was involved in an industrial accident. His body was never provided for burial.'

Louise paused and choked back a few sobs. 'Elsa is very old and frail now. I would love to give her a final gift of knowledge. She investigated the death many years ago, but got nowhere except he was involved in a... Project Hedgehog.'

The General looked impassively at Louise. 'Well, it is irregular, and the name means nothing to me, however 1964 was a long time ago. Let's see.' The General opened up an MOD archive application on his computer.

Louise watched as his eyes went wide, not quite out on stalks, but with a noticeable shock.

Crowley took a breath and looked back to the screen. Project Hedgehog 1962 - 1965: Ultra Black. Experimental tests to determine existence of psychic powers. Closed down after notable disappearances. Tests were universally unsuccessful. Linked to Platoon RZ3.

General Crowley had never come across an Ultra Black rating before, even from his days in SAS operations; neither did he know what Platoon RZ3 was. 'Elsa must have been tenacious, even to find out her brother may have been on this project, but I cannot confirm anything.' He paused. 'I am sorry, Mrs Harding, but this project is top secret. I'm not even aloud to repeat the name. There's nothing I can do. Sorry.'

After Louise had thanked him and left, the General sat alone for a while. Given Project Hedgehog had an Ultra Black rating, he needed to make a formal report to the MOD Internal Affairs team. He really should not have confirmed Hedgehog existed, much less told Louise it was top secret.

He phoned the MOD Internal Affairs team to notify them of the security breach. An old colleague was soon on the phone and the General explained the full story regarding Louise's presence and her questions.

The MOD Internal Affairs man told the General that he had logged the event and marked it as *no need to follow up* as there had been no material breach of security.

Later in the day, an automated process sweeping the MOD files generated an alert to the MOD G60 team.

And a second alert was created by a passive observation programme running within a Gadium mini-bot which was happily sequestered in one of the main MOD datacentres in

Basildon. The small size of the robot meant it had to be quite ingenious to get its message out, as its transmitter arrays were tiny and only suitable for short range communications. It couldn't risk trying to hide in the MOD wireless network, as the MOD security was pretty good at detecting active tampering. However, the security guard with his swanky new mobile phone provided a short range Bluetooth connection which allowed the mini-bot's message to get into the phone and then hitch a ride out on the 4G connection into the wider world. A Gadium watching programme running in a UK network provider data centre picked up the message and forwarded it onwards.

CHAPTER 15

In the crew room, Aytch was eager to review the data on Jack Bullage. He called across the room to Justio. 'How long will we need to wait for data?'

There was a pause before Justio replied. 'A small number of weeks.'

'Would you like support updating the data aggregation feeds?'

Again, Justio let the silence stretch for a few moments then looked up. 'It's fine, Aytch, I've got it covered.'

Aytch stood and started to pace the room. Justio flashed a look of annoyance. 'Aytch, just get on with your revision. Why don't you read through a few intervention scenarios?'

Gadium training focused on data collation and analysis. Aytch knew they needed to wait for sufficient information before they could make a judgement on Jack Bullage. He sat back down. 'Computer – Chapter 6.1.A.'

The computer generated text on the wall and narrated at the same time.

Chapter 6.1.A – Intervention Tenets
Overview

1. *Gadium is committed to introducing new worlds into the galactic population*
2. *New worlds must successfully navigate a Full Emergence*
3. *Gadium will help any new world through its Full Emergence only if it is determined the new world can take a meaningful place in the*

galaxy

4. *Until a Full Emergence is clearly underway Gadium intervention must be kept secret, irrespective of the new world's attitude to aliens*

5. *If a successful outcome is at risk then produce models based on a 10-generation, 100-generation and 500-generation isolation. Where no clear advantage shows, act in favour of the longer isolation*

This was basic material, and Aytch had memorised these many years previously. The onus was on Aytch to understand (through investigation of case studies and through hands-on experience) why these tenets were critical. The material on alien exposure was of particular interest. It was an area in which he had once watched Sharnia discipline his brother for a wrong answer. She'd lost her temper and not stopped far short of tearing him in half. He still had the scars. *Never let them see us until the right time.* Certainly the histories were full of case studies where a civilisation had collapsed utterly through the confluence of knowledge of alien worlds, and inability to join. The civilisations tended to revert to animalistic basics.

Chapter 6.1.D – Intervention Tenets
Professor Harkin Commentary

'The act of Emergence for a species is a rebirth, the gains from Emergence are astronomic (literally - as they will gain the ability to perform inter-stellar travel). However, the inferiority complex usually sustained when not able to join is usually fatal to the …'

The narration and display froze as a high priority incoming message overrode the screen. Aytch had received a QET message.

The energy required for storing QET particles in a stable state was immense. The Gadium Earth team, like most other missions, had only enough quantum entangled particles to be able to encode a few hundred short messages (and their mission lengths were typically hundreds to thousands of years). Each QET particle could only be used once, after which it was useless, so once all the QET particles were used the communication reverted to tight beam laser. Given the power requirements, a regular Gadium ship could only generate a laser broadcast for distances less than fifty light years (and it was slow... only operating at the speed of light). Effectively, over these distances, once your QET ran out you were on your own.

It was marked as personal, and Aytch routed it to his communications tablet. Once decrypted, the message displayed in normal text. It was from Commander Sharnia.

> Vantch. Monitoring indicates conflict, perhaps
> Triple Alphas. I suspect GF. No supporting
> evidence yet. Be alert.

It was big news to receive a second QET within a month, Sharnia very rarely wrote to him. Aytch reflected on the actual message. *Conflict*. It wasn't unusual, particularly when Gadium forces were not yet on station to keep control. *Gadium First*. That was bad news, although Aytch noted with a grimace his grandmother did tend to suspect everyone of being covert members of GF. The planet Vantch was interesting though, it was a new mission in a star system relatively close to areas where Gadium were not well liked. Aytch was not 100% sure if the Gadium mission team had actually arrived on Vantch yet, but it was certainly due there sometime soon.

Justio looked at Aytch from across the room. 'Anything interesting?'

'Just a note from my family head, general concerns only – reminding me to focus.'

Justio held Aytch's gaze for a few moments. 'So nothing about Vantch?'

'How did you know?'

'I had a note from a contact back on Gadium earlier today. The GEC are trying to keep a lid on this, but they're nervous. There is potential war on Vantch and it appears our mission team is still a few years away.'

Aytch nodded, although he couldn't remember hearing the alert of another recent QET. *Perhaps while I was meditating?*

Anyway, he knew Justio was well-connected. You could hardly fail to be well-connected once you had been on 30 missions. 'I'm sure we'll sort out Vantch. What do you think the GEC will decide to do?'

Justio shrugged. 'It depends on the severity of the conflict. If there are many self-aware Triple-Alphas on Vantch there may not be much we can do.'

'Standard procedure is to remove them.'

'Fine if there are only a few… but very difficult if there are millions of them. It's not unheard of for a 0.5% Alpha Population to find out about Triple Alpha abilities and convert themselves, leaving the other 99.5% as Betas.'

Aytch nodded. He'd read a few case studies on those situations. The Gadium doctrine on those was generally to isolate the planet and wait for a long time. While any Triple Alphas remained there were no new Beta to Alpha transitions. In these situations, infants were born as Betas. So, after a while, tens of thousands of years, the Triples died out and the planet was left in a Beta state again. The Gadium mission would remain hidden and covertly interrupt any significant advances by the host planet in the areas of space travel, AI or stasis development. However, fundamentally, planets with high levels of inequality across the population typically didn't have the energy to do anything much more than enforce their positions, bemoan their inequality and look out for themselves. It really was normally a simple quarantine – a forest-fire burn out. *Unless.* Unless the planet's population *knew* about the Gadium mission holding them down, and gave the planet a common enemy to unite against. Then it was more difficult.

Aytch remained silent. Justio continued to talk. 'Once they have 99 per cent Alphas, then we deal with them: treaties limiting AI, acknowledgement of Gadium primacy in galactic exploration. You know the drill, they get interstellar travel and enormous gravity-warping stasis machines.'

Aytch nodded. The 99 per cent limit was important for all sorts of reasons, not least as it was the level after which all new-borns were Alphas. *Fully Emergent.*

He opened up a few more Gadium bureaucratic texts; then he stopped and turned to Justio. 'What would you do?'

'I'd have to find out exactly what's happening on the ground in Vantch. Currently, we know nothing, just a few QET messages from the mission team. We don't know what's really happening there.' Justio turned his full attention back to his own screens.

ЦЩ

'But, Madam Chairwoman, we don't actually know what's happening there!' Councilman Smitter looked around the table for support and got a few murmurs which seemed to embolden him. 'How do we even know for sure they haven't reached Vantch?'

Sharnia forced herself to remain in her dangerously creaking chair. It was all she could do to stop herself from vaulting the table and ripping his whining head from his shoulders. The QET message from Vantch had come through a few days earlier, and already the information war was in full swing.

The Chairwoman stood up, also bristling with rage. Smitter sat down quickly. 'We have three Gadium officers of the highest integrity on the mission. Their few QET messages have been consistent for the last 50 years. Their families are convinced of the veracity of their QET messages. I'm convinced too. There will be no more talk of failed mission cover-ups. So Councilman Smitter, do you have anything more to add?'

Smitter was not the brightest, he stood up. 'I do not mean to cast aspersions on the integrity of our officers. However, the mission should have got there five years ago. All I am saying … it's unusual and we should have full disclosure.'

The Chairwoman remained standing, still furious. She looked around the room and took a few deep breaths before continuing. 'I wish I could offer the council full disclosure but, quite simply, I can't.'

The intimation that the Chairwoman was holding back information from the ruling council flashed around the room. The murmuring rose again, with words such as *GF* and *sabotage* and *failure* bubbling up. The Chairwoman sat down.

Sharnia looked around for the reactions of the key players. The Deputy was characteristically passive, whispering the odd message to one of his aides who, as ever, stood in readiness behind his chair. Sharnia's gaze swung around the table. There was no hard support here for the rumour that the Vantch Mission were covering up their own failures, but more evidence would gain it momentum. Her eyes came to rest on Commander Jenkins. *Exemplary service record but with over-liberal tendencies.* She was concerned about him; a few references over the last ten decades needed to be reviewed.

The landmass of Vantch was almost a single supercontinent, similar to Earth's Pangaea period. But on Vantch there were two continents currently separated by about 10 miles of ocean. The sentient inhabitants were very similar to humans, basically: mammalian, biped, heads, hands, faces, noses, etc.

The technology prevalent on Vantch was on a par with mid-20th century Earth. A closer inspection of the cities on Vantch showed the current sentient species appeared to be the second sentient species to have made this planet their home. There were residues of a previous owner, long since departed. Many of the buildings found were made from technology far in advance of the current incumbents. The new inhabitants had simply moved into the buildings left behind by the previous owners but had not learned the technology required to improve them.

At the northern end of the continent of Harfi, within the second largest city, a conference was being held to confirm the status of a new religion, led by the self-styled Prophet. The religion, *The Many Paths*, had, for the last five years, been gaining enormous traction.

The Palace of Infinite Wisdom, set in the middle of the city, was the focus for the conference; around the building large crowds had gathered. Mostly the members of the crowd were dressed in the orthodox clothes of the ruling party; full grey cloaks with hoods thrown back. However, there were pockets of people wearing the white trousers and green shirts of the Disciples of the Prophet. These small crowds were surrounded by armed soldiers.

In one such small group, the leader, Klope, one of the original converts to *The Many Paths*, pulled up his green shirt to reveal a tattoo of the sign of the Prophet – a single star circled by eight identical planets all equidistant from the centre. Klope called out above the noises of the crowd. 'Freedom in my world. I walk the many paths.'

Just a handful of metres away, across the other side of the line of soldiers, an old lady dressed in the grey cloak stood resolutely facing Klope, holding her home-made placard. It read 'One world. One god. One path.'

Klope made eye contact with the old lady and shouted to her. 'The Prophet walks amongst the sick on Lokis. Healing them and succouring them. What does your Prelate do for you?'

'He prays for us. As he prays for you also. There is one world, god's world, and one path, god's path.'

Klope felt the rage build. He remembered the old ceremonies, with this Prelate. Familiar and comforting, but lies… and now Klope's eyes were opened. The Prophet had walked out of the crystal caverns of Dunsat and his words had shown the glory of the myriad of possibilities out there – *The Many Paths.* Yes, the simple monastic religion of *The One* was still prevalent here, but its days were numbered, its fires were burning low. 'You have been misled, old lady. The Prelate does not pray for anyone but himself and his continued corruption of this world. Emancipation is near. Truth is near.'

The old lady's eyes did not waver. 'Was it truth driving your Prophet to order the atrocities in the monastery of Fairport?' There was a murmuring from the crowd around the old lady. A swell of support for her words. The grumbling grew as they noticed Klope was not backing down. There was a general movement towards Klope's group; the soldiers held the line, but were not quick to push the crowd back.

Klope noticed the looks shared between the soldiers and felt the animosity. This was not the day to make a stand, he decided, and turned away, back to his group. *This is not your world, old lady. This is my world. And in my world the Prophet brings freedom to all of us.*

The old lady saw Klope turn away, but called after him. 'Is this your world? Is this what you have shaped for yourself; for us to share with you?'

Another Disciple close to Klope noticed the exchange and moved up to comfort him. 'I, for one, am proud to be in your world, brother.'

Klope looked gratefully at him. 'And I in yours, brother.'

Their moment was broken by a trumpet call from the Palace, and the crowds hushed as a delegation came out from the main doors and worked their way down to a large podium close to the main gates.

CHAPTER 16

Louise left the MOD unhappy with her achievements. She'd been so pleased with her performance of the heartbroken mother story. Yes, she'd managed to get confirmation Project Hedgehog had existed. It was obviously something the MOD was trying to keep quiet, and the General had looked pretty shocked when he read whatever he'd found. But she'd not walked away with any significant new information.

She got back to the Daily Record and started to write up the interview. Midway through, Harry Jones came to her desk.

'Hey, Louise. How did it go?'

'Pretty well. We've got the piece, with decent anonymous quotes. I'll have it finished by 4pm.'

'You've been flat out for ages now. Get me the first draft by 3pm, then go home and start the weekend early.'

'Thanks, Harry, I appreciate it.'

By 3pm, the draft was in Harry's inbox and Louise was out of the door.

Outside the tube station, Louise called Jeff to see how he was doing. Unfortunately, he was deep inside the University campus where the phone signal was severely restricted by the vast amounts of scientific equipment and electromagnetic shielding. So Louise left a message. 'Hey, love. How are you doing? How's the school of lust?'

Back home, Louise booted up her laptop and, with a cup of tea next to her, started more web sleuthing. *Something more on FibonacciEddie perhaps?* Louise loaded three different search engines and started surfing. She reviewed some of the old web postings and made some new searches.

After three or four hours, using very diverse searches, Louise found nothing of note related to Project Hedgehog. *Nothing there, or just well hidden?* The more she searched, the more frustrated she became. There was nothing there. When Jeff came home, Louise related her disappointment.

Jeff soaked it up. 'I would take the lack of information as a positive sign. We know there is something real and so there should be something coming up. Looking for the holes can be rewarding.'

Louise brightened. 'Maybe the lack of references means the information has been cleansed. But we're no closer to finding out what it actually means. Were there positive results? Are they just very embarrassed about wasted money? Were there unnecessary deaths?'

For a few moments Jeff was silent. 'Did you search on drugs and mind-control? There was some whacky stuff postulated in the 60s.'

'I tried all that.'

'Well, no harm done, every loose end chased down means we are...' Jeff paused.

'We're what?'

'Not sure, I was hoping you would finish the sentence with something utterly motivational.'

Louise arched an eyebrow and, although her heart wasn't in the retort, she made it anyway. 'You can't rely on me to do everything.'

Jeff leant over and gave her a kiss then disappeared into the living room.

Louise heard the television go on, and returned her attention to her laptop.

A few hours later, in his cabin, Justio saw one of his private email addresses had received a new message. It was an alert notifying him that searches were being made on the internet with a combination of words indicating interest in Project Hedgehog. Justio recorded the information and then checked to see if the UK Ministry of Defence had any alerts.

Interestingly they had a totally separate alert generated by MOD personnel accessing information on Project Hedgehog purely internally. *Two separate incidents.* Justio made a note of the details, and considered what to tell Aytch.

CHAPTER 17

Jack stood in his kitchen looking out over the back garden. Although it was past lunchtime, he was still dressed in his pyjama bottoms and t-shirt. He nursed his fourth coffee of the day. He was desperate to drive away the constant feeling of exhaustion; the doctors had told him it would take time to get over the trauma. *Am I traumatised? Or just tired?*

It had only been two weeks since the crash, but it seemed to Jack he'd already spent a lifetime in hospital taking part in physical and mental assessments. He knew he'd been emotionally shaken by the crash, obviously, but he also felt, somehow, physically changed by it. Outside he could see the sun shining brightly, low in clear blue late autumn skies. His memory returned to the crash, and he felt panic rise. Remembering his treatment, he concentrated on his breathing. *In for a count of five then exhale and count to ten – then repeat.*

Jack moved to the kitchen table and finished his coffee, sitting in silent reflection. *Oh, Sarah!* He was tired, and put his arms and head down on the table. *You were all I ever wanted. I can still see your sleeping face, serene and beautiful, as I was dragged out of the car. Dragged out and saved. Why was I…* But before he could finish the thought, the doorbell rang.

Jack's head came up abruptly. He turned in the direction of the front door. In the same movement he put the cup down on the table, or at least he thought he had. It wasn't until he was a pace away from the table he instinctively thought about the cup; he hadn't put it securely down on the table. He turned and watched the mug teeter precariously on the edge of the table. As he started to turn back towards the table, it fell.

Time slowed and Jack watched for what seemed like an age as the mug tumbled downwards through the air. A myriad of concurrent thoughts flitted around his subconscious and, here and there, a few pushed forwards for consideration.

Damn, a broken mug.

Sarah bought it for me at John Lewis.

It's certain to smash now.

It might not.

Yes, it will.

Jack's consciousness seemed to detach slightly and in the tiny instant between the cup almost hitting the floor and it actually hitting the floor, he worried about when, where and how he could get a replacement; as well as blaming himself for putting it down incorrectly.

I won't be able to get a replacement until Saturday.

I'll park behind the chemist.

Jack took stock of the situation and at the moment of impact he was convinced it would break, but it didn't. The cup landed on one of its corners and did not smash, it just bounced a few times, rolled a little bit and then it came to rest in the middle of the kitchen floor.

Jack let out his long held breath. *Lucky break … lucky no-break*

He picked the cup up, returned it to the table, and then went to answer the door.

CHAPTER 18

Aytch lay on his bunk trying to sleep, but he was restless. He wondered if he was really ready to take an equal role to Justio in managing an Emergence on Earth. It had been different when they'd just arrived, he hadn't expected to be an equal partner and Justio had made all the calls. But now... now he was determined to make a meaningful contribution. He rolled over on his bunk and lay staring at the wall, then he rolled over and looked at the other wall. *Vantch! We're going to be under such scrutiny to get it right on Earth.*

Sleep wasn't coming, and Aytch had already done his meditation trance; also he was reticent to take any drugs – a sign of weakness. He got up and started to pace the corridors. As he passed the main crew room he looked in. The walls were showing real-time feeds of the main news channels from around Earth, with no sound. Justio was working away on his communications tablet. Aytch paused at the doorway to say something but shook his head and walked on.

Pulling out his own communications tablet, he browsed some of his revision notes on counter-terrorism associated with Gadium control of Full Emergences. The Gadium definition of terrorism was pretty broad, encompassing anything going against the point-in-time Gadium view on any particular situation. In some cases it could just be a host species uprising against Gadium in the name of independence and self-determinism. In other cases it was a local group who simply had more to lose from the entire host population becoming Triple Alphas as part of the Full Emergence. Occasionally it was interference from within the Gadium ranks itself – Gadium First.

Aytch had some experience of GF; one of his ancestors had joined in an era when membership of Gadium First was not illegal, but a legitimate political party, and membership was only distasteful. The ancestor had claimed it was a reasoned personal protest against Gadium oppression of a particular planet he'd been connected with. However, the official position, and the family position, was that he'd unfortunately suffered animustosis – soul death. Aytch remembered questioning Sharnia on the subject. She had gone on about the difference between absolute truth and relative truth. Aytch couldn't remember the details but her position was clear, this ancestor had flipped out. *Well, I'd better make sure I know my enemy.* Aytch pulled up the summary on the GF.

Chapter 11.1.3.A – Gadium First Tenets Overview

The Gadium First (GF) believes fervently that Gadium must play no part in the wider Galactic civilisation. Their reasons are varied and typically each member of GF will align to one of the principal tenets. The tenets are (in the generally accepted order of popular moral acceptability):

1. *Emergence monitoring and support activity proved by Gadium individuals greatly interfere with their own social responsibilities (marriage, parenthood, etc.) due to the significant amount of travel and time in stasis.*
2. *Helping species evolve into a fully emergent state interferes with the natural order which would tend to slow the Emergence of some species and halt others; more species (perhaps unworthy ones) get through with Gadium assistance.*

3. *The Gadium people were the first species to fully emerge and have a prominent position in the galaxy. As more species join Gadium in Full Emergence the preeminent position will weaken.*

Aytch shuddered. Except for the last tenet, they all seemed so reasonable. However, Aytch knew the GF had been responsible for devastating activity over the previous few hundred thousand years. He read on.

Chapter 11.1.3.D – Gadium First
Professor Harkin Commentary

'Their goal is bring about a retrenchment of Gadium through realigned political and moral will of the population. In general they do this by secretly sabotaging Gadium missions to make the cost of intervention seem prohibitively high.'
'The best result for a GF is when a Full Emergence appears to be mismanaged by the Gadium mission. This allows for GF sympathisers to create popular momentum against the general Gadium approach for intervention. Over the hundreds of thousands of years in which Gadium has been active, there have been substantial periods where GF pressure has effectively stopped all Gadium missions.'
'It should be noted that, statistically, civilisations do fare better with a Gadium support during an Emergence. The GF doctrine openly acknowledges this but says Gadium bears an unacceptable price for this.'

Rubbing his temples, Aytch tried to get his thinking straight; nothing could justify some of those GF reported actions. Unfortunately, events like Trogia meant pro-GF sentiment always factored in Gadium politics. He shook his head. *I'm stuck here, and at home they're not even united I should be here at all.*

Aytch's walk took him down to the stasis room where he double-checked the instrumentation before returning to his cabin. As he passed the crew room, Justio was still immersed in his work. It seemed unlikely Justio had any GF tendencies, although he did remember Justio had bemoaned the loss of Gadium family values. And Justio had once said Gadium interventions were becoming less considerate of the host population's lives as a result of the general breakdown in Gadium empathy. But Aytch was sure Justio had only meant the comment as a gentle reminder to stay sympathetic towards Earth. *Justio's been doing this longer than most other Gadium personnel. He'd hardly do so much if he didn't truly believe.*

As he lay on his bunk, Aytch stretched his limbs, working through the major muscle groups. After twenty minutes he stopped. The exercise had helped clear his mind. He had his duty, which was to help all other species, through their own Emergences, become full members of the overall galactic civilisation. *It's all for the best.*

As Aytch drifted off to sleep, a small voice sounded from the depths of his subconscious. *Best for whom?*

116

CHAPTER 19

Jeremy Benedict got up Saturday morning very happily. He was on a handsome retainer from Merrily Associates. The phone rang in his flat. It was his old school friend, double-checking he was going to make their usual golf game later.

'Sorry, but I'm working today; chasing down cheating husbands and wives. It's my best client and they need it by Monday.'

Jeremy sat on his sofa and reviewed the email requesting him to investigate Jack Bullage. He hadn't been able to start his investigation earlier in the week due to other work conflicts and he was running out of time to meet the deadline.

His first approach was the various social networks. Within a few hours he had built a reasonable picture of Jack Bullage's circle. There clearly was a relationship of some type with Sarah Dukes, who had perished in the same crash which Jack had escaped from. But Sarah was single – never married. *It's unlikely to have been her ... who else, then?*

Jeremy expanded his search. The name Louise Harding came up a few times. Firstly, on the web-site for the Daily Record, where she had written some incredibly damming pieces about Glowview, and Jack Bullage in particular. Secondly, on a recent archive of the local county court where she had been the subject of a civil suit from Bullage on the grounds of intimidation and stalking. There were also conflicting reports about an attack with a brick: with one paper intimating a premeditated personal attack, while another played the whole affair as vandalism gone wrong. Louise Harding was married, but her behaviour towards Bullage made it an unlikely affair – unless they were creating the mother of all smokescreens.

Jeremy decided to do a site visit. He wasn't sure what he'd get, but he thought he always benefited from looking his quarry directly in the eyes – to see what he could see.

Remembering Louise Harding's news articles, Jeremy arrived at Jack's street in Chiswick half-expecting to find a house wreathed in flame with a driveway lined by victims encased in medieval torture equipment. As it was, Jeremy found a very non-descript semi-detached house in a quiet looking street with neighbourhood watch stickers, and a small well-tended front garden.

There seemed to be lights so Jeremy took a clipboard from his rucksack and walked up to the front door of a house a few doors down the street. He knocked and politely performed a short retail shopping survey on the person who answered. Then he moved down the road on to the next property. After ten minutes or so, he knocked on Jack's door and Jack answered.

Jeremy held out an identification badge indicating he worked for John Lewis. 'Hi there, my name is John Rivers; I'm a retail marketer. I'm surveying this neighbourhood. I've got a good number of responses, I was hoping you could give me a clean sweep.'

Jack shrugged. 'Sure, if it's quick.'

Jeremy pulled out a new survey. 'It will be no more than five minutes of your time – and you'll be entered into a free draw to win vouchers.'

The survey consisted of 15 questions to determine buying patterns. Jeremy meticulously wrote down Jack's answers and associated comments. 'The initial responses to our questions indicates you are a fairly instinctive purchaser; has this always been the case?'

Jack shook his head. 'I'm not sure really. Up to fairly recently I would have said I was a careful purchaser. Lately... things have been a little more volatile.'

'Ah, well, life is strange. You never know what's going to happen next.'

Jack chuckled amiably. 'That's the truth.'

Jeremy tried to discretely look past Jack to get a clue of the inside of the house, and therefore another view on Jack's personality. The hallway was mostly obstructed by Jack, but Jeremy could see the trappings of reasonably ostentatious wealth. It wasn't solid gold toilet territory, but the telephone on Jack's hall table was clearly a top of the range designer item. There was also what appeared to be an original abstract oil painting hanging on the corridor wall. Jeremy couldn't see any further into the house.

Jeremy made a few more notes and took a record of Jack's email for the prize draw. Then he left, noticing Jack's sports car, before continuing his charade by moving down the street to survey some of Jack's other neighbours.

Way above Jack's house, Aytch received confirmation the mini-bots had detached themselves from Jeremy Benedict and had headed for their pre-assigned stations. He set up the computer to suck in and perform basic analysis on all the data the mini-bots would be sending.

Within a few hours, the mini-bots had infiltrated Jack's landline, mobile phone, laptop and internet. Additionally, they had set up small monitoring stations in every room and calibrated themselves to measure a host of standard day-to-day activities Jack would be involved in.

CHAPTER 20

On Monday morning James Chambers walked into a small unmarked office block in a sleepy backstreet of Basildon. He was wearing his standard office clothes: jeans, black t-shirt and black trainers. He walked down a few corridors until he reached an unremarkable door with the sign 'G60' embossed on a small brass plate.

James fumbled in his pockets for various keys and security passes. The office contained space for about four people to work in relative comfort but, in practice, there were two of them living like kings. Looking around, James saw his workmate.

'Hey, Max. How did the weekend shift go?'

Max glanced up from his monitor. 'Nothing much. Just sifting the data. I'm a bit tired of it all, really.' He stood up and started to pack up. 'I'll be off now.'

James flopped down into his seat and booted up. 'Well, it suits me fine. A cosy job close to my home, and I get to read Sci-Fi magazines as genuine research.'

There were a few standard department-wide MOD reports in James' inbox and he skimmed them. Although he was in a very minor department of only two people, technically he was a Department Head and so was kept abreast of security matters. *Nothing interesting.* The next item was a budget submission reminder. That would take a bit longer. James needed to come up with plausible reasons why he should keep the budget as high as it was. He started to jot down some corporate nonsense when his eye caught on an unusual email.

Interesting. There was an email addressed to the 'G60 Department Head'. It highlighted a *General Crowley* had made an internal search on the subject of Project Hedgehog. James had been responsible for some G60 cataloguing a few years previously. He remembered Project Hedgehog - it had been shrouded in secrecy.

James accessed the archives and brought back the summary.

```
Project Hedgehog 1962 - 1965: Ultra Black.
Experimental tests to determine existence of
psychic powers. Closed down after notable
disappearances. Tests were universally
unsuccessful.
```

In fact, the summary was the total sum of everything James knew about Project Hedgehog.

There was no specific action allocated to G60, but he couldn't let it go. He picked up the phone and, after referencing an internal directory, put a call into the MOD Internal Affairs team. 'Hi, this is James Chambers. I'd like to speak to someone about a recent alert referenced to G60.'

He went through the various security protocols and, once cleared, a senior risk officer related to him the story about General Crowley and Louise Harding. *An investigative reporter on a fishing trip.*

This was suddenly feeling more risky. MOD Generals could be trusted to be discreet, but investigative reporters could not. Logging on to the MOD mainframe, James set up an extended search of Louise Harding. Then he went to the kitchenette to make himself a cup of tea while the computer whirred on in the background. When he returned to his desk a few matches had been collated.

```
Louise Harding
```

```
Swindon County Court (Nov 2011) - Trespass
Blackfriars Crown Court (Feb 2013) -
Harassment
MOD (Nov 2015) - Security Breach
```

A door slammed and James was snapped out of his line of thinking. He looked up. 'Hi Max, why are you back?'

'Forgot my keys.' Max walked over to his desk and started rummaging. 'What're you up to?'

'A bit weird.' James paused. 'There's a security alert about a reporter who's been looking into Project Hedgehog.'

Max looked blank. 'Never heard of it.'

'It was something we ran in the 1960s, secret and unusual. I'm going to have to make a report to the controller. It's too close to budget season to allow for loose ends.'

James had regular contact with his MOD controller. Every month (for the past five years) he had sent a one-line report stating *nothing unusual found*. He'd always got a one word response; *acknowledged*. He'd met the controller once, and was reasonably sure the man hadn't a clue who he was. But in large bureaucracies this was not unusual. Frankly James got what he needed: his monthly pay cheque, access to ground-breaking technology, and every Friday afternoon off – so he didn't ask questions of the government system.

Max turned back. 'Well, my bed is calling me. If you need me to do anything on the night shift then leave me a note.'

'Or send you an email?'

'Not as secure as leaving a note under my keyboard.'

'Cleaners?'

'They don't read our stuff.' And, with a chuckle, Max left the office.

James went back to his computer. *I'm going to need to file an internal report, just to acknowledge the security breach.* After checking the operating manuals on security breaches (there'd not been any in the previous five years) he realised he'd also have to report on why Louise Harding was looking into

Project Hedgehog, and to determine if there was a breach in G60 security. James considered referring the investigation back to the MOD Internal Affairs team, but quickly came to the conclusion: no oversight was good oversight, it was his job, and he'd be better off doing it himself.

But what was Hedgehog really all about?

After another hour searching all the various G60 and MOD databases, James had no more than the three-line summary he had seen at the start of the day. He flicked off a request to the MOD archivist to dig out any paper records in easy-access storage.

Louise Harding?

CHAPTER 21

Within a few days of infiltrating Jack Bullage's house, the mini-bots had collated sufficient data for Aytch to start a review. Sitting in the crew room, Aytch ran the initial matching analysis.

Mostly, Jack's behaviour looked consistent with a normal person dealing with grief. But there were a few tantalising technology markers potentially indicating early Triple Alpha activity. In particular, Aytch honed in on Jack's computer which showed elevated levels of reboots. It could just be a virus infested computer but it may be the start of uncontrolled Triple Alphas interactions. *Technology and unaware Triple Alphas don't mix.*

Aytch waved across the crew room to get Justio's attention. 'I'd like to start the formal evaluation of next steps related to Jack Bullage.'

Justio did not look up. 'Two days is too early. A few more days are required.'

Aytch turned towards Justio. 'This may be the most important operational decision of my career. As a mission, I'd like us to avoid a rerun of the Bill Jones rush. And I really need to be part of the process.'

Justio kept looking at his communications tablet. 'Bill was a confirmed Triple Alpha who was under close investigation by the UK government, and he was moments away from becoming self-aware. We had to act. Now is different. Jack may, or may not, be a Triple Alpha. But, irrespective, he's not yet under any investigation. The government is paying him no attention.'

'But… if he is a Triple Alpha, then he's only a few weeks away from becoming self-aware.'

Justio sighed and looked up. 'Okay. In the spirit of your revision, and specifically not related to any perceived rush on Earth, what are the options?'

Aytch generated a screen and listed out a shorthand of options.

1. *Bullage not Triple – continue to observe*
2. *Bullage is Triple – kidnap and secure him on Earth*

Justio reviewed the two options. 'Agreed, although there are many options related to *securing* him.'

'I suppose we may need to kill him if he fails to comply.'

'I didn't mean that.' Justio shook his head. 'Why don't we kill all of them then? Make our lives easier.'

What did you mean? 'I apologise, Commander, I wasn't being flippant. It's just that a loose self-aware Triple Alpha would be very dangerous.'

Justio waved a hand to accept the apology.

Aytch waited but Justio didn't elaborate on what he actually meant, leaving Aytch a little wrong-footed. *I have to act as an equal.*

'The kidnapping will mean one of us going to the surface. Considering my extra mobility, I'll go.' Aytch brought a few maps of the south east of the UK up. 'We've lost assets in West Devon, the RAF Base installed new hard-wired computers and we haven't redelivered any mini-bots yet.' Aytch opened up some more screens and highlighted an area of the southern UK. 'But we have created a decent gap in their defences in Norfolk. Those radar stations are fully subverted and we have control of the NATO base at

Northwood. So an infiltration across Norfolk into North London would be very possible.'

'And if he becomes dangerously uncooperative?' Justio looked at Aytch. 'Now, on the understanding that termination is a last resort. Have you any specific thoughts?'

So I am supposed to consider kill options. 'To be clear, we'll do everything we can to avoid killing. But, if required, we'll use one of the following options.'

Again Aytch listed out a shorthand of options.

1. **Override car computer and crash at speed**
2. **Cut gas pipe in his house**
3. **(last resort) reconnaissance drone AM missile**

Justio nodded approvingly. 'Very last resort. We cannot risk detection, and the last I'd heard the humans didn't have anti-matter missiles. Where's the recon-drone?'

'It's hidden under Jeremy Benedict's car, but I agreed it's a last option.'

Justio stood up slowly and walked towards the doorway. 'Let's pre-authorise self-destruct sequences for all of our mini-bots. Ready to cover our tracks.'

Conciliatory gesture? 'It may make us seem prematurely aggressive, or nervous, to authorise all of them now.' He looked around the crew room.

Justio smiled. 'Agreed. I'm going for some regenerative meditation. Let's see the results of analysis first. Ah … the Jeremy Benedict report was mostly empty, but I suggest we keep him sniffing around for a few more days, get some more background on Bullage. It'll feed into any extraction plans.'

'Okay, I'll finalise some safe house options.' Aytch turned back to the main desk and typed on the communications tablet.

At the doorway Justio stopped and turned. 'You know, once we extract him, we could bring him here. Just have a think about it.' Justio left the room.

Was that a test? Surely Justio didn't mean it. Aytch knew a successful Full Emergence would look good on his record, but he had to consider the risks. *No, Earth's not ready.*

Aytch instructed the computer to record to the vault and then spoke aloud. 'Current view, possible Triple Alpha identification but Earth's not ready to survive a Full Emergence. Their energy debt is significant, they're not democratic enough globally and there are too many factions. I'm focusing planning on capturing any Triple Alpha and rehousing them on Earth.'

Managing a Full Emergence may get an immediate promotion but keeping the status quo would reduce the risk of a significant mistake.

Closing down the formal recording, Aytch decided to refresh himself on the decisions taken during the 1960s. He sifted through some of his own old notes.

'1962 Nov 12 (am) Reports of people falling out of moving cars at high speeds and walking away. Earth news services surmise their relaxed state through recreational drugs usage was the reason for survival... they bounced... probably Alphas.'
'1962 Dec 12 (pm) Bill Jones may be a Triple Alpha. The UK government are putting him through intensive tests. Observation needed.'
'1964 Jan 07 (am) Most UK and US mind control programmes now infiltrated and are being wound down. Can't allow this level of self-awareness in a pre-Emergence civilisation.'

Aytch spent a little time checking the status of various safe houses where he could allow Jack to live a secluded life of luxury if required. He also checked a few options where Jack could be kept sedated for the rest of his, significantly extended, biological life with no other human contact. *I mustn't imply this as a first choice to Justio.*

Opening up a screen showing the stasis room, Aytch checked on Bill Jones. If they were forced to kill Jack then it was possible they could send Bill Jones back to Earth. Unfortunately, reintroduced Triple Alphas were usually much less effective at suppressing host Beta to Alpha transition. Aytch shook his head. It was unlikely Bill Jones could be used to stall the Emergence.

Justio hobbled back to his cabin. It was interesting that Aytch was starting to proverbially flex his muscles, trying to take a larger share of the decisions. But it was a good thing. Aytch could be relied on to trot out the standard Gadium doctrine.

Justio opened up his private communications channels. FibonacciEddie had received an email from an anonymous user about Project Hedgehog and Jack Bullage. *Not yet.*

Finally, Justio looked over his own encrypted notes. Aytch was blissfully unaware about many decisions made without his input.

CHAPTER 22

Late on Tuesday afternoon Louise received a message on one of her anonymous email accounts. Unable to concentrate, she left work immediately. It was a reply from FibonacciEddie.

Walking back from the tube her phone buzzed. A text from Jeff asking her if she wanted dinner. She replied.

What makes u think I'd be home by 6pm! See u in 5. Pizza.

She met Jeff at the front door and, kicking through the junk mail on the floor, led him to the kitchen table. A few minutes later, she'd booted up her laptop and was displaying the email.

Subject: Hedgehog
I'm pleased to have a collaborator. Project Hedgehog ran in the 1960s. They tested soldiers and civilians for mental powers. But the test participants had to be special. They had to be crash survivors. No idea why. They used some basic luck tests, coin flips? Hard to believe, but I think they had some successes with special people. Keep digging, I'll try to send you more info. No idea about Jack Bullage...Fib

Jeff looked at Louise with exasperation. 'You sent an email to FibonacciEddie, naming Jack Bullage! Louise, you're out of control. Everything is monitored on the internet.'

Louise shrugged. 'I used all the standard anonymity protection. Anyway, look what we've got. We've got a lead.'

'This guy could be anybody. All we know is that the MOD are trying to hide it. We don't know if they found anything. Maybe they just killed a whole bunch of men, women and children in their experiments.'

'Look, this FibonacciEddie is probably a conspiracy nutcase. But he seems to be well informed, and he's given us a lead. Why not follow it for a little while?'

Jeff raised an eyebrow. 'To get to Jack Bullage?'

'To get to the truth! I truly believe he's a shithead, but my priority is the Hedgehog story.' *And I need a big story to get momentum behind my career.*

Jeff sat down at the table. 'I'm having a drink with Mike tonight in The Three Kings; why don't you come along?'

Louise bustled in with Jeff following in her wake. A combination of low lighting and blown bulbs meant the pub was half shrouded in darkness, which Louise considered to be a good thing, given the usual hygienic state of the place. A quick look around revealed Mike sitting in a corner, with drinks for all of them already on the table.

They took their seats and gave the requisite thanks for the drinks.

Once seated, Jeff did a stage whisper. 'As the old Chinese curse goes, we are now living in interesting times. There have been developments...'

Mike arched an eyebrow theatrically. 'Do tell me all, young Harding.'

Louise leant forward. 'I got into the MOD on Friday, and confirmed Project Hedgehog was a real top secret 1960s programme.'

'You broke in?'

131

'You know perfectly well I got it from a very senior army general.'

Mike nodded gently and Louise reacted with mock anger. 'What?! I get top secret information from the MOD and all you give me is a small nod!'

'If it gives you any satisfaction, internally, my stomach is doing somersaults.'

Louise ploughed on. 'Secondly, last night we got an email from none other than... FibonacciEddie. He said Project Hedgehog was real and tested mental powers. He didn't mention the word *luck* but he did mention *coin flipping* tests.'

'Or was it *flipping coin* tests?' Mike tutted, but after getting no reaction sat back in his chair. After a few moments of thought he exhaled dramatically. 'I'm just going to order food. Who wants what? Louise... cheese and ham, or ham and cheese?'

A few minutes later Mike returned with sandwiches. He beckoned the others to lean forward. 'Do we need to start considering our own safety? If Project Hedgehog is as big and black as seems to be indicated, things may get dangerous.'

Jeff nodded. 'Not sure. Louise has come across a few mystery disappearances.'

Louise snorted. 'You've changed your tune. I remember you telling me it was nothing to get worked up about.'

Mike took a sip of beer. 'I'm not an expert in national security, but there does seem to be something a little strange going on. It wouldn't hurt to take a few basic precautions.'

'Okay, like what?'

'For a start, only research online using internet cafes. Secondly, only stay online for ten or fifteen minutes. Thirdly, wear a hat and dark glasses.'

Louise was a little unconvinced but nodded. 'Mike...
FibonacciEddie mentioned some actual testing of mental
powers. Could we do some tests?'

'I'm always up for an experiment. Although I have to
reiterate the slimness of the chances of finding anything.'

'Understood, so what would we do?'

Mike pulled out a notepad and started jotting. 'We've had
a few big hints: use crash survivors, use a simple luck test.
Our decisions are whether we want to try to stimulate fear, or
address the *half-asleep* references you found... We can start
planning, and maybe we'll get some more focused
information from FibEddie in the next few days. Jeff?'

Jeff pulled out a coin and started flipping it. 'We can use a
simple heads or tails test, but build up massive amounts of
data across multiple participants and crunch the numbers.'

Mike nodded. 'I agree. Measure and analyse. For the
experiment we have two choices. The first is the participant
either tosses the coin, or watches it tossed and calls the result
in mid-flight. The second is the coin is tossed out of their
sight and they call the result.' Louise indicated for Mike to
explain, and so he did. 'Basically, the first one may possibly
give positive results if the participant has super-enhanced
reflexes or eyesight. Whereas the second one will be pure
luck.'

Louise nodded, but was unconvinced. 'Just tossing a coin
feels a bit lame. Shouldn't we try to stimulate fear or some
sort of survival instinct?'

There was a silence, and it stretched. Finally, Mike spoke.
'I'm not sure we're professionally ready to stimulate the levels
of fear generated in a car accident. I think we just start with
simple tests.'

They kicked a few ideas around before agreeing to meet
up later in the week. As they were leaving the pub, Louise
confirmed the plan. 'You guys continue to design a test. I

know I'm rushing you, but we should aim to run it next Wednesday in Mike's garage. Jeff will source student participants from the Uni. I'll try to convince a few genuine crash survivors to join us. And I'll see if I can get more from FibonacciEddie.'

It was agreed. The test was on. Louise left the pub.

Mike hung back for a few moments, pulling Jeff to the side. 'Don't let her get her hopes too high.'

'She really needs a story.' Jeff shrugged and hurried after Louise.

CHAPTER 23

It wasn't until Thursday morning that James Chambers received a file from the MOD archivist. It was a disappointingly small file and came with a hand-written note from the archivist.

> *Chambers (G60)*
> *Re: Project Hedgehog*
> *It is not without precedent for old projects to have official records in such poor shape. Governmental reviews in the 1970s and 1980s both deleted information related to frivolous projects to reduce the risk of being accused of profligacy.*
> *V. Princey (Archivist)*

James picked up the file. It was woefully thin and, even against the backdrop of the archivist's note, he could not believe a project lasting so long could have left a footprint of only two pages.

James sat at his desk and tried to read a summary report dated 1965, and entitled *Interim Findings*. It was clear that the report should have been much longer; many pages were missing, making it difficult to follow, but there was one section which did stand out.

> *3 February 1965*
> *The tests have been repeated on Subject G for a continuous period of 8 hours. Subject G has been subject to both a hypnotic trance and strong FT. The subject appears to be interacting with the apparatus and more than 90% of measurements are*

falling within the 'seriously affected' range. This seems to be significant given his fairly average results from the previous sessions on 1st February 1965 when he was only being stimulated by drugs.

The rest of the page simply listed columns of numbers with no markings or headings to inform the reader what was being measured, or how it was being measured.

The second page contained more columns of numbers dated to March 1965. It also included some scribbled notes in the gaps between the columns. Much of the writing was illegible but there were a few interesting phrases.

'FT providing notable results'
'Subject G disappeared? Soviet?'
'Professor X wants to save his soul'
'Subject C dead!'

It made very little sense. James leant back. Except for himself, the office was empty. *What is FT? How could I find out? How am I going to make progress here?*

Although there had been no additional noise from Internal Affairs about the security breach, James was concerned. He needed to ensure Project Hedgehog would not surface in the public domain and preferably not within the MOD either. He really needed to work out what had happened.

He took a photocopy of the report and scribbled some notes in the margins. *Fatalities, but how many? FT?*

Picking up the phone, James dialled the MOD archivist. 'Hi there, it's James Chambers here. Many thanks for the report you sent through. Is there any more primary material available?'

The archivist's somewhat reedy voice came back over the phone. 'Sorry, Mr Chambers, what I sent you was all of the readily available materials. I would need special authorisation to search the deep storage for more.'

James rolled his eyes. The concept of getting budget approval from the MOD was an anathema to him – G60 never asked for any additional budget, as it might make the executives review the current allocation. 'Okay, thanks. How about the personal archives of the old G60 directors? Do you have access to those?'

'The personal archives are stored in the MOD for national security reasons, and they're never shared with anyone other than the archive owner, or the Prime Minister in the case of national emergency.'

'Okay, thanks. I'll consider another angle. And thanks again for what you did send.' James put the phone down and turned back to his computer to determine the name of the G60 Director for 1962 and 1965. The search was straightforward and he soon found out Molly Saunders had been the chief in the 1960s. Unfortunately, Molly passed away in the early 2000s. James continued his investigations and managed to get the name of the Deputy Director who had been active through most of the 1960s and 1970s. His name was Dougy Raddlestone. His personnel record gave very little information except that he was still alive, and he was living in Surrey. James sent an email to the MOD Human Resources team asking for contact information for Dougy on a matter of national security.

Now to the leak?

Given that Louise Harding was a reporter, if she was asking questions it was likely she had a reason. He needed to find someone to investigate her. There was no way he could approach her work place, The Daily Record, they were the enemy. James considered his options.

James returned to the MOD report that he'd run earlier in the week on Louise Harding. There were a few other items, over and above the mention of her court appearance for harassment. She was registered as married, and she had been listed on a Home Office system as a hunt saboteur. *Not sure if there's an angle there?*

The afternoon wore on, with James browsing various social media sites on which Louise was registered. James was fixated on keeping the search entirely within G60; it was too much of a risk to his budget if he came to the attention of people higher up. G60 received the same amount of budget as a small hospital A&E department, and James spent that money looking for aliens and investigating paranormal activity. No-one with any sense could be allowed to become aware of his existence.

James continued to search.

Bingo!

The husband, Jeff Harding, was a science lecturer at North London University of Science and Technology. *NLUST! The MOD has worked with them a few times before.* This was a route in.

James called up the MOD academic coordination manager and between them they looked for someone at the university who had sufficient security clearance. They found Bob Reaple, who worked in a similar department to Jeff. *Well, both in Materials Science.*

The coordination manager gave James the contact details, and James gave him a call. 'Hi, Bob. This is James Chambers. I'm a department head within the MOD. I believe you worked with a colleague of mine, Major King last year?'

'Yes, that's right. I think I remember the drill. I'll call you back through the MOD switchboard and give them my identification number?'

James smiled to himself. The voice that came back over the phone had sounded very certain and competent.

A few moments later they were securely connected. 'Hello again. Thanks for being so prompt. There's a possibility the

MOD will benefit from some informal support from you over the next few weeks. Nothing too onerous, we hope.'

'By informal, I assume you mean unpaid?'

'I'm afraid so, but it shouldn't be more than a few hours.'

'So what's it about?'

'National security, I will have to come and discuss with you face-to-face. Can you make tomorrow? I can come to near you, say Hampstead?'

'Sure - Heath Street Baristas at 10?'

'Great.' James put down the phone and resumed his investigations of Louise Harding.

The following day James walked up towards the coffee shop rehearsing the meeting in his head. He needed to get Bob on side, but without telling him anything, while also not giving away the fact that he himself actually knew nothing anyway.

James recognised Bob from the MOD photo he'd received from the MOD academic coordination department. Although Bob didn't appear to be wearing glasses. *Contact Lenses?* And Bob appeared to have lost what little hair he'd had when the photo had been taken a few years previously. Still it was definitely the right guy.

'Bob Reaple? I'm James Chambers.'

'Good to meet you James.' Bob had the easy air of a man used to being listened to and obeyed. They shook hands.

Bob had already secured a table in a deep corner of the café. James shuffled his chair around to Bob's side and took out copies of the various official secrets forms from a few years previously. 'Just to remind you what you've signed up to.' Then James showed his MOD Identity Card. Bob looked a little nervous, that was to be expected; the documentation was plastered with aggressive wording.

Bob remained silent and James continued. 'Within the North London University of Science and Technology, there is a professor called Jeff Harding, do you know him?'

'*Junior* professor.' Bob corrected James. 'I know *of* him, but he works in Metallics. Our paths don't really cross.'

'Ok, not perfect, but we'll work with what we have.' James took a breath. It was tenuous, but it was all he had, and he had to start somewhere. 'Jeff is under observation by the MOD. He and his wife, Louise, are poking around a sensitive 1960s programme called Project Hedgehog.' James paused. *Mostly true.* He continued. 'The UK government wants Project Hedgehog to remain hidden. It had some troubling aspects.' *Probably true.* 'We want you to use your connection to Jeff through the university to find out what he knows without alerting him.' *Absolutely true.*

Bob nodded. 'So there is a programme…'

'Was. It closed down 40 years ago.'

'So there was a programme, and the MOD wants it to remain hidden. You want me to find out what Jeff and Louise know.'

James nodded.

'So what was the project about?'

'I'm sorry but I can't tell you.'

Bob persisted. 'Surely you must be able tell me something? Even if it is top secret. I'm likely to find out what Jeff knows.'

James shook his head.

Bob broke eye contact with James and looked around the room. Then he turned back to him. 'Can you give me any leads?'

'I just need you to find out what they know, and ideally how they found it out.' James took a zip drive out of his pocket and passed it to Bob. 'These files give you an idea of the Hardings' recent online activities, but it's not complete, mostly just their search queries.' James passed over a piece of paper. 'That's the password.'

Bob put the zip drive and the paper into the inside pocket of his jacket. 'Okay.'

'Also, it would be useful if you could find out if the Hardings are limiting their activity to Project Hedgehog, or if there are other MOD projects in their sights.'

'I guess I have a few avenues to see what Jeff is up to. If it's harmless then it will probably come up in a conversation. If it's not harmless then he'll be more guarded.'

James stood up to leave and Bob stood also.

Bob shook James' hand. 'I'll contact you next week, James.'

Once James had left, Bob sat down and pulled out his laptop. Booting up, and inserting the zip drive, he started reading through the files. The Hardings' activities had included searching a significant number of conspiracy websites as well as some more bona-fide science discussion forums. There were no posts left by the Hardings at all. Bob noted that pretty much all of the searches relating to conspiracy websites stopped several days earlier, on the previous Sunday. His interest was also drawn to the large number of searches they had waded through on mind control and telepathy. *Well, it gives me a hook to start my investigation.*

High above the earth, the Gadium mission stored the transcript of James' conversation with Bob courtesy of a mini-bot secreted on James' clothes. G60 were old friends of the Gadium mission.

CHAPTER 24

Back on Gadium, Commander Jenkins sat at his desk fiddling with his personal communications tablet, in a grim mood. Looking up from the tablet his eyes rested briefly on the hologram of his daughter. Yes, he needed something to take his mind off the various missions that were shaking his conscience. He opened up his personal folder.

His daughter, Katrina, was currently on-station at Trogia, and Jenkins had five video diary entries that she'd recorded during the first tranche of her mission. These large video files were delivered the old fashioned way, by courier ship, and so they were all at least 12 years old (just to cover the physical journey back from Trogia).

He'd been rationing them, only watching a new one each year – if Katrina had something critical to say she would say it via QET. *Ah, it's just about time for the next one. It may give me the courage I need.* He flicked on the relevant file and an image of Katrina came up on the screen. Her big green scaly face filled the screen with an enormous smile and wide white eyes hosting very green irises surrounding her pitch black slit pupils.

'Video Log 3 – Katrina to Daddy. Hi, Commander Daddy!'

Jenkins reflexively smiled and his shoulders relaxed, he settled back in his chair and the video log continued.

'I hope your duties on the GEC are not too onerous and you are keeping to our stasis agreements. All in, I reckon I'm going to be away for about a hundred years but I'm still planning to meet our agreement to only age two years. I've about a year so far, I'm on target unless there's some unexpected Emergence.' Her face screwed up into a mock grimace. 'Yeah, right! Like I'd get that lucky!' Katrina's smile washed away her previous serious expression. 'Anyway... you'll see the official stats on Trogia, so I won't go into them, but the mission Commander here,' Katrina frowned, 'has said we are not going to start removing Triple Alphas for at least five hundred more years – I'll be long gone by then.'

This was not new to Jenkins. The GEC had ordered Trogia to be left fallow for a fairly arbitrary five thousand years to allow the population to stabilise and forget about the previous Gadium interference. Trogia was still stuck in a Partial Emergence with around 1% of the population in Alpha status (and the rest Betas, excepting a small number of Triples). There were a handful of Alphas each century who spontaneously transformed into Triple Alphas but these were left to their own devices as long as they did not exhibit any signs of turning into Despots. It was undoubted that those few Triple Alphas were continuing to hold down the Beta to Alpha transition rates. Jenkins turned his attention back to the video then, realising he'd missed a section during his thoughts, he rewound.

'... five hundred more years – I'll be long gone by then. It's all stable now, we've pretty much removed all consequential alien and Emergence references. We're just a myth to them now.' Katrina's face was uncharacteristically still for a moment and then she continued. 'They're just back to the basics: eat, sleep and screw.' She paused. 'They seem quite happy; I'm not sure we shouldn't just leave them to it... anyway, I'm continuing with my studies, mostly on the probability wave harmonics and double conscious resonance factors.' Katrina shook her head and smiled. 'Impenetrable doesn't even come close.'

Jenkins paused the video, carefully savouring this new interaction with Katrina. He knew that within a few months he would have utterly memorised every word and facial expression. He smiled ruefully, reflecting on her views. *Why? Because it's our obligation to the universe to interfere.*

He leant back in quiet contemplation. He'd never pushed any interventionist message with Katrina. He had been very careful to keep her safe from any of his more risky activity.

Suddenly, Jenkins was brought back to the present by one of his aides coming into his office.

'Sir, an emergency subcommittee has just been called by the Chairwoman. Apparently, the Rolumpus Sector is having a freedom uprising.'

Jenkins got up immediately and marched out of his office, his aide trailing in his wake. Rolumpus was a problem. They were only a few hundred light years away and had always resented Gadium controls. 'How big is this uprising?'

'Hard to say, sir, but the current estimate is that four or five star systems are involved, but it's mostly centred on Rolumpus itself.'

Jenkins thought for a moment. 'The usual grievances and demands?'

'Yes sir, their demands came through a few hours ago. They want to have access to three of their neighbouring systems, all of which are denied due to the presence of unemerged sentient species.'

'So what's this meeting for? Approval of capital force?'

'Yes sir. The feeling is a short sharp attack on the main industrial bases will deter them. We've got enough assets on-site to make a decent impact.'

'And our comms limits?'

'The QET Grid is fine, sir, plenty of bandwidth.'

A short time later, Commander Jenkins entered the meeting room. The Chairwoman had not arrived, and unusually, the Deputy was not huddled in a corner of the room with his entourage. He was standing at the conference table, behind the Chairwoman's place, and was deep in conversation with Commander Sharnia.

As Jenkins approached the table, he caught the tail end of the point Sharnia was making. '… and so, Deputy Chairman, given that the Rolumpus are demanding the right to develop AI, this could be the time to restart internal discussions on whether we can use more advanced technology ourselves.'

The Deputy nodded at Sharnia while waving Jenkins into the conversation. 'Good afternoon, Commander Jenkins. Are you up to speed on the current set of events in the Rolumpus Sector?'

'It seems like a standard suppression activity.'

The Deputy turned away from Sharnia, and focused fully on Jenkins. 'Standard… I suppose… But difficult. The Rolumpus Sector has been gearing up its military capability for 20 years. We've got much more advanced weaponry, but the difficulties associated with reinforcements mean we can't afford to go too easy on them.'

Sharnia eyed Jenkins intently. 'A short sharp shock is the best option. Treason will not be tolerated.'

As usual, Jenkins strained to meet her eye. *Best option for who, though?* Had Sharnia been self-reflective, she may have concluded that the sharp shock was best for ensuring that the Gadium population were able to fulfil their destiny. But Jenkins was not sure that she wouldn't go further and say it was best for all of the species under the Gadium protectorate

– they receive peace and prosperity. *But at the cost of self-determination.*

He turned his attention back to the conversation.

The Deputy nodded. 'Quite so, Commander… an object lesson in not biting the hand that has fed you … if you will excuse us.' The Deputy manoeuvred Jenkins back towards their own seating area.

As they started to move away, Sharnia obstructed Jenkins' path. 'Commander, my grandson Aytch is on the Earth Mission with Justio. You were with him on Darth, weren't you?'

Jenkins nodded. 'Yes, he was an excellent team member. I'm sure Aytch will learn a lot from him.'

Sharnia took a minimal step out of Jenkins' way. 'Not too much, I hope.'

Jenkins manoeuvred around Sharnia and quickened his pace slightly to catch up with the Deputy. The Deputy took his usual seat and motioned for Jenkins to lean in. 'This betrayal by the Rolumpus cannot be endured. We gave them everything. They will be punished.'

'The original treaties are many generations old for them now, even with the longevity. Their new guard don't feel quite the same way about us, and are looking to make their legacy.'

The Deputy hissed. 'Their legacy will be a decimation, perhaps one of their planets erased by a mini-bot replication swarm, perhaps something else.' He paused. 'There may a little hand-wringing before the order is confirmed, but it will be confirmed.'

Commander Jenkins's eyes flashed wide but the rest of his face remained impassive. He leant in close and whispered. 'Rumours are starting that the Vantch Mission ship was sabotaged, which is why it's running slow.'

'Those rumours are not to be heeded, repeated or discussed here.'

'I'm concerned about the potential impact on Vantch.'

The Deputy closed off the topic. 'Not here, Commander.'

Suddenly the doors to the meeting room were flung open and the Chairwoman was announced.

The Chairwoman swept in and headed to the head of the table. Sharnia watched her approach and their eyes locked. Sharnia gave an imperceptible nod of support and got one in return.

The Chairwoman opened the meeting. 'I call this emergency session to order.'

Sitting next to the Chairwoman as the meeting was opened, Sharnia looked around the table. *Where are the traitors?*

Her gaze came to rest on Jenkins. Highly regarded, very highly decorated, but she had her doubts about his allegiances. Doubts she felt the Deputy Chairman shared. She looked across to the Deputy Chairman, but his face was a mask, as usual. They'd discussed Jenkins, and nothing was said outright, but she'd felt the Deputy's disquiet.

Sharnia could not understand why she was concerned, but she had an itch, an instinct. When she'd originally seen Aytch's posting she'd checked Justio's background to assure herself he was a good influence for her grandson's first mission. There had been some grim history in Justio's past, an incident on the Marhok mission, but nothing so very unusual by Gadium standards. She'd been reassured by the Gadium authorities that Justio had made a full recovery. But during these checks on Justio, she'd come across Jenkins' name many times, and there were a few inconsistencies in his behaviour.

Further, subtle investigations – Jenkins was a hero after all – had uncovered a little more, and there was too much at stake for her to ignore her initial gut instincts. They'd served her well in the past.

She looked back at Jenkins. *Is there a link to GF? A secret?*

CHAPTER 25

On Friday morning Bob worked his way down the campus corridors clutching a few print-outs he'd made at home detailing Jeff's online activities. The corridors were crowded with students moving between classes. He grumbled to himself as he pushed through the would-be graduates. His thoughts flitted between: *it's their fault, I'm a senior professor,* and the more self-admonishing, *I did time my arrival badly.*

Eventually, he got to the sanctity of his office and took stock. Although he'd never heard of G60, working with the MOD would be good for making connections. He threw his papers on to his desk and walked over to his personal coffee machine. *Double shot.*

After his caffeine fix, Bob opened up his email and started to type an email to Jeff (copying Jeff's Boss, Sophie Raymond, Head of Metallics).

> Subject: Strength Modelling
> Hey Jeff – Your name came up in conversation
> earlier this week as someone who may be able
> to help. Can you spare me (and the Organics
> team) about an hour of your time, please?
> We're doing some spider-silk strength
> modelling and want to run through the
> calculations just to make sure we're not
> setting up any false assumptions. Just a quick
> bit of peer review please.
> Bob Reaple

Bob was pretty sure Jeff would have the required knowledge, or at least enough to make the request seem natural. Jeff wasn't the leading expert on strength modelling but he would be sufficiently competent to peer review a few assumptions and equations. Plus he knew Jeff would be pleased to mix with his department, as Organics was the current hot ticket. *And, of course, I'm on the cross-university funding review board.*

A few minutes later he had his reply. Jeff would be over in the early afternoon. He took a book out of his bag and placed it strategically on his coffee table. *Nothing too obvious, but this may get him thinking.*

After having spent the morning at Mike's discussing the experiment set-up, Jeff walked into the university campus at just after 2pm. He paused for a few moments to chat to Jim, on the reception desk, but then continued through the corridors, stopping at his own office long enough to drop off his rucksack and pick up a book on strength modelling.

Paging through the book to refresh his memory, he continued on to the Organics department and knocked on Bob's door.

'Come in.'

As Jeff walked in, he took a moment to look around; the walls were covered with citations, official-looking photos, and academic certificates. It was clearly the office of a senior professor.

Bob got up from behind his desk. 'Thanks for making time for me. Please, take a seat.' He indicated to a couple of comfy chairs in the corner of the room.

Jeff's eyes lingered on the walls a few moments more, there was a photo of Bob meeting Stephen Hawkins and another with the current Archbishop of Canterbury. *Eclectic mix, but nothing wrong with his self-image.* Jeff sat down and Bob took the chair next to him.

As he continued to sweep the room for interesting items, his gaze stopped on the book on Bob's coffee table, *Shadows of the Mind* by Roger Penrose. Jeff jerked a little. Mike had mentioned it that morning – something about a new way of looking at brains.

Bob picked it up. 'It's a bit radical, not really mainstream biological thinking, but it's Penrose's thoughts on the possible differences between big computers and human brains. Heavy stuff: academically, metaphorically and physically.' He hefted it back onto the table. 'I'm probably taking a sabbatical in the next few years to do some investigation into the fundamentals of computation.'

Jeff nodded, uncertain. He hadn't expected this. He waited.

Bob continued to talk. 'So… organic materials... We're doing the whole spider-silk review again. Mostly for a nature documentary, but funded by a couple of industrial companies. We need someone neutral to review our biaxial tensile test. Could you give me a few hours a week for the next month?'

Jeff was momentarily lost in thought, looking at the Penrose book, but as the request registered he snapped back to the present and nodded. 'Sure.'

'Do you want to borrow it?'

'Ah, no thanks. But I agree it is an interesting subject.' Jeff paused. 'Mike Littlejohn and I are doing a little extracurricular investigation ourselves.'

'I know Mike reasonably well, we sit on a few committees together. Anything I would have a view on?'

'I'm not sure, we're doing a bit of informal research.' *I can't say anything.* 'Nothing worth bothering you about.'

'What sort of investigation? Brain power, consciousness, AI computer modelling?'

Jeff looked around, his stomach was now doing somersaults. He was trapped. This guy controlled a lot of budget, and a lot of popular opinion amongst the other professors. Should he lie or risk appearing to be a whacko?

The silence stretched a little. 'Nowhere near that conventional. It's an informal investigation into mind control.'

'Mind control?'

Need to bluff it out. 'Telepathy, telekinesis, clairvoyance.'

'Why?'

Jeff forced a chuckle. 'I can't really tell you why, sorry. It's an informal look into possible reasons behind some people believing they have unusually good luck.'

Bob smiled. 'Is it for one of those awful television programmes? Well I can't judge you, I'm taking money for the spider silk. Your secret is safe with me... So what do you actually mean by mind control, then?'

'Just… controlling things with your mind.'

Bob held Jeff's gaze. 'Mind control… It's a broad subject with whackos at both ends and not much science in the middle. But there was a paper written in 1988 by Professor Choots in this university, back when it was a Poly.' He went to his computer and started typing. 'Give me a second, I'll find the summary.'

Bob scanned the screen and summarised. 'The gist of the paper was there were three buckets you had to consider.

(a) Genuine mental powers causing a physical effect,

(b) Some type of instantaneous transfer of information into your brain so you think about an event, not before it happens, but before you actually see it happen,

(c) Misprocessing of memories in the brain so you think you've seen something later than you actually did.'

Jeff paused to take this in. 'That sounds about right, certainly the third one is basically a derivation of *déjà vu*, right? Anyway, for your information, I'm interested in option A.'

'Aren't we all? I'd love to be able to wake up in the morning and magically conjure up good weather and a healthy spine. But, don't worry, I won't tell anyone you're a nut!' He smiled and winked. 'Have you done any testing so far?'

'I have no idea how we could test any of it. So far, all I've done is kick a few ideas around with Mike.'

'Well, to get you started, off the top of my head, I would say if you assume some people have genuine mental powers then your options would be… your brain physically emits a particle to interact with the outside world… God knows what type of particle.' Bob paused for moment. '… or some type of influence over random events, and that could be anything… but we'd have to start looking at quantum mechanics. There's enough uncertainty there to come up with some hokum.'

'Any pointers?'

'None with any formal scientific credibility, but Copenhagen has a role for an observer and Many-Worlds lets anything happen.'

'I don't really remember that part of my degree. What about the Many-Worlds?'

'Do you want me to teach you the 2nd Year syllabus? Or do you want to understand how it could be twisted to allow people mental powers?'

Jeff squirmed.

Bob relented. 'The Many-Worlds hypothesis states that at every event (whatever it may be) the universe splits to create new downstream universes in which each possible outcome of the original event happens. So if we postulated that your brain allowed you to choose which downstream universe you swept into, you'd effectively be choosing your future, and choosing the outcome you wanted… this would break pretty much every physical law we know.'

Some of this chimed with Mike's musings from the morning discussions. Jeff wrestled with his desire to take out a notepad and write down Bob's information. *Act casual, just try to remember it.*

An alarm on Bob's desk rang and he stood up. 'Sorry, Jeff, but I've got an appointment. Thanks for agreeing to look at my tests. And I actually would be very pleased to talk more about your experiments… if you want?'

Jeff stood up. 'Sure thing, perhaps next Wednesday evening in the pub?'

They shook hands and Bob walked Jeff to the door. 'The Many-Worlds is a moral minefield.'

What does that mean? Jeff murmured a goodbye, and left.

After the door closed, Bob returned to his keyboard and typed up his notes for James Chambers. *He's either very naïve or a criminal genius.*

CHAPTER 26

At 10am on Saturday, Louise's self-imposed intensity was ratcheted up to eleven. She paced around the kitchen glancing alternately at her wrist watch and the clock on the wall. 'Jeff! We're going to be late. Get down here!' Louise was barely hanging on to reasonable language and considered actions. *For fuck's sake*. 'Jeff! Come on!'

Jeff came down the stairs. 'Sorry. I can't find the laptop thingy.'

'The one I asked you to find last night?' Louise shook her head, muttered expletives under her breath, and opened the front door.

'Mike will have one.' Jeff locked up and managed to get to the car just as Louise was pulling out into the road.

'Sorry, Louise… but I was working last night.' Louise didn't answer. She chewed her lip and studied the traffic. Jeff silently flicked through a pile of papers. 'Mike and I will run a prototype test today. We're using his garage.'

Louise continued to stare directly ahead. 'I have lined up interviews with a few crash survivors for tomorrow and Monday. I'll see if I can convince any of them to come to the tests on Wednesday evening.'

'What time are you meeting Bullage?'

This got a reaction. Louise turned and stared at Jeff, but he smiled and she couldn't stay angry. She grinned. 'I'm pretty sure the restraining order is still firmly in place. But I have three other people… genuine miraculous crash survivors from the last five years.'

They sat in silence for a few minutes until Jeff broke the silence. 'Don't you think if Project Hedgehog had made any significant advances then it would have been leaked in the last 50 years?'

'Not if they're ashamed of what they achieved, or ashamed of what they had to do in order to achieve… whatever they achieved.'

They drove for a few minutes and, on arrival at Mike's house, found him smiling on the driveway. 'Welcome to Chez Mike. Are you ready to earn yourselves a Nobel Prize?'

Louise climbed out of the car. 'I'm after a Pulitzer, but I'll make do with a Nobel if it's all that's on offer.'

Mike led the way to the garage. Once inside he was forced to walk around two heavy wooden benches to the back wall, where lines of immaculately labelled boxes sat, equally distributed across the shelves. Louise nodded in appreciation and gave the rest of the garage another look. The floor was spotless, and the wooden panels on the door frames were painted beautifully. *Mike is meticulous.*

'Now, you need a DC power supply for a MacBook?' Without waiting for an answer, Mike selected one of the boxes and, after a minimal amount of rummaging, brought out the right piece.

Louise walked over to Mike and accepted the lead. 'Thanks.' She shot a withering look at Jeff and then pointed at the benches dominating the central floor space. 'So, Mike, what's all this?'

'Just our work area for the impending tests.' Mike picked up a wooden box from one of the benches. 'I'm not sure how much Jeff has told you about the experiment design. Basically, each participant will have a box. We wanted to make the subjects subconsciously influence the result of a random 50-50 event.'

Jeff stepped forward. 'Like the subliminal advertising they used to have in cinemas, we tweak the subconscious using faint lights on the surface of the box. To make the participant want a certain result.'

'Pedantically speaking it's not quite *want*. It may be more accurate to say *expect*. The lights can be configured to either give a shape reminding the observer of a head or a tail.'

They dimmed the lights slightly and ran a test with Louise. She matched seven matches out of ten. Mike spoke. 'Not amazing, but we tested this yesterday with a much higher sample and we were getting seven to eight hundred out of a thousand. Do you want to try another nine hundred and ninety times?'

Louise shook her head. 'I'll take your word for it. Okay, we can trick the participants into thinking about a particular result. What happens next?'

'There's a simple mechanism which re-tosses the coin when you shut the box; just a metal spring flipping it.' Mike opened and closed the box a few times showing the coin being tossed.

Louise watched as Mike and Jeff shared a look. *What now?*

Mike held the box just under Louise's nose. 'Just before you open the box, you cannot know if it is heads or tails … right?'

'I guess.'

Mike opened and shut it a few times. Each time Louise saw the head or tail of the coin as the box was opened. 'So when the box is closed, quantum mechanics says it is both heads and tails… until it's opened and we see the coin.'

'So…'

'Schrodinger's Kitty!' Mike paused. There was a chuckle from Jeff.

Mike waited for a few moments and then continued. 'We know, well, we assume, the lights will alter the subconscious.

Therefore, if the results come out skewed from a 50-50 split we can infer that the subconscious affects the coin-tossing results.'

Louise nodded slowly, turning over the experiment design in her head. 'Why not just show them the lights and get them to toss the coins themselves?'

'We're pretty convinced the experiment needs to have a single instantaneous observation of the result to keep it clean.' Mike paused. 'There's nothing in classical physics to give us any hope here, but the uncertainty principle gives a bit of wiggle room.'

Louise smirked. 'My hope stems from the fact that scientists always seem to be entirely certain about why something is impossible, right up to the time it happens.'

Mike frowned. 'Maybe historically, but it was generally more a cultural inertia rather than a deficiency in the craft of science.'

Louise nodded; she'd been lectured by Mike on the public mistreatment of scientists a few times. Generally after too many glasses of red wine, and heaven forbid you got him started on the subject of Alan Turing. It was the one time that Louise had seen Mike actually lose his temper.

Mike turned to Jeff. 'So what about Bob Reaple?'

'I don't know, he seemed genuinely interested…'

Louise cut Jeff off. 'So will the police be if they think I'm trying to steal military secrets.'

Mike waved his hands in a conciliatory gesture. 'It seems that Jeff is stuck betwixt Scylla and Charybdis. You never know, we might get something useful from him.'

Louise shook her head. 'We have to keep this tight.'

For the next few hours, they tested the various boxes that Mike had made, including the connections to the laptops and the programme Jeff had written to collate and analyse the coin-tossing data.

By the middle of the afternoon Louise felt the set-up was good enough to risk bringing in some test subjects. Now all they had to do was get those subjects.

While Louise and Jeff were at Mike's garage, Jeremy Benedict slowly drove past their house on Exeter Road. He parked and had a snoop around the outside of the front of the house. A few moments later the curtains from the next door house twitched and he made a hasty exit. Nothing achieved from his point of view but, within a few minutes, there were 15 mini-bots inside the Harding house.

CHAPTER 27

Jack woke up on his sofa in the pitch dark. He lay for a few moments just breathing slowly, getting his bearings. He remembered lying on the sofa mid-evening; he'd been exhausted; but he wasn't sure how the lights had been switched out. Trying to get back to sleep would be futile now – his adrenaline was already surging, even though nothing had happened.

Resigned, Jack got up and stumbled around the room, narrowly avoiding knocking over an expensive vase that Sarah had given him earlier in the year. He managed to find the light switch. It was 3am, pretty much the worst time to wake up; his body felt as though it had had a full night's sleep. He considered watching a film; a stack of Blu-ray discs lay on the carpet under his television. Wandering over, he sorted through them, but found he didn't have the required enthusiasm even to select one.

He dimmed the light and lay back down on the sofa – adrenaline raging. His mind was racing.

As his attention was drawn away from the interior of his lounge, Jack became aware of noises outside. He could hear the wind howling and barking in the distance. He got up and looked behind the curtains. There was a little light from London's always-on ambient light reflected off the bottoms of the clouds. The trees at the back of the garden were swaying; the wind was strong. He peered intently towards the trees. *Is there something out there?* He drew back from the window and paced around the room. After a few moments he returned to the window and looked again. Nothing had changed. Jack thought he saw a different movement from the back of the garden, and again he stared, but nothing emerged. *Am I imagining it?* There was another unusual movement. But after a few moments it turned out to be just another bush, so he turned away from the window and walked around the room again.

An hour later, he was still pacing indiscriminately. He couldn't settle. This time, he flicked on the television. His large wall-mounted flat-screen hummed to life, but the signal seemed to flicker and race; it appeared to be displaying two channels at the same time. He switched channels, and eventually the picture settled down, but Sunday morning television at 4am was not stimulating. Jack turned it off in disgust.

Another hour later Jack was still lying on his sofa, staring wide-eyed at the ceiling. *Am I going mad?* Suddenly, he jumped up, threw on a coat and walked out of the front door. The clouds still remained, but the wind had died down. There was no noise. Silence. Stamping his feet to get the blood circulating, he walked down his driveway and on to the road. It was narrow, with no pavement and no lights. There was a faint drizzle, but it gave him no discomfort as it settled on his face. It was comforting, a gentle reminder of normality.

The drizzle turned to heavy rain and Jack walked faster. As he reached road junctions he took arbitrary left and right turns. He knew the area well, so there was no real chance of getting seriously lost.

After a while, Jack came to a larger road with street lighting. Most of the houses had lights coming from their downstairs rooms. *6am on a Sunday?* Jack stopped outside one house, trying to discern if there was any activity. He wasn't really interested; he just wanted to keep his mind distracted from the growing, gnawing fear. He'd been out of the house for a while now. He needed to keep his brain occupied, actively focused on something mundane. And what could be more mundane than a sleepy Sunday morning in a safe suburb of West London?

Nothing seemed to be happening in the house. The downstairs lights were on, but the curtains were shut and there were no tell-tale silhouettes for Jack to interpret. About to move off, his eye was caught by a flash of colour. Through a small gap in the curtains, he saw a definite movement in the front room.

He decided to take a closer look. He crept up the driveway to the front room window. Through the gap in the curtains he could see a man wandering around half dressed, attempting to squeeze into a set of yellow cycling gear, while his television pumped out some generic Sunday morning programme. The man was fully engrossed in putting his cycling shorts on; Jack kept at the window – just watching, feeling reassured by the normality of the scene.

But, clearly, Jack watching a complete stranger getting dressed at 6am was not normal and, when a rumble of thunder made the man look up, *Shit!* He ran.

A few moments later the door to the house opened and he heard a shout. 'Bloody pervert!' And then much louder. 'Bloody pervert!' More lights started going on at other houses. Windows opened. Shouts of 'What's going on?' reverberated up and down the street.

Back on the pavement, Jack looked around; the street lamps were still bright and illuminating him. *Can't stop to explain.* He ran up the road. He could hear the prelude to a hunt behind him: doors opening, shouted exchanges. He dreaded the sound of a car starting, but it hadn't come yet. Another shout from behind him. 'There! On the pavement. Heading toward Farmely.'

Looking around again, Jack noticed the streetlamps were giving away his position. *Damn those lights!* He looked ahead; it was about 100 metres to the end of the street and into the comparative safety of some darkened lanes. He needed it to be darker. He had to be in darkness so they wouldn't see him.

With 50 metres to go, Jack heard a car engine starting. *Shit!* He turned back to look and, at the far end of the street, he could see the car pulling out of a driveway. A few houses down there were two men seemingly waiting at the side of the road. One of the men looked up, straight into Jack's eyes.

Jack looked at the street lights giving him away; suddenly, they went out – all of them. There was confusion as the men waiting for the car suddenly couldn't see much at all, and they certainly couldn't see him. Within a heartbeat, he had doubled his speed and made it to the end of the street. He threw himself sideways into the bushes and lay, panting, in the comparative safety of darkness.

Seconds later, the car drove past Jack's hiding place without stopping; they hadn't seen him jump off the road. The car followed the main street and disappeared from sight. Jack lay on his back. His legs and feet were painful, and his chest was tight. He breathed heavily, waiting.

The rain was constant, and he was soaked to the skin; but he felt safe. His breathing returned to normal quickly, and the muscle ache in his legs disappeared. He looked for signs of the returning car, or other pursuit. There was none.

All the streetlamps were still off when Jack crawled out from the bush. There was a small amount of light coming from some of the houses, but nothing much. Sensing noises in the far distance, he retreated to his hiding spot. Minutes later the car returned, stopping at the end of the street, where all the men got out. Jack stood up quietly and made his way back up the road, back to his home.

At home, he went into the bedroom to change out of his drenched clothes. Looking down at his legs, he could see one of his socks was soaked, but with what appeared to be blood. Jack inspected his legs, and there was a reasonably deep gash in his calf. He had a closer look, but the blood was only gently seeping out of it. Jack was amazed and concerned. The wound looked deep but also it looked a few days old. He shook his head. *That's not right.*

Grainy pictures from the night walk were beamed into the Gadium crew room. The house was set up with multiple mini-bots providing image overlay and reinforcement so, although the images of the outside chase were poor, footage of Jack around his home could be seen quite clearly.

Justio watched Jack inspect his legs and then followed the intermittent conversation Jack had with himself. There wasn't much to go on, but Justio could tell Jack was only just holding on to his sanity.

Although Justio still had many options, time was running out. Aytch had made a formal vault-recording of the decision not to progress a Full Emergence. It was technically a good decision from Aytch, but not one Justio would have expected Aytch to make unilaterally. Aytch was growing in confidence, and this would only become more and more restrictive for him.

Justio reviewed his contingencies. Aytch would not sanction Jack Bullage's removal, so the obvious next step was to kill Jack surreptitiously – set Earth on a path to a Full Emergence. A Full Emergence that Earth would not successfully negotiate.

But Justio had to move fast. Judging from experience on other planets, it could be that Jack Bullage was only a week away from becoming fully aware, after which it would be very difficult to kill him secretly – Aytch couldn't be allowed to find out about Justio's hand in the matter.

And there was always a back-up; use the threat of Jack becoming a Despot as a means to get Aytch to agree to a purge.

Justio smiled. He had plenty of options; but it had to be made to look as though a genuine, well-intentioned Gadium intervention went wrong through mismanagement. *Time to intensify the manipulation.*

CHAPTER 28

Aytch sat in the crew room reviewing materials from the previous 48 hours, his exam revision forgotten for the moment. There were real-time feeds from Louise Harding's house, but nothing much of substance seemed to be happening. Both Louise and Jeff seemed to be working at their kitchen table, but the voice feeds were not effective and Aytch couldn't make out what they were saying. *Once the mini-bots infiltrate their laptops we'll have all the data.*

Aytch had inferred the gist of the proposed test structure from snippets of conversations he had captured, and from hand-drawn diagrams observable on the Hardings' kitchen table. The tests seemed to be well short of the structure required to get results. However, the next time Jeff went to Mike's garage he would be couriering some mini-bots specifically to cover the tests.

At Jack Bullage's house, it was a different matter. The data from Jack's was not comprehensive, but it seemed likely he was a Triple Alpha. *He must have spontaneously converted during the crash.* On the positive side, assuming it was true, then, as a Triple Alpha, Jack would be suppressing further Alpha Emergence – Earth was not ready for Emergence.

Justio walked in, sat down and looked up the screens. There was a video showing Jack appearing to shut down the street lights, and some footage of the aftermath of Jack's probable subconscious self-healing of his leg.

Aytch stood up and started to pace around. 'The extraction process must be run before he becomes self-aware.'

'And without Earth finding out about us.' Justio waited for a moment. 'You haven't changed your mind about a Full Emergence?'

Aytch was silent for a while. He'd got another QET from Sharnia, intimating things were tough at the GEC – a good news story would be a real boost. He wavered. 'Can we leave the final decision for a few days?'

Nodding, Justio stood. 'Sure, we've got a few weeks before Jack is likely to become self-aware; he'll probably follow the standard lifecycle. He'll worry that he is going mad well before he wonders if he is developing superpowers.'

'So, the extraction plan.' Aytch displayed the various safe corridors in the airspace.

Justio looked up at the data on the walls. 'There's no mad rush. We take him in about a week. In the meantime, we'll just keep a watchful eye.'

'During which G60 finishes their investigation, which will lead them to a null test result from Louise Harding.'

'Exactly, everyone finishes what they're doing, with no positive results or leads.'

Aytch went back to his cabin and, once it was decrypted and enriched, reviewed the most recent QET message from Sharnia.

> *GEC issues remain. GF are up to something, I sense them everywhere. AI question may get traction. Think about it. Its time is coming*

```
again. Keep an eye on Justio, he has
complicated history - Darth and Marhok.
```

Darth and Marhok? Pulling out his communications tablet,
Aytch opened his Grandmother Sharnia's archive. Nothing
on Marhok, but he found a file with a reference to Sharnia's
Darth investigation. He accessed the video and set it running.
It was from about 20,000 years previously. Aytch watched a
close up of Sharnia's face looking tired. Sharnia spoke slowly.

> *'Not a great few months. I was ordered to perform*
> *a full investigation of the Despot disaster on Darth,*
> *whose inhabitants are now condemned to a*
> *lengthy quarantine.*
> *I've reviewed the mission notes and questioned the*
> *three Gadium participants. They all behaved*
> *absolutely correctly. Additionally, they all have*
> *perfectly clean records, with the exception of*
> *Commander Justio who had some personal issues*
> *a long time ago.*
> *Speaking to Commander Hunla about*
> *Commander Justio, she was convinced he'd*
> *suffered full animustosis... total soul death... on*
> *Marhok.'*

Aytch thought for few moments. This was from a period
of time when GF activity had been either totally absent or
not attributed. So Sharnia had been working in a position of
very low suspicion. *Not like now...*

Aytch looked for a follow-up on the subject but there was
nothing. It wasn't unusual; although computer memory was
almost infinite, all Gadiums were quite frugal when it came to
creating records, as it was all too easy to end up recording
your whole life. Then, as well as your descendants looking
upon you as a self-absorbed narcissus, they were also left
with data which was unsearchable, because of the severe
restrictions of Gadium usage of computer search capability.

He hunted around, but there were no more entries tagged with Justio's name. He spent a few more minutes flicking through other files. Nothing caught his attention.

Sharnia watched as the Chairwoman swept into the GEC meeting, passing the Deputy Chairman without acknowledging him.

As she sat down next to Sharnia she leaned across and whispered. 'My source has confirmed Rolumpus was instigated by GF agents. We think we know where they are.'

Sharnia nodded her receipt of the message and then stared out towards the meeting's attendees.

Next to her, the Chairwoman gathered her thoughts and then stood, addressing the meeting. 'Fellow Gadiums, we've had an ultimatum from the Rolumpus sector. They have demanded we give them unfettered access to a volume of space about 50 light years' radius centred on their main home planet.'

There were rumbles of disapproval around the room and a few half-whispered threats. The Chairwoman let the committee rumble on for a few moments then raised her hands. 'Well, let's hear the case of leniency. Delegate Smitter, I believe you think we should open up a dialogue with them.'

Smitter stood and bowed to the Chairwoman. 'Madam Chairwoman, giving them a mere 50 light years' range will only encompass a few dormant sentient species. I cannot see the harm.'

There was silence around the room. There were no signs of approval or support. Smitter looked around, trying to catch the eye of other committee members. Everyone looked away. Smitter turned to the head of the table. The Chairwoman looked down at her notes.

My turn. Sharnia stood up. She was a full metre taller than him and well over twice his weight – all muscle. Even from across the room, she loomed over Smitter, who, in fairness, was unnaturally small for a Gadium.

Sharnia took half a step towards Smitter, then stopped. Smitter sat down, struggling to get his breathing under control. Satisfied that he was subdued, Sharnia addressed the room. 'These requests are on the increase, and are fed by GF insurgence, giving places like Rolumpus courage to take us on.' She paused for a moment. 'No deals. Ever. No concessions. Ever. No special cases. No investments in good will. No pragmatism.'

After briefly, but meaningfully, letting her gaze rest on Jenkins for a few heartbeats, Sharnia turned to the Deputy Chairman. 'Mister Deputy, have you tabled a response?'

The Deputy Chairman looked to the Chairwoman for permission to speak. The Chairwoman gave a small nod and the Deputy addressed the committee. 'We have real-time communications with the Gadium mission on Rolumpus. Our analysis shows about 30% of the Rolumpus wants secession, and the remainder would prefer to remain with us. A short, sharp shock will bring them back in line, with minimal risk of a protracted guerrilla war.' He paused. 'I must add that some of their intercepted communications indicate they are aggressively developing Artificial Intelligence.'

The Chairwoman leant forward and gazed intently at the Deputy. 'What's your definition of a short, sharp shock?'

'We have embassies located in all major cities on their home planet. Each one has a high grade plasma bomb concealed inside. We detonate three or four of them, causing a few million deaths. Additionally, we destroy all of their ships. As you know, we provided them with their star-drives and, as per usual, we added a little something to each one for this eventuality.'

There was a murmur around the table. This was a little more severe than the standard response to species secession demands. Smitter stood up. 'How can we know they don't have all these devices under their own observation? How can we know they don't have AI capability to over-run us?'

The Chairwoman raised her hand. 'Smitter, much as I admire your judgement and guidance, this is not a time for leniency. The Rolumpus may think we have softened, we have changed. We have not.' The Chairwoman looked around the table. 'Votes in favour of *a* military response?'

Watching Jenkins, Sharnia noticed him flinch, ever so slightly, but milliseconds later his usual military face was back in place.

Meanwhile the vote went on. Sufficient hands went up. The Chairwoman stood. 'The motion is passed. However, as the Chief of the Executive, I reserve the right to use my judgement in the choice of targets, on the basis that the extent of the damage is similar to that proposed by the Deputy.'

Councilman Smitter raised a hand. 'Madam Chairwoman, can you tell us the targets?'

The Chairwoman smiled, all teeth, her voice dripping with menace. 'Why, councilman, do you have any friends in the Rolumpus Sector that you would like to warn?'

Back in her offices, Sharnia reviewed the evidence she had been accruing against the GF movement. She had a strong ally in the Deputy Chairman, but was resolutely against his occasional intimation that the Chairwoman was a secret sympathiser. *No, he doesn't know her like I know her.*

As for Jenkins, the Deputy had never really pointed a finger at him, but neither had he leapt to his defence when she'd laid out some of her concerns. And Jenkins had reacted to the Chairwoman taking executive control of the Rolumpus targeting.

Sharnia turned her attention fully back to the reports on her desk, and quickly let out a growl of frustration; the data aggregation and analysis was a nightmare – too much data and no sensible analysis. They were going to need to harness some limited AI capability to bring the galaxy to heel.

It had been a well-established fact within Gadium culture for half a million years that using AI brought in a large unknown element. Sharnia grimaced. *When you're already the de facto ruler of the Galaxy, then unknown is bad.*

Her personal communications tablet lay on her desk. She unlocked it and looked at the last QET message she'd sent to Aytch. Yes, Justio had acted correctly on Darth, but Hunla had seen first-hand Justio's rage many years before, on Marhok.

> *Personal Log – Commander Hunla*
> *I felt the slash of claws across my face. Although it was only a feeble strike, it still drew gouges into my skin. I tightened my own fingers around the wretch's neck and lifted him off the ground with one hand.*
> *I said, 'She's dead, Commander. You have your job to do here.'*
> *I released my grip, and Commander Justio slumped to the ground in front of me, struggling to regain his breath. His wife Graxa was dead. Dead to him. Not in stasis back on Gadium. Old. Old and dying. Great grandchildren all around her bedside.*
> *I said, 'Justio, get to your assigned position.'*

*Lying on the ground, Commander Justio lashed
out at me with his foot – striking out with the force
of an infant. I stepped backwards, evading the
kick, and then showed him how a kick should be
executed.*

*At this stage, I still felt compassion towards my
crew member; he'd been deceived.*

*I said, 'Don't let the animustosis take you. Get up!
You have your responsibilities!'*

*The fool screamed at me. 'My responsibilities can
burn!'*

*Any renouncement of responsibility is very unwise.
I kicked him again, not so hard, but squarely in his
genitalia. I swear I saw his eyes actually roll back
into his head as he passed out.*

*As I walked past his twitching but thoroughly
unconscious body, I whispered down to him.*

*'Careless kick, I seemed to have missed both your
legs.'*

These young ones, no respect.

Sharnia smiled, Commander Hunla had been a role model
and a wise counsellor. The evidence was tenuous: Jenkins
was under suspicion, Justio had a history of instability, and
they'd worked together a lot.

CHAPTER 29

By the time Jeff woke on Sunday, half of the morning had gone. He rolled over and was not surprised to find Louise wasn't there; he wasn't sure she had even been there overnight. He glanced around; her clothes from yesterday were on the chair.

After taking a few moments to take stock of the situation, he called out. Louise was not in the house. Jeff dragged his feet through his late-morning routine and only felt perkier after his 11 o'clock cigarette break with Mrs Saunders. As he walked back into the house, Jeff congratulated himself. He felt he'd nodded, shrugged, mumbled, commiserated and smiled all in the right places to effect a nice social exchange.

Then, picking up his notebook, he left the house to meet Mike. A text arrived from Louise. She was on her way to her first targeted accident survivor.

In The Three Kings pub, Mike sat with two drinks on the table. He waved Jeff over. 'We're ready for Wednesday. I've set up 10 sets of test equipment.'

'Sounds good.' Jeff picked up the beer. 'Louise is off chasing after survivors.'

Mike winked. 'As long as they do as she says, they'll remain that way.'

Opening his notebook, Jeff doodled a picture of a coin box. 'Do you honestly think anyone could alter a coin toss within a closed box?'

'You mean inside Schrödinger's Kitty!'

Jeff smiled, Mike's enthusiasm was a little infectious. 'But without a meaningful interaction, an exchange of some sort of force. How?'

'We agreed to suspend disbelief.'

As he thought about it, Jeff's smile slipped. 'I guess I did agree to assume it's possible. It's just a bit much…'

Mike leant over and gently closed Jeff's book. Jeff looked up and Mike held his gaze for a few moments, then Mike spoke. 'Everything we know now about the universe is true and irrevocable, right? They'll never be any new theories and never be any improvement on what we know now, right?'

Jeff remained impassive. *Well there's open-minded and there's mentalist.*

Mike continued. 'Newton, Copernicus, Einstein should have all respected the received wisdom of their age.'

Jeff's could feel a Mike rant coming. Could he hold it off? 'Well, Newton was a fervent alchemist and astrologer…'

'Come on, this is a chance to do something big. Jeff?' Mike imitated an over excited football commentator. 'You want your Bjørge Lillelien moment right? Pierre Simon de Laplace, Pierre de Fermat, Blaise Pascal, Christiaan Huygens… Your laws took one hell of a beating!'

Jeff laughed. 'Okay, not really their laws but I'm in.'

'Has Louise got any more from her informer on Project Hedgehog?' Mike scribbled some notes. 'Are we even close to the same type of test?'

'We've not had any more. Project Hedgehog was a military initiative, so I suspect their tests were quite edgy; probably a large fear element.' Jeff paused for a moment, thinking. 'Assuming Louise convinces the accident survivors to participate, we can't expect to replicate the fear they felt in their own escape situations.'

'Agreed, given we can't be honest with them; I can't see how we could drive those levels of fear. But there's definitely some tweaking we could do related to fear, if we felt suitably empowered.'

'We can't. Most of the participants are just volunteers from the university; our control population.'

Mike conceded the point. 'Okay. I'll cancel the order for scorpions.'

The evening wore on with general discussion.

Just as they were getting ready to leave, Jeff's phone received a text. 'It's Bob checking if we're still meeting next week. Shall we invite him?'

Mike thought for a moment. 'He's a solid thinker. A little political in places, but generally a decent scientist. And from what you've seen he seems to have an interest in the workings of the brain.'

'But… he also sits on the funding committee. I don't want him thinking I'm a loony.'

Mike laughed. 'We can sound him out, I think he'll welcome any experimentation that might push back the frontiers of knowledge.'

'So we invite him.'

'It couldn't hurt.'

CHAPTER 30

At lunchtime, Louise arrived in Wolvercote, looking for James Hollander's home. Parking on the edge of Port Meadow, she soon found the relevant house. Rather ominously, it looked run down and had no signs of life. She walked up to the front door and peered through the crenulated glass, but could make nothing out. She rang the doorbell and waited, then a few moments later rang it again. The house had a high wall, blocking access to the back garden. After five minutes, Louise tried a neighbour's house.

The door was quickly opened, by a middle aged woman. 'May I help you?'

'Good morning, madam, my name is Louise Harding, and I work for the Daily Record.' Louise showed her identification. 'I'm writing an article on survivors of dangerous traffic accidents and was hoping to speak to James Hollander, who I understand lives next door.'

The lady's body language gave the distinct impression to Louise she wasn't about to be invited in. 'Sorry to tell you, but your information is a little old. Lucky Jim was found drowned in a canal 18 months ago.'

'I'm sorry to hear that.' Louise kept a respectful silence for a few moments. 'You referred to him as Lucky Jim. Was there any other luck... other than the car crash?'

'Well.' The lady paused. 'I'm Sue, by the way. He survived cancer about 10 years ago. He told me about it. He said one day the doctors were talking about making his last days comfortable, and then a few months later the tumours had disappeared.'

'That is lucky. Anything else?'

'He talked a bit about his gambling friends. I got the feeling he did quite well.' Sue paused.

'Oh.' Louise made notes and then looked back towards Jim's house. 'His death didn't come up in my research. I was going to ask him about the crash. Was there anything unusual about the story, anything Jim may have told you?'

Sue shrugged. 'He'd been travelling in a friend's car on the way back from a concert. He always said he was very drunk and one minute he was singing along to the radio, and the next moment he was sitting by the side of the road while the car had been burned to a crisp. He was the only survivor out of six people in the car.'

'Was there much interest in his death?'

Sue shook her head. 'A few suspected foul play, but it all died down in a week or so.'

'And, pardon me for saying something which may sound strange, but did Jim ever talk about hedgehogs?'

Louise noticed a faint reaction from Sue, perhaps a twitch of recollection. She held her breath.

Sue paused. 'Actually, Jim did mention once he had contacted some other crash survivors. I think there was a hedgehog club, something to do with deaths on the roads.'

Louise nodded. 'I think it was a road safety thing. I have come across some references. You don't remember the names of any of the members of the club, do you?'

'There was an old lady called Mary Jones who lived in Banbury. I remember her because she's got the same name as my goddaughter. I don't have any contact details; sorry.'

'I'm sure I'll track her down.' Louise passed over a business card. 'If anything else occurs to you please give me a call. Also, not to be too dramatic, but could you drop me a note if anyone else starts asking you about Jim? I have a professional adversary, nothing serious though!'

Louise called the newspaper and asked an assistant to look up contacts for Mary Jones. Then she headed north towards Woodstock. After 10 minutes her phone buzzed: Mary's phone number and address.

Louise dialled the number and a few moments later the phone was answered. 'Hello?'

'Hello, is this Mary Jones? My name is Louise Harding, I'm a reporter for the Daily Record and I was hoping to get 10 minutes of your time.'

The voice on the other end of the phone sounded unsteady. 'What's this about?'

As Louise approached her turning she switched the phone into the other hand. She checked her rear-view mirror, checked the road ahead, and made the turn. 'I'm doing a piece on road safety.' Louise grimaced, the irony was not lost on her. She completed her turn right and continued talking. 'I heard your name in conjunction with a safety campaign and was hoping to get some of your thoughts. I'm close to Banbury. Could you do 10 minutes face-to-face please?'

There was silence for a moment. 'If you're here before 4:30pm. I lock up at dark and I don't open my door after then.'

'Okay, thanks. See you then.' Louise put the phone down. It was 3:45pm, plenty of time. She looked in her rear-view mirror. There was a car 50m behind her doing a 3-point turn. She hadn't noticed anyone in the street, but the light was fading fast and she couldn't make out any details. The car had turned around and was following her. Maybe.

There was a flash of blue light. Louise groaned and started scanning the road for somewhere to stop.

A few moments later Louise pulled into a bus stop and wound down the window. She watched as the policeman made a slow circuit of her car, finally stopping at the driver's window.

'Good afternoon, madam, I suspect you have an inkling of why I pulled you over.'

Louise tried her best to look contrite. 'Sorry, officer, I'm usually very careful about my driving habits.'

The policeman mumbled a polite acknowledgement and turned his attention to his phone before speaking. 'Are you Louise Harding of Exeter Road, London, NW2 3UU?'

'Yes, officer, I am.' Louise waited with growing trepidation as the policeman flicked through a few screens on his phone, then he frowned and sighed. 'And your comment about being a careful driver… do you count the six points you have for speeding, or not?'

Louise's shoulders sagged, and fumbled in her purse. 'I'm sure this won't make a difference, but I'm trying to get to an old lady in Banbury of a matter of urgency. I'm a reporter.' Louise passed over her identification card.

The policeman studied it then smiled. 'You are quite correct Mrs Harding, this doesn't make a difference. I am going to issue you with a fixed penalty notice. If you could just answer a few questions, please.'

Louise looked at her watch in frustration and then closed her eyes to get under control. *I can still make it.*

At 5pm, Louise pulled up outside the house of Mary Jones. Although in her 80s, Mary still lived in her own house in a quiet side street of Banbury. The house was in complete darkness. *She can't have gone to bed this early.* Louise looked through a downstairs window. There was no movement within. She checked the address; this was the place.

Louise called through the letter box. 'Mrs Jones. I just want to ask some questions about road safety... and hedgehogs.'

A few moments passed, then a light came down the corridor. Mary Jones stopped and talked through the front door. 'So who are you, exactly?'

Louise posted her identification badge through the letterbox. 'My name is Louise Harding. I'm a journalist. I'm investigating people who survive road crashes. I'm focusing on people who survive and then go on to have other unusual occurrences.'

Mary paused for a few moments. 'I believe you, but I'm not sure I'd let the Mother Teresa into my house after dark. Perhaps you could come back tomorrow?'

'Well, Mrs Jones, if my only option is to come back tomorrow then I will.' Louise stood, turned and walked back down the path.

After taking a few steps, there was a click behind her, the front door opened. Mary Jones leant out and scrutinised Louise. 'Okay, then, you can come in for five minutes, no longer.'

Louise followed Mary into the back room. Once seated, she turned to Mary. 'Thank you very much for agreeing to see me, Mrs Jones.'

Louise took her notepad out of her bag and opened it up at the next blank page. 'So, Mrs Jones, I have been looking into road safety and I came across a reference to a Hedgehog Club. Your name came up and I know nothing about it, is there anything you can tell me?'

Mary sat quietly for a moment, apparently thinking, then leant forwards towards Louise. 'Well, my two boys — my husband, William, and my son, Thomas… do you know their story?'

'Sorry, I don't. I'm in the very early stages of the investigation, Mrs Jones. Perhaps you could tell me about them.'

Mary's eyes narrowed. 'I'm not sure how you got to me without hearing their story. I'm also concerned about your use of the word hedgehog.' Mary looked at Louise in an appraising manner.

'Sorry, Mrs Jones, I got your name and the hedgehog reference from a neighbour of James Hollander… Lucky Jim. I know very little more.'

Mary went over to her desk, took out an old local newspaper cutting from the late 1970s and passed it to Louise. 'Well, firstly, take a look at this.'

Local Father and Son Disappearance
Local father and son, Bill and Tom Jones disappeared in the mid-1960s without a trace. Bill's wife, Mary Jones, has been searching for her missing family ever since.
Bill miraculously escaped from a serious car crash involving over 15 vehicles in late 1962. Following his escape, he was invited to participate in some government studies into road safety.
On the way home from the first session he disappeared. His son Tom disappeared a few days later.
Now, after almost 15 years, Mary says she's giving up. 'The UK Government aren't telling me anything.'

Louise passed the newspaper clipping back to Mary. 'I am sorry for your loss.'

Mary gently shushed Louise. 'No matter. I've given up the chase. Many years ago I got a few visits from a senior civil servant who implied Bill and Tom had been involved in espionage and they'd been eliminated by a foreign power.' She shrugged and concentrated on her hands.

Around the room there were a few old photos Louise assumed were Bill and Tom. 'So what about Lucky Jim and Hedgehog?'

There was a pause as Mary collected her thoughts, then frowned slightly. 'Four or five years ago I got a visit from a man who had a totally different spin for me to consider.'

'Lucky Jim?'

'Yes. He said he'd been investigating for many years and had come across a Project Hedgehog. This was a military experiment run in the 1960s and there were a number of people involved in the experiments who were car crash survivors. He thought it was linked to mental changes people suffer under trauma. Lucky Jim said he was pretty sure Project Hedgehog had taken Bill and Tom.'

'What did you do?'

Mary sagged back in her chair for a moment and then pulled herself together and leant forward. 'Nothing much. I wrote to the government, I pleaded they let me put my ghosts to rest. I asked explicitly about Project Hedgehog. I got no replies, and I was unable to drum up any support. It was another dead end.'

Louise nodded sympathetically.

Mary looked resigned. 'A year or so later Jim called me and said he'd some more information. He implied he'd spoken to a government official, and there'd been talk about psychic powers and aliens... Well, I asked him to come round to discuss it, but he never showed up.'

'Aliens?' Louise kept a straight face and looked carefully at Mary.

'I didn't believe him either. I didn't try to investigate.'

'Was there anything else?'

'No, dear. That's all.'

Louise stood up. 'Well, if I find out anything about Bill or Tom I promise I will let you know.'

'That would be kind.'

Mary walked Louise to the door.

A few moments later, Louise was on her way to her hotel.

Louise rented a room in a motorway hotel. Entering the bedroom, she threw her laptop and overnight bag down and jumped onto the bed; her phone was dialling before the bedroom door had closed shut. 'Jeff, I've made some progress. Lots more about Project Hedgehog, plenty of references to the MOD, mentions of psychic powers and aliens.'

'Aliens… are you sure?'

Louise spoke back tersely. 'I'm absolutely sure it's what I heard… look, let's both do a little internet searching and see if we get anything.'

Although it was getting late, Louise drove into the centre of Oxford to find an internet café. She paid for an hour of browsing in cash, and was careful to keep her baseball cap pulled down over her face.

After an hour of browsing with all her new search words she managed to achieve pretty close to zero except re-hitting a few web forums which had the old postings from FibonacciEddie. There was nothing on aliens at all.

In the morning Louise headed to Bath. After just over an hour of driving, she found the house of a fairly recent crash survivor called Ashley Davidson. Ashley had had a miraculous car escape in 2009.

He lived in a quiet side street off the main high street in Bath. He was in his mid-thirties, very personable and chatty. Louise gave him the high level story and, as the conversation moved on, it became clear there was a resonance.

'I'm not sure I should be saying this to anyone, let alone a news reporter, but I have always felt I was a little special.' He paused and chuckled. 'On reflection, I'd prefer to tell this to you than a psychiatrist. Okay, so … I do feel generally that 50-50 chances go my way more often than they should.'

'Have you ever tested this?'

Ashley looked a little sheepish. 'I did try a few years ago… rolling dice… nothing. I haven't tried recently, but I'm still convinced things generally go my way.'

'You shouldn't feel weird about it. I'm doing investigation into this very thing and I've met a few other people like you.' *Well, I've almost met them.*

Ashley gave a tiny nod, an indication, perhaps, that he was not averse to believing her. Louise pressed on. 'Would you be prepared do some formal tests with me and the scientific team I am collaborating with?' *Can't say husband and his quiz partner.*

'Maybe, what are the specifics? What's this other team?'

Louise did not miss a beat. 'I've put together a small research team with some professors from a north London university. It's a small team, but we're determined to get to the bottom of our investigations.'

For a few moments Ashley was silent. 'Where and when?'

'We'll be running our first session this Wednesday evening in North London. Clearly that's very short notice for you. So you could come to another one instead. But if you're good for this Wednesday then I'll pay costs.' *Please.*

Silence.

'You may get some helpful insights, plus we're testing other people from similar circumstances.'

'Okay.'

Louise smile broadly. *Thank god!* Louise provided additional details of where and when, then said her goodbyes and left.

On her way back into London, Louise noticed she was gripping the steering wheel very hard. She really needed this story. Although Harry constantly denied it, she was under pressure at The Daily Record. All Harry's talk about her being his star reporter was true… to him. But he wouldn't be around forever, and alternative sponsors were notable by their absence.

One genuine crash survivor; hopefully one more tomorrow.

CHAPTER 31

As Louise was driving home, Mike settled down in The Three Kings. Jeff was late. He nursed his beer and reflected on their current situation. It was fun! The intrigue and speculation really got him excited. Of course, nothing would happen at the tests on Wednesday, but they would have created a story of failure they'd savour for years.

Mike was brought out of his contemplations by Jeff's arrival. Jeff sat down with a thud. 'Louise just called. She's got a crash survivor.'

'Good news.' Mike opened up his notebook and took a pen from his inside jacket pocket. Not any old pen either, it was his lucky pen. A shiny Montblanc, given to him by the Fermi Research lab for a paper he'd written almost 20 years previously. 'So, what shall we say to Bob?'

'Do we even need him? Louise was a little scathing when I spoke to her earlier.' Jeff took a sip of beer. 'She's worried about leaks.'

'I did a little digging over the weekend into my records: emails, notes from university meetings, memories! Etcetera.' Mike consulted his notebook. 'I did come across an old email in which he was named as our liaison with the MOD.'

'So you're suspicious?'

'Not really; we should try to use his expertise.'

Jeff looked concerned. 'Louise was adamant about secrecy.'

Mike was about to respond, when he noticed Bob walk in. Maintaining his usual gait, Bob marched across the pub –

shoulders back, chin up – he'd perfected the small man charge. Mike stood up as he approached. 'Welcome, Monsieur Reaple.'

'Mike.' Bob turned to Jeff. 'Jeff.' Without waiting, Bob sat down, a look of intrigue on his face. 'So, how are the mind control experiments going? Go on – tell me which TV production company it's for.'

'I can't say too much.' Jeff eyed him warily.

'You haven't said anything yet.'

'We're planning some experiments to see if participants can somehow influence a coin tossed in a closed box.'

Mike watched the conversation unfold, concentrating on Bob.

Bob leant forward, accusing. 'So what makes you think there could be anything to be found? Surely it goes against pretty much all we know about the way the human brain interacts with the world. There are no scientifically plausible records of mind control or telekinesis.'

Jeff looked chagrined. 'A null result will be a valid result. We just need to make sure the experiment is tight, and the data is well controlled.'

'So you don't *actually expect* to find anything out.' Bob paused for only a second, before charging on. 'You must be aware that there are billions of dollars spent on gambling every year – all of that would be defunct if people could skew the results.'

Jeff nodded.

Mike was suddenly nervous. They hadn't prepared well enough for this. Bob was steam-rolling them. *Need to get some breathing space.*

Bob continued. 'So the most pertinent question is... why did you start this investigation at all?'

Mike interjected. 'Bob, surely you've already computed that we're prostituting ourselves to a wacko television programme.'

Bob did not miss a beat. 'Are you?'

'We're…'

Jeff cut Mike off. 'No. We're genuinely trying to investigate luck.' Jeff paused. 'Actual luck.'

'Why?'

'My wife is a journalist. She investigated a guy who had miraculously escaped from a car crash. She found other miraculous escapees. She found references to special powers. One thing led to another and we're trying to replicate the activity.'

'I hope you're not planning to crash cars, are you?'

Jeff smiled. A disarming smile, self-effacing and open. 'No, of course not. We will try to set up simple experiments to investigate luck. We're expecting null results, but we've come across…'

Mike interjected. 'Hedgehog!'

Bob was an excellent scientist and an effective political mover, but Mike allowed himself a satisfied smile as Bob proved to be a terrible actor. He jumped in his seat, visibly startled.

Mike raised an eyebrow at Jeff. *Now turn on the indignation.*

Jeff stood and started to collect his things. He whispered at Bob angrily. 'You have set me up in some way. I don't know how, but I'm leaving now. Shame on you for taking advantage of our professional connection.'

Bob was startled for a moment. 'Wait Jeff, Mike, I know it looks bad, but there's no entrapment going on here. I will be honest with you … well, as honest as I can be without going to jail. Give me two minutes to explain.'

Jeff made no move to retake his seat.

Bob looked at Mike imploring. 'Come on, Mike, we go back a long way.'

Mike nodded and Jeff retook his seat.

'You guys went snooping around the government, and the internet, using code words which have been buried for 50 years. There are some very concerned people at the MOD worried about security leaks.' Bob looked to each of them in turn, and then continued. 'The most reasonable person, my boss, decided a few tacit questions from me would be significantly preferable to black masks, tear gas and guns in the middle of the night.'

Mike chuckled. 'Come on, Bob. We may go back a long way but half an apology and half a threat is not sufficiently conciliatory. Let's put all of our cards on the table.'

Leaning back, Jeff folded his arms. 'I want to know about Project Hedgehog. What do you want to know?'

'When your wife tricked the General into giving information about Project Hedgehog an alert was generated.' Bob stopped to take a sip of his beer. 'They want to know how you got the code name Hedgehog.'

Jeff looked at Mike briefly then shrugged. 'Louise was investigating this guy who had survived a nasty crash. She was looking at all angles. She's under pressure at work. Anyway, she picked up the phrase Project Hedgehog from an internet conspiracy site. The…'

Mike cut in over Jeff. 'What *do you* know about Hedgehog, Bob?'

Bob shook his head. 'Nothing at all. My boss has told me nothing, except it was top secret.' They looked at each other for a few moments. He smiled. 'Look, I have to report back to him. But I will tell him there's no leak. You just got it off the internet. Can you give me the URLs?'

'It's rather hard to reconcile the fact that you've been sent by the MOD with your claim that you are blissfully unaware of any background to Hedgehog.'

'Have you ever worked with the government? It doesn't even know it has a left hand, let alone what it's doing.'

Mike smiled. 'Perhaps there's a modicum of truth in that. Okay, then, Mr Reaple. We believe you.' Mike turned to Jeff, who shrugged. 'Now, can we buy you another drink?'

'Sure, a strong one.' Bob chuckled. 'I wasn't completely lying about being interested in the mind control stuff, though. I am open to scientific controversy and I'd be interested in talking more about it.'

Jeff looked at him. 'It depends on your further orders for this investigation.'

'Well, I can't be sure what those orders will be at the moment.'

Jeff replied. 'We would be interested in your thoughts. Maybe once you've done your report we can talk further.'

Mike leant forward. 'Nothing at all about Hedgehog, really?'

Bob spread his hand wide, palms up in supplication. 'As I said, nothing. My boss has given me nothing to go on.'

Jeff's phone pinged. It was a text from Louise. She was home. He jumped up and collected his things. 'I'll speak to both of you tomorrow.'

Mike and Bob sat in amiable silence for a few minutes, finishing their drinks. Mike had worked with Bob quite a few times before on university funding committees. They knew each other. As Bob made ready to leave, Mike felt the need to say something more. He felt a little guilty about entrapping Bob earlier. 'Cards on the table, Bob. This all started as therapy for Louise. She feels she's struggling at work and just wanted a big story. But it's morphed into something a little more interesting; there are a few tantalising bits of information all teasing us as to the existence of something bigger.'

Bob grimaced. 'But the science…'

'We're just doing a little research. We may find something, we may not.' Mike stood up. 'It would be great to see the Hedgehog results. Please could you try to orchestrate something?'

'I have no idea how. My boss doesn't seem to know anything. I'll try. Let's keep communication lines open.'

'Do you want to review our experiment set-up?'

'Let me think about it. I'll give you a call tomorrow.'

On Tuesday morning, Louise stomped around the kitchen making her breakfast in the loudest way she possibly could. Jeff's revelation the previous evening about how much he'd told Bob Reaple had annoyed her immensely. He just didn't understand about confidentiality and control of information. *Bloody naïve scientists.*

Jeff came into the kitchen looking a little bedraggled. His night on the sofa had not been comfortable. Louise eyed him guardedly, daring him to say anything to lighten the mood.

After a few moments searching through his jacket pockets, Jeff lit a cigarette and went into the garden. Louise watched him through the kitchen window. The drizzle was falling incessantly and she could see him getting drenched. She opened a window. 'Come in, Jeff.' He wasn't really to blame; Mike and he were trying their best. They just weren't seasoned at snooping.

Jeff came back in. 'We know now our investigation has something going for it.'

In a blink her burgeoning sympathy evaporated, she simply couldn't stop herself. 'We knew already. Mary Jones confirmed it. General Crowley confirmed it.' She reached for her coat and walked to the front door. 'Now you've told them, they know we know.'

Jeff followed her down the corridor. 'Where are you going?'

'I'm off to Acton to track down another crash survivor – well, not a crash exactly. Willis Fereepe – gang fight survivor.'

'What's his story?'

'Willis and his gang were ambushed down a dead-end alley. Initially only a half-serious attack; just pot shots with small airguns. But one of the rival gang had managed to get his hands on a black-market stun-grenade – or so he thought.'

'So he thought?'

'It was a high-powered fragmentation grenade; Willis had six close friends ripped to shreds while he had no more than a few deep scratches. It was characterised as a mistake, a tragedy and a miracle all at the same time.' Louise opened the front door, then turned. '*You* need to ask Mike if there's anything you can do for tomorrow's tests.'

Jeff nodded. 'I'm going to speak to him later this afternoon.'

Louise mouthed. '*Now!*'

Jeff opened his mouth to make his excuses as Louise pulled the door shut.

CHAPTER 32

Returning to the crew room, Aytch found Justio deeply immersed in studying the data feeds from Jack's house. Jack was mostly wandering around the house and talking to himself. He did appear to be more relaxed than on the previous few days: there was less compulsive straightening of furniture, less double-checking of door locks, and a generally slower pace of wandering.

Aytch sat down. 'Are there notable developments I should be aware of?'

'Nope.' Justio looked up. 'I'm just studying his movements… considering ways to lure him up to North London.'

Fiddling with his comms tablet, Aytch brought up some technical statistics related to Jack's electronic appliances – no degradation in the last 24 hours.

'We're missing a mini-bot. Given the last recorded position, when it stopped transmitting, I'd guess we lost it down the shower plug hole.' Justio shrugged. 'It shouldn't have been there.'

'I can take a few hundred more when I go down for the extraction. We need to agree a date and time for that.'

'A week or so.'

Aytch turned to face Justio. 'I would really like to formalise the time and date.'

Justio did not meet his gaze, instead concentrating on his own comms tablet. 'I will provide some options within the next 24 hours.'

'Thank you.' Aytch involuntarily looked to the ceiling, where he pretended that the Gadium recording machinery was. Although, in reality, it was embedded into his chair.

A new set of screens appeared on the main wall. Justio had projected the recent G60 and Harding transcripts. 'So we're agreed to let them run their experiments, find nothing and lose interest.'

'Assuming Louise doesn't create a problem when Jack disappears.'

'Disinformation will be easy, Aytch, we'll fabricate a story – send Louise an anonymous email saying Jack has relocated to Buenos Aries.' Justio brought up the screens showing Louise's progress in recruiting crash survivors for their tests. He directed Aytch's attention to the relevant screens. 'She's met Mary Jones and Ashley Davidson. She did get an alien hint, so we'll have to monitor them.'

Aytch scanned the transcripts. 'She also got a fairly strong lead on Hedgehog.'

'There's nothing there for her to find.' Justio made a calming gesture. 'We've seen their experiment design, they're nowhere: they don't have the right people, they don't have the right conditions, and they have no idea what they are looking for.'

'If they get close, we'll need to take action.'

'They'll give up. If not, we have plenty of options. Murdering reporters and old women is not the first one.'

Yet again Aytch felt a twinge, the Gadium dictates were very clear. Everything was focused on the greater good. Sometimes it was necessary to take drastic steps. *Why does Justio paint me into a corner?*

'Formally noted and agreed.' Aytch paused. 'But I will instruct the mini-bots to start cutting into the Mike Littlejohn garage gas pipes.' There was an itch in the back of Aytch's subconscious; he'd overlooked something.

Justio spoke again. 'It will go smoothly. My only real concern is the talk of aliens. It would be a genuine disaster if we had to quarantine the planet for a hundred generations.'

'There are other failures too: Despots, war and animustosis.'

Justio started closing down the transcripts on the main wall.

There! 'Can you freeze, please, Justio?' Aytch pointed to a section of the transcript. 'That's new – James Hollander – have you come across him before?'

'I don't think so.' Justio paused and checked his comms tablet. 'He came up on a Potential Alpha event log about ten years ago… ah, yes, you were in a stasis break. It was too tenuous to investigate.'

Silence settled on the crew room and Aytch continued to review the video footage from Earth related to Louise Harding. It was not as clear cut as Justio would have him believe. Yes, the historical precedents were clear, if host populations became aware of the Gadium mission before most of the population were Alphas there was often war. But an open mind towards aliens in general helped cultural assimilation.

Aytch looked across the room; Justio continued to work, his head buried in his own communications tablet. Aytch preferred to use the main crew room walls, it encouraged consensus.

With a shrug, Aytch turned back to his own work. He reviewed the locations and statuses of the Jack Bullage mini-bots – yes, there was one missing. He started a search for it using the other mini-bots' active electromagnetic probing. It seemed a safe option, it was not as if Jack Bullage was scanning for stray signals.

Aytch couldn't settle. He looked back across the room at Justio. *I'm not suggesting we kill everyone who suspects anything. But the GEC cannot afford another failure.*

CHAPTER 33

Arriving early at the pub in Acton, Louise parked and went in to wait for Willis. The pub had a nice atmosphere, well-loved and, judging from the décor and lack of corporate branding, independent. She sat down at a table and unbuttoned a few buttons of her shirt, enough to let her crucifix necklace show, but not enough to compromise her principles.

She frowned slightly to herself. *If you fail to prepare* …

Taking her phone out of her pocket, she checked she had a signal. Then she manoeuvred her chair around to face the doorway, and fiddled with her phone while waiting.

Within minutes, a man entered the pub alone; black hair, black face, black clothes, and a large silver crucifix on a pendant. He instantly saw her, and came over, holding out his hand with a friendly smile. 'Louise?'

Louise shook his hand. 'You must be Willis. Thanks for making time for me.' She held out her ID. 'I was hoping to get some first-hand commentary from you. Can I get you a drink? I'm having a diet coke.'

Willis sat down. 'Sure thing. But you don't need to go to the bar.' Willis turned to the bar. 'Hey, Marie, could we have two DCs please?' The girl behind smiled an acknowledgement. Willis turned back. 'I'm very pleased to have any opportunity to spread my anti-gang message.'

Willis retold the basics of his story. It was just as Louise had read: a gang, a grenade, a few scratches and six corpses.

Louise made a few notes. 'How did you feel when the grenade went off?'

'Well the experts told me I couldn't have seen anything as it would have happened so quickly. But I believe I saw it explode. Somehow I knew it was real.'

'How scared were you?'

'I was in total terror. I was about to be shredded. I had no idea about the Holy Ghost and his plans for me, so I didn't know about my inevitable safety.'

'Did time seem to slow?'

'Yes, it almost stopped. It felt very strange. Of course now I know it was the Holy Spirit filling me and protecting me.' Willis paused for a moment, while Louise made notes. 'You know, Louise, normally by this time people ask me about the strength of my belief.'

Louise smiled. 'I will come to that, but faith is a very personal thing and I was waiting until we had got a bit more comfortable with each other.' She paused. 'Have you had any subsequent situations in which you've also felt lucky?'

The drinks arrived and Willis took a sip before replying. 'It wasn't luck. It was God's hand protecting me, to let me spread his message.'

He certainly is devout. 'I understand. So have there been other situations where you have felt God's protection in a similar manner? Or situations in which you have felt something unusual happening, not related to actual safety – more paranormal.'

Willis thought for a moment. 'Sorry, no, nothing similar.'

Louise waited, smiling at Willis. It seemed to her the wheels were whirring wildly within, and behind his calm eyes and gentle smile he was struggling to make a decision. Louise swayed gently, trying very surreptitiously to cause her crucifix to catch his eye. *You never know, it may swing the balance.*

Willis did not give any indication of noticing anything, but seemed to reach a decision. 'Interesting you use the word paranormal. I was contacted a few months after the event by a paranormal expert. He said he wanted to test me for super-paranormal powers. However, by then I had found my true calling, and I refused him. He bugged me for a few months, then disappeared.'

Louise wanted to get more information on the guy but did not want to risk making Willis suspicious. She also needed to get Willis to come to the experiments. She decided on almost telling the truth – a speciality of hers. 'Look Willis, the piece I'm doing is not sensationalist. It's part of a controlled set of scientific experiments investigating whether certain people are luckier than others.' Louise paused. 'I understand the depth of your faith, and I don't want to insult you by talking about science when you clearly feel spiritual about your situation… but science and faith can coexist.'

'I'm not sure they can.'

Louise took stock of the situation, this one seemed to be slipping away from her. *One step at a time.* 'I am planning to write a big piece for the Daily Record. If you come, I'll put aside a decent paragraph to support your anti-gang message... I'm not sure how at the moment, but we'll work it in somehow.'

Willis took a sip of his drink and then leant back, folding his arms. 'If I said yes, what would it mean I had to do?'

'Well, I've a few colleagues I'm working with. We're running tests to see if certain people are luckier than others. I'd love you to come tomorrow evening to North London to participate.'

The silence stretched, then Willis seemed to come to a decision.

Louise willed him to make the right one, for her.

'Okay. On the condition there could be no angle in the eventual write-ups ridiculing my faith… or any faith.'

Louise used her hand to gently wave the crucifix on her necklace. 'No concerns there. There is only respect and tolerance in our activities. She paused. 'I will send you an email with the details. Plus, I'd be glad to make a donation to your charity or church.'

They shook hands in agreement. Louise left the pub, happy. *One more down.*

Willis sat finishing his drink. Her smiles didn't fool him. He knew a predator when he saw one. But exposure for his message was paramount, it was God's will.

CHAPTER 34

A siren broke the calm of the ship, Justio, sitting alone in the crew room, watched as a priority QET communication from the Gadium Emergence Committee appeared on the crew room wall.

Unusual.

He started the decryption process. Given that Aytch was not in stasis he would have to include his security key to release the message. *Any moment now…*

Aytch ran into the crew room, eyes wide. 'Zeta Prime. I've never seen this before.'

Justio did his best to appear nonchalant. It was a real-time QET, simultaneously to over a hundred Gadium missions across the entire galaxy. It included the instruction for ships to forward on the QET message where they had entangled pairs with places other than the Gadium home planet. *Such a massive expenditure of communication energy.* He nodded slowly. 'Rare indeed.'

Aytch entered his own personal code to release the message.

Then Justio enriched the message using the mission's one-time pad. It displayed on the main crew room wall. Full text.

```
All Gadium Commanders - HIGH ALERT
Vantch. Additional evidence indicates a Gadium
mission may have been on-site for three years.
Information uncorroborated but, either way,
indicates a resurgence of GF activity. All
```

Aytch turned with a look of wonder. 'Gadium First terrorism.'

Justio felt relieved to see surprise on Aytch's face, rather than suspicion. 'Perhaps. Or maybe an honest mistake by the mission commanders.'

They both turned back to the text, absorbing the implications.

Aytch broke the silence. 'The recent statuses from the Vantch mission indicated they hadn't arrived yet.'

Accessing the relevant sections of the Gadium operating manual, Justio pulled up the requirements for enhanced security processes. He looked across at Aytch, then made a decision; speaking casually as he navigated the menus. 'And maybe they haven't.'

'Sorry, Commander. It says they have.'

'It may be a limitation of our translation, but the text says *a Gadium mission* not *the Gadium mission*. The implication may be that there is a separate ship.'

Aytch remained silent for a while. 'I suppose so, but an independent GF ship?'

'There've been rumours of one.' Justio was conflicted; highlighting the potential existence of a separate ship was giving away information about the GF operations. However, the identification of an obvious external threat could draw Aytch's attention away from dangers closer to home.

Aytch assimilated the data. 'A second ship, staffed with traitors, could cause trouble.'

'But there is always the chance the Gadium mission really has been on Vantch for a while and has made mistakes. Now they're using the GF as a convenient excuse.'

'Sharnia's convinced the GF are on the ascendant. She sees them everywhere, and thinks they will make some legitimate political moves soon.'

'She's a strong force for stability. One of a kind.' *Except for all the other maniacs just like her.*

By now, Justio had brought up a screen detailing the additional security protocols required in conjunction with a security alert indicating Gadium First sabotage. Step 1 was a review of the relevant manual sections.

Justio brought up the screens and then stood up. 'I'll leave you with these to review. I'm going to stretch my legs.'

'But you need to authenticate that I have refreshed myself on the manual.'

'Ship – This is Commander Justio. Zeta Prime acknowledged and executed by Commander Aytch.'

'And I need to authenticate that you've done it.'

Justio looked at the screens for a few seconds, then turned back. 'Done it.'

He didn't wait to see if Aytch would log the cross-authentication. He left the room. Walking down the corridor, he felt the initial pangs of concern. He'd seen the look in Aytch's eye, and he wasn't one hundred percent sure that Aytch would give him the authentication.

As the crew room door slid closed, Aytch turned back to the screens. Something was bothering Justio, that was for sure, but what? It was no surprise that Justio made a show of cutting corners of the official process; he'd been doing that the whole mission. *If I had his sponsorship I could get away with it too. Not that I'd want to.*

'Ship – This is Commander Aytch. Zeta Prime acknowledged and executed by Commander Justio.'

Then Aytch turned his full attention to the screens and initiated the narration.

Chapter 11.1.3.A – Gadium First Sabotage Overview

Noting membership of (or affiliation to) GF is illegal, sabotage will usually come in one of the following formats:

1. *Official GEC orders giving bad advice, due to GF manipulation of the GEC; some people feel this already happens on a daily basis*
   a. *Mitigation: All decisions subjected to statistical analysis*
2. *Forged orders to Mission teams appearing to be from the GEC; arising from the subversion (by blackmail, bribery, etc.) of the QET operators*
   a. *Mitigation: Mission teams have executive control over operational matters, they do not expect, nor always obey, orders from GEC*
3. *Mission teams infiltrated by GF sympathisers; considered to be rare due to intensive training required for all Gadium teams, however, the wide lassitude of operational decision making means a skilled GF operative can sabotage and often has a good chance of covering his or her tracks*
   a. *Mitigation: Two-member Mission teams with significant four-eye validation and authentication*
4. *A GF Mission ship on location; separate from, and unknown to, the on-site Gadium mission; existence disputed, but analysis implies one to three GF ships in existence*
   a. *Mitigation: Hope and vigilance*

Aytch shook his head and turned back to his comms tablet. *Disaster on Vantch…*

On Vantch, Klope watched as the Supreme Prelate of the True Faith walked out of the Palace of Infinite Wisdom. Flanked by six guards, he walked slowly up to the podium set out in front of the palace. There was a murmur in the crowd. They had expected a simple sermon preaching *The One*, with perhaps some reference to the Prophet, and the way he'd strayed from the One Path. However, the presence of another member of the Prelate's retinue indicated something more significant was to happen.

Behind the main entourage another guard, the seventh, followed, carrying the Staff of Wisdom cradled across his outstretched arms.

The guard, a giant, clad head to toe in black leather armour, walked up to the Supreme Prelate and knelt in supplication. The presence of the Staff meant judgement was about to be given. Klope looked around at the soldiers with growing consternation. They didn't seem to be getting ready for anything, but their faces betrayed uncertainty. He turned to look at the Supreme Prelate.

The Prelate took the Staff and then addressed the crowd. 'Blessings of The One upon you all.' He paused while the crowd returned the greeting, replicating the words, then continued. 'There can be no reconciliation with the Prophet. There is no middle ground. There is one God. One Faith. One Path.' His blue eyes glittered with life and he held out the Staff. 'The so-called Disciples, the followers of the Prophet, are hereby banished from the continents of both Harfi and Lokis. Those who proclaim their allegiance after the setting of today's sun will be executed without trial.'

Most of the crowd cheered and pockets of people started shouting abuse at the Disciples. Klope stood waiting for the soldiers to disburse the crowd, but the Supreme Prelate had not finished. The seventh guard went to a doorway at the side of the palace and returned after a few moments dragging a Disciple, whose green and white clothes were caked in mud and blood.

The guard threw the Disciple down in front of the Prelate, and then, taking hold of him by the throat lifted him easily off the floor with one hand. The Prelate turned to the crowd. 'This Disciple has been found guilty of treason against the True God.' He paused. 'The punishment is death.'

Klope felt his stomach cramp, and he watched in growing fear; if the giant guard were to squeeze a little harder, his brother would die, and then the crowd would turn on all the other Disciples. *I hope I can find a safe path through The Many.* The soldiers around Klope and his few Disciple brothers, began to finger their guns. Klope looked around the crowd. Other groups of Disciples were also being focused on by soldiers. Klope turned to his closest companion. 'I am proud to be in your world, brother.' They shook hands. Klope couldn't help but notice the sweat on both of their palms.

But the Disciple looked back at him, with his grip firm. 'And I in yours, brother.'

A shout rang out across the courtyard. 'I am the Supreme Prelate of the One Path. And only I shall judge in God's name. The other Disciples gathered here today may leave in safety… but not before witnessing me carrying out the judgement here.' The Supreme Prelate took a step towards the prisoner and reached out his own hand. The seventh soldier lowered the Disciple slightly, allowing the Prelate to take the Disciple by the neck.'

A gasp rang across the crowd.

Klope felt his chest tighten. Breaths were hard to come by, as if his own neck was being squeezed. *The Prelate is holding my brother up with one hand!* The Supreme Prelate turned back to the crowd. 'I follow the One Path. God's strength is in my arm, his wisdom is delivered to my mind, and his judgement is mine to carry out.' The Prelate effortlessly flicked his hand and a loud crack washed across the silent crowd. The Disciple's head lolled forward.

The Prelate dropped the body to the ground and gave his benediction to the crowd. 'Blessings of The One upon you all.'

Klope turned and ran.

CHAPTER 35

By Tuesday, James Chambers couldn't shake the feeling that he should have found out more about Project Hedgehog, but there was simply nothing recorded. He called Bob to see what had been gleaned from the Hardings.

Bob relayed the information about Louise's obsession with Jack Bullage and the car crash.

James took this in. *Probably no leak.* 'I remember the reports of the crash, people seemed incredulous anyone had survived. But that said, Louise Harding is a seasoned reporter. Surely she didn't think it was anything more than a simple, albeit horrendous, accident.'

'Well, given your department is nominally in charge of investigating the paranormal, you don't have much of an open mind...'

James conceded the point. 'What about their sources? Did you get the web sites?'

Bob gave the information he had, including the user name FibonacciEddie. Then probed for more. 'Is there anything you can tell me, James? They're doing luck experiments now. If I knew more about the actual Project Hedgehog scenarios I could compare the set-ups...'

Silence. *Do I really care about their experiments?*

Bob continued. 'They've assumed Project Hedgehog was linked to mental powers of some sort, telekinesis or altering reality in some way. They have extrapolated, tenuously, but on advice from FibonacciEddie, into a wider investigation of luck.'

'I'm just happy there's no leak.'

'But you're in charge of paranormal and aliens. You must be a little interested.'

'The programme was closed down. The records are all gone.' James paused and stopped himself. *No need to mention the disappearances.*

'So it's over?'

James thought for a moment. It couldn't hurt to keep an eye on things, even if just to cover his back. 'Try to stay close for another week.'

'Okay.'

Putting the phone down. There was no leak, the investigation was over.

But…

The Hedgehog file summary. James referred back to his notes. He had to admit there was still an intellectual irritation that needed soothing. Of course, he wasn't going to make his position worse by giving any information out, but he could still have a look around internally.

James turned to his G60 technology hardware and, within a few moments, some of the most intrusive and powerful computers in the MOD were looking for FibonacciEddie. The scale and complexity of interpreting and cross-referencing data across all the impacted systems ensured that most of James' afternoon was spent tweaking matching algorithms.

As the results started to drip in, James felt a sick feeling. FibonacciEddie was a paradox.

A smoking gun?

Jack sat in his lounge staring into space. He had tried for three hours to log on to the internet with no luck. He'd spent thirty minutes on hold to his internet service provider. He'd walked around the block twice to clear his head. His iPod had quit on him, and he definitely felt he was being watched. *Deep breaths. The shrink said the shock may cause me to suffer from paranoia.*

He ate a microwave dinner and then, at only nine o'clock, went to bed exhausted. And yet, again, sleep did not come easily.

At 11 o'clock, he was still awake. *Two hours looking at the bedroom ceiling covered in sweat.* He smiled wryly.

By midnight he managed to drift off to sleep. He dreamt. There was no respite.

He was in a corridor. There were doors, so many doors. He had to find the right room. Jack reached for a handle, but the door wouldn't open. He tried another door, which was also locked. He cried out in frustration. 'What's going on, Connie? Where are you?'

He started to run down the corridor, but it was an endless, colourless tunnel. Lots of doors, but whenever Jack stopped to try a handle, it was locked. 'Where are you, Connie? You said you'd help me!'

Running faster, Jack could hear a sound up ahead, but which door was it coming from? He had to remember how to help himself. 'I love you, Connie!'

Still the doors remained locked. He kept running. The corridor was shrinking, and he was brushing his head on the ceiling. A growing dread had settled in. He was being followed. Not quite chased, but definitely followed. 'I know you love me, Connie!'

He was starting to feel squeezed. The walls were closing in. He stopped. The next door seemed to give a little, but remained shut. As he pushed, the door bulged inwards slightly, as if made of rubber, but it did not open.

Jack could hear the ticking of his bedside clock. 'Is this a dream, Connie? I said "I love you".' No, that was not it; Jack ran down the corridor – he was close to remembering. But the corridor was closing in on him again, the ceiling grating against his head.

'You love me!' He tried a door. It gave slightly, but did not open.

He had to remember. The ticking was louder. The corridor still shrinking. He looked behind, there was a darkness swallowing up where he'd been. Oblivion!

'You love me!' He tried a door. Still locked.

He remembered. 'I love me too!'

The next door opened, warmth flooded in.

Jack woke up. He lay in a pool of sweat. It was 3am. He'd had a nightmare. He couldn't remember much of it. He got out of bed and walked into the bathroom. For a few minutes he rubbed water on his face and just looked at himself in the bathroom mirror. 'Do you have to torment yourself?'

But, deep down, he felt something good had happened.

CHAPTER 36

Justio sat in the crew room and reviewed his handiwork. The walls were covered with maps and projected routes for the incursion to collect Jack Bullage. They'd agreed on Newgate Golf Course, in North London. They would deploy multiple mini-bots for tracking and also take one of their remaining military reconnaissance drones with tranquiliser missiles.

Aytch highlighted the preferred track of their re-entry craft. 'I believe that is route sorted. It should be no longer than six hours to get there.'

'Sunday night, plenty of time to get countermeasures in place.' Justio paused. *Looks good and with Aytch in the re-entry craft, I will have control.* 'I'll ensure he gets there.'

'We're using the psychiatrist?'

'Yes, Jack will be invited, at very short notice, for stress counselling. With a last-minute spot coming up on Sunday evening. Jack will drive himself, arriving after dark in the car park.'

The Gadium technology to fake emails, telephone voices and postal letters, made it easy to ensure Jack got a very official invite from England's finest.

Justio pulled up some additional screens. 'Invite on Friday evening, giving minimum time for Jack to get any formal corroboration – but his phone will be hacked anyway. We'll do a Sunday night snatch.'

'Will five minibots, plus the reconnaissance drone, be enough?'

'Plenty. With me in manual control we'll overcome their limitations.'

Aytch gave an uncharacteristic chuckle. 'It's funny, on Earth they use the phrase *it's not rocket science*, with the implication that rocket science is difficult. Our minibots are stupid, but great at rocket science.'

Justio raised an eyebrow in acknowledgement. *Not actually funny but…*

Aytch had not finished. 'But our mini-bots struggle with intuitive deduction by abstract pattern matching built up from repeated measurement of experience.'

'Is that a quote you've learned for the exams?'

Aytch nodded.

'You know the rules, no technology which could even get close to independent thought.'

Aytch was silent for a moment. 'Sharnia thinks we could use limited AI to cement our stewardship.'

Justio remained silent. *Stewardship… a nice word for hegemony.*

Aytch continued. 'She said AI could be used for better data analysis, improved allocation, and ultimately driving better decisions.'

Justio nodded. *She's also a total psychopath, second only to my very own Deputy Chairman in the mouth frothing stakes.*

'What do you think, Justio?'

'Let's ask the manual. Harkin is pretty good on these things.' It took a few moments, but Justio brought up a new screen, this time muting the narration and reading the second paragraph himself.

Chapter 29.3.D – Alphas (Commentary)
Professor Harkin

'Some believe it may be the active removal of the Triple Alpha which triggers the Emergence acceleration, rather than only the passive existence

*of the Triple Alpha suppressing the wider
Emergence – I am not convinced.'
'Utterly outlawed for over 700,000 years (even
during GF Ascendant Periods) but theoretically
possible is the possibility for a Triple Alpha to
tunnel into an Alpha to effect the transformation of
Alpha to Triple Alpha.'*

Justio waited for a few moments for Aytch to catch up.
'You knew this?'

Aytch nodded. 'I'd heard of it before.'

It was known certain advanced AI could perform SISR
with the same level of competence of a biologically based
Triple Alpha. So many replicated AI machines could
revolutionise the speed of moving a planet of all Alphas to be
a planet of all Triple Alphas.

Justio struggled to his feet. 'If you're looking for a reason
to defend reintroduction of AI, then that's the best one - to
simplify and secure the transition process. But independent
thinking machines capable of SISR could prove a risk to
Gadium.' *I'm not sure anyone wants that, even GF.*

Justio left the room.

Once Justio had left, Aytch reflected on the AI Tunnelling.
He knew about the theory; it was in the manual, it wasn't a
secret. But within his family, there was a little extra history
connected with AI studies. Unfortunately, it was also mired
in GF history.

Aytch turned to the manual and started paging through it,
mostly to take his mind off the uncomfortable family
memory.

Tunnelling. The act of mentally stimulating a probability
state reduction within the body of another living thing.

216

Illegal. Aytch shuddered and instinctively flicked to the most read section of the manual – Chapter 8.1.A. This section was read at least three hundred times by every juvenile Gadium in the 10 or so years between their coming of age and their own conditioning programme.

Chapter 8.1.A – Juvenile Conditioning Overview

All Gadium children shall undergo significant subconscious treatment to ensure they do not (and mostly cannot) activate probability state reduction to hurt a fellow Gadium. This is done via operant conditioning and results in the individual's subconscious being unable to directly or knowingly indirectly harm a fellow Gadium. Other non-Gadium organisms can sometimes be tunnelled into without pain. It depends on the imprinting within the specific Gadium subject. Certainly, non-Gadium but bipedal reptilians should be treated with caution.
This conditioning is run hand-in-hand with the instruction required for the juvenile to safely manage the enhanced physical capability which Triple Alpha status confers.

Aytch knew what the operant conditioning felt like. He could still feel the echo of unbearable, crippling pain from his own treatment as a juvenile – the mescospoline burning through his veins, not just in his arms, but his eyes, his throat and his heart. Threatening to blind him, choke him, cripple him, and ultimately destroy him, just as he took his full place in the Gadium society.

Even now, the conscious consideration of trying to alter a probability function inside another Gadium being brought bile up into his mouth. He smiled to himself ruefully. *Agony. I won't forget… ever.*

Back in his own cabin, Justio took stock. He hadn't pushed firmly about trying for a Full Emergence, but he felt Aytch was wavering slightly. *His sense of galactic duty probably.*

Justio didn't think that Aytch would change his mind. But Aytch didn't need to change his mind, Justio could kill Jack Bullage anyway. Removing Jack Bullage could make way for a Full Emergence to develop; after which, the Earth would probably manage its own destruction. Of course, he'd have to stop Aytch stalling the Emergence with other Triples, but that would be doable – once the Alpha population got past 5% it went so quickly anyway.

Justio had a few days to act; he couldn't afford to have Jack retrieved to a safe house on Earth. Given Jack was a Triple Alpha, it would bring stability to Earth transitions for a few thousand years. Additionally, it would be impossible to kill him surreptitiously.

He needed Jack dead... or turned into a raging Despot, in which case Aytch would be quick to assist in the removal.

There was additional complexity. Any future audit of the Gadium Mission would need to clearly show that both he and Aytch had acted honourably, and according to Gadium standards, at all times. Difficult, but possible – after all, he'd done it before.

Option 1 - Jack never makes it to Newgate.

Then there was the matter of Louise Harding. She was a second piece of the puzzle. She would be his mouthpiece, but it needed to be a mouthpiece utterly devoid of any reference to aliens. And untraceable back to him.

James Chambers had sat in the G60 offices for the best part of 20 hours. Every time he was about to leave, the mainframe spat out another paradox. Max had come and gone, although James had not involved him in any of the discussions.

Who is FibonacciEddie?

Any messages captured passing around the internet infrastructure, either referencing FibonacciEddie, or directly from him, were heavily encrypted. Plus their information trails were obscured to a level that James had only seen in military grade software. The message routing went through public, government and military systems both within the UK, and other countries, with equal ease. Without the hardware that James had access to, FibonacciEddie would have been untraceable.

However, where James did manage to find source materials, he also found that timestamps (and other reference data) had been altered in an incredibly amateur way. The levels of complexity simply did not match up. Even after all the analysis, James was no closer to identifying the background to the online persona FibonacciEddie. But he could see that the person who created FibonacciEddie had almost ultimate access.

James tried to forget about it. There was no leak!

But he couldn't forget. Primary investigation was required.

CHAPTER 37

On Wednesday evening, at 5pm, the volunteers arrived and congregated inside Mike's garage, each of them automatically finding a seat in front of a coin-tossing box. They looked like a pretty standard set of students to Louise, neat and presentable. She watched as Mike took Ashley and Willis aside, briefed them and reminded them to keep quiet about luck.

Mike led the briefing. 'Okay guys, today we are at the start of a large study to investigate shape recognition and various cognitive functions within the brain.' He looked around the room, trying to catch the eyes of each of the participants. 'I won't deceive you, this is not an official university experiment. It's a bit more commercial in nature. So volunteering does not count towards any course credits; but the good news is we will be paying you in cash, and these experiments could run and run.' There was a murmur of appreciation from the participants.

Picking up a coin box, Mike explained as he showed its workings. 'The experiment is simple. You will each open a small drawer in a box three thousand times. In the drawer is a simple coin. You will record whether the coin is *heads* or *tails*. In future sessions we will be measuring brain patterns, eye movement and ultimately shape recognition in various mental states. I recognise this control is very boring, but we do need a set of accredited controls. Let me demonstrate.' Mike put the various bits through their paces. 'There are switches on the boxes for you to record the results. There is no speed requirement, and no concept of reaction time in this run of the experiments. Just get yourself into a steady rhythm, open the box, observe the coin, flick the switch then close the box, then repeat.'

Most of the students nodded and when Mike asked if there were any questions, there was only one. 'How do we get paid today?'

'Good question. Well after you have finished your three thousand coin tosses you get to keep the coin… No, it's cash in hand, and please don't talk about this to other students… or lecturers.' Mike looked over to Jeff. 'Jeff will get in trouble if this gets out, and then your cash flow will dry up.'

One of students checked the apparatus. 'Why is there a picture of a snake on top of the box?'

Mike replied. 'It's for experiments in a few weeks when we'll be stimulating various areas of the brain during the shape recognition exercise. The image of a snake will be used to reset your brain's thought patterns.' He paused and looked around the room, there were a few nods of understanding. 'I said reset but that's not really a very good word. Using a snake picture is very powerful, because as mammals we are hard-wired genetically to be frightened of snakes. So showing a snake forces our primordial subconscious to do a little bit of work overriding the hoity-toity cerebellum and effectively resetting our cognitive function.'

So far, so good. Louise noted to herself. Then she retired to a tiny office area, which Mike had partitioned off from the rest of the room, and primed the laptop.

From the other side of the stud wall, Louise heard Mike announce the start of the test. 'Thanks, guys, off you go.'

A few moments later, Mike joined Louise in the office area. He nodded back in the direction of the experiment area. 'Jeff is troubleshooting.'

The noise built as the participants started opening and closing the boxes, and recording the results of individual tosses by clicking their switches left or right. The results fed through to the laptop with Louise.

The ten participants all worked through their three thousand coin tosses, and with arm resting, toilet breaks and cigarettes all eating into the productive time, it was four hours before the last of the participants had finished their allocation. At just after 9'o'clock, they were given £40 for their troubles.

Once the students had left, Louise walked through to the main garage area. Willis and Ashley had stayed behind. 'How do you think it went?'

Willis shrugged. 'I'm not sure, we were just recording what we saw.'

Mike's voice came over the partition. 'Three minutes, guys.'

No-one spoke for a while, then Mike called them through and everyone crowded around the laptop while he took them through the results. 'Overall, we have each candidate tossing 3,000 coins, a good sample size. Assuming it's random, then on average, each would correctly guess 1,500 tosses.'

Louise looked over Mike's shoulder. 'So what is the result? Did any of our subjects show any variation from the expected average?'

Mike gave a tiny shake of his head. 'One of the students, Ben, got 1545 calls correct, Ashley 1524, and Willis 1482.' He paused for a moment. 'There's no smoking gun... so far.'

Louise frowned. 'What would have been needed?'

'If any of them had managed to get 71 more than the average 1,500 correct then according to the chi-squared test, given there is one degree of freedom, we could say the coin was not acting randomly - assuming the subliminal stimulus is working.'

Louise's frustration bubbled up. 'Thanks for the nerd-a-thon description.'

Willis pointed at the laptop. '71 additional correct answers doesn't seem like too big a target.'

Mike eyed Louise. 'Given her ladyship's current predisposition, I won't go through the maths, but I can assure you the chances of you getting 1571 correct are very slim unless you are somehow influencing the result.' Mike paused. 'So, Ashley, Willis, are you happy to stay on and try again, but this time actively trying to affect the results?'

The second set of tests was slightly more complicated. Willis and Ashley had to record two switch flicks for each coin toss; the first recorded their expected outcome and the second recorded the actual outcome. The tests ran on for a few hours, after which Mike crunched the results. 'Sorry, no better.'

By now it was past midnight, so they agreed to ramp down for the evening. Jeff and Mike tidied up while the others walked out.

Louise took a few moments to speak to Ashley and Willis on the driveway. 'Hey, guys, many thanks for coming. We may re-run the tests this Saturday. Could you make it?'

Willis nodded amiably.

Ashley stood for a few moments in contemplation. 'No problem. Unfortunately, I felt normal today, not the state of mind I would need to do something unusual. I'd love the chance to go again.'

They shook hands and Louise went back inside. Mike was staring at the laptop. 'I will run some additional analysis overnight, there may be something hidden amongst the data, like runs of good luck, etcetera.'

Louise let out a sigh. 'I had higher hopes for Ashley, – he felt positive about influencing coin tossing.'

Mike shrugged. 'He probably just has an excellent self-image, so he focuses on the 50:50 chances that fall his way. He simply forgets the ones which go against him.'

Jeff returned from a cigarette. 'I assume I will just tell Bob the truth, unless something comes up in Mike's overnight data crunching. Mike?'

'We could invite him for Saturday?'

Louise kicked out half-heartedly at a table leg. 'If we even bother running it. We've no new information.' She took a few deep breaths. 'Okay, reconvene tomorrow lunchtime and make a decision.'

Mike passed Jeff a zip drive. 'You take a look at the data as well. You may find something I miss.'

CHAPTER 38

Justio walked slowly down the corridor towards the QET room. He'd waited a few hours for the opportunity, and now that Aytch had returned to his own cabin, Justio could get to work.

Although he'd been resting in his cabin, he was emotionally tired; he flexed his hands nervously as he walked. Recent conversations had underlined a couple of things: Aytch was getting more proactive, and there was genuine momentum within the Gadium hierarchy to take the fight to the GF. Time was running out.

Once inside, Justio overrode the control panels and examined the message logs. There was no record of his own recent communications, which was good, he'd taken great pains to delete them.

Unusual. There were two recent QET messages from Sharnia to Aytch. The one he knew about, referring to GEC issues, GF concerns, AI, and Sharnia's concerns about himself. But there was a second message, time stamped from only a few hours previously.

Justio started to decode it. Aytch had security controls and strong encryption, but given he was alone, it was straightforward for Justio to open it. *I'll find a path, one in the many.* He concentrated on the secure decryption password – a 20-character alphanumeric. As usual he felt a fuzzy detachment as the possibilities opened up before him.

Visualising himself typing the code into the decryption screen, Justio tried to hold all the possible future states in his mind. The code didn't matter though. One code would lead to a green light, for success, and the other billions and billions of codes would lead to a red light, indicating a lock out.

Justio moved his consciousness past the point of entering the code, and visualised himself a step further into the future. He focused on the path in which the code would be accepted and would return a green light. He followed it. A matter of seconds later, a green light, and the decoded message was enriched and displayed.

> *Recent Zeta Prime message a total 'decision by committee' disaster. Most recent communications from Vantch Mission estimate they are only three years away and now passively receiving communications from Vantch indicating a religious movement is active based on Parallels doctrine. GF are there. The GEC is in turmoil. My investigations into Jenkins have uncovered significant evidence, but not quite enough yet to challenge him directly.*

After cleaning away traces of his intrusion, Justio walked back to the crew room. He'd received a QET earlier in the day, affirming some of the Vantch information, and also demanding he finalise the Earth activity. But the fact that Sharnia could pounce on Jenkins at any moment gave him cause for concern. His own links to Jenkins were so deep his past would soon be under immense scrutiny. *And if Aytch received a direct order to subdue him…*

Justio settled himself back in the crew room and considered his position on Earth. If he couldn't manage to kill Jack Bullage then he would engineer a full blown Despot-based conflict. There were probably 10 or so million Alphas on Earth, plenty to cause issues if the Earth governments were to discover how to identify Alphas (very difficult) and convert them (quite easy). Obviously, Justio would then have

to hack the Gadium logs to show that, with the best
intentions, the Gadium Mission had accidently let the
Emergence knowledge proliferate. The crux of the issue was
there could be no sign of aliens to the humans, as it would
unite them against the alien force – the power of the tribe.
But a Despot solution was still only the back-up plan.

It was a delicate balance. Keeping Louise Harding warm,
while also being ready to close her down, and also killing Jack
Bullage.

Justio was snapped out of his contemplation by Aytch
marching into the crew room looking troubled. He walked
over to his flight chair and started browsing data feeds. He
did not appear to be settling.

Justio broke the silence. 'What's up, Aytch?'

'I received *another* QET from Sharnia. She's pushing me
to investigate aspects of Emergence doctrine.' Aytch looked
around room nervously. 'The Parallels.'

Justio put a suitably shocked expression on his face.
Aytch would expect it. The Parallels were mostly forbidden
from even being discussed. *Sharnia must be feeling the pressure.*

Aytch nodded, and returned to his screens.

Justio considered his position. 'I know we shouldn't but
I'm happy to discuss it, if you'd think it would help you.'

'I'm not sure; the mission recorder…'

'Isn't networked into the QET. Just local storage, and
eminently hackable. I've been around, Aytch, I may have
some views that would help your understanding.'

'There's nothing of substance in the manual.'

'Let me start you off, after which it's mostly down to your
own thinking.' Justio reflected on his own experience of the
Parallels. *Might as well start with truth.* 'The received wisdom is
that a Parallels-based doctrine always leads to disaster. I
suspect someone as old as Sharnia will have come across
situations contrary to the received wisdom.'

'Her log file references Sarkol.'

'The case-study of Sarkol was removed from the manual a few hundred thousand years ago. They'd assimilated a Parallels-based philosophy, integrated with extreme stoic acceptance.'

'How did the Emergence go?'

'It went on without us... we arrived well after their successful Emergence. They'd already come up with equivalent interpretations to Parallels v SISR. Their scientists had chosen Parallels based on aesthetics.'

'Did they accept our stewardship?'

Justio smiled. 'Stoically.' *After a few months of orbital bombardment.* 'Our actual technology was far in advance of theirs.'

Aytch stood up and started to pace. 'What about within our own culture?'

The silence stretched as Justio put on a show of thinking, but inside he was churning. 'Some have been known to choose Parallels as a comforter.'

Stopping in front of Justio's chair, Aytch looked intently. 'But what about the truth? You've mentioned a few times that people choose to believe.'

Justio snorted and stood up, forcing Aytch, from the standpoint of politeness, to step backwards. 'The truth is unfortunately not experimentally provable. Incomplete. Unknowable.' He walked towards the door. 'No, Aytch, what we freely choose to believe is all we have.'

Aytch did not follow Justio, but returned to his chair. 'There was a postulation that the Parallels interpretation was better at explaining Triple Alpha suppression of transitions.'

This was safer ground. Justio stopped and turned. 'I haven't heard of that one.'

Aytch's face brightened. 'Well, it stated that for a specific Triple Alpha... discounting a third-person supreme being...

basically SISR demands some type of subconscious awareness and the active suppression of the states of all other individuals. Whereas the Parallels just requires subconscious awareness of the states of all other individuals with an accompanying future-path selection.'

Justio made a show of internalising this. 'That hangs together logically, but the end game is the same. A choice of belief is made.' He paused. 'But let's back up. I suspect Sharnia is not interested in choice or belief, and actually she just wants to understand operationally how a Parallels-based doctrine can be controlled.'

Aytch appeared to twitch, but Justio could not be sure. *What else does he know? His family line has a history with the Parallels. But has he been told?*

Sitting back down, Aytch brought up the screens they'd been using to plan the Jack extraction. 'Well, we'd better get to the Jack question.'

Jack Bullage? Justio had been struggling to set up a surreptitious kill of Jack Bullage. Could it go a different way? Ultimately, to protect Aytch from an audit, Justio was going to erase this morning's conversations from the logs anyway, so he may as well be brazen. 'Given the GEC tensions, and your own ambitions. I think we should reconsider pushing for a Full Emergence.'

Aytch looked up, directly into Justio's eyes. 'I can't deny that I've been thinking about it. My heart says yes, but my head says no.' He paused. 'We do the right thing, each time, and in the long term we're stronger... so my formal answer is no. We progress with Emergence suppression.'

'Agreed.' Justio nodded and left the room. *Decision made... again.*

CHAPTER 39

For Gadium citizens, there were places where you knew for
certain your conversations were being monitored (e.g.
government buildings and mission ships). There were also
places on Gadium where you suspected your conversations
would be monitored; this set of places included everywhere
other than the places where you knew for certain it was
happening. However, within the highest echelons of
government, there was a tacit understanding that there must
be a few places which were explicitly not monitored.

And against this backdrop of realpolitik, Commander
Jenkins waited patiently for the Deputy Chairman. The
restaurant was designated quiet. All of the rooms were
shielded against electromagnetic radiation and there were no
electronic machines either used in the restaurant or allowed
inside it. It was a haven of privacy, albeit you had to trust
your immediate dining companions. Theoretically, the
restaurant was not shielded from QET, but the apparatus
was so large it couldn't be concealed. *Of course, if a small QET
machine were available, who'd know?*

Jenkins looked around the restaurant; he wasn't exactly a
regular there, but the staff knew he was a dining companion
of the Deputy Chairman, so service was attentive, and
obsequious. Jenkins growled quietly at the waiter who'd
come to refill his drink for the third time in as many minutes,
irrespective that it hadn't been touched.

He wasn't nervous, Jenkins had been dealing with the
Deputy for many years. He was well able to defend himself.

But... there was always a risk with the Deputy. *It should be fine. Except Katrina.* The Deputy knew he had leverage there. It didn't seem to matter to the Deputy that Jenkins truly believed in the mission; if he slipped, he would fall... be pushed.

The Deputy was late. Jenkins re-read the menu for a fourth time and looked around the room again. There was no-one here he recognised. Then the entourage appeared; three executive assistants led the Deputy over to the private alcove. Once he was seated, they quietly disappeared leaving Jenkins and the Deputy alone.

The waiter brought some nutrient tubes, which they inhaled. Jenkins opened the conversation. 'That's the nutrients covered, now we get to enjoy the tastes.'

The waiter took their orders. 'Sirs, today our special tasting menu is thirty tiny slices of animal heart-flesh. Mostly they're simply marinated in their own blood, but some are sweetened and some are spiced.'

The Deputy Chairman signalled for two specials.

Once the waiter had disappeared, Jenkins checked there was no-one in ear shot and then started the discussions. 'The incoming Vantch mission is still unaware of the GF team. Evidence has been planted on Vantch to suggest failed interventions with messages implying the late-arrival was faked.'

Time stretched for a few moments as the Deputy focussed. 'So it's time for our operative to hijack the ship and *go dark.*' He paused. 'Triggering a few selected people in the GEC to raise questions about animustosis and failed stewardship.'

Jenkins nodded; this was a standard tactic, and this time the mere implication of failure may be enough for the GF to gain legitimate political ascendancy. 'The misinformation is working as planned.'

Unblinking, the Deputy held Jenkins' gaze. 'We are at an inflection point; we can't afford for the deception to unfold when the next team arrives. We have many hundreds of years, but it must still look like a genuine failure under close forensic investigation.'

Jenkins nodded. This made sense. The likes of the Chairwoman and Commander Sharnia could not be underestimated. If they could hold on to power for a few hundred years more, they could check Vantch and Earth.

The Deputy had not broken eye contact. His green irises, and vertical black pupil slits bored through Jenkins' sense of calm. 'Additionally, order the ground-based team to up the tempo significantly. I need more atrocities on Vantch.'

'Is it necessary?'

'It's an order, Commander. The doctrines used on Vantch should allow for religious fervour to boil over. Relay it via your other cell members.' He paused. 'Yes, the Parallels-based revolt seems to work very well.' The Deputy rolled his eye dismissively. 'Greedy and needy.'

Jenkins remained silent. He knew of a few broken individuals who took great comfort from the Parallels interpretation.

The food arrived and the Deputy took five pieces of heart-flesh while Jenkins waited. He remained silent while the Deputy ate his first portion. The Deputy smiled appreciatively and then indicated to Jenkins to start eating. While Jenkins took some food, the Deputy spoke. 'We've decided the time is right, but is our operative on the incoming ship ready to act?'

Momentarily lost in savouring the delicious meat, Jenkins replied. 'Ready and willing. Total crew is three – our guy and two normal Gadiums, both unaware of any danger.'

The Deputy Chairman looked up sharply, frowned and spoke in a very harsh hiss. 'What did you say?'

Jenkins stopped chewing. *What did I say?* The room started to feel distinctly chilly as the Deputy Chairman became agitated.

'We are the *normal* Gadiums! This current majority is an abomination to nature; it has no respect for the family unit, no concept of love and a deep-rooted and insidious level of entitlement. The Gadium civilisation – and our Chairwoman worst of all – cannot be allowed to continue this façade of Galactic Keeper.'

Bowing his head, Jenkins mumbled an apology, the Deputy Chairman accepted it and the mood thawed again. 'But, as you say, it should be easy for our team on Vantch. So, what of the Earth mission?'

'We're in good shape.' Jenkins put his drink down. 'At this moment he's trying to trigger an Emergence and then surreptitiously mismanage it, but the fall-back is to trigger a Despot-based war. If he's uncovered, he's ready to overrun the other crew member and go dark.'

There was a standard set of prioritised options. Although not documented, it was clear to all GF operatives.

'Are you sure about his capability?'

Jenkins took his time before answering; he wanted to ensure the Deputy knew he was taking the question seriously, and not simply rushing out an automated affirmation. 'He'll try to find the path of least violence towards his crew mate, but he's committed. If it comes down to the wire, he has what it takes to make the kill.'

The Deputy bared his teeth. 'Do you know how many kills I've made in the name of righteousness? We have to make sure Earth is an unmitigated disaster for Gadium.'

Jenkins nodded solemnly. 'I completely understand, sir… and we do have truth on our side. We're all ready to make sacrifices. It's just that killing our own does not sit well.'

'Killing Aytch will cause repercussions, he's one of Sharnia's.' The Deputy paused. 'She's suspicious of you with regard to Vantch. Not helped by the timing with the Earth mission, given your long time connection with Justio, and her protective instincts of Aytch.'

Sharnia. 'She broke one of our cells some years ago and got a few names. Nothing directly led to me, but in conjunction with the other factors it now seems compelling... to her. Perhaps we should deal with her.'

The Deputy waved a hand dismissively. 'She's tenacious and has admirable instincts, but she's a blunt tool and I prefer to keep her around.' He leant forward. 'Better the psychotic killer you know, and can steer.'

Jenkins didn't really want to ask, but his military background had bred a straightforward nature. 'But are you steering her towards me?'

The Deputy appeared mildly amused. 'I am not trying to dissuade her, you are guilty after all. She trusts me well and I cannot risk two exposures. But do not worry, I will not let her have you.'

There was nothing to say, save challenging the Deputy's ability to make good on his commitment. Jenkins returned his attention to his food.

After a short while the Deputy looked up. 'All we need is those two big successes, Vantch and Earth. The GEC is fractured, there is discord – our time is near.' He paused. 'But it's not all straightforward. The GF Executive also has an issue to deal with. We need to address the propaganda saying that GF doesn't want to help other civilisations in order to keep Gadium's galactic dominance.'

Jenkins was lost for a moment in his food. 'I am not surprised; there are some who quite enjoy the status of ruling the galaxy. As more civilisations emerge, we will have more competition. It's inevitable.'

The Deputy stood up abruptly, knocking over his chair, which clattered off the back wall of the alcove. He leant over the table and strained in a harsh whisper, with spittle emanating for every well-enunciated word. 'Never. Never. Never. We do not kill people, pervert justice and destroy planets for power. The current prevalent Gadium behaviours are an abomination to nature, the longevity, the break-up of the family unit and the degradation of natural selection. Without our interventions most of the species would not have emerged successfully. Our meddling has given power to these species long before they have any concept of how to account for it. Our desire to shepherd in other planets is wrong. It must be stopped and never in the name of some galactic overlord role.'

The Deputy swept out of the restaurant and Jenkins was alone.

Back at his desk a few hours later, Jenkins played the next video diary from Katrina. He should have left it for at least 6 more months but … He was under orders to escalate the Vantch team activity, and Earth was about to intensify. It was a lot for his soul to bear. He needed the strength.

He opened the file and Katrina's blue eyes filled the screen, slowly the camera panned back to show her scaly face sporting a very new and significant scar.

'Video Log 4 – Katrina to Daddy. Notice anything new?'

Jenkins' eyes went wide, and he leant in towards the screen. The scar came very close to Katrina's left eye. The video log continued.

'I've only spent 20 more days awake in the last year, so I'm well on target. But as you may see, it's been eventful. All is well now… I'd hardly leave you a message with a cliff-hanger.' She laughed a little ruefully and continued. 'So I made a joke, *her ladyship* Commander Kuper didn't like one bit. We were sitting in the crew room, just observing some of the Trogia activity and she said – Commander Kuper –' Katrina paused. 'She said the Trogians were at least three hundred generations away from having the controls released. And I said it may just start happening. And then she said she was ready to convert an Alpha to a Triple Alpha and then put it back to ensure Alpha rates were held down for a few *thousand* more years. And I asked why, and she told me to shut up and not to question her.' On camera, Katrina looked left and right; then she leant in to the lens so her face filled and overflowed the screen. 'Then I said …'

Jenkins shook his head, he knew Commander Kuper; she was not someone to toy with. He returned his attention to the video.

Katrina continued. 'Then I said *I hope another Trogia gets better treatment from Gadium out in one of the Parallels.*'

Jenkins paused the video and swore under his breath; any reference to the Parallels was considered borderline heretical. The SISR – Single Instance State Reduction – was the ultimate doctrine. *Stupid girl, she's lucky to keep her eyes.* Jenkins restarted.

'Anyway, I got twelve months' stasis and the scar was specially treated so it wouldn't heal. And I got a massive beating… which was allowed to heal. When I was revived the Commander had already executed her actions.' Katrina paused. 'Over a period of nine months, Commander Kuper had kidnapped around 300 Trogians and held them in a secure facility. She was working on the assumption that even in a stuck Partial Emergence there would be a few Alphas in a group of 300. She put each of the Trogians through the standard Alpha to Triple Alpha operant conditioning. The

Betas were unaffected, but there were a few Alphas in the group. Kuper managed to create two new Triples. In fairness to Kuper, the Betas were released without much clue about what happened. They never saw any Gadiums.'

Katrina looked off-camera for a few seconds, she looked pensive and her trademark smile slipped into a frown. 'But it was a different deal for the Triples. They're being held at the secure facility. They've been lobotomised and are held in semi-comatose conditions. Their subconscious will keep regenerating their cells, and they'll live for 50 generations. Just brains in jars.'

Katrina started to cry. Her voice got harsher. 'She said she'll take a few more hundred next year to make sure. She said she regretted letting the Betas go – too much risk of discovery – and she wouldn't make that mistake again.' Katrina took a few moments to pull herself together, wiping her tears away. 'I'm sorry Daddy, I'll try harder, I'll do my best – I promise. I won't make any more trouble. I'm just praying to avoid soul death.'

Jenkins paused the screen. His own tears were now washing down the front of his highly medalled military uniform. He checked the message logs – the video was nine years old. She had recorded it only days before the transport ship had returned the video logs to Gadium. Jenkins checked the last few QET messages from Katrina. She'd been in stasis for much of the last nine years. *I could send the order for her to return… but I don't want to shame her.*

Jenkins penned a QET message. 'Katrina. Trust your instincts. I am very proud of you.'

It wasn't just the active kills that bothered Jenkins. With Gadium artificially restricting Emergence on Trogia, there were billions of Trogians who would live pitifully short lives; 50, 60, or 70 years, whereas, had Trogia successfully navigated a Full Emergence those same people would be living for thousands.

Then he sent the orders for Vantch, with a second set to the back-up cell.

CHAPTER 40

Jack Bullage's trauma counsellor had suggested he get back in a car as soon as possible so, after a quiet but tense week of recuperation at home, he took to the streets. He drove randomly around West London for most of Thursday morning.

As lunchtime approached, the roads got busier and the road users less friendly. The gradual build-up of passive aggression began to take a toll on Jack's sense of peace. He could feel the tell-tale signs of a panic attack creeping up. He was very aware of his breathing, almost to the point where it was a conscious decision, rather than reflexive. He was gripping the steering wheel too tightly. His hands were sweating. *I need to get home now.*

Jack got his bearings and took the next turning to head homewards. *I just need to get over the M4 and I'll be home.* The traffic was heavy and the going was slow. Jack revved his car in frustration but it was bumper to bumper. Ahead, Jack could see the railway crossing looming. *Please, no train!*

He edged forward, closing in on the railway crossing. But the car in front was dawdling. Jack could see the driver fiddling with the car stereo, making no effort to keep up with the car in front. Suddenly the level crossing lights began to flash and the barrier lowered. Jack's car was the last one not to make it across. *Shit!* He waited, the barrier obstructing his way. Several minutes passed, and there was still no train. From his position, his view up the tracks was blocked by houses, but he couldn't see any hint of a train. He waited. His breathing began to speed up. His heart was beating more quickly. *I can't breathe.*

Jack loosened the first two buttons on his shirt and wound the window down, concentrating on his breathing. *I have to get home.* There was a group of about five pedestrians waiting for the barrier to raise. One pedestrian looked into Jack's car. 'Are you all right love? You're looking very pale.'

Jack forced out a smile. 'Just in a hurry to get home.' A baby in a stroller started to cry. He tried to block out the noise. An argument broke out between two school kids. Their mother tried to intervene. The shouting increased. The baby cried louder. Still no train. *I have to get away.*

Jack looked at the signal posts next to the barriers. The red light was flashing. He craned his neck forward. Still no train yet. He tried to listen for it but the baby's cries and fighting kids made it impossible for him to hear anything. He was finding it difficult to breathe. *I have to get away from here.*

There was a shout from the pavement. 'Fuck you!' Jack turned sharply towards the shout. A man had come out of a shop straight into the crowd of pedestrians. He'd barged into the crowd, knocking the baby-buggy. There was pushing. Jack eyed it nervously. *Could they get angry with me?* His pulse was racing. There was a whoosh inside his head as blood rushed to his brain. His hair seemed to stand on end. Adrenaline coursed through his system. His hands started to shake on the steering wheel – he gripped harder.

Jack observed the scuffle, trying not to appear interested. Turning away, he looked around the car. A flashback – a cracked windscreen – another – Sarah's sleeping face. *I have to get away from here.* Another loud scream came from the pavement, a baby's scream. He turned reflexively. *Shut up!* Jack looked at the baby, now in its mother's arms. The baby looked directly back at him – screaming. *Shut up!* Jack turned back to look at the barrier; it was still down. He turned back

240

to the baby and their eyes locked. *Shut up!* The baby's head jolted slightly and the screaming stopped. A few seconds passed. Jack fought to get his breathing and mind under control. He turned back to the barrier. The baby's piercing shriek cut through all the other sounds again, a cry of rage. Jack felt himself losing his battle over his breathing. He suppressed a retch, but a small amount of vomit and bile refluxed up into his mouth. *Oh, God!*

Out of the corner of his eye Jack saw the signal flashing and the barriers in front of him starting to rise. He moved the car forward, half hearing one of the pedestrians say, 'But the train hasn't come yet.'

The barrier on the opposite side of the rail track was also raised and Jack accelerated. He heard a shout from behind him and half turned, in doing so he got a glance down the railway track – there was a train coming. It was close. He could see the fear in the train driver's eye. His stomach wrenched with fear. It was all he could do to keep his hands on the steering wheel. He wanted to throw his arms across his face and let oblivion take him.

But self-preservation won over, he gripped the wheel and, yet again, time seemed to slow as he pushed his foot full down on the accelerator. The car leapt forward. He crossed into the middle of the tracks. The train was bearing down, was too close. And then… and then he was over the other side of the rail track. His car shook violently as the train passed noisily behind him. *Holy shit!*

Jack did not stop the car, but drove straight on, hardly daring to think about anything except getting home – and remembering to breathe. *In, hold, out, wait.*

Twenty minutes later Jack lay on his back in his bedroom, with the curtains shut and the lights turned off. He remembered back to only a few years ago when he'd been at the Grand National. He'd scoffed at the fact that thoroughbred horses appeared to be happier when wearing their blinkers. He understood it now; the darkness was comforting, kindly, warm… safe.

He used calming exercises and controlled breathing to bring his fear under control. Two hours later he still lay there – breathing – counting – breathing – counting – not thinking – not thinking of anything – breathing – counting – breathing.

By late evening Jack felt calm enough to venture into the kitchen and make some toast and a cup of tea. He looked out of his kitchen window on to his silent garden with a wry smile alternating between a mindless grimace and caring self-admonishment. *Rule 1 – Never leave the house.*

Even later, Jack lay awake on his bed. *Did I do something to that baby? I felt a connection.*

Justio sat in his cabin smiling ruefully to himself. He'd been waiting for a few days for Jack to get back in his car so he could engineer a crash. In the end, Jack had almost killed himself unassisted. As it was, with Aytch watching the whole event sitting next to him, Justio had had to sit back and watch; still, he had plenty of time.

CHAPTER 41

Just as Jack was driving home from his railway incident, James Chambers drove sedately down a quiet country road in Surrey. The fact that the handwritten reports he had received from the MOD archivist were so obtuse, and incomplete, smacked of intrigue. The fact that Project Hedgehog was rated Ultra Black smacked of intrigue. This hadn't been enough to spur him into action, however. No, it was the paradox of the FibonacciEddie username that had got him intrigued. *Such unparalleled technical access.*

There was an indication of some additional primary source material held in deep storage somewhere. Unfortunately, it would require senior budget approval to initiate a search of those places, and James felt an acute need to keep out of sight of the budgetary bean counters. *Well, my job title is Head of G60, and this is a G60 programme; so I'm going to investigate.*

Driving carefully, James wound the car through postcard villages with cricket greens and parish churches. What could Project Hedgehog have really been about? *I need to control the information – protect my patch.* James grinned. *Protect my 30-hour week and two-hour lunch breaks!*

James had tracked down Dougy Raddlestone, Molly Saunders' deputy from the 1960s, to a retirement home near West Byfleet in Surrey. He was ushered into Dougy's small sitting room. The room was lined with books and family photos. 'Mr Raddlestone, thank you for making time for me.

I'm not here officially, but I'm James Chambers, the head of G60.' James showed his security pass.

Dougy was dressed casually in cords and a heavy jumper. He looked at James with a smile. 'Please call me Dougy. Are you not here *officially*?... Or... Are you *officially* not here?' There seemed to be a twinkle in Dougy's eye as he spoke.

'Ah, well... a bit of both really. I would prefer you didn't go out of your way to tell anyone of this visit, but I'm definitely not asking you to lie on my behalf.'

'It's nice of you to consider my conscience.'

Settling into an armchair, James set out his stall. 'Firstly, thank you for agreeing to see me, and secondly... what I'm about to ask you may be a little unusual.' Dougy nodded and waited for James to continue. 'Recently, there's been some... some internal interest in a project from the 1960s. Project Hedgehog.'

Dougy opened eyes wide for a few seconds and then he grinned, stretched his arms, scratched his leg, still waiting. James waited too. Dougy broke the silence. 'After you, James.'

It only took James a few minutes to summarise the little he did know: the government agencies were triggered to react to anyone investigating it, there was almost no written information, it seemed to have something to do with telekinesis, or telepathy, and it had fallen foul of some type of Cold War action. James looked around the room before returning his gaze to Dougy. 'And so, here I am. I don't know much at all.'

'It certainly seems like bugger-all squared to me.' Dougy paused. 'Well, on the assumption you have internal clearance for this, albeit I don't really give a damn if you don't, since you are the Head of G60... There are a few things I remember about Project Hedgehog. I have to confess I have thought about it quite a lot in the past twenty years. Every time an aeroplane goes over this place late at night.'

'So you can help?'

'Perhaps I can share some information. Whether it helps or not … Well you can be the judge. I was in G60 during the time, but there was still such severe security I knew very little. However, a rumour emerged from the labs; a few people I greatly respected believed it.' Dougy waited for a few moments, took a sip from his tea cup and then continued. 'Are you ready, James?' James nodded, took out a pencil, took out his notebook and opened it. Dougy leant forward, closed James' notebook, and gently shook his head. 'Well, the research experiment was trying to develop super-soldiers with extraordinary mind powers… and it got closed down due to alien sabotage.'

James tried hard to stop himself from gasping, but didn't succeed. 'Aliens?'

'Let me continue… there was no explicit proof. But there were a few very competent scientists I knew well who genuinely believed it. The stories were quashed and the experiments were closed down. There were a few significant disappearances. Blamed on Russia, but I'm not so sure.'

There was a long pause as James collected his thoughts. 'Why did you think aliens were involved?'

'There was a test participant who showed special mental abilities. He disappeared. There were persistent rumours of abduction. The MOD pushed the story that it was a Cold War tit-for-tat, but internally there were groups of scientists and military who believed he had been taken by little green men. Some of them disappeared too. The rumours dried up.'

'Well, any alien species with technology to travel across the galaxy would probably have no problem stealing a few humans.'

Dougy shrugged and so James continued to talk. 'Dougy, when you say special mental abilities, I saw a paper on Hedgehog which made little sense. It said something along the lines of… Subject G has shown success in the tests with a drug-induced trance and strong FT. Can you shed any light?'

'I don't know what the actual tests were sorry. But they were definitely focused on making an individual influence an event simply by thinking about it.'

'But what about FT?'

Dougy arched an eyebrow. 'FT… well I don't remember seeing the note you're talking about, but they used two stimuli, drugs and fear; perhaps FT relates to one of these.'

'F for fear, maybe, or something along those lines, maybe being scared focuses the mind. Although we're just guessing really.'

'No. We're not guessing... Sorry, I didn't realise you didn't know.' Dougy looked hard at James. 'Perhaps I misspoke earlier. The key trigger was not fear, it was *terror*, and not *terrified of spiders*. Genuine terror, when the blood drains from your face and your stomach knots, and your bowels evacuate… or churn at the very least.'

James remained silent, enrapt.

Dougy looked at James and chuckled. 'You thought it was all about smoking pot and meditation in the 60s, didn't you? We did have tests trying to unlock the power of the mind solely through the use of drugs but, depending on the drug used, the test participant either went to sleep, attacked the door or started rutting with the furniture.'

'And you say some of the experiments were successful?'

'I heard there were successes, particularly regarding the guy who went missing. As I said, the disappearances weren't limited to one guy. I can't remember exactly who else.' Dougy tapped the side of his head. 'The theme is fresh but some of the details have evaporated, most of us knew to keep quiet.'

'Dougy, do you know the name of the key guy who disappeared?'

'At the time there were no real names used, just codes. But in this case there was quite a public splash by the wife in subsequent years and so I put two and two together. Her name was Mary Jones. The man was her husband Bill Jones. Her son, Tom, had disappeared as well.'

James sat back. 'Thanks, Dougy, this is really useful. Do you have anything more?'

'I don't think so, but if you ask a few more questions you may jog something out of me that I don't currently know is in there.'

'Well... why was the name Hedgehog? Was it just a prickly subject?'

Dougy chuckled. 'Well, not all the people involved in G60 or Hedgehog were as charming and friendly as me. There was a senior MOD guy who was given the job to kick off the project. He told one of the secretaries in the typing pool to write it up as Project Erinyes. Well this jumped-up shit of a general had pinched one too many bottoms and the secretary *misheard* and called it Project Erinaceus.'

James looked bemused.

'It was funny to us anyway. But then again, we were all ex-Oxbridge classicists. It's where G60 recruited from in those days. No longer, I take it?'

'Sorry, no, I read information system management at Brunel.'

'Shame... Erinaceus is the Latin for hedgehog. Erinyes was one of the furies.'

James smiled in what he took to be a polite manner, but he felt it was coming across as all teeth so he stopped.

The silence stretched and James stood. 'I really appreciate you making time for me Dougy. I will let you get back to your crossword.'

'Well it's been very nice to meet you, James.' Dougy got up a little unsteadily and walked James as far as his door. 'Good luck.'

'Thank you, Dougy. I'll let you know how things develop.'

Dougy winked. 'If you're around to tell the story.'

After saying goodbye, James walked out to his car and called Bob. 'I can't speak, but we need to meet now.' They agreed to meet at the university campus later in the afternoon.

A little later on Justio frowned as he read the transcript of James Chambers' meeting; any strengthening of alien rumours was unhelpful. But given that it was still limited, and uncorroborated, there was no need to get worked up. After all, there were thousands of humans who were already convinced they'd been seen, spoken to or probed. The big issue would be if humans found alien artefacts, or if Jack was to give credibility to the notion while also displaying Triple Alpha powers.

However, Gadium dogma was absolutely clear, any pre-Emergence civilisation cannot know about aliens before a Full Emergence. Events on Trogia had underlined how widespread knowledge of aliens before the Emergence had led to disaster.

Justio reflected on how this could change his own approach. The GF view was that, as Gadium individuals shouldn't be away from the Gadium home planet, it really didn't matter what anyone else thought. But for his mission, at this moment, he needed to keep alien existence a secret. Given that he was currently trying to make the process look like a failed Emergence, he would need to follow the formal Gadium approach.

In any case, without a common alien foe, they'll fight each other more willingly.

CHAPTER 42

Early on Thursday at the Harding house, Mike arrived to find the place a mess. There was a sea of dirty plates in the kitchen and papers scattered all over the sitting room. Louise was in the kitchen hacking away at her laptop, while Jeff lay on the sofa with a tea towel across his face.

'Hey, Boss, where should I set up my laptop?' Mike wandered over to Jeff, and gave him a nudge. 'I said, where should I set up the laptop?'

Jeff pulled the tea towel off his face and sat up. 'Boss? I assumed you were speaking to Louise.'

Louise called through from the kitchen. 'When you two clowns have stopped the double act – which incidentally I totally saw coming – I've made tea.' Jeff and Mike filed through and sat down at the kitchen table. Louise continued. 'If you think I look ropey it's because I haven't slept. If you think Jeff looks great it's because he's had ten hours of peaceful slumber.' Louise gave Jeff a withering look. 'So, Mike, did you look at the data?'

Mike nodded. 'Before I talk about the data, Willis came back to the garage last night and we stayed up half the night, consciously trying to make the coins come down heads or tails... We were successful too...'

Louise gasped. 'No!'

'We tossed over a thousand coins and... all of them came down heads or tails.'

Louise rolled her eyes. 'Idiot... so you got nothing.'

'I analysed the data and found no unusual patterns at all, sorry. What about you, Jeff?'

Louise interrupted. 'The only interesting patterns Jeff saw were on the inside of his eyelids. As for me... well, my night, surfing the web, was useless. Nothing new on FibonacciEddie or Hedgehog.'

It was Jeff's turn to interrupt. 'She did stay up all night, though. Superstition.'

Louise looked a little sheepish. 'I'm not proud of this but I take the view if I sacrifice my personal comfort then the god of reporters may take pity on me and give me some more clues. I found nothing.'

Chuckling, Mike took a sip of his tea. 'Well, as long as we're all being thoroughly rational and scientific, I can't see how we're going to fail.'

Louise stood up and started pacing around the kitchen. 'But with no hint of encouragement from the data analysis, do you think we should give up?' Her gaze swept from Mike to Jeff. 'Well?'

Silence.

Louise continued to pace. 'None of us is compromised yet. But if this got out...'

Jeff shrugged. 'It's looking a little futile, unless you want to try with other survivors – widen the testing pool. You know Ashley and Willis are just one-off survivors.'

'So who do you suggest?'

'Bullage? He survived the court case, the brick and the M40.'

Louise shook her head. 'He'd never come, he hates me and, anyway, I'd never ask him for help.'

Jeff chuckled. 'Normally I'd say you were overacting, but in this case...'

The phone call from James Chambers had annoyed Bob more than intrigued him. James' unwillingness to share any information about Hedgehog went against the principles of the scientific community. Then there was the added realisation that James was clearly not a mover and shaker within the MOD.

So Bob found himself waiting with ill-concealed impatience as James Chambers walked into the university reception.

James smiled as he approached and held out his hand. 'Can we go somewhere private, please?'

Bob shook James' hand quickly and turned, leaving James to follow. As they moved down the corridors towards his office, Bob asked, 'How private do you mean?'

James mumbled. 'Very private, secure from electronic prying.'

NLUST being a scientific university, there were a few different options. Bob led James into one of the high-energy experimental laboratories. Once inside, he shut the door. 'These laboratories are used for energy particle experiments. They're shielded, Full Spectrum Faraday's Cage, many layers of copper and steel, and electrified when required.' Bob turned the switch to activate the shielding. Then he took out his phone, showing James the display that indicated zero coverage.

James looked at Bob's phone. 'Just like being in the countryside.'

'So we're secure. What's new?'

Bob listened to a summary of the information James had got from Dougy Raddlestone. *Extreme fear? Aliens?* 'It sounds implausible. Are you sure that Dougy wasn't just getting on a bit?'

'Possibly, but I looked the guy in the eyes, he seemed straight up.' James paused.

So do we have proof of the alien angle?'

James shrugged. 'There's been a whole lot of uncorroborated alien information over the last fifty years: the 1947 Roswell, the 1977 WOW signal, and many others. I find it believable… But I have to admit I want to believe it, so I may not be the most objective of observers.'

Bob remained quiet. *I want to believe it as well, but…*

James continued to talk. 'We have to carry on investigating Louise Harding.'

As the amazement subsided, Bob found his frustration returning. 'I'm not sure, really, James. I investigated the leak for you, national security. Fine. But you haven't exactly been on the level with me. You clearly knew much more about Hedgehog than you let on.'

'I was bound by my perceptions of national security as well. I apologise. I will be more open from now on.'

It would be the scientific discovery of the century. Bob leant in. 'So what now?'

'We act as if Dougy is correct; that we are under alien observation. Then we try to get evidence, assuming that if they had wanted to talk, they would have.'

Bob nodded. 'And the disappearances?' *Not so good.*

'We have to assume they were real as well. We can't pick and choose.' James continued. 'Step one is to assume all conversations are compromised and all emails are intercepted and decoded. We also assume any communication we get, voice call, email, or letter, could be a fake.'

Bob grimaced. 'That makes life difficult… What about step two?'

'Step two is to escalate internally within the civil service…
but with such little evidence I'm holding off just now. And
before you go all *Battlestar* on me, we assume there is no
prevalence of doppelgangers on Earth, face-to-face is *bona
fide*.'

Bob had no idea what *Battlestar* meant but let it go. 'Step
three? Surely something about the tests?'

'I'm not sure. However, if Louise Harding is close to the
right track then we can benefit from what she finds without
initially implicating the government too much. It would be
good to get everything she discovers, just to keep us on the
front foot.'

What about personal security? 'And back to the
disappearances Dougy mentioned? You know, thinking back
Mike may have intimated something when I spoke to him.'

James found a chair and sat down. 'I got a few names, Bill
and Tom Jones were two of them. I haven't got anything
more from G60 records on Project Hedgehog. Dougy gave
me some more ideas where I could get some data. I have
requisitioned the full set of Molly Saunders' diaries in the
name of national security.'

'So our best bet is to stick with Louise? Tell her about
extreme fear and aliens?'

James paused for a moment. 'Yep, provide them with the
support.'

'And what about the concept of alien surveillance? Do we
take precautions or not?'

'I don't know. I think the answer is we take precautions
like this. Try to make things a little harder where we can.'

Bob escorted James out of the building and then waited at the entrance until James had left the car park. Then he turned back towards his office.

I don't believe him.

But the entrance hall was lined with posters, paintings and photos. Not only of NLUST alumni, albeit there was a picture of Mike (much to Bob's annoyance), but also from history. A history that had not always been kind to new ways of thinking.

Surely I don't believe him?

As he walked, Bob also passed a display from the Royal Society and the 17th century birth of experimental rigour. And, finally, one from the Hubble telescope; 100 billion galaxies, each with 100 billion stars.

They can't all be dead.

Involuntarily Bob sped up as he walked back to his office. *Scientific discovery of the century!*

CHAPTER 43

As James had left the electromagnetic shielded room, the mini-bots on his clothes had locked on to the university Wi-Fi and transmitted. It had only been a matter of minutes before Aytch had the full transcript.

Sitting in the crew room, watching the transcript unfold on the wall, Aytch had quickly realised it was not good news. Although the initial Harding tests had been a failure, G60, with critical new experiment information, was actively lining up to support Louise.

Aytch put a call through to Justio's cabin. 'Justio, would you mind meeting? I can come to you.'

The voice came back over the speaker. 'I'll be there in ten seconds.'

A few moments later, Justio walked into the crew room. He looked at the transcript. 'Okay, that's not so good.'

Not so good. It's a disaster. 'I knew we should have closed down G60.'

'We agreed to keep it active to corral the conspiracy theorists. There were always going to be risks. We've had fifty years of good behaviour.'

Aytch took a breath. 'This has to be reported real–time to the GEC. It's a potential material breach of anonymity.'

'What? No. They just happen to be right. But they have no evidence. Nothing.'

'I must insist.' Aytch could not stop his gaze flicking to the crew room ceiling. *No, this is not about scoring points.* 'We have to report.'

'And say what exactly?' Justio had been standing in the doorway. Now he walked into the room and sat down. 'They have no evidence. No Jack, no mini-bots, nothing. We should get Jack, then, in a few days, we'll send a message saying everything is under control.'

Maybe.

Justio continued to pile on the pressure. 'A message now will look like panic.'

Aytch started to pace around the room. 'You're genuinely ready for the Jack invites?'

'Of course, we discussed this already, standard misinformation, we'll send him emails and fake phone calls tomorrow to get him to a meeting point up near Newgate on Sunday. Then, in the darkness, we lure him into a secluded spot… and you grab him.'

'And if he doesn't agree to come?'

'We'll use limited police involvement. Have him arrested and taken somewhere secluded for special interrogation… and you grab him.'

'Sunday evening?'

'Agreed, just a few days.'

Aytch nodded, and felt his anxiety lessen. Justio did seem to know what he was doing. He had a very calm head; still, that was to be expected after so much experience.

Okay.

On Thursday afternoon, Louise marched into the university reception with Mike and Jeff trailing in her wake. Perhaps the god of reporters did exist after all; Mike had received a call from Bob Reaple asking to meet them in his office, 'a matter of gravest urgency.' Louise was unclear if Mike had been directly quoting Bob or not. She suspected not.

As they moved through the corridors, Jeff forced them to do a little detour to pick up coffee from the canteen. Then it was all business. Marching full-speed.

Louise was forced to slow down a few times to get directions from Mike, or Jeff, with regard to the location of Bob's office. But soon enough they were outside his door, and Louise walked straight in.

Bob jumped up from his desk in shock.

Without preamble, Louise took a seat. 'So, you're on our side now?'

Bob looked intently at Louise. 'Everything we say is probably being listened to by a third party.'

He does look serious. Louise nodded an acknowledgement, and then allowed herself to be led, by Bob, to a nearby laboratory.

They all waited while Bob shut the door, and activated a switch on a control panel nearby to the door. Then he took out a black box from his pocket and appeared to take a reading from it. After a few moments he turned to the group. 'Just scanning for unusual emissions of electromagnetic radiation. There are none.'

Mike tapped the wall. 'No EM at all, I hope, given the cost of the shielding we put in here.'

Bob shrugged. 'Thanks for coming. Firstly, the government knows almost nothing... Project Hedgehog did run in the 1960s. It was focused on investigating mind-powers. The material is all lost, destroyed, gone.'

Louise was unimpressed. 'We knew most of that.'

Bob nodded. 'Some people genuinely believe that there were successes. Additionally, some people genuinely believe there were mysterious disappearances.'

Louise frowned. 'Successes?'

'The few surviving records mention successful tests, but not what the tests were.' Bob paused. 'But the key is that intense, almost uncontrolled, fear is a mandatory condition.'

Jeff nodded. 'Our set-up is certainly a little weak there. And the disappearances?'

'From what I've been told, at least one participant, probably two, plus a few scientists who were too vocal. Bill Jones was mentioned – and taken.' Bob looked at Louise, their eyes locked and he spoke again. 'Taken.'

Louise gasped. *Taken?* Surely Mary was not right about the other bit. She felt the blood start to drain from her face. Her skin tingled. Christ, she could feel tears welling up. 'No… God, no!' Her knees went weak.

Jeff took a step forward, a look of amazement and fear on his face. 'Louise?'

But Bob was already there, leading her gently to a chair.

Louise put her hand over her mouth, trying to stop the squeaks that were embarrassing her, and also trying to slow her breathing down. *This is it, my way back: redemption, Harry's office…*

She looked over to Mike, who was white as a sheet. *He's made the connection.*

Bob turned to face them all. 'We have no proof. It may all lead back to the same mistaken source. But there are very strong rumours regarding the shutdown of Project Hedgehog in the 1960s.' He looked down at Louise. 'You believe it.'

Louise looked over, and Mike was whispering to Jeff, who, in turn, was looking less surprised than she felt he should be. She felt slightly foolish over the strength of her initial reaction so, taking a few moments, she gathered her thoughts. 'I spoke to Mary Jones, Bill's wife. She believed both her husband and son had been abducted by aliens. Do you believe it, Bob?'

'I'm not closed-minded. Certainly this new information makes the experiments worth progressing, if we can get the right conditions.'

Mike stepped forward. 'And fight off the inevitable wave of little green men.'

Standing back up, Louise felt normality return, as the adrenaline marginally loosened its control over her mind and body. 'Jeff?'

Jeff shrugged. 'I don't know, it seems a little implausible...'

Mike walked over and took Bob's scanner. 'I choose to believe it, and this won't help. They'll have suitably advanced technology to fool passive scanners like this.'

Louise turned to Bob. 'So do you want to be on the team?'

'If you'll have me?'

He'd given her a lifeline, but Louise was still Louise. 'And you know if you double-cross us I'll exact some terrible retribution.'

'I won't willingly put myself in opposition to your preferred path.'

Louise held Bob's gaze. 'You won't oppose me, willingly or unwillingly!'

Bob remained silent.

Louise came to her decision and held out her hand. 'Welcome aboard, then. I'm assuming Jeff's 2016 budget requests are going to sail through...'

Bob smiled. 'We'll see about that... but I'm not sure he's earned it yet.'

Jeff looked a little chagrined. 'So if aliens are involved – what's their angle? Should we be in fear of our own safety?'

Bob shrugged. 'Pragmatically, we should assume if the aliens wanted to harm us then we'd be dead. That said, we should try to keep future experiments secret.'

Walking over to a whiteboard, Mike sketched a few thoughts. He wrote the words *fear* and *aliens* on the board. 'Assuming we run more tests, we need to understand how much additional fear is needed and whether we are ready to compromise ourselves professionally to get those levels.'

Jeff picked up a whiteboard pen and wrote up the word *superpowers*. 'Maybe we need humans with super mental powers to protect us from the aliens.'

Louise shook her head. 'Assuming Bill Jones had these powers, and was taken, it didn't trigger a concerted alien attack.'

Bob interrupted. 'It may be they do want Project Hedgehog activity which produces people like Bill Jones, who they then farm. Then once they've got their man, they let the project dwindle until it's time to get another. Maybe they want us to find another Bill?'

Then everyone started to talk at once.

Louise tried to keep the conversation focused, as the three scientists drifted into conjecture and supposition.

Thirty minutes later, they'd agreed they had no idea what the aliens wanted. But, usefully, they'd also agreed to have a detailed experiment-planning session later in the day.

Louise wanted to double-check her contact records to see if she could get any other crash survivors to the new tests, scheduled for Saturday. Willis and Ashley had already made themselves available. They needed a few more. She and Jeff left the laboratory, while Mike and Bob remained.

Once Louise and Jeff had left, Mike turned to Bob. 'Do you believe?'

Bob threw up his hands. 'Almost. I certainly believe it's our scientific duty to investigate. What do you think the best course of action is?'

Mike grinned. 'Wishing for the best required outcome totally depends on where you draw the boundaries of the measurement. For example, the best for me personally would be if an alien walked in through the door and offered me the job of Earth Emperor with an alien army to enforce my rule.' Mike smiled. 'You see... I would make an excellent benevolent dictator.'

Bob laughed. 'But... I suppose in a few years there would be plenty of heads on spikes for people to look at.'

'Well if they had it coming... but you see the best outcome for your G60 friend would be for him to safely negotiate a peace treaty with the aliens. It would give G60 serious political clout within the UK Government.' Mike paused again. 'Whereas, the best thing for the UK Government may be for the aliens to disappear with no evidence of their arrival or their leaving; this would make their lives easier, they being the MPs and the Civil Service.'

Bob smiled again. 'Point taken... How many more are you going to do?'

'Two more! Firstly, the best thing for the whole world may be a treaty in which all disease and poverty were removed by advanced alien technology; however, it would put the western world at a substantial disadvantage.'

'And?'

Extracting a packet of chewing gum from his pocket, Mike offered one to Bob and then took one for himself. 'Cue the sinister music; the best thing for Planet Earth may be for all humans to be exterminated to stop the pollution, defoliation, hunting, and depletion of the ozone layer. And depending on exactly what the aliens want, it may be best for them as well... '

'But I suspect you still prefer option one, Emperor Mike?'

'All hail me!'

Mike picked up Bob's scanner again and fiddled with it. 'Who knows how they could be monitoring us?'

Having spent most of Thursday with the feeling he was being shadowed by Aytch, Justio managed to sneak off a couple of QET messages overnight and then clean down traces of them in the QET room. But he'd still had no time to progress his primary task, to kill Jack Bullage.

On Friday morning, however, once Aytch went back to his cabin for a meditation session, Justio returned to his cabin and used his communications tablet to review real-time feeds from Jack's house.

I mustn't procrastinate any more.

Justio watched as Jack went through his morning routine, before climbing into his car and driving to a nearby supermarket. Once Jack was rolling, Justio scanned the nearby motorway for a large lorry or coach coming into London. He quickly found an Italian coach and, remotely hacking into the Satnav of the coach, saw that they were bound from Windsor to Central London. The coach was modern, with all aspects of its driving supported by computer-controlled hydraulics.

Justio relayed new instructions to the coach and the driver dutifully followed the Satnav instructions, turning off the motorway and heading towards the supermarket Jack was inside. *Okay, so we've got the mechanism to scrub the crime scene.*

Justio waited for Jack to get back into his car and then accessed the highly encrypted self-destruct instruction to the *missing* mini-bot currently residing in Jack's inner ear, having negotiated its way up his nose and Eustachian tube. The explosion would kill him, and then the coach crash would mask the real cause of death.

Justio sent the self-destruct message and waited.

A few seconds passed.

Justio checked the other mini-bot signals in Jack's car. They were transmitting normally, the sounds and pictures were still real-time and indicated that Jack was now driving out of the supermarket car park.

Justio resent the self-destruct message.

Still nothing.

Justio pinged the mini-bot up Jack's nose. It reported itself to be online and functioning.

Justio swore. *His subconscious must have some limited awareness of the device.*

Justio covered his tracks, deleting the messaging logs and erasing records of the recent activity. He wasn't worried yet; he had plenty more options.

As the coach pulled into the supermarket, he considered overriding the coach controls and ramming Jack's car. But it would be futile. A crash like that would not do anywhere near the damage required to kill a Triple.

CHAPTER 44

On Friday lunchtime, Mike met Bob in the university café. They studiously avoided all talk of the experiment design.

As they walked from the café down to Bob's office, Mike noticed that Bob was walking a little slower, a little smaller. 'Out with it, Bob, what's on your mind?'

'Can't talk about it now.'

Fair enough. And Mike resumed watching the daily life of the university pass by as they made their way deeper into the campus.

Louise and Jeff were waiting outside Bob's office. He unlocked the door and they went in.

Mike took a quick look around. 'I like what you've done with the place.' The office appeared to have been *hardened* in the previous few hours. There were copper meshes over the windows, and a small amount of steel panelling on a few walls.

'Thanks, the university estate manager owed me a favour. I told him I was doing experiments that required additional shielding in my office. But, it's probably not enough.'

Mike smiled. 'I suspect he thinks you've flipped and you're trying to protect yourself from cosmic rays.'

Jeff wandered over and inspected the windows. 'They've got this mesh on the windows in the Particles Building.'

Louise coughed loudly, drawing their attention. 'So are we safe here or not?'

Bob shook his head. 'No. But I thought that to be extra safe we could leave all of our electronics here; in that way, if they have infiltrated our technology we get additional protection.'

There was quick agreement, and a few minutes later they were all back in the same laboratory they'd used the previous day; shielded.

Mike did a stage whisper to the others. 'Well, no-one was taken by little green men with laser guns in the night; that's a plus.'

Bob gave a disapproving stare. 'It's no laughing matter.'

'I've got to laugh about it. The alternative is crippling from a self-esteem perspective.'

'How so?'

'Well, assuming Earth has been under alien observation for at least the last fifty years, if we believe about Bill Jones, don't you feel a little insulted they haven't even bothered to contact us?'

Bob shook his head. 'Rubbish! There are lots of good reasons why they wouldn't have contacted us yet. Fifty years may be a very short time frame for them. They may be waiting for a particular trigger…'

'And?'

'Those are perfectly good reasons.'

'Gentlemen!' Louise had her arms folded and was tapping her feet. 'Save your wishy-washy philosophising for your own time. One question – can we run a test to generate sufficient fear?'

Bob shrugged. 'Honestly, I'm not convinced. Ashley and Willis know what we're doing and so there will be a massive requirement of willing suspension of disbelief.'

Mike chuckled. 'I'm not having anyone staring…'

'Michael!' Louise stared angrily. 'We must be able to do something.'

She really needs the story. Mike waved an apology. 'Sorry. I don't think we can spook Ashley or Willis sufficiently. They both know too much.'

Bob stepped forward. 'We would have to put them in actual mortal danger. It's beyond us. And we don't know enough about the drugs route.'

Louise started to pace around the laboratory

Picking up a pen Mike wrote on the whiteboard. *Brainstorm.*

A few minutes passed but no-one wrote anything else up.

Then Louise turned to the group. 'A lucky person, who we could frighten the living shit out of quite easily. I do know one.'

Silence.

'Jack Bullage.'

There was a groan from Jeff, and Mike scribbled a few bullet points on the white-board: special relationship, restraining order, harassment, attempted kidnap and attempted murder. Mike pointed at Louise. 'Most of them done by her ladyship, there.'

Bob looked concerned. 'Murder?'

Louise went over to the white-board and erased Mike's list. 'He got some thugs to throw a brick through our front window. I went to his house and threw it back through his front window.' She shook her head. 'According to a reporter from one of our competitor newspapers, it was an attempted murder and they wrote a piece about the brick narrowly missing his head. The courts saw things differently, but I did get charged with harassment.'

Mike took a moment to consider the angles. 'Actually, I like the idea. But it's a one-shot attempt because, once he realises Louise is involved, he's not going to participate willingly.'

Louise nodded. 'I thought a little about it. Clearly, he won't respond to me. However, if he gets an invite from the university, courtesy of Bob, to attend some sort of review of physical reactions…'

All eyes turned towards Bob.

Bob was silent for a few seconds, then he smiled. 'It probably is time to put some skin in the game.'

CHAPTER 45

Information chaos reigned when Aytch arrived to take over from Justio. Every wall in the crew room was covered in facts and figures. Raw feeds pumped out various Earth statistics, aggregated feeds showed cross-references between countless activities across Earth; it was a data mess.

Where's Justio?

Aytch sat down and looked around. Most surprisingly, over and above the sheer volume of open screens, was that there were over ten chapters from the Gadium intervention manual projected onto the floor by Justio's seat. He never looked up Gadium policy; he was the authority, ten thousand years of experience. True, Justio had a grudging respect for Professor Harkin, but the rest was often described by Justio as 'sludge'.

Interest piqued, Aytch walked across the room. Justio's communications tablet was sitting on the central bench, screen blank. He looked down at the projections closest to Justio's seat; it was a Gadium manual entry on the use of mini-bots for surveillance and intervention.

Chapter 35.2.A Destruction of Surveillance Overview

All surveillance machinery must be equipped with comprehensive auto-destruct capability. As mentioned, (Chapter 3.2 – Risks of Discovery), it is imperative that Gadium does not unwittingly give pre-Emergence civilisations access to ascendant technology. The destruction of mini-bots must be

controlled by dual Gadium officer authorisation
codes. In the event of incapacitation...

The text went on, but Aytch was clear on all of this, as
they'd recently pre-authorised many of the Earth mini-bots,
both as potential weapons, and to erase evidence of alien
technology.

Aytch opened a ship management screen, which gave
Justio's position. He was in the QET room.

He daren't close down the screens. He didn't know what
Justio was doing. But this level of information overload
obscured his ability to see anything.

Focus on the critical items.

Aytch opened a search filter: *Jack Bullage*. The feeds
showing his house opened – nothing unusual. Aytch sat
down, waiting for Justio to come and perform the handover.
He looked at the screen; Justio was still in the QET room.
What's taking him so long?

His comms tablet pinged. The search had found another
hit. A conversation transcript from Louise Harding. Not
unusual.

She hardly stops talking about him.

A corner of a screen was highlighted on the main wall.
The screen was obscured by another data feed, but, out of
curiosity, Aytch brought it up to the front. It was the full
transcript of the recent Harding discussions.

They are trying to test Jack Bullage!

His stomach churned. Frantically, Aytch jumped up, then
patched through to the ship-wide comms. 'Justio!'

Opening up the screens controlling the Gadium re-entry
vehicle, Aytch set the system for immediate departure. They
had to collect Jack tonight. *Six hours...*

'Justio!'

The ship overview screen showed Justio was heading
back to the crew room.

'What did I miss?' Justio arrived and, following Aytch's pointing, saw the offending items. 'Ah! Jack Bullage has been remembered by Louise Harding… Interesting.'

Aytch couldn't believe his ears. How was Justio being so calm? 'It's a disaster! We have to stop it.'

Justio remained silent.

Aytch paced around the room, unable to conceal his discomfort. 'I will send a message to GEC to formalise our approach.'

'Slow down, Aytch. Nothing has changed from our discussion yesterday. We secure Jack, then we inform the GEC. This is just normal operational activity. No need to over-react.'

Aytch paused for a moment. He didn't want to look overly dramatic in front of Sharnia. 'But, if they test Jack…'

'They'll probably find nothing.' Justio didn't look too sure. 'However, as long as we can stop the test without feeding rumours of aliens, then it would be best if Jack wasn't tested.'

'So what do we do?' Aytch was already regretting his outburst. The recording would not be favourable in the eventual audit. Maybe he could ask Justio to delete this one as well.

Justio sat down on his chair, taking deliberately care of his injured leg. 'We try to collect Jack tonight. Once we have Jack we report in.'

'I'd better get ready to go.' Aytch walked towards the door.

'You've still got half the day. We can't go until night-time. We'll re-run the Hampstead snatch option. You'll get to the heath by just after midnight. Once you're in position, I'll arrange for the police to arrest him from his house, and bring him to you.'

On Vantch, the threat of attack from the Prelate's troops was constant, but Klope, and 10 other Disciples he had escaped with, kept moving steadily northwards. They'd travelled through the heavily forested northern parts of the continent of Harfi to a seaport. From there, Klope had managed to secure passage on a ship for all of them across the straits to the southern tip of Lokis.

Arriving in the southern city of Fairport, Klope approached a dock worker. 'Good sir, peace and contentment in your world.'

The dock worker looked Klope up and down, spat into the dust and mumbled the reply. 'And in yours.'

The remaining Disciples, their green and white robes dirty and torn, bundled up behind Klope, listening into the conversation. Klope nodded to the dock worker to acknowledge the correct form of response. 'Do you have news of the Prophet's whereabouts?'

The dock worker looked at the Disciples and then around the harbour. Klope followed his gaze. There were no other people in the green and white robes. There were, however, plenty of soldiers, although none wearing the black uniform of the Prelate. The uniforms worn by the soldiers seemed to be a local militia. The dock worker spat again. 'We don't hear much about him nowadays, he's not too popular in these regions. Further north maybe?'

Klope was concerned. 'Further north maybe what… kind sir?'

'Further north you may find news of him… but not here. There are too many who blame him for the bombings.' The dock worker left, leaving Klope and his fellow Disciples to consider their position.

Klope shook his head. 'I thought the entire continent of Lokis was behind him. What changed?' The Disciples had no answer, and they moved off. They walked for a few hours through Fairport. The city seemed relatively unscathed physically, but the few open shops showed extremely inflated prices for foodstuffs.

As they walked on through the city, Klope's group were being watched by anyone who happened to be out. It didn't seem like an organised observation, just the green and white robes were acting as a beacon. Klope looked around, and here and there were local militia, also watching. At one point Klope thought he saw a flash of a green and white robe, but in an instant it was gone. Klope shook his head. *I'm seeing things.*

At a coaching station, they were turned away – no travel out of the city without a licence, a precaution to stop looting of nearby farms.

By lunchtime the Disciples were attracting the explicit attention of soldiers. There were now four soldiers trailing the group. Klope turned to the other Disciples. 'It may be that they're waiting for reinforcements, or maybe not, but I don't think we're welcome here.'

One Disciple, named Unzer, nodded. 'I am not welcome here. I fear for you all. I will be protected in my world but I cannot vouch for you also.'

Klope walked over to Unzer and gently squeezed his arm. 'Do not be alarmed, my brother, it is the same for all of us. And just because we are all players in each other's worlds it doesn't mean we do not feel empathy for their suffering. In my world, you will be saved. Come!' Klope turned and, moving at faster pace, they trotted due north towards what appeared to be a city gate a mile or so away.

Within five minutes there were eight guards following them, still 100 metres behind. Up ahead the gates were visible and open. There appeared to be a few guards but they did not seem to be paying much attention to the group of Disciples.

Klope closed his eyes and offered a short prayer to the keeper of the Parallels. *Please find me a safe path through the possibilities.*

The gate guards started to take notice of the Disciples. One of the gate guards unshouldered his rifle. Behind the Disciples the group following were similarly taking out hand guns and rifles. Klope's heart started to race.

Within 50 metres of the gate, one of the gate guards called out. 'Stop there. You're under arrest.'

Klope raised his hands in supplication. 'Good sir, we are just Disciples of the Prophet travelling north to be with him.'

The gate guard's face remained impassive. 'Kneel on the ground. We're taking you in.'

Klope looked around, the guards behind them had stopped 50 metres short of them; many weapons were being aimed. To the north, Klope thought he could see movement on the main road, a few miles outside the city, but he couldn't make out any details. He turned to the others. 'I think we trust in The Many to keep us safe in custody.' There were a few nods of agreement.

Unzer shook his head. 'I am sorry, brothers, for your fate in my world, but I cannot guarantee a safe route for you. I have learned something over the last years about riding the parallels. I have to go.' Suddenly he screamed and ran towards the gate, shouting. 'By The Many, I travel the paths to my safety.' He ran towards the gate, but between him and the gateway five heavily armed guards raised their weapons as one. Shots rang out, Unzer was shredded and his body slumped to the ground.

Klope shook his head, tears in his eyes. 'Perhaps in his world he survived, but I cannot see how it could be – and certainly not in mine.' *What did he mean, riding the parallels?*

The soldiers had their weapons all trained on the Disciples. One move, one reason, and they would be cut down too. Klope watched as one of the gate guards walked up to Unzer's body and tapped it with the toe of his boot, Unzer was finished.

The gate guard jerked his rifle at the Disciples. 'On your knees, now!'

The other Disciples all kneeled. Klope kneeled. He looked north, the dust on the highway travelling towards the city resolved into a few jeeps. They were coming fast. The gate guards began to take notice. A rifle was raised. Shots were fired. The shots were returned, but where lead slugs were being sent towards the approaching jeeps, the returned fire was fire, great bolts launching through the air. The Disciples scattered, and all the guards started to shoot, some at the jeeps but some at the Disciples.

Klope felt a pain radiating through his body, and then his world went black.

CHAPTER 46

On Friday afternoon, Mike drove himself, and a quietly humming Bob, to Jack Bullage's house. Mike looked anxiously for road signs announcing they were getting close to Chiswick. 'Stop humming and help me look for the house.'

'I can do both, you know. He's just round the back of Chiswick House; we could walk it in twenty minutes.'

Mike gave Bob a sidelong glance. 'Keep up the humming and you'll be testing your assertion.'

Bob smiled. He also stopped humming. 'I've arranged for the Pryson Lab this weekend. It's got the required EM shielding.'

'The Pryson, nice choice. The observation office makes me feel like I'm in a virus movie.'

'That's the one.' Bob paused. 'So, will Jeff come and help us set up tonight?'

Mike nodded. 'And I've got all the kit in the boot.'

'And I've got this.' Bob took out his portable scanner. 'Bugs beware.'

'Have you found anything unusual with it?'

'Nothing yet.' He swept the inside of the car. 'But the world is awash with radiation, and I don't know what I'm looking for.' He put it back in his jacket pocket. 'Inside the lab it may be useful.'

'Don't start pointing it at Jack today.' Mike paused. 'So let's go through the story again.'

'Just as we said, we're doing a government sponsored investigation into stress, trauma, mental cognitive function and physical reflexes.'

'And he bought it?'

'Well, we're invited over.'

'Have you had any more thoughts on the science?'

Bob shook his head. 'I don't think this is a case of hypothesise and then test. I think it's a case of test and then retrofit. But if Jack can influence a coin in a closed box, or similar, then we'll have to start with Schrodinger.'

Mike smiled to himself. 'Or Many-Worlds?'

'Maybe, but I worry about the near infinite energy requirement to fuel all those new universes.'

'We got a Big Bang in our universe, from nowhere.' Mike paused. 'And we find it pretty normal to divide by zero when required.' He raised an eyebrow, no reaction from Bob.

'We're tearing up the rule book.'

'Not entirely, if you were to combine Many-Worlds with some type of time smearing, there could be the concept of a sneak preview of the possible outcomes.'

'Time smearing? So no conservation of energy; no 2nd Law.'

'H bar, delta E, delta T… maybe?'

'Bollocks… Okay, so you have some free information; how do you influence the choice of which future you play out in?'

'No idea.' Mike looked straight ahead. 'So what's your great idea?'

'I don't have one.'

'But you hate my time-smeared-many-world.'

'To paraphrase an alumni of, and poster-boy for, NLUST, I *choose* not to believe it.'

'So guess something else.'

'Carrier waves, hidden variables, observer interaction, anything *but* MWI.'

'Why?'

Bob did not reply but started to hum.

The notes were wrong, and the tempo was wrong, but Mike was pretty sure it was *I vow to thee my country*.

Jack looked out of the window for the fifth time in as many minutes. They were not here yet. He pulled out the printed confirmation email and gave it another look. *Government investigation? Well it couldn't hurt.*

He'd returned from his daily drive at 2pm and spent the last hour tidying, tweaking, and wholesale rearranging his front room furniture. He looked at his mantelpiece again. *Should I take away the photo of Sarah?* He paused and then walked back into the kitchen, leaving the photo as it was.

There were a few unopened letters on the table. They looked like insurance claim correspondence – he couldn't face the stress right now. He went back into the front room and sat down on the sofa. He turned on the television; after a few minutes he flicked channels, and then again, and again; there was nothing of use on. He turned it off. His eyes drifted over to the mantelpiece, his prescription sedatives. *Maybe just one pill to help me relax before they arrive. Then none tomorrow.* Jack reached for the diazepam but stopped short of picking up the packet. Every morning he woke up determined to get off the damned pills and went to sleep each evening with very peaceful resolve to give them up the next day. *Not today.*

He picked up a book; it held his attention for a minute and then the frustration hit him and it was returned to the pile. He got up and paced around the room, stopping only to look at the photo of Sarah on his mantelpiece. *Sarah, Sarah, Sarah.* He walked around the room again, looked out of the window and wondered just when they would arrive and what they were going to do to him. He switched on his computer. The hard drive was acting up and he had to switch it on and off four or five times before it actually got through to the home screen. *Technology hates me.*

The doorbell rang. Jack invited Bob and Mike in.

Bob held out his identification card. 'Jack, thank you for agreeing to meet us. Hopefully, after we've explained our position, you will be happy to take part in some clinical tests we're doing.'

Jack nodded, and led them into the front room.

Once they were seated, Bob continued his introduction. 'We understand you don't have any physical damage to inhibit your motor neurone skills, so we think you are a prime candidate for us to test to see if there is a stress-related impact.' Pausing for a moment, Bob looked around the room.

Jack noticed Bob's eyes came to rest on the pills on the mantelpiece. *Shame may be the best incentive to get off them.* 'I'm trying to get off them, but it's hard, they're really a safety blanket. I don't take many.' He looked down at the floor.

Mike interrupted. 'Given what you've been through, it's a totally understandable transitory usage.' Then he looked to Bob to continue.

'Sooner is better as, if you'll pardon my expression, we need you fresh. So we'd like you to perform some basic tests tomorrow – mostly focusing on eye recognition and reflexes.'

Again Mike interrupted. 'Have you noticed any degradation in your hand-eye coordination?'

'If anything, my hand-eye coordination is improving. But, overall, I'm not coping too well with the stress. I feel very different since the crash.'

'Different?'

'I feel removed from reality, as if I'm watching myself in a movie, not actually here.'

Jack caught Bob and Mike sharing another meaningful glance. 'For instance, I saw the look you just shared. I'm not mad. Not yet, anyway.' He paused, and Bob nodded for him to continue. 'It's just some strange things seem to be happening to me. Technology failures, and other stuff, strange stuff... Okay then, show me your forms; I can tell you all about it tomorrow.'

Pulling out the waiver forms he had drawn up, Bob passed them to Jack.

Jack reviewed them quickly and signed.

Mike leant forward. 'How do you want to get to us on Saturday? You can come directly to the university by yourself, or if you'd prefer I can pick you up from here?'

'No, it's fine, thanks. I'll drive to the university. My doctor's orders are to drive a little each day.'

'Can you give an example now of a strange thing that has happened?'

'As I said, I'll tell you tomorrow but, as an example, my catching seems to have really improved in the last few weeks. Twice I have dropped something from a kitchen cupboard and managed to catch it before it fell to the ground.' He paused. 'I almost wonder if I'm developing super-hero reactions!'

Mike smiled. 'Maybe you should buy a mask... and a cape?'

Jack smiled half-heartedly.

After a few more pleasantries, Jack walked them back to
the door. Shutting it behind them, Jack felt a sense of relief.
It couldn't hurt…

Molly Saunders' diaries arrived as promised and James
Chambers immediately started scanning them for references
to Project Hedgehog. His interest had been piqued by the
information relating to FibonacciEddie, and then further
stimulated by Dougy Raddlestone.

James found a number of chapters associated with the
1960s. He skipped past comments about Cold War spy rings,
deals with Castro and regime change plans for a number of
European countries (not all Eastern European). In total, he
found only eight lines under the title Project Hedgehog.

> *'The Hedgehog farce continues and, although the
> results are amazing, the programme is plagued
> with technical glitches and strange occurrences.
> PM has asked for us to close it down; this is a
> massive reversal from last year. He is worried
> Subject G disappeared after showing impressive
> results particularly when subjected to fear and pain
> stimuli. The service was slow to put a lid on this. A
> shame to close it down; it would have given us the
> jump on eagle and bear. We'll have to disband
> Platoon Z00A, they'll return to the SAS.'*

James searched the MOD databases for references to
Platoon Z00A. It was unclear whether the unit was currently
active or not; there were tantalising hints, but nothing
substantial. However, he did find a service roster from as late
as 1999 listing four soldiers. James cross-referenced them
and a Lieutenant Sebastien (now Major Sebastien) appeared

to be operational. His personal record on the MOD systems was almost blank.

He hadn't forgotten about the report he would have to make to his controller but, on reflection, decided to wait until he had a bit more to say. He didn't want to expose himself to ridicule, or budget oversight, until he was certain.

James picked up the phone to contact Major Sebastien. He left a message explaining his position, saying that he was trying to build up a picture of Project Hedgehog and explicitly asking about Platoon Z00A's role.

CHAPTER 47

Justio sat in the crew room at the main desk. The walls were covered with video footage and associated data, including transcripts of recent conversations of the main Earth participants. He positioned his chair to see the main wall and the entrance doorway. Aytch was preparing for his trip to Earth, but could come in at any moment.

The recent two public transcripts from Gadium concerning Vantch were displayed on the wall. The content was trite – Full Emergence Conflict – Potential GF Insurgence. However, a new message from his GF controller was more serious. *They're closing in on Commander Jenkins.*

If Aytch was to find out Commander Jenkins was a senior GF operative then trouble would be close behind.

A flash on his communications tablet warned Justio that Aytch had left his cabin. He quickly killed a few data feeds on the wall before leaning back and taking up a relaxed posture.

Aytch was not relaxed. He powered into the room. 'I'm ready to go.'

Justio indicated the recent conversations Mike and Bob had had with Jack Bullage. 'They're all set for testing tomorrow, but Jack will be at home tonight.'

Aytch growled. 'We have to get him now!'

'I will set up the arrest for midnight and he'll be delivered to Hampstead by 1am.'

'You're sure you can get him into the Heath?'

'I'm sure, I'll just cut into the police radio and say a woman's screams were heard, can they have a quick look.'

Misdirection was easy when you were able to replicate any message, sounds, content, format and style – even voice could be 100% effectively imitated.

'Anything else?'

'They've got themselves a passive EM scanner. I've recalibrated all the mini-bots to high security: short distance, directional, burst transmissions. I will be fine. On the other hand, their laboratory is high tech and the black-out inside will be total – so we'll not be getting real-time feeds.'

'Well, they won't have Jack Bullage by tomorrow, anyway.'

'Exactly.'

Aytch spent a few moments looking around, and then left.

Alone again, Justio looked back at the various feeds. The increase of activity related to Jenkins had influenced him to alter his plans. The original idea was a Full Emergence that was just generally mismanaged, ultimately leading to a catastrophe, but in baby steps – maximum reputational damage to Gadium. *Bad stewardship.*

But with time pressing, he was happy to move to a second plan. Jack would be at the tests on Saturday. The Gadium mission would have failed to keep a Triple Alpha away from intrusive tests. And soon, the humans would discover Emergence all for themselves. There were plenty of Alphas on Earth to convert and it would lead to devastation. Less good propaganda for GF, as it could simply be labelled as personal failure in his and Aytch's actions. *Good enough under pressure.*

He just had to ensure that it all looked accidental, and that nothing indicated actual GF intervention. And he had to ensure that aliens were not identified by the humans.

Justio tuned into the real-time feeds of Mike, Bob and Jeff. It was early evening, and they were arriving at the campus. They emptied two large boxes from Mike's car and headed into the building. The feed signal started to struggle as the team went deeper into the campus, then, as they entered the Pryson Room, the signal died. *What is their new test?*

Turning to another set of feeds, Justio watched the ship management screen showing Aytch making final preparations for the re-entry craft. This was good; the message Justio had received warning him about escalations related to Jenkins had also told him to send a back-up escalation message to Vantch. Justio couldn't access his hidden Vantch QET pairs without going into the QET room.

He waited.

'Justio, I'm leaving now.'

Justio turned to see Aytch in the doorway. 'Good luck. Mission Initiated.'

With a formal salute Aytch turned and left. Moments later the re-entry vehicle detached and headed down to the surface.

Six hours.

As Justio walked down to the QET room, he reflected on the interactions he'd had with the Vantch. He was not the primary controller – that was Jenkins. He was the back-up, which was just as well. The use of religious fervour to instigate failure in the official Gadium mission jarred with his principles.

Once in the QET room, and accessing the hidden partition, Justio checked the bandwidth. *Barely enough.* These missions took a lot of coordination, and they'd only managed to hide 1000 characters' worth of entangle pairs on his current ship. It had been an incredibly arduous task, over 1000 years ago, to transport the pairs in total secrecy between him and the roaming GF ship.

Justio wrote the message.

Copy. Vantch. GEC Suspicious. Escalate Now.
Full. Enemy Close V. 3 Out.

Justio felt the blood drain out of his head as he pressed send; it could mean a nuclear exchange on Vantch.

Returning to the crew room, Justio saw a transcript on Bob and Mike's discussion in the Pryson Room. The mini-bots had recorded everything inside the laboratory, and then pushed the information out when Bob had returned to Mike's car for more equipment. The transcript was dull, they were clearly keeping quiet about the details of the test. But whether this was due to fear of alien intrusion, or because they were wrestling with their own consciences, Justio could not tell.

Klope's head felt as though someone was hammering on it. Either his eyes were shut or he was in pitch black, he couldn't tell. Outside of his skull, there was silence. But he felt safe. He was clearly in a bed of some type, with soft warm covers. He drifted into a light slumber.

There was a noise of movement close to him, and a voice whispered in his ear. 'Friend Klope, you have been faithful and resourceful. I am proud to be in your world.'

Euphoria flood in. *My prophet!*

The words of response came automatically. 'And I in yours, my Prophet.'

The rustling continued for a moment and then the light began to increase. Klope was in a tent which seemed big enough for five or six people. There were three beds and a few very solid wooden chairs. The tent canvas was black and the light came from a few globes dotted around the ceiling.

Klope looked towards the Prophet. His green and white robe was identical to the one Klope wore, if a little cleaner.

The Prophet pushed his hood back to reveal his face. He looked younger, more vigorous and more joyful than Klope could remember anyone ever looking. He radiated power and certainty. 'I look well, don't I brother? It's the power of righteousness within me – not just a placebo from positive thought – real power; the power of truth.'

Klope relaxed back on to his bed in rapture. His Prophet was with him. The Prophet picked up a chair nonchalantly with one hand, put it down next to the bed and sat on it. Klope tried to keep the shock off his face. *I don't think I could have lifted that with two hands.*

The Prophet leant forward. 'You were lucky in my world, friend. I got to you just in time and, although you were gravely injured, I managed to find a world-path in which you survived.'

'I am honoured to be in your world, my Prophet.'

The Prophet smiled broadly. 'I have to confess I had a little help getting to you in the first place.' The Prophet turned and a shape moved up behind him.

Klope looked at the new arrival. He could not tell if it was a man or woman; it was shaped similarly to a Vantch inhabitant, but much larger than anyone Klope had ever seen before... well, almost. Klope's eyes went wide as his memory returned to the day in the Square outside the Palace of Infinite Wisdom – the giant seventh guard carrying the Staff of Judgement. Klope drew back into his bed, fearful.

The Prophet raised his hand. 'Don't be afraid. This is my loyal friend and servant.' He turned to the newcomer. 'Please show yourself to Klope so there are no secrets amongst us.'

The newcomer unwound the green and white hood. As the cloth came away, Klope saw a large green reptilian face: eyes, mouth, ears and teeth – so many teeth.

The Prophet turned to Klope. 'Brother, Jasang here will just do a little investigation of your brain. It won't hurt, please relax.'

Taking Klope's head in his monstrous hands, Jasang stared intently into his eyes. After a few moments Klope felt an itching in the back of his skull. Jasang nodded in affirmation. The feeling in Klope's head became more abrasive and it began to hurt.

The Prophet looked on in silence, he gave Klope a reassuring smile, but it was all Klope could do to keep focused. The pain was becoming unbearable. Jasang noticed the discomfort and offered some support. 'Just a few short moments to go; hang on.'

The pain grew for a few more seconds and then was gone. Klope's head cleared, and there was no pain. He felt very tired and turned to the Prophet. 'What just happened?'

'You just joined my personal retinue. You will need to rest for the next few days but then you will be amongst my most favoured. My army of truth... I have much to attend to now, so I will leave you in Jasang's company. He will explain what has just happened and our immediate plans.' The Prophet stood up. 'Jasang is only known to my closest Disciples; my Paladins; you must not discuss him with anyone else.'

The Prophet left the tent. Klope heard him start to give orders. They were distant and muddled, but Klope was convinced he'd heard the expressions *righteous fire* and *destruction*.

Jasang took the Prophet's chair, although it hardly looked as though it could take his weight. The chair creaked ominously. Jasang chuckled. 'If I were a female of my species, then this chair would have been reduced to splinters by now.' He paused and smiled. 'So let me tell you about the changes I have just made to you, and what you need to know to ride the parallels.'

CHAPTER 48

With the lights off, Jenkins sat in his office and looked out over the Gadium capital city, silently reflecting on the GEC meeting from which he had just returned. Out there, life was going on as normal, but the Chairwoman's speech could well be the herald of a seismic change in Gadium life.

Early on in the meeting, councilman Smiiter had openly charged the GEC with restricting free speech. He'd made a lengthy speech on the subject of command and control. He claimed the Gadium people were fed up with the stringent legal controls around aspects of Gadium life, notably the forbidden subjects: use of AI, family regulation and Emergence treaties.

Rather than just closing the conversation down with some platitudes about *the ends justifying the means*, the Chairwoman had responded. The response was now being broadcast on every channel across the planet – and soon it would go further.

> *Although we are the most evolved species in the universe, we cannot presume to have been designed to ever fully comprehend it... in aggregate, or, most particularly, as individuals. Leading up to the First Great Congress, almost 700,000 years ago, the knowledge amassed by our civilisation was so complex that the role of the lady amateur had, even then, long since become unattainable. Only specialists could meaningfully contribute on the intricacies of any particular subject, whether this was science, humanities, law*

or galactic expansion.

Many avenues were considered to allow each Gadium citizen to know more, do more and participate more. Our limitations around AI made it complicated but, even so, self-augmentation was considered, hive-minds were considered.

But through all this there was one overruling tenet – we are individuals.

After lengthy contemplation, the decision was taken to simplify our lives, to allow us to retain our individuality.

The First Great Congress legislated away our rights to discuss selected subjects, those considered unassimilable. For those few subjects, the rights of the individual were removed; people were silenced.

Nothing has changed. The complexity around these so-called forbidden subjects still remains too great for any individual to genuinely understand the depths of any given situation and to make valuable decisions based on meaningful analysis of historical data.

I believe this has allowed us to retain the ability to devise self-validated views on the subjects left open for discussion, and therefore to retain our individuality.

This has led to a much lower amount of group assimilation, hive-mind and general cult creation. The evidence from looking at other cultures across the galaxy reinforces this. As our civilisation is reaching its millionth sentient self-aware year of existence, we remain gloriously individual.

Jenkins grunted. At the meeting, most of the GEC members had nodded knowingly, each assuming they were not one of the individuals who were unable to grasp the whole truth.

Fundamentally, most of what she'd said was acknowledged intellectually within the more philosophical Gadium circles. However, her speech was now in the public domain and there would be repercussions. The general Gadium populace would not react well to being called stupid… and that is simply what they would see. Jenkins resolved to talk to the Deputy later in the day to build a plan. There would definitely be a way to capitalise on this for Gadium First.

Particularly if we agitate a little, build a bit more antagonism towards the ruling party. Maybe even offer some alternative policies from Gadium First.

Jenkins stood up, and walked over to the window. Sharnia had also been at the GEC meeting. He'd mostly ignored her stares, but he knew she was getting close. The Deputy seemed to be letting it all happen. Jenkins looked back to the holograph of Katrina on his desk.

Her most recent QET grid message indicated she was getting on a transport home within the next few months – ships were fairly constantly shuttling between the Gadium and Trogia, a benefit of their proximity. *I miss her.* He considered going into stasis but he knew he'd be needed to coordinate the information war on Gadium while they decided how to react to Vantch and Earth.

A buzzer sounded. A voice was patched through. 'Five o'clock meeting cancelled.' The line went dead – the dreaded code.

Jenkins looked at the door, and took a deep breath. The next 30 minutes would be a painful wait, and then the visit he was now expecting would be even more painful. Would he even survive it?

Running never crossed Jenkins' mind. He reached across the desk and picked up the holograph of Katrina. Then he accessed his private comms network and reviewed the last QET message from her. Jenkins shook his head almost imperceptibly. *She really should have left QET bandwidth for people remaining on-station.*

Well – you've obviously watched all the tapes now.

292

I have been good, there's been no more talk of 'the parallels'. I've agreed the return trip with Commander Kuper and she's allowed me to go into stasis now and remain there until I get back to Gadium. I've not enjoyed seeing things first-hand here, it's too big. I've continued my research into harmonic resonance of the probability waves. I think a few hundred thousand years ago we made a breakthrough around double observation interference – but it seems to have been lost. I found a very oblique reference hidden away postulating a link to safety controls which could pave the way for AI reintroduction.

Jenkins shook his head. *It's not about the AI ability to collapse the probability waves. We can control AI, if we really want to. No. The AI questions considered by our ancestors had two parts: the first was simple – would they ever turn on us? The second more complex – can we create immortal beings? What sort of life would they have? How long before they went mad?*

There was a motion at the doorway and suddenly it was filled by the imposing bulk of Sharnia. She strode into the room alone. There was no squad of soldiers to arrest Jenkins. This was a personal visit.

Bad news.

Sharnia reached Jenkins' desk in a few strides and slammed her massive hand down on the desk, causing it to creak ominously. She looked down at Jenkins.

'Justio was in Marhok, where he suffered a serious mental breakdown. Then he was with you in Darth. And there are rumours of his involvement, somehow, on Vantch. And now he's on Earth, and Aytch tells me things are complicated. Too much to be a coincidence.'

While waiting for Sharnia to arrive, Jenkins had wondered whether to go on the attack or plead ignorance. He decided to attack. He tried to remain calm under Sharnia's gaze. 'I have no idea what you're talking about. You're the family with historic links to the GF. Any evidence you have on me has to be circumstantial; I'm innocent. You're driven by a desire to protect your own family's honour.'

Sharnia growled. 'You're obviously worried about the shame of a public trial, so you're trying to get me angry enough to kill you right here. Don't waste your energy. I am going to kill you right here anyway.' Sharnia picked up the hologram of Katrina and examined it. 'Your daughter, Katrina; how sweet. Are you still deluding yourself she loves you as much as you love her? It's a one-way street, you know. She only loves you as much as you currently love your own parents.'

Sharnia grabbed the desk and flung it against the wall. It smashed into a thousand pieces. 'And, just for reference, I had my mother euthanised.'

Jenkins watched, frozen to the spot, as the hologram of Katrina hit the wall along with the desk, the base shattered and the image faded. Katrina! He snapped back to the present. Sharnia took a step forward and Jenkins lashed out at her leg, but not physically – it would have been futile – he mentally tunnelled into her knee and stimulated the nerves. Her leg collapsed.

Sharnia's eyes went wide; unable to support her huge bulk on one leg, she tumbled to the floor. 'Bastard!'

'My reconditioning was necessary, and it was to fight the GF, not to support them. I'm innocent.' He grimaced to himself. That's a long shot... Jenkins looked around the room. He had to escape.

Sharnia fought back the pain and started to drag herself across the floor towards Jenkins. 'Liar!'

She was between him and the doorway.

Suddenly, there were noises in the outer offices, and a squad of Gadium soldiers filed into the room with looks of profound respect on their faces when they realised

Commander Jenkins seemed to have overpowered Commander Sharnia.

After the soldiers had filtered in, the Deputy Chairman also entered. He looked around, quickly taking stock. 'Take Commander Jenkins away to the maximum security holding cells, he's to be treated as a potential GF agent.'

Jenkins allowed himself to be led away.

Standing up, Sharnia eyed the Deputy warily. 'He used SISR on me. How can he be anything other than GF? I'd heard rumours some GF agents had had their conditioning switched off.' She was stretching out the pain in her leg and her back. 'What led you here and now?'

'We've had Jenkins under observation for a few weeks now. No definite links to Vantch or Earth, but certainly links to other suspected GF activity. My agents told me of your impending visit and so I knew I had to get here before you killed him. We need to use him to get to the others.'

'Well, there's nothing wrong with your instincts... I understand your desire to use him, but he's a tough soldier – he won't crack.'

The Deputy looked blankly. 'Everyone cracks.'

'I'm not convinced.' Sharnia looked around at Jenkins' room. Her eyes alighted on the hologram base of Katrina. 'Still, we will have some quite useful levers.'

The Deputy walked over to the window. 'There's a build-up of GF momentum. We have to act now.'

Sharnia continued to work the feeling back into her muscles. 'What do you suggest?'

'A purge.'

Sharnia looked at the Deputy for a while. 'Well, you can have Jenkins for questioning, but if the names don't flow then…'

The Deputy looked her straight in the eye; he was one of the few Gadium males who could do this without flinching. 'You'll get your names.'

Close to midnight, Aytch rechecked his instruments. His descent had been uneventful, but slow, to avoid giving away his position. Many of the feeds from the main crew room were being piped down to his retrieval craft. It was all quiet in Jack's house. *Justio should set the police off soon.*

Suddenly, an alarm went off. Aytch checked through the various data and radioed through to Justio. 'What's your understanding of that alarm?'

'Just checking… inbound interceptor fighters. They look as though they're on a direct intercept.'

'What's the call?'

'You're the active officer, but my suggestion is we abort and go again tomorrow.'

'Can't you perform an override on their systems?'

'Not these ones, they're all locked down tight.'

Aytch looked at his readouts. Even though he'd come down slowly, he was still a sitting duck in the infrared spectrum. Escape upwards would be relatively straightforward. But, if he was seen, he'd have to destroy the fighters and even then they may get readings on him. A confirmed alien sighting would be bad. 'Any other options, Justio?'

'I could try to kill Jack overnight.'

Aytch shook his head. 'No. We should disrupt the tests, get them put off. Perhaps a fire at the university. Then I'll come back on Sunday, with additional decoys.'

'Understood. I'll look into stalling techniques, but I'm more mindful to let them go ahead, they'll be suspicious of random meddling.'

Back in the crew room Justio watched the retrieval craft make its way back into orbit. His hand hovered over the buttons he could push to send it to oblivion.

He breathed deeply.

For five minutes he sat there, but it wasn't going to happen.

CHAPTER 49

At 9am on Saturday morning Louise got her first look at the experiment set-up. The walk through the corridors had darkened Louise's spirits; this deep into the campus the decoration budget had run out. The walls were blank, the windows covered in copper mesh, and strip lights illuminated everything in a dull sheen.

However, the Pryson Room itself was exactly as Mike had described it: high tech, clean and professional. *Good.* When Jack arrived, they needed to give a good impression to avoid raising his suspicions. Not that he would be meeting Louise.

Within the laboratory there were three distinct areas, two partitioned experiment zones and a separate observation room, with a glass window onto the coin box testing equipment. The area where Jack's experiment was situated was hidden from the observation room.

Mike walked Louise around the equipment. 'So it's Ashley, Willis and Jack in here – the coin boxes first. Then we take Jack around the back.'

'Jack can't see me.'

'Don't worry, during coin tests we'll set the office window to mirror mode.'

Louise nodded approvingly; that sounded good to her.

Bob came in with Jeff, Ashley and Willis. He took out his scanner and swept all of them individually, picking up the passive pinging, or simple EM leakage from all of their personal electronics. He collected them all up: phones, iPads,

Kindles, digital watches, everything. 'I'll lock these in my office. Back in five.'

Louise went into the observation room with Jeff, while Mike briefed Ashley and Willis about the high level plans for the day and reminded them about Jack's own reasons for being there.

Inside the observation room, Jeff and Louise looked out on to the coin box area. They tried a few experimental waves but, as Mike had said, the glass was one-way, and they were safe from being spotted.

A few minutes later Mike waved towards Louise, signalling he was going to collect Jack from reception.

Ten minutes later, Louise's heart sped up as she saw Jack being led into the coin box testing area and introduced to the others. Jeff gave her hand a reassuring squeeze.

After shaking hands with Willis and Ashley, Jack followed Bob to one of the coin box stations and settled in. He looked around the room. 'So this is mostly a University campus rather than a high-tech government laboratory, right?'

Bob looked a little embarrassed. 'The government can't afford to maintain lots of separate research facilities so it's very common for collaboration, grants, space, expertise – it all gets shared out.'

'Makes sense, resource sharing and all that.' Jack paused for breath. 'Well I'm just pleased you're having another look at me. During these last few weeks I have begun to think something wasn't quite right… my stress counsellor seems to think the passing of time, in conjunction with emotional heart-to-hearts, will get me cured. I'm not so sure.'

'Can you expand on… something wasn't quite right?'

'Just a hunch really, and perhaps it's all trauma. I lost someone special in the crash; I'm beginning to recognise what a shit I was at Glowview. God knows.' Jack glanced quickly at Bob and then concentrated on his breathing. 'But the fact remains, over the last few weeks, I feel I have been slowly letting go of reality.'

'Have there been any particular incidents?'

'No… well, yes… well, maybe. I don't know. Let's just do the tests.'

Bob looked towards the mirrored glass of the observation room.

It didn't take Bob long to show how the coin box apparatus worked. Jack quickly got the hang of it, although he wasn't sure what it was for.

The uncertainty must have shown on his face because Bob answered his unspoken question. 'This experiment is just a little motor skill, eyesight and shape recognition test. Willis and Ashley are doing the same; they're not recent trauma victims, but both were in bad accidents a few years ago.'

Jack had a closer look at the coin boxes. 'It's not what I expected. I was thinking more along the lines of brain scanners and such like.'

'There will be something like that later, but for now we start simple.' Bob paused. 'Jack, have you done anything today to help you deal with stress and worry?'

'I'm sedative free.'

Once all three participants were settled at their places, Mike dimmed the lights. 'Okay guys, firstly can you do five hundred normal open and closes. Then we will do five hundred with you going as fast as you can.' The others murmured their agreement and the experiment started.

Back in the observation room, safely shut away, Louise was getting real-time results of the tests. She turned to Jeff. 'Anything?'

'We need a larger sample size, but Jack's numbers do look a little odd.'

They waited. After just under 65 minutes, Mike walked into the control area. 'So Louise, how's the journey towards investigative immortality?'

She looked at Jeff. 'Jeff?'

Jeff ran the numbers. 'Jack has recorded one thousand tosses.' He paused. 'For the 500 in which we were subconsciously pushing him to think about heads, he got 277 heads; looking at the chi-squared analysis, it's not quite statistically significant... but it looks promising.'

Mike looked over Jeff's shoulder. 'Not amazing.'

'But if we were to assume that the subliminal trigger is not very efficient then Jack could be hitting 80%.'

Louise interrupted. 'What do you mean he's got 277 from 500... close to 55%.'

'Yes, but that assumes there are 500 in which he tries to get heads; what if the subliminal trigger only works in 350 cases?'

Mike shook his head. 'We wouldn't know if the heads were from the other 150...'

Jeff was undeterred. 'Sure, that's true. But the fact is, these results are almost statistically significant. We're on to something.'

'Okay. On that we can agree. We continue the tests.'

Louise intervened. 'What about Ashley and Willis?'

Jeff looked at the results. 'Nothing unusual.' Then Jeff turned back to Mike. 'And before you ask, there was no difference between the fast and the slow box opening speeds.'

Louise watched with growing consternation from behind the mirror. Outside, Bob had given the participants a break. He'd brought out soft drinks and biscuits for them. *Don't say anything incriminating.*

Then Bob organised a restart to run another 1,000 coin tosses. Mike went out to help administer the tests.

Jeff gave Louise a hug. 'Something will come of it. You're too special not to get the results.'

Louise wasn't sure. The adrenaline, surging earlier, was now ebbing. A discovery was no longer inevitable.

An hour later, the results had not changed meaningfully. Ashley and Willis had nothing, while Jack was still borderline significant.

Bob took Jack to the cafeteria to get coffees, while Mike, Willis and Ashley joined Louise in the observation room.

Willis looked at the figures. 'Just getting a few extra 50:50 chances correct doesn't seem too hard.' He pointed to a run of correct answers.

Mike looked up from the figures. 'So you never heard the one about the old Indian chess player and the Maharaja?'

Willis shook his head.

Louise interrupted. 'Short version Mike.'

'This poor man was challenged to a game of chess by the Maharaja, and offered a herd of elephants if he won. But the poor man said…' Mike switched to his best Welsh accent. 'Kind sir, I would like rice, not elephants, if I win.' He drifted into generic Scandinavian. 'If I win, you will give me one grain of rice on the first square of the chess board, two grains on the second square, four on the …'

'Mike!' Louise had had enough. 'Enough of the lazy racism. And I said short version.'

Mike feigned a look of innocence. 'All right, Big Brother; anyway, the Maharaja agreed, lost the game and then was asked to provide enough rice to cover the entire country of India a few feet deep in rice. Two times two times two… etcetera, sixty-four times in a row, is a massive number.'

Jeff stepped in. 'Just the chances of getting 20 correct in a row is half a million to one.'

Willis appeared satisfied, and Louise's attention turned back to the experiment room. Bob and Jack had returned. Mike went out to meet them. After a short conversation Bob and Mike came into the office, leaving Jack momentarily alone.

Willis spoke. 'I'll go and keep him company.' Ashley followed.

Louise looked at Mike and Bob. 'So how about the heightened fear experiment? Are you ready to push the buttons?'

Bob looked a little concerned. 'If we do this additional experiment then we are all really professionally compromised.'

'I'm committed now. We've been told fear is the key. So let's turn it up.'

Bob paused for a long moment, and then nodded. 'The die is cast.'

As Aytch approached the main Gadium ship in the re-entry craft, he looked at the screen read-outs for a sixth time. It was already late morning in London, and the docking had thrown up one problem after another. Not only had Justio sent him on a circuitous route back up to orbit, but they'd had to abort two of the docking manoeuvres. It was now a case of third time lucky.

The first one was an honest mistake on Justio's part. But the second was plain carelessness.

Justio's voice came over the speakers. 'I'm sorry to mess you around Aytch. I was trying to do too much at once. Your second approach came just as I was setting off the university fire alarm system.'

Aytch swore under his breath. The re-entry craft was built for stealth and speed; but really, it needed a more advanced computer system to make the flying manageable.

'So did the fire alarm distraction work?'

'No, it didn't. The tests are running ahead.'

Aytch was too busy engaging the engines, working on the docking process to really internalise Justio's response. Got to concentrate.

The docking was effective. He waited anxiously as the locks and seals all operated. Then he tore out of his seat and rushed through the corridors to the crew room.

As he arrived in the crew room Justio stood up. 'Sorry again.'

Sorry doesn't cut it. There would be a formal analysis, report and perhaps a charge later. 'Okay, Justio. We'll go through it later. What's up here?'

The screens showed most of the CCTV footage from the university campus, plus transcripts from the few conversations that had been captured and sent.

Justio played the previous three hours of recordings at high speed to bring Aytch up to date. Occasionally, there was a grainy picture from inside the Pryson Room when one of the doors was left open for too long.

There was some indication that a second test was being prepared for Jack Bullage, but zero information on what it was.

Justio spoke. 'They've mentioned fear quite a few times, but a self-aware Triple wouldn't need any fear stimulus. Actually…'

Aytch cut him off with a grunted noncommittal reply. *I'm not interested in musing.*

But Justio continued. 'Actually, if their results from fear related experiments are positive, it may slow down their understanding of Triples.'

Aytch snapped. 'Actually, it would be better if you had done what we agreed and cancelled the tests.'

'Okay, you're angry. But there is no problem here.'

Aytch stood up. 'None except… except all the extra complication from allowing Jack Bullage to be tested by the Harding team.'

Justio spoke slowly and clearly. 'It will be fine.'

Aytch's comms tablet beeped. *Another QET from Sharnia.* He stood up and left the room.

Justio watched Aytch leave the room and then opened video links across the ship to track him real-time as he walked back to his cabin.

He knew he'd over-stepped the mark when he was delaying Aytch's return. But he was confident it looked like incompetence rather than sabotage. *I'll have to show Aytch some mental frailty to convince him the mistakes were genuine.*

But there was also the matter of the most recent QET message.

Once Aytch had shut his cabin door, Justio hobbled quickly down the corridor to the QET room and hacked the main database to get the decoded message.

Egg. I arrested Jenkins. He claims innocence but his fingerprints are all over the Vantch debacle. He has a long history with Justio. Double check Justio's activity.

Not good.

Justio walked back to the crew room as fast as he could. Apart from his heavy-handed delaying tactics earlier that day, he'd been very careful with all his tampering and scheming. He was comfortable Aytch couldn't find anything directly incriminating. But if Aytch looked carefully, he would find lots of circumstantial evidence; lots of items didn't quite fit.

He opened up links to the main ship command centre and loaded some programmes to allow him override controls of the key systems.

CHAPTER 50

In his cabin, Aytch read over Sharnia's message for an eighth time. There was a little resonance; Justio had been controlling, albeit in the name of leadership, and did say the occasional odd thing. In particular, he showed sympathy to the impact of deep space travel on families, but his circumstances were special in that regard. *Plus there was that debacle today.*

Aytch did not feel ready to accuse Justio openly although, undoubtedly, Sharnia would want him to. *Investigate irregularities?* Justio was often fiddling around in the QET room. Any serious GF activity would include irregularities in the transmission logs.

He set off to the QET room. As he passed the crew room, Justio came out into the corridor. 'Aytch, they're about to run the second set of tests.'

'I'm just going to stretch my legs first.'

Justio paused as Aytch walked by; then he called out. 'Actually, I need a little help with the analysis of the data; can you give me a hand?'

Aytch slowed and called back over his shoulder. 'I'll be back in a minute.'

Justio shuffled after Aytch. 'We can walk and talk.'

Aytch frowned to himself. *This was unusual.*

At the entrance to the QET room, Aytch turned. 'I just want to check the sync of my tablet with the QET logs.'

Aytch walked over to the QET command panel. The statistics looked normal. They had 35% of their bandwidth left; there were no obviously unusual messages – noting that Justio's private ones were encrypted.

Aytch took out a multi-tool, and started unscrewing a panel on the main server.

'Aytch, what are you doing?'

'I'm just checking the hardware control panel.' Aytch continued to unclip the panel that would allow him to check the physical status of the QET pairs.

There was a noise behind him; he also noticed movement out of the corner of his eye and turned. He turned and saw a definite glint in Justio's eyes. He shifted his weight subtly; there was no chance Justio could physically overpower him but a hundred million years of evolution alerted him to the early stages of confrontation. 'What's the issue, Justio?'

Justio said nothing.

'I'm just going to check the hardware log integrity, just to make sure there isn't a glitch between the physical states and the automated reports.'

'I have a confession to make.'

Aytch stood and turned fully facing Justio. 'What do you mean?'

Justio leaned heavily on his good leg and looked down at the ground. 'Come into the crew room, and I'll explain.'

Aytch followed Justio back down the corridor.

Once seated in the crew room, Justio brought up the official message logs of the QET grid, detailing messages sent and remaining bandwidth. It showed they had about a third of their entangled pairs left, plenty for a hundred short messages – easily enough.

Aytch looked at the statistics. 'So what's the confession?'

'I've tampered with the numbers. We're actually down to about five per cent bandwidth.'

Aktch felt his chest tighten. 'You'd better have a good explanation!'

Justio's eyes went wide and he took a step backwards, stumbling slightly on his bad leg. 'I'm not a GF agent, or anything bad like that. But I've been sending extra messages in secret… Personal messages.' Justio looked down at the ground.

'This is very serious. Misuse of QET bandwidth. Court-martial. Prison.' *Not to mention a serious reprimand for me, because I did not spot it.*

Justio did not respond.

'This has to be reported immediately. It is utterly unacceptable. I will need to see every message you've sent.'

Justio nodded.

'So, why have you sent all these additional messages?'

Justio held out his hands in supplication.

Aytch slowly shifted his weight and tried very hard not to be obviously getting into a fighting stance. But he couldn't stop himself.

Justio's shoulders sagged and he looked down at his hands, which appeared to be shaking. 'I've been sending illegal messages, not just on this mission, but for the last ten thousand years. I have…' Justio paused, apparently fighting for the words, 'distant descendants alive on Gadium.'

What? Aytch felt sick. 'Post-fourth-generation communication is utterly forbidden. It's criminal and morally reprehensible. It's forbidden. It's sick.' Aytch stopped to draw breath. 'Do they know who you are?'

Justio shook his head. 'No, they don't know. It's all done via messaging, and I have a go-between on Gadium who scrubs my identity. They think they're talking to an old academy buddy. I just need to keep in touch.'

Justio sagged further. 'I have no-one. I have nothing. I left my wife and children when I went to the galactic rim. She promised to go into stasis. She lied. I came back and they were all gone. All dead to me. I was so alone, and I knew I was breaking the law, and I tried not to do it. I tried so hard not to do it. I forbade myself. I…' Justio's voice tailed off.

Aytch looked at Justio. He appeared so weak and pathetic. *Not GF, just a delinquent.*

Suddenly Justio looked up, this time with defiance in his eyes. 'I try so hard not to do it, but I need to be connected to what I lost.'

Justio's hands were really shaking now. 'I set myself ultimatum after ultimatum.'

He continued to force his words out. 'And the stronger the ultimatum, the quicker I broke it.'

Justio chuckled ruefully. 'Like some sort of morality based Uncertainty Principle.'

Aytch had had enough. 'I can either throw you into stasis… or keep you around with reduced privileges.' Aytch loomed over Justio. 'What will it be?'

'I'm a loyal subject of Gadium. I want to help here… I can help here.'

'And your relationship with Commander Jenkins?'

Justio looked surprised. 'What about it?'

He's clueless. 'Jenkins was arrested as a GF agent, and you have a long history with him.'

Justio paused for a long while, apparently searching for his thoughts. 'Look, Aytch, after the Marhok expedition I suffered what can only be described as full animustosis. Part of the rehabilitation was coaching by Jenkins.' Another pause. 'He took me on the Darth mission and, while there, he tutored me and helped me deal with the pain. He never mentioned GF.'

For a few moments, Aytch tapped away on his communications tablet. Then he held it out to Justio. 'You are now forbidden from using the QET grid. Please confirm the order.'

Justio entered his authorisation and Aytch took back the communications tablet.

His first instinct was to report this back to Sharnia, but she would only criticise him for being too lenient. *Once Jack is secured, or maybe later.*

'There will be a full enquiry on our return, so I suggest you start building up some goodwill.'

Justio, with his eyes cast downwards, set about tidying up the crew room.

A tiny spark of pleasure built within Aytch as he watched. *Justio's subservience could work for me.*

CHAPTER 51

Jack walked with Bob through to the 3rd area of the laboratory. Ashley and Willis were not doing this experiment today, and he'd left them repeating the morning's activities with the coin boxes.

The first thing he noticed was that the room was very dark. The second was Bob's current demeanour. Jack stopped Bob in midstride. 'You seem a bit on edge.'

'I have to be honest, I am a little nervous. This is the part where we do the control experiment concerning fear reactions.' Bob paused. 'We're going to make you think you're going to die, while obviously not harming you in any way. I'm worried we may be pushing you a little too hard.'

Nodding, Jack looked at the chair he was obviously going to be sitting in. It looked very sturdy, basically immovable. It was a steel construction with leather restraining straps.

Mike arrived and helped Jack into the chair. Then Mike started firmly attaching leather straps locking his arms, legs, body and head into place. Jack felt his anxiety start to rise, he half-turned to Bob. 'Shouldn't you tell me what is going to happen first?'

'Your uncertainty and restraint is all part of the set-up of the tests. You will consciously know you are in no danger. But we are going to convince your subconscious you may be fatally injured.'

Jack nodded very slightly, partially through uncertainty and partially because, by now, the leather straps were severely restricting his movement.

'The experiment will only take fifteen minutes. Mike and I will put recording electrodes all over your body to measure nerve impulses and then subject you to severe stress.'

Mike fitted the patches to Jack's skin to measure heart rate and sweat emission.

Jack started to become aware, hyper-aware, of the leather straps restraining him. *Control your breathing; this is part of the cure.*

Bob wheeled out a second piece of apparatus. It was a large tripod, about one metre tall, with what looked like a video projector on the top of it. Bob wheeled it up to within two metres of where Jack was sitting. Bob pointed to the projector on the top of the apparatus. 'This lens you can see is pointing at your left eye.' He pointed around the side of the projector. 'On the other side of the projector is another lens you can't see, which is pointing at a screen on your right.' Bob then took a piece of glass and slid it into place on top of the front facing lens. 'I have now added a diffusion filter on the front lens, this renders this laser beam harmless. Try to forget it.'

Now Bob dimmed the lights right down. 'Okay, Jack, we have a safe word in the room, *banquet*. If you say the word then we will stop the test. But try to get through it.'

Turning to the right, Jack was able to move his head just enough to see the screen Bob had mentioned on his right-hand side.

'When I activate this machine, an enormously high powered laser will fire a laser beam. Either it will fire at the screen, vaporising part of it, or it will fire into your eye.'

My eye!

Bob came back to the tripod and fiddled with some settings. 'There is a switching mechanism controlled by the computer within the projector. The computer randomly chooses *red* or *blue*. If it chooses red then the red light on top of the box will go and your eye will be fried. If it chooses blue then the blue light on top of the box will go and the screen gets vaporised.'

What did he say about the filter?

Then Bob pointed to another part of the projector. 'However, there is also a switch to override the laser.' Bob flicked the switch and the laser hummed for a millisecond before a large flash of heat and light appeared on the screen on Jack's right. 'In about one minute we will start a test in which we will fire the laser twice only. Then we'll wait for a while and then we'll fire a hundred times. Good luck!'

Breathing in and out, to stay calm, Jack tried to say *good luck* back to Bob but the leather straps restricted him to a mumbled croak. 'ood uck.'

In the low light, Jack vaguely saw Mike walk up to Bob and whisper in his ear. Then Mike walked away fast, followed by Bob.

What was that?

Jack thought he had made out the word *intruder*. Jack tried to look around but he was thoroughly strapped in.

The lights dimmed further. He had heard the word intruder. *Intruder… what did they mean by intruder?* The projector started to hum. *First shot.* The red light went on. The laser fired. There was a gentle flash of light in his eye, but there was no pain. *A little uncomfortable but manageable.*

The projector started to hum. *Second shot.* The blue light went on. The laser fired. There was a flash of light and an intense burst of heat from the screen on Jack's right. He flinched. He concentrated on his breathing. *It's okay, there's a protective filter.*

There was a movement in the darkness at the back of the room. Jack strained to look. It seemed to come closer. There was a rustle in the dim light behind the machine. Jack called out. 'ob? ob? ike?'

Silence.

Jack fought to control his breathing. It was too dark to see what was happening, but there was definite movement from near the machine. A hand seemed to loom out of the darkness behind the screen and tamper with the front diffusion lens. 'ob? Ike?'

Silence.

Jack began to feel sick. *Keep breathing.* Bile was rising in his throat.

The movement subsided into the background. Jack strained to hear. The footsteps were now behind him.

Someone was tightening the neck strap. Not actually cutting off the blood and air, but it made breathing a strain. He could smell a faint perfume; it hadn't been Bob or Mike.

The person in the darkness slipped back to the projector mechanism. Jack strained his eyes. Long hair, perfume. *A woman?*

The laser began to hum. A blue light went on illuminating the side of a face. *Louise Harding!*

The laser flashed and the screen on Jack's right flashed in light and heat. For a nanosecond Jack could clearly see Harding standing there. She had the diffusion filter in her hand. She turned with a leer. 'Justice Bullage, this is for all the old people you left to rot in their own piss and shit.'

Jack screamed. He tried to speak. *I'm sorry.* But the straps distorted the sounds. 'Orry! Orry! Ankit! Ankit!' Louise laughed gleefully as she ran out of the room. 'Bob's not coming. But a red light will indicate a laser is coming to fry your brain.'

Jack almost blanked out in fear. His heart was racing. He felt the beat in his brain, as if the blood pulsing around his head would push his eyes out of their sockets. The projector started to hum. *It has to be blue.* Blue – A flash of light and heat from the screen. *It has to be blue.* Blue – A flash of light and heat from the screen. He strained against the leather straps in the chair. They were stretching a little but the leather held. He strained again.

He knew it was only a matter of time before a red light fried him. Jack felt as if he were in a trance as the sparks and flames from the screen on his right kept flashing into his peripheral vision. The heat from the laser bursts on the screen was singeing his eyebrows.

Please god, blue!

Jack held onto consciousness. He strained against the leather straps in the chair, but they held him.

After what felt like eternity, the projector stopped firing. Jack slumped back in the chair.

Back in the control area, Mike could not believe what he was seeing. *There must have been some mistake.*

Jack's biological readouts went off the charts. His heart had been beating at well over 350 beats per minute. *Impossible.*

And that level of impossibility was dwarfed by the second order impossibility showing on the laptop screen.

Jack had somehow influenced all 100 random red/blue choices to come out as blue.

Bob looked dumbstruck. 'Surely, we must have made a mistake. Maybe Louise flicked the switch accidentally.'

Louise shook her head. 'I didn't touch it.'

Back on the Gadium ship, the comprehensive electronic black-out within the laboratory was continuing to make things difficult. Justio watched all the feeds for signs of the second set of tests. There was nothing yet.

He looked over towards Aytch, sitting in his flight chair. Aytch had not moved for the last two hours. He'd not even acknowledged Justio's existence, and he hadn't shown the slightest bit of empathy.

Justio had to remind himself that he wasn't actually contacting his long lost descendants, it was just a ruse. But he also felt it would have been completely understandable if he had been. *Bad laws be damned. But that's not how he sees it.*

He's an emotionless automaton. An empire toady.

The misdirection he'd delivered to Aytch had been well prepared. But Justio was surprised about how little emotion he'd had to fake. He blamed Aytch. That, combined with the obvious escalations on Vantch, made him feel very unsettled.

What is Aytch going to do about me?

Even with the reduced bandwidth, Aytch was almost certainly going to report him. And Sharnia would make it clear what to do.

At that moment, Aytch turned. 'Have you accessed and decrypted all your QET messages yet? I'd like to see them all.'

And I'd like to wipe your smug face off your head. Of course he hadn't, he would need to do a bit of cleaning first. 'Not yet, I was waiting until after these tests.' He indicated the feeds coming from the NLUST campus.

'Start on them now, I need to check them.'

Justio stared intently on the screens, trying to block out Aytch.

'I said, start on them now, I need to check them.'

Justio stared intently at the screens. 'Yeah, yeah, you need to double-check on my activity.'

Aytch did not reply.

What?

Justio looked up and Aytch was walking towards the exit, at the doorway he turned. 'Call me when we get some new data.'

Aytch left the room.

Then it dawned on him. *Shit! I said double-check on my activity! That was the exact wording in Sharnia's last QET.* Justio quickly brought up video footage of the corridor. Aytch was marching purposefully towards the QET room.

The decision was made in a split second. From the crew room, Justio accessed the QET grid. He sent a message to Gadium.

```
Jack Bullage, Triple Alpha, becoming self-
aware due to freak combination of events.
Local government has discovered Jack. Despot
organisation may be only weeks away. We are
intervening.
```

Then Justio dumped all of the remaining QET Grid bandwidth.

They were alone.

###

Aytch was suspicious. Justio was acting strangely, and Aytch needed some thinking time. He was going to start reading Justio's messages himself. He could use SISR to decrypt them himself.

Entering the QET room, Aytch saw a series of warning light illuminating the instrument panels. On closer inspection, he saw all of the QET bandwidth had been erased. Full decoupling from pair-mates back on Gadium. *Sabotage!*

Time seemed to slow.

Turning sharply, Aytch ran out of the room and charged back up the corridor. The blast doors in the middle section of the main corridor were closed. He went to the door panel, but the instruments were overridden.

He was trapped in the aft section of the ship with just the QET Grid and the stasis machines.

Justio's voice was projected into the corridor. 'I have made an executive decision. We're going for a Full Emergence. Be reasonable and put yourself into stasis for six hundred years. I will revive you when we get back to Gadium.'

Raging, Aytch struck the blast doors. 'You sabotaged the QET Grid! You've been a GF agent all along!' The door was immovable and Aytch slumped down on the floor next to it. *If I go into stasis he'll kill me.*

After 10 minutes of self-pity Aytch resolved to escape. There was an override panel on the wall. He tried the electronic code, tried a number of combinations, but the doors would not open. Aytch focused all his consciousness on the panel, a Single Instance State Reduction probability attack. *Surely I can use SISR to randomly find the right combination?*

It didn't work. The blast doors remained resolutely shut.

Justio must be observing somehow and stopping me from taking control.

He needed to force the doors open. He wouldn't budge.

Justio won't weld them shut as he'll need the stasis tubes for his return journey.

Turning away, Aytch walked back towards to the stasis area.

Justio's voice came over a loudspeaker. 'I give you my word. I will not harm you in any way, assuming you don't try to stop me.'

'Traitor.'

'History will decide that. I say freedom fighter.'

Back in the crew room, Justio looked around and reflected on his options. He didn't have any. It was clear what he had to do.

The first step was allowing the humans to discover Triple Alphas. The second step would be well-meaning, but ineffective, controls of the proliferation of Triple Alphas. There were overwhelmingly high odds that plenty of Alphas existed on Earth. It wouldn't take much to get them fighting. And then, of course, he would run… leaving Earth and forcing any incoming mission to assume they'd left in shame.

Must still keep alien intervention a secret.

Although Justio wanted to see Gadium mismanagement of Earth, he didn't want to consign 1,000 generations of humans to early graves. And any incoming mission would be forced to grow-out the knowledge of aliens in advance of a fully controlled Emergence.

Hopefully, it wouldn't come to that anyway, as the GF would have political ascendency and the missions would stop.

Justio looked back to the screens. Aytch was prowling the corridor. He'd do all he could to avoid killing Aytch. But it depended on Aytch's good behaviour.

He continued to scan the feeds. In the university campus, it was quiet. The team had still not left the shielded laboratory.

CHAPTER 52

The lights went on and Jack opened his eyes

Mike and Bob were standing in front of him. He couldn't even gather his thoughts; they were muddled and chaotic. His head felt like spaghetti. And there was pain: his arms, his neck, and his legs. Where he'd strained in terror against the bonds.

His heart was racing, and his mouth was dry. Confusion. *Louise Harding?*

Bob stepped forward. 'Well done, the test was a great success. We'll explain everything once you have had a chance to calm down.'

Bob took off the main leather strap restricting Jack's head. The pain in his neck started to ease. And the confusion began to evaporate, to be replaced with rage. *Harding?*

Jack stared at each of them in turn. *Step one, get free.* 'Untie me now!'

Jack noticed a silent exchange of glances between Bob and Mike. *Step one, get free.* He forced himself to appear relaxed, even though his heart was racing. 'I'll hear your side of the story, but please untie me.'

Stepping up to the chair, Mike untied the rest of the leather straps. As the electrode patches and leather straps came off Jack methodically rubbed life back into his face, shoulders and arms. There was blood where the leather straps had dug in so deeply they'd broken the skin. He rubbed his wrists; the bleeding seemed to have stopped.

He looked at Bob and Mike in turn silently for a long while. 'You nearly killed me... I understand the laser was harmless – just a trick – but my heart... it nearly burst out of my chest.'

Bob looked remorseful. 'Well, we did strap you in to keep you from hurting yourself, as well as to heighten the fear. We were also monitoring your vital signs.'

Jack stood up and paced around the room, never taking his eyes off Bob. 'I saw Louise Harding! Is she part of a government investigation into stress and trauma?'

'Well, yes... almost. She's involved because you're involved.'

The confusion of the last few weeks came flooding back to Jack. Nothing really fitted, all the strange events. 'And are any of you even doctors?'

'Medical doctors... no.'

Jack looked around the laboratory. He was struggling to stay calm. 'Jesus, guys, I told you I was struggling with my mental health and you do this. What the fuck! Do you have any idea what I've been through?' Jack walked up to Bob and pushed him in the chest. 'What's the full story?'

Bob stumbled back slightly and opened his mouth to speak, but Jack overrode him. 'No, Bob. I think I'll hear it from Louise.'

Mike went to the doorway and called. A few moments later, Louise and Jeff walked into the room. Louise stopped a few paces away. 'Hello Jack... Well, I guess this is a very strange situation we find ourselves in.' She paused. 'You were a shit to do the things you did at Glowview.'

'Typical Harding, attack first.' Jack turned and walked towards the exit.

Louise stepped forward and spoke in a rush. 'Sorry! Don't go now, you may be in danger. We need to stay together. It all sounds unbelievable, but you have some special powers and we think there are aliens involved as well.'

Jack sneered. 'If it's true, then I'll take my chances with them over the likes of you.'

'Look, I admit the original Glowview investigation became too personal. I was trying extremely hard to get you thrown into jail. I crossed the line a few times.'

'You've crossed a few more lines now. The only reason I'm not going straight to the police is that I trust them less than I trust you.' Jack turned to open the door, but it was locked. 'Let me out now!'

Mike came forward. 'Look Jack, we have information about a possible alien presence… observing us. We don't really know for sure; or, if they're there, whether they're dangerous or not, but we should stick together.'

Jeff had been quietly standing in the background, playing with Bob's scanner. 'There seems to be a signal emanating from Jack.'

Mike turned. 'What do you mean? Let me see.' Mike waved the scanner over Jack's body. 'Jack, do you have any irritation inside your nose area?'

Jack had had enough. 'What? Open the door!' He felt his breathing speed up.

Mike scratched his head. 'I know it's a lot to take in. It's about drugs, mind control, telekinesis, alien abduction, superpowers… and now we think there may be a radiation source up your nose.'

'Are you mental? There's nothing up my nose.' Jack looked around, there were four of them. If they turned on him, could he overpower them? He shook the door.

'I promise I'll open the door, once you've listened for two minutes,' said Mike.

Jack stopped rattling the door and turned back. 'One minute only.'

As fast as he could, Mike gave Jack a brief summary: The Crash, FibonacciEddie, Hedgehog, Bill Jones, the MOD, G60, alien rumours, and finally, the results of the laser test.

Jack was incredulous. 'So you started investigating my luck because Louise was sad I had survived a crash, and you've ended up discovering I have special powers, and we're being watched by aliens?'

Jeff murmured in the background. 'She wasn't sad. She needed a story.' Jack looked over to see Louise walk over and take Jeff's hand.

Mike spoke again. 'You are now as confused and amazed as we are. Do you believe us?'

'I don't know. But I'm not staying here to discuss it. Not after what you've done.'

'Do you know the chances of getting one hundred blue lights in a row?' Jack shrugged and Mike continued to talk. 'If we took ten thousand trillion people, so fifteen million times the population of Earth. Then we asked them to do this experiment ten times every day. Well ... after the approximate lifetime of the universe so far, about fourteen billion years, one of them may have achieved it once.'

'So I'm lucky. I'll make sure to buy a lottery ticket.'

Bob spoke. 'Look, Jack, I'm not sure what you are, or what you have done. But if you want to leave, we can't stop you. I'm hoping that, once you can see our intentions were purely scientific, you may go easy on us. And I'm slightly worried about the radiation in your nose.'

Jack looked around the room. His breathing was evening out, and he could feel the adrenaline start to drain out of his system. His eyes lingered on Louise for a while before he spoke. 'They say a drowning man will grab for what he knows to be a concrete ring, if it's painted to look like a life-ring.' He paused. 'But I'm not putting myself under your control.'

Bob unlocked the door and opened it. Louise stepped forward. 'Please, Jack, reconsider.' She reached out to take his arm.

Jack knocked her hand away. 'Haven't you heard anything I've said?' Jack left.

Jeff followed. 'I'm going for a cigarette anyway, I'll make sure he finds the car park. And I'll get some coffee on the way back.'

Louise followed Mike and Bob back into the experiment area. They went over to the chair; the metal was buckled, the leather straps stretched thin.

Bob looked at Mike. 'I'm not sure what we've got into here.'

'I'm not sure either.' Mike's face was unusually grim as he walked around the chair a few times shaking his head.

Bob ran his hands through his hair and sighed, looking around the laboratory. Then he picked up a leather strap stretched so thin as to almost having been snapped. Bob held it up for Mike to see. 'Mind over matter.'

Mike looked up, his frown slowly transforming into a smirk. 'The placebo crowd will love this!'

Louise remained silent. *Well, I've got my story. What next?*

A few minutes later, Jeff returned with coffee. They all sat around in the laboratory discussing the next steps. Ashley and Willis had come through from the coin-tossing area to join in the discussions.

But Jack was gone. What could they do?

Louise turned to the group. 'Shall we try to re-run the laser test with either Willis or Ashley?'

Mike shook his head. 'There would be no fear.'

Ashley nodded. 'Honestly, I'd rather head home if it's all the same to you guys. I'll go back to Bath but I promise I will keep quiet. You get the exclusive in the next few weeks and then I clean up on the chat show circuit.'

Willis shrugged. 'I'll stay, maybe try another test.' He turned to Ashley. 'I'll call you in the next few days; you owe me that conversation, right?'

'I promise. You'll get your chance.' Ashley and Willis hugged, then Ashley headed for the door.

Louise noted the closeness. *They seem to have become friends.*

Jeff stepped forward. 'Okay, Ashley, I'll take you back to the car park.'

Again Jeff left the room.

Bob stood with the scanner in his hand; he turned to Mike. 'Scientific discovery of the century ... and that's even excluding the possible alien discovery.'

Louise watched Bob as he walked around the experiment desks; then she turned to Mike. 'What's your thoughts?'

Mike smiled. 'Without a doubt, the discovery of the century. But the evidence seems to have just stormed out.'

CHAPTER 53

Justio sat at the main desk in the crew room looking at the blitz of data received from the mini-bots transmitting from Jeff's clothes: video feeds, recorded conversations and data sucked out of the laptop. Jeff's mini-bots had aggregated from across the whole mini-bot swarm using short-range data sharing. Justio had it all.

The material covering the coin tossing was inconclusive, but the laser test was significant. Skimming the footage of the laser test, Justio could make out the colours as the laser fired. *Red lights or blue lights initially, then only blues.*

The discussions after the laser test were problematic, they'd clearly discovered Jack's powers. Not bad in itself, but the last five minutes of the recordings were a disaster. *Discussions about aliens!* They'd found a signal emanating from Jack's nose. The mini-bot had not been contactable since Justio had tried to detonate it a few days earlier.

This changed everything; the humans could not be allowed to find definitive alien proof. The historical case studies showed very clearly that knowledge of an alien presence would give the Earth factions a common enemy to rally against. It would be nigh on impossible for him, individually, to sow discord.

Plus, although he wanted a little war to underline failed stewardship, he didn't want to condemn Earth to the enforced fallow period.

He now had two clear objectives: remove any evidence of alien existence, and silence any humans who could credibly propagate stories about alien technology.

Justio opened the mini-bot communication panel and instructed all of them to move to the most sensitive levels of security. They would now self-destruct if tampered with in any way, or if they did not get a *stay alive* signal each day. The mini-bots inside the shielded laboratory would get their instructions passed on to them when Jeff returned from his coffee break.

The mini-bot up Jack's nose would not respond to his instructions; it would have to be destroyed another way.

An alarm went off in the crew room and Justio turned to the screen showing the Gadium ship main corridor. Aytch was walking up to the main blast door. Justio focussed his attention on the electronic locking mechanism. Aytch seemed to tamper with the override lock. Justio opened up a communications link with the corridor. 'Aytch, stay away – or I will vent you into space.'

Aytch retreated back to the stasis area.

Justio reviewed his priorities. *Jack Bullage mini-bot.* The others could wait, all they had was a list of numbers: they didn't have Bullage, and they didn't have a mini-bot.

But contingency was always good, so Justio refreshed his memory of the mini-bots in Mike's garage – cutting the gas pipes, and in Louise's car – infiltrating the brakes.

Now to deal with Jack.

Justio turned back to the screens. Jack had got into his car. He would be heading home soon.

The crew room walls filled with databases and map overlays of the various fuel delivery companies. *Which tankers are close by?* Results soon started flowing in. He found a tanker containing liquid propane. Then Justio picked an ambush spot based on his prediction of Jack's route home. He hacked the fuel truck's satnav. He'd have to remember to erase all traces of the control overrides after the crash.

More contingency required.

Calling Jeremy Benedict, Justio asked him to stake out Jack's house. He assumed Jeremy would take his car, under which was residing a golf ball sized reconnaissance drone. The drone had two tiny, but operational, antimatter missiles, each capable of vaporising Jack's head. Jeremy's phone diverted to voicemail.

Need to avoid using AM if possible, too exotic.

Then Justio accessed the mini-bots stationed in Jack's sports car. They were all online.

For 10 minutes Jack sat in his car in the university car park, trying to get his head together. He rubbed his wrists where he could feel the leather straps had cut into his flesh. He could still sense the lingering feeling of the restraints, but when he inspected his wrists there was no damage. *I was sure they'd drawn blood.*

He started the car and pulled out into the road. As he drove, he reflected on the morning's shocks. *Aliens? Mind-powers?* He shook his head. He wished he didn't believe a word of it, but he'd seen some of it with his own eyes. Even if Bob had faked the test, he knew he'd been the focus of some strange occurrences recently: the lights going out, the railways crossing, and the techno-glitches all around the house. He kept looking back over his shoulder, half expecting to see Louise Harding following him, but she wasn't there.

After only a few minutes of driving, Jack hit a high street and quickly got stuck up behind a large white van, it appeared to be blocking the road entirely. After a few moments it edged forward. *Just normal traffic.*

But Jack was sweating. The reduced visibility, because of the massive car in front of him, was making him nervous. He forced himself to slow his breathing and looked around; the pavements were crowded with Saturday shoppers. But they were just ordinary people going about their business.

Driving down Christchurch Avenue, Jack thought back to the number of times Sarah had teased him about having such a girly car – his little two-seater sports car. He shook his head to clear the memory of her gently chiding expression as she tried to convince him to get something manlier. He'd always told her he was so much of a man he could roller-skate around in a pink tutu and no-one would doubt his manliness. He didn't feel manly now; he didn't feel invulnerable now; he didn't feel like a master of his own fate. Things felt uncertain and volatile. *Volatile is bad.*

A few miles south of Jack, Ajay Moss pulled out of Wormwood Scrubs Sports fields after his morning on the soccer pitch. He and his team had won their seventh league match in a row and, after a quick drink, he was making the short trip back to his home. Turning north, Ajay swore under his breath as he was brought almost to a standstill behind a slow moving fuel tanker dribbling along at only a few miles an hour.

Ajay swung out into the middle of the road to take a look, but the steady stream of oncoming traffic stopped him from overtaking. He nestled back up behind the tanker and edged forward.

After only five minutes of driving, Jack pulled off the high street and headed south. He had a nagging feeling he could not shake, as if his subconscious was trying to tell him something he was incapable of understanding. *I just need to get home.*

Up ahead Jack could see a bridge, which he knew took him over the canal, and further down the road he could see a large fuel tanker moving slowly towards him. At 70 metres away, he started getting a really uncomfortable feeling. His memory flashed back to the inferno a few weeks earlier. A fuel tanker had been involved in the pile-up.

At 50 metres away Jack thought the tanker was edging onto his side of the road. *Am I imagining it?* The memories of the crash came flooding back. *Sarah!*

Jack let out an involuntary shriek and slammed on the brakes. Nothing happened. He was still moving towards the tanker.

Ajay noticed the tanker swinging towards the middle of the road. Oncoming cars were mostly slowing down, but one car swung across the road and passed the tanker on its right-hand side. With the car coming towards him, Ajay instinctively swung his car to the left. Mercifully, he missed the oncoming car, hit the side railing on the bridge, scraped for a few moments and then came to a stop. He looked up at the tanker; it was near the middle of the bridge now and had veered all the way across the road. The far side lane was blocked and there was little space on his side of the road.

The tanker stopped.

Jack passed a garage, the last building before the bridge. He saw the tanker stopped less than 30 metres away, almost blocking the whole road. There was a small gap in the road, on the right of the tanker, and Jack swung the wheel hard. The electronic steering did not respond. Jack screamed and pulled harder.

Something gave. His car swerved right, narrowly missing another car in front of him. He swung on to the right hand side of the road, but when he tried to straighten the steering, nothing worked. The car left the road. There was a gap in the railings and he sailed through it, and down a short grassy bank into the canal.

The water was only a few metres deep but, as he hit it, all the windows opened half-way and the muddy canal water came flooding in. *Shit!* Jack lunged for the window controls but they were not responding. Jack kept pulling on the switches but the windows did not respond. The car was filling with water.

There were a few tiny explosions within the car. Jack looked through the flood of muddy water filling over three-quarters of the car's interior. The dashboard was dark. He turned his attention to the doors. They wouldn't open.

He hit at the window glass, but it resisted.

I'll drown.

Now he was totally under water except for his mouth and nose. The water was hampering his movements, so that he couldn't get any force behind his blows. He lashed out again, but still nothing gave. Involuntarily he drew a breath, and took in some water. He overcame the urge to draw in more water, but he knew he was drowning.

I must survive!

Somehow, the urge to breathe lessened, but Jack didn't know how long he could hold on.

⚎

Justio accessed the remaining mini-bots within Jack's car. He had very limited video feeds. He opened up a feed from a nearby CCTV camera. The car was totally submerged. Nothing had come out of the car or the canal.

A text message from Jeremy indicated he couldn't get to Jack's until 7pm. Justio shrugged; hopefully it wouldn't be needed. *When the ambulance arrives, I'll make sure they put the body near the tanker.*

Justio watched, via the CCTV, as a crowd started gathering around the canal.

⚎

Ajay started running towards the canal. He had seen the car go in, and hadn't seen anything come out. He slipped through the gap in the railings and down the grassy bank. Then, without a pause, he jumped into the canal and put his head under.

The water was murky, but he could see movement within the car, a body wildly thrashing around. Ajay tried the door; it was stuck. He felt a reverberation as the person inside the car seemed to land a hit on the driver's window. Ajay couldn't see much. *Is there just one person in there?*

Ajay pulled at the door again, but it didn't budge. He looked into the car. There was still one thrashing shape. Ajay swung his legs up and gave a kick at the window. The window seemed to give a little. Desperate for breath, Ajay pushed upwards and his head broke the surface. A crowd had gathered. Ajay shouted for help. 'There's a guy in there!' And he dived back and kicked the window again. It seemed to give a little more. A few more kicks and he was forced upwards again.

Ajay could feel a numbness creeping into his hands, and his limbs felt heavy. He dived down once more. *There's still movement inside!*

Ajay was hit by something cutting into his face. Ajay felt a hand clawing at his clothes, reached out, grabbed an arm and pulled.

Soon hands from the canal side were pulling them both on to dry land. Ajay looked at the man lying beside him in disbelief; he must have been under for more than 6 or 7 minutes.

He reached down to do something. *Anything.*

Jack was being shaken. He vomited. He couldn't stay; it had been no accident. He got to his feet and looked around. There was a man shaking him, clearly wet with blood dripping from a gash on his face. 'You okay?'

The man nodded with a look of incredulity. 'How did you hold your breath for so long?'

Jack wretched and vomited up a load more water, it was excruciatingly painful. 'I'm not sure I did.' He looked up at the roadside and the bridge. The tanker was still there, looking menacing. He turned back to the man on the ground next to him. 'Thanks.'

'You're welcome. Nice car.'

'You can have it, the keys are in the ignition.' Jack turned and made his way, slowly at first, but with increasing rigour, up the slope.

Back to Louise Harding? Or wait for the aliens to try and kill me again?

Justio watched via CCTV as Jack ran up the side of the grassy bank. Then, turning away from the tanker, Jack ran fluidly up the road, picking up speed easily.

Justio knew that, deep within each and every one of Jack's individual cells, overseen by his subconscious, his metabolism was responding to an ongoing perceived threat with 100% efficiency.

He smiled ruefully to himself. *The short-term benefit of overclocking… he might overheat?*

But Justio knew that wouldn't happen. He needed a new plan.

CHAPTER 54

Louise paced around the laboratory, her gaze flicking between the coin boxes and the whiteboard that Bob was scribbling on. She almost had what she wanted. It was so close. The results were astounding – Jack could control luck – but he'd gone. And, without Jack, all she had was a list of numbers.

And who'd believe anything I said about Jack Bullage anyway.

They'd drag her off to a padded cell if she tried to publish anything without clear, irrefutable proof. She paced on.

'Nothing from Willis.' Mike had returned from the laser test. 'We tried but we got nothing.' A few moments later Willis came back around the partition wall and sat down at one of the benches.

Louise hadn't expected it to work, not least because of Willis' unshakable faith.

Mike walked over to the whiteboard. 'So, Master Robert,' he said, 'what the bleeding hell is happening?'

Bob put down the pen. 'Assuming the test was true, and we didn't set up the experiment incorrectly, Jack clearly interacted with the laser, and caused one hundred fifty-fifty events to go his way.'

'We know that. But what happened… deep down? What really happened… in the ether?

Bob flicked a gaze towards Louise and the others. 'Quantum mechanical state reduction.' He shrugged his shoulders.

'So, we should discount the idea that the alien machine up Jack's nose was doing it?'

'We don't know it was a machine. We don't know how long it's been there. You could be right. But I suggest we start with Jack.'

Then Bob wrote up on the board. Copenhagen or Many-Worlds.

Mike shrugged. 'Yeah, I see the problem. Untestable.'

Louise stepped forward. 'What do you mean, untestable? What do you mean, Copenhagen or Many-Worlds?'

Mike answered. 'They're just two interpretations within quantum mechanics. You see Schrodinger's Kitty here.' Mike picked up a coin box. 'When we open the box, something happens. Sure, there's a 50:50 outcome. But Copenhagen has an observer causing the universe to choose a result. While Many-Worlds has the universe split and both results happen in two different new universes.'

Bob coughed gently. 'Or it could just be Newtonian derived rotational and gravitational dynamics.'

Mike turned back to Bob. 'If a tree falls…'

'Back in this room, Mike.' Louise picked up her own coin box and banged it on the desk to get his attention.

Mike focused on Louise again. 'So, ignoring Bob, when I open the box, there is an apparent choice made. With the laser, it appears that Jack was making the choice on behalf of the universe.' He turned back to Bob. 'The laser randomiser was as QM as we could make it.'

'So we need to find out how it works, this Copenhagen thing, or the other one?'

Mike shook his head. 'No, it's untestable. We cannot step outside our own universe to watch from the side-lines. We have no way of knowing if other universes are created. Incompleteness.'

Louise couldn't really tell where this was going but she needed facts to back up her story. Maybe she could distil the information down into a story. 'Does it only work with 50:50 chances?'

Mike smiled. 'There are a few good thought experiments: The dragon behind the door and the paint mixing are my favourite.'

'Not the dragon story.' Bob turned to the others. 'Every time we do a fundraising he wheels out this anecdote. It's got nothing to do with physics, it's just semantics... do the paint.'

'As an illustration to Copenhagen versus Many Worlds.' Mike paused and smiled at Louise. 'Keeping it very brief. I could pour red paint and yellow paint into a tin and mix them together. I've now got a tin of orange paint. There are zillions and zillions of tiny individual, red or yellow, paint particles all mixed up - to us, the whole thing looks orange.' He paused. 'If I cover the pot and shake it vigorously for a few minutes, when I uncover it, there's a statistically tiny chance they could have separated out again half red and half yellow right down the middle of the tin. The chances are astronomically low – but it's mathematically possible.'

Louise nodded. *That's clear enough.*

'So in the Copenhagen view, the paint (with the lid on) is held in a superposition of all states and just resolves when I look at it – a state reduction. In the Many-Worlds, we assume all possible futures play out in the totality of reality, say the multiverse, because every time something happens the universe splits into almost identical copies of itself, with each copy carrying a different outcome of the event that caused the split.' Mike paused. 'So, somewhere there are zillions of universes, and in one of them - a very rare universe - the paint had randomly separated out and split down the middle, yellow and red.' Mike paused again. 'I don't do anything to the paint. I just happen to live in the universe in which the random outcome I wanted had occurred… and there are other Mikes living in universes with orange paint in their tins.'

Shit. It resonated with some junk Jeff had been spouting earlier in the week. The punchline had been; it was untestable.

Yet again, dread settled into Louise's stomach. She looked at Mike, who appeared to be very happy. He didn't have a story to write to save his career.

Willis stepped forward. 'There is only one universe. God's universe. And each of you only has one soul.'

Mike shrugged amiably.

Reflexively, Louse felt a tiny subconscious urge to share her pain. 'But, Mike, weren't you saying just the other day that your atheism allowed you unparalleled promiscuity, as you didn't have to worry about a soul?'

Willis looked shocked. Mike went red.

Bob chuckled. 'From what I remember of Mike's frottage around the common room, his soul is quite safe.'

Mike was about to reply when there was a knock at the door.

Jeff was first to it, and found it was Jim from reception. 'Jim, what's up?'

'There's a Mr Jack Bullage at the reception, asking for you.'

Before she could think, Louise had barrelled passed Jim and Jeff.

Jack flinched as he saw Louise Harding running towards him. But she slowed within a few metres, and the others appeared behind her.

She approached. 'I'm sorry.'

He nodded and, without any discussion, they filed back to the Pryson Room.

Bob closed the door, and engaged the EM shielding. Jack recounted his journey: crash, canal, drowning. 'A coincidence?'

'I'm not sure anyone believes that now.' Louise looked at Jack more closely. 'Would you like one of us to run you up to A&E for a check-up?'

'No I'm fine; physically anyway – but thanks.' Jack and Louise locked eyes for a few seconds. A flicker of understanding flitted between them – a truce.

'Are you sure? Maybe you did it to yourself.' Bob turned to Jack. 'Have you had problems with your car before? Do…'

Mike cut it. 'Bob, it's aliens. Accept it.'

Jack sat down. 'Nope, but then again, recently I've had trouble with most of the other technology in my house.' He sagged. 'Aliens… Trying to kill me… and, if so, why?'

Mike walked over to Jack and laid a hand on his shoulder. 'Hang in there Jack. We'll find a way out of this.'

Bob was agitated. 'But if they're dangerous?'

Jack ignored Bob, he was panicking. Jack knew all about fear. 'What about my nose?'

Mike disappeared for a few minutes and then returned with the scanner and an enormous magnet. He sent Jeff for some hot water and three minutes later they had Jack inhaling the steam, while they manoeuvred the scanner and magnet around the outside of his nose to try to get it out. After 15 minutes, the source of the signals appeared to be stuck to the magnet. To the naked eye, it was the size of a large grain of sand, but nothing else could be seen on it, it seemed to be just a tiny metal ball. Mike put the magnet into a reinforced glass beaker and then placed a metal sheet on top. 'We should take a magnified look to see what we're dealing with.'

Again Mike left the laboratory, and they all waited until he'd returned with a portable microscope. They didn't want to take the tiny metal ball off the magnet or out of the glass beaker, so it took a lot of fiddling for them to get an image, which in itself was severely distorted by the curvature of the glass beaker.

After examining for a few minutes, Mike looked up from the microscope. 'It's hard to say, it's probably about a millimetre in diameter. There seem to be some tiny protrusions, but basically it's a metal sphere. I couldn't say for sure it's alien... or what it does.'

By now, Bob had calmed down. He took a look. 'It may not be alien, but I've never seen anything like it before. Earth based nanotechnology?'

Mike shook his head. 'What's more likely? It's alien... or an Earth based government has this technology, and we've not heard anything about it.'

For a few minutes everyone took a turn looking, but there was nothing really to see, just a tiny distorted metal ball.

Jack felt a little better. 'So you're sure there's nothing up my nose now?'

Jeff did a sweep. 'All clear.'

There was a quiet cough from over by the whiteboard. Bob utterly calm now, had written the word *Evidence*. 'We've got some sort of evidence with the metal sphere. Now, I think we do need to rerun the coin box test, see if we can get some repeatable evidence on Jack's powers.'

Jeff shook his head. 'Come on Bob. The guy's just almost been killed. I don't think the right thing to do is to test him again.'

Jack looked around. There were mixed emotions showing on everyone's faces.

Mike spoke. 'I know it seems harsh of Bob but, actually, if Jack has some special power then the best thing he can do for himself is train it... for his own safety.'

Okay. One more test. Jack nodded his acquiescence.

Mike brought the laptop out of the office and set it up next to a coin box. The subliminal lights were turned off. Then he gave a printed list of 500 *heads* or *tails* to Jack. Everyone else just stood around.

Mike turned to the crowd. 'Back a bit and, in the interests of purity, please, no-one try and look over Jack's shoulder. He has to be the only observer.'

After reading the first item off the list, Jack operated the box willing the drawer to reveal the required side of the coin. He ensured he was the only person to look at the result initially, and then he showed it to Mike, who recorded the value. He turned to Mike. 'For the first hundred I will simply think hard, willing the result to happen.'

The two of them settled into a rhythm and, after one hundred tosses, Jack had correctly selected 60 results. Mike held up his hand for Jack to stop. 'Jack, it's good, in the one to five per cent range, but not off the charts. Can you try a different way of thinking?'

'I think so. I can try to replicate my mind state when strange things have happened to me in the recent past.'

'How do you describe the required state of mind?'

'With difficulty.' Jack sighed. 'I don't really know, but if I try to keep the result I want in my mind for about a second and then just as the box is opening, just a split fraction of a second before I see the coin I try to forget the image, sort of push it away.'

They continued the coin toss double act, with Jack opening and looking. He did the first ten.

Ten right in a row.

Mike was looking surprised. Jack continued.

Twenty right in a row.

Jack's hands were sweating, he had to concentrate to keep a grip on the drawer.

Thirty.

Again, unbidden, Jack's heart rate started to rise. *Not now.* He didn't want to have a full panic attack. He stopped the test. Looking around he said, 'I need to take a break, I'm getting panicked.'

'It'll be okay. Frankly, thirty in a row is job done.' Mike put an arm around Jack. 'Funny how the morning coin tosses were so bad. Maybe the subliminal influencing was off.'

Mike let go of Jack and turned. 'Or perhaps his conscious mind is just stronger, and the subliminal worked but he ignored it.' Then he chuckled. 'Of course, Jack's subconscious did fine when the lasers were firing.'

As the others all gathered around him, Jack looked at each in turn. 'So, what now?'

Louise looked at the glass beaker on the table. It held an alien artefact. Then her gaze swung to Jack. He could influence random events.

What now, indeed?

Everyone started to talk at once.

'Stop!' It was Bob who took control. 'Stop. First, Jack, what's your view?'

'No police, no government, no public story. Two months of cooling off, to give me a chance to get adjusted.'

Bob turned to Louise. 'I guess that doesn't work for you.'

No it doesn't but… perhaps there is a middle way. 'I'm a reporter. This will get out. It's my story. But I can commit to

Jack's anonymity. Assuming I get to use the alien artefact as proof.'

Her eyes locked with Jack, again there was a brief connection.

Jeff came up and put an arm around Louise, whispering in her ear. 'Nice decision, boss.'

Jack spoke. 'I'll need Mike to help me work through these powers. See how they can be used to protect me. I'll disappear. What about you, Bob?'

'Once we've agreed our position here, I'll report to G60. Then Mike and I will work on the artefact.' He nodded towards Jeff. 'With Jeff, of course.'

Mike chuckled. 'Until the government break down the door and rip it from our still cooling hands.'

Bob walked over to the whiteboard and started cleaning it.

Jack called over to Bob. 'How long before you speak to the government?'

'I have to say something this weekend, but I can leave it until Sunday. The best I can do is warn James Chambers tomorrow morning about the article... once it's too late for them to stop the publication.'

Louise did not agree. 'Sorry, Bob, but if you want to be part of the discovery team then you have to commit to silence until we say so.'

Bob looked uncomfortable. He started to speak but stopped himself.

Louise looked at Bob warily. *Probably just worried we'll cut him out of the discovery.*

Mike turned to the others. 'Are we ignoring the point about Jack having been targeted a few hours ago? How will we protect ourselves? If the aliens really did try to kill Jack, then we may all be in danger.'

As Mike mentioned the danger of aliens, Bob flinched. Louise faced the group. 'We're as safe here as anywhere. Probably more so. I'll call Harry Jones to warn him a big story is coming.' She motioned to Mike and Bob. 'Can you guys get some enhanced photos of the alien bug? And, Bob, can you retrieve my phone from your office, please?'

Jack informed them he wanted to stretch his legs, and left with Bob.

Willis also followed Bob. 'It's probably time for me to get home. Assuming you all trust my word. I promise not to speak to anyone.'

Louise came forward and gave Willis a hug. 'Sure, Willis. Be careful, and thank you.'

Everyone split up to their assigned tasks. But Louise watched Bob carefully as he left the laboratory. *It's not that I don't trust him, but…*

Alone with Mike, Jack and Jeff now, Louise voiced her concerns. 'Do we totally trust Bob?'

Mike replied. 'He won't dare miss out on the find of the millennium.' He looked back at the jar containing the alien artefact.

Louise wasn't so sure. She met a lot of chancers in her line of work.

Way above London, Justio watched the sounds and pictures coming in. Since Jack had returned from his canal dipping, Justio had been receiving very little information from the room.

Then the bad news flooded in. Justio watched as Bob and Jack walked down to Bob's office. The mini-bots pushed the previous hour of activity onto the crew room wall.

Bad news. They had alien proof. They knew about Triple Alphas.

Justio knew his options were limited. *First the very loose ends.* He tracked Ashley Davidson's position.

An alarm sounded.

Justio turned his attention to the relevant video feeds to see Aytch coming back up the corridor towards the blast doors. Justio switched on the communications channel. 'Aytch, I'm venting the corridor in ten seconds if you don't go back.'

Aytch looked determined for a few moments but then went back towards the stasis area.

He turned his attention back to the university. They'd shut the door to the Pryson room, but Bob was in his office with Jack.

Justio accessed the real-time sound feeds.

> *Bob – Look, Jack, I appreciate your position, but I think that the government will offer you better protection than Louise Harding.*
> *Jack – I've had plenty of dealing with government organisations before. They're mostly well-meaning, but also strangely blinkered.*
> *Bob – But Louise's treatment of you?*
> *Jack – She's passionate and committed. And I trust her word.*

Nothing more was said. Bob stayed in his office, while Jack made his way back to the Pryson Room.

Justio opened up the mini-bots distribution screens. There were plenty covering the team, but even if they self-destructed the explosions would be insufficient to kill them. The mini-bots had to be internal to make a kill. He needed a bigger bang.

Although the university was full of exotic materials, there wasn't too much of danger near them.

When Jack let himself back into the Pryson Room, the scene was very peaceful. Mike and Jeff were huddled by the whiteboard covering it with strange notation. Louse was sitting on the floor scribbling on a notepad.

He walked over to Louise. 'You may have to keep an eye on Bob. He tried to tempt me to elope.'

Louise looked up sharply. 'Has he gone?'

Jack shook his head. 'Not yet. I don't think he'd leave without some proof. And I'm not going with him.'

Louise went over to the alien artefact in the glass jar. She picked it up and hid it under one of the experiment benches. Mike and Jeff noticed her; she gave them a shushing noise and shook her head.

Mike and Jeff returned to their work. Jack made himself comfortable on the floor. 'So we wait for you to finish your story?'

Mike called over to Jack. 'We can start discussing your training anytime.'

Jack was tired. 'I think I'll take a short break.'

Twenty minutes or so later, Jack opened his eyes to see Bob come back into the room. He was carrying Louise's phone. 'I thought you'd come for this.'

Louise jumped up. 'Sorry, I thought you were bringing it.'

Jack noticed Bob's gaze sweeping the room. *He's noticed the missing jar.*

Bob spoke. 'I'd like to do a bit of prodding on the alien artefact.'

Louise replied. 'We'd prefer you didn't take it out of this room.'

Bob nodded. 'Okay.'

Jack relaxed. Bob seemed to have calmed down.

Louise pointed out where the glass jar was hidden. 'I'll put a call into Harry to warn him of a big story. I won't give any details yet.'

Then she took her phone outside into the corridor.

Jeff followed.

They were back a few minutes later, and Jack returned his attention to trying to get some sleep.

CHAPTER 55

BANG! BANG! BANG!

Jack was awakened from his doze by commotion. As he came round he picked up scraps of an ongoing conversation.

'… Crash …'

'… Ashley …'

'… Dead …'

Awake fully now, Jack saw Willis standing in front of the others. Willis was out of breath, his clothes apparently soaked through with sweat.

'As I walked to the tube, I checked the news feeds. Something looked odd, and then I tried Ashley, and then I called his home number. He'd been on that coach.' Willis sobbed. Mike went over and gave him a hug. 'It turned out, I was the one to tell his wife the news.'

Jack scanned the room. *They're picking us off.* Everyone was subdued, everyone except Bob – who looked spooked.

Jeff was standing at the doorway, fiddling with his phone. 'The coach crashed, there's talk of failed brakes.'

'We have to stay together… here.' said Mike.

'No way!' Bob pushed passed the group. 'We have to tell the authorities.'

He left the room.

'Traitor!' Louise sneered. 'You'd better warn him never to see me again.'

Mike sat down heavily on to a chair. 'He did what he felt was right; he didn't take the data, didn't take the alien bug. Give him a break.' He paused. 'So what now, do we stay, or

349

go? Personally, I think we're as safe here as anywhere. All the dangerous activity so far seems to have been contained to motor vehicles: the attempt on Jack, and now Ashley's crash.'

Jack stood up. 'If Bob has gone to the government, then the police, or army, will be here soon. I'm going to leave. I'm not ready for any government probing.'

Mike took his phone from the pile that Bob had left on one of the tables. He walked over to the whiteboard and took a few photos. Then he started collecting the laptop and various other materials together. 'We have a little time; let's try to clear up this place. Jeff, you start to dismantle the laser.'

Jack and Willis followed Jeff through to the second area, where they spent ten minutes dismantling the apparatus as best they could.

Suddenly, Louise put her head around the partition wall. 'More information. Come round.'

They gathered around Louise. 'A text from FibonacciEddie, it says "army on the way to university, suggest you run".'

Mike stood again. 'It may be a trap.'

Louise frowned. 'Not sure... he's helped before. But we need to move; the SAS will be kicking down the doors soon.' Louise started to gather her things together. 'I need time to finish the story. I'm going on the run. Who's with me?'

Jack put up his hand. 'I'm in.'

Mike threw up his hands in exasperation. 'Bloody populist politics! Okay, we're all in, we have to stay together. But remember what I said... so far the danger has been on the roads.'

Louise sped off, walking fast towards the university entrance. The others followed.

Halfway to the reception area, Jeff suddenly stopped. 'We forgot the bug! I'll go back for it and see you in the car park.' Jeff peeled off from the group and retraced his steps.

They momentarily stopped as Jeff left the group. Mike took a moment to get his breath back. He turned to Louise. 'Where do you think we can go to be safe?'

A few hundred miles straight up, Justio listened in. 'Where indeed can you be safe? Nowhere springs to my mind.'

James Chambers waited for Bob with growing nervousness by the ticket booths in Liverpool Street station. The message from Bob had been incredible; he didn't know what to think. *Positive tests for aliens and superpowers?* He'd always believed in aliens, but at a distance – the conceptual existence of other life somewhere in the 100 billion other galaxies.

Suddenly, Bob appeared, looking panicked. James led Bob towards a coffee shop, but Bob shook his head and pointed downwards. They passed through the barriers and went down a staircase towards the underground platforms. Halfway down the stairs, James stopped. 'So tell me what happened.'

Bob sat down on one of the steps and recounted the events of the previous 24 hours. He summed up. 'Jack has special powers. We are being watched by an alien force. Apart from that, I don't know what to think.'

'Jack won't come quietly?'

'Definitely not. I had to abandon them.'

'And you didn't bring the drone?'

'No, in my panic I forgot it, but it's in the laboratory. I'm sure we only managed to capture it because of the EM shielding. I've got a copy of the data, but without Jack it's probably meaningless.' Bob passed over the zip drive.

'Have you theorised what may be happening?'

'I've discussed it with Mike, but it's a minefield.' Bob shrugged. 'I wanted to see you face-to-face, phones can't be trusted. But I don't want the others to think I'm a deserter. Tell me the next steps and I'll return.'

'I'd better call Major Sebastien.' James massaged his temples. 'Saying that, I'm actually officially in charge of government activity on alien contact.'

'I suspect you're only in charge until some extra-terrestrials are actually found.'

James smiled ruefully. 'Spot on. But let's get our twenty minutes in the sun anyway, before the fun police take it away.'

They travelled back up to ground level. A few seconds later Justio had a full transcript of the conversation.

James called Major Sebastien. This time the phone was answered and, after a short conversation, the Major asked James and Bob to go directly to the MOD building in Whitehall. Bob was explicitly forbidden to return to the university.

CHAPTER 56

It was dark when James and Bob exited Westminster tube station. As they were getting their bearings a large soldier dressed in black camouflage fatigues approached them. He was conspicuously armed: pistol, rifle and knife.

'James Chambers, please follow me.'

James and Bob followed meekly and were led into a side street where at least 14 more soldiers stood in readiness. One of them stepped forward. 'I'm Major Sebastien. I'd better hear the full story.'

Five minutes later, Sebastien dispatched two soldiers to the university campus, two to Jack Bullage's house and two to Mike Littlejohn's garage. Then he turned back to James. 'We have contingency plans for this type of thing. Our first job must be to secure the participants. There can be no publication of information unless fully vetted by MOD chiefs – national security.'

James and Bob were then invited to get into a large black truck, which had a command centre set-up in the back, complete with a table and multiple screens fed from cameras on the soldiers' helmets.

As they were settling into their seats, James asked many questions, which were roundly ignored. However, once the truck started moving northwards, Sebastien spoke. 'I am not much more informed than you. There are records from the 60s about possible alien incursions, but there's never been any hard evidence. However, my unit has a constant watching brief for this type of thing - Platoon Z00A's real

353

job is counter terrorism. Rule one is that we cannot trust any communications, so we'll all drive up to the University. Until we get Jack Bullage and the alien bug we've got nothing.'

ЩЦ

Justio received a message from Jeremy Benedict. He'd finished his golf early, and was on his way to Jack Bullage's house. Justio redirected Benedict to the vicinity of Mike's house, albeit not giving the exact address or name, and then programmed the reconnaissance drone to detach once it got within a few hundred metres.

Justio then turned his attention to the Harding team. Firstly, he re-routed all of their phones into the Gadium crew room. They couldn't send or receive anything without his explicit permission.

Secondly, he tracked Jeff's movements through the university.

Thirdly, he followed the progress, and conversations, of Louise, smiling ruefully as they discussed the morality and logic of the alien interventions.

And finally, he kept a watchful eye on Aytch.

All by myself, no AI support, a hostile partner… and I need some sleep.

ЩЦ

As they approached the entrance, Mike turned to Louise. 'If the aliens do mean us harm, then it's probably to silence us. So there's a gamble to be played… tell everyone everything

354

right now. Use social media, and don't wait for tomorrow's exclusive.'

Louise thought for a moment, and Willis chipped in. 'It may be a moral test by the aliens. While we look for personal gain then we're vulnerable to reprisals.'

Mike blew out his cheeks. 'I'm not sure we can ascribe human motivations to them. But they're unlikely to destroy the whole world… if they wanted to they'd probably have done it a long time ago. Remember, there were only a few unexplained disappearances in the 1960s – not wholesale slaughter.'

Willis added more. 'Maybe they repress the knowledge to keep their own ruling position in the galaxy?'

Mike reached out to Louise. 'So, Louise?'

'So, I have a story to write. I'm giving Jack his anonymity, and that's all.'

Louise's phone buzzed and a text came through from Jeff.

Have seen soldier out of window. Run! I will meet you at Mike's.

They ran. Then, piling into Louise's car, set off for Mike's house. Mike tried to call Jeff but the phone diverted to voicemail.

Jeff picked up the glass jar with the alien bug and started to walk back down towards the car park. His phone buzzed, a message from Louise.

Soldiers in the car park; go out the side entrance and meet us at Mike's. Run.

CHAPTER 57

Justio watched with growing frustration as Louise's car pulled up in the street outside Mike's house. Jeff hadn't arrived yet. He needed to get them all together. He turned to another screen, and watched Jeff going into a corner shop!

Justio had banked on getting the whole team to take refuge in Mike's garage while they finalised their plans. Unfortunately, Louise and the others just stood by the car, and Jeff was absent. Justio thought for a few moments and then texted through to Louise.

> *Hey, love, I'm a few minutes away, suggest you take cover in the garage. Jx.*

Then he texted through to Jeff.

> *We're at Mike's. See you in the garage.*

Then he checked the other data. The reconnaissance drone had detached from Benedict's car and was a few minutes away from the garage. The 5,000 antiprotons in each missile would be plenty to vaporise someone's head, but he still wanted to avoid using it, or at least save it to erase the alien proof being carried.

The perfect scenario would be for Jeff to see them entering the garage, and to follow them in just as Justio detonated. Justio checked Jeff's progress. He was ambling along with a cigarette hanging out of his mouth. He was still at least a minute's walk away from Mike's garage. That would work, but something itched in Justio's subconscious.

Louise, Mike, Willis, and Jack walked towards the garage.

Justio cursed. He'd forgotten that they'd smell the gas. Ruefully, he rubbed the area on his face where humans would have a nose.

Louise, and the team, continued towards the garage. A few steps away, Willis turned to the others. 'Something doesn't feel right.'

Everyone stopped.

Willis took half a step towards the garage. Trying to look through the small windows inside. He took another half step forward, then turned and gestured for the others to hang back. 'Something's odd.'

Jeff came round the corner and started walking up the driveway. 'Hey, guys!'

Willis reached out to the garage door.

Justio still thought there was a chance he could get all of them. *Slow down a bit, Willis.*

But Willis turned, and shouted, 'Gas!'

Growling in frustration, Justio authorised the mini-bots within Mike's garage to self-destruct immediately.

The explosion from the garage flooded outwards sending everyone flying. Jack was the first to pick himself up. He looked around, quickly taking stock of the scene.

Mike seemed to be unscathed, but Louise was badly injured and Willis was not in sight.

Jack looked at Louise. There was a gash in her leg and what looked like arterial blood spurting out. He pulled off his jumper and put pressure on the wound, trying to staunch the flow of blood. 'Mike, help!'

Mike ran over. 'Try your luck powers!'

Jack focused. He looked down at the leg, willing the blood to stop flowing. There was no immediate change. Louise gasped in pain. He focused again. *What do I do?* Louise was going very pale. Jack focused in on the wound; he didn't want the blood coming this way. Surely, some of it could clot, or slow down. He pushed hard on the wound.

'Jack!' Mike had found Willis

Jack looked over, Mike was crouched over a body, half-concealed in burning bushes on the side of Mike's garage. *Jesus, he's been thrown 20 metres*

Mike appeared to be checking for signs of life, but shook his head.

'Louise!' The scream came from Jeff as he finished the last few metres at a flat sprint. Dropping the glass jar on the lawn. 'Louise!'

Jack looked up at Jeff. 'I'm trying to save her life. Push down on the wound.' He focused back on the wound. It seemed to have stopped pumping, but Jack couldn't tell whether that was a good or a bad thing.

There was a car horn. Mike had started his car. 'I think we need to get moving.'

Jeff jumped into the back seat, and then, with Jack's help, pulled Louise in next to him. Jack got in the front.

Jack turned. 'Willis?'

Mike shook his head. 'I found the body. I checked for a pulse… I think.'

From the back came the sound of coughing. Louise was coming round.

Jack looked in amazement. 'How are you doing?'

She patted herself all over, wincing when she touched her thigh wound. 'My leg aches like mad, but I feel okay. A bit weak, but okay.'

Jack pulled out his phone and tried to call for an ambulance. 'No signal.'

Louise said a prayer for him, with Mike giving a heart-felt. 'Amen.'

Mike drove northwards. 'You've lost a lot of blood, Louise, we need to take you to a hospital.'

Louise shook her head. 'I have to get the story out.'

Mike looked around. 'Maybe it's time to go directly to the authorities.'

'No. They'll just close everything down. Just give me tonight to write my exclusive.'

'Social networks?'

'No.'

'I'll try to find you the time,' Mike scanned the road ahead, 'but I suspect there are others who won't.'

CHAPTER 58

Bob and the others arrived at Mike's house to find the garage in flames and a crowd of people beginning to congregate. There were sounds of a fire engine in the distance, but approaching.

James, Bob and Major Sebastien all got out and investigated the smouldering ruins. Sebastien ordered a few soldiers to secure the area.

A glint in the grass drew Bob's attention. It was the glass jar with the alien bug in it. He picked it up. Peered closely, but it was dark now and he couldn't tell if the artefact was inside or not.

At the same time, Willis' body was found. He was alive, just. Bob rushed over. 'Willis, stay with us. Help is on the way.'

Willis reached out with a badly burned hand and took Bob's hand. He smiled through the pain. 'I feel cold.'

Bob felt his eyes filling up. 'Don't worry, Willis. Help is on the way. Stay with me.' He squeezed Willis's hand gently. In the distance, a siren could be heard, getting louder. Bob gave Willis a reassuring smile.

'I see you found the jam jar.' Willis nodded at Bob's other hand.

Bob could see the light fading from Willis's eyes. 'Stay with me.'

Willis took a deep breath and started to whisper prayers.

There was a shout from the army truck. 'We've got a lock on their mobile phones; they're only a few miles north of here.'

Major Sebastien looked around. 'Bob, you stay with Willis and one soldier. I will go with James in pursuit.'

Bob acknowledged with a slight wave of his free hand. 'Stay with me, Willis.'

Major Sebastien walked toward the truck. A moment later, the truck was coming towards him far more quickly than he was walking. He hit the side of the truck hard. Turning as he landed, he looked back across the garden. There was a gaping hole where Bob and Willis had been just moments before. An explosion had ripped that small part of the garden to shreds; not widespread, but utterly devastating within the blast zone.

Justio let out a breath he'd been holding in for some time. The reconnaissance drone had been knocked aside in the garage explosion and he'd missed the opportunity to take out Jack Bullage, but he managed to achieve something. *Missing mini-bot dealt with. One more antimatter missile if required.*

He sent the drone northwards. *Jack Bullage next.*

A small alert indicated Aytch had walked up the corridor. 'Justio, can we talk?'

'What's to talk about? I guarantee your safety if you go into stasis. But I have to sleep soon and I cannot leave you roaming, so if you're not in stasis within an hour I will vent you into space. I have no choice. My mission is critical.'

Aytch stood at the blast door and started randomly typing in passcodes. Justio looked on in amazement. *He's losing his mind.* 'Aytch, there is no chance of you overriding it.'

Aytch started hitting the blast door with his bare fists.

'It's no use, you're not getting back in here. I genuinely believe in the GF movement. We should not be interfering with all these other planets - like that zoo we've ended up creating on Trogia, and that's just one of many planets we've screwed up. Across the galaxy we dispense awesome technology: stasis machines, instantaneous communications, and close to light speed travel. But then we restrict their usage, stop their expansion, curb their ambitions. We're just dressing up our dolls in pretty things.'

Justio paused for a moment. 'But, really, I don't care so much for all the other planets we're spoiling... my reasons are racially selfish... our society is dying due to the breakdown of the Gadium family unit. The GF movement will usher in a retrenchment and more stable era for Gadium.'

Aytch hit the door again. 'The ends do not justify the means! What about our responsibilities of stewardship? What about my life, my wife, my parents. I'm not disappearing for five thousand years.'

'I would not ask you to give up anything I haven't already done.'

'But you were never given the choice. You are asking me to choose abandonment.'

'You have no choice either. You're staying there. You have thirty minutes to go into stasis, otherwise I'm venting your air supply.'

Aytch turned his back to the door and leant against it, slowly lowering himself to a sitting position.

Justio focused back to the action on Earth; but there was unfinished business with Aytch. He turned back to the feed of Aytch. 'You're blinded, Aytch. Blinded by the Gadium dogma. It's not about stewardship, it's about power and control. The AI laws… why are there no AIs?'

Aytch's face was impassive. He was ignoring the question, pretending not to hear; he remained sitting on the floor.

Justio continued to push. 'What did they teach you? AIs were outlawed to avoid rogue computers replicating and turning on their masters? AIs were outlawed because they were found to be able to consciously observe, to be able to control probability, like us, only faster and better?'

Aytch remained silent.

'Maybe the real reason was that our ancestors couldn't bring themselves to create sentient immortals, because they feared the inevitable despair would lead these beings into madness.'

Still nothing.

'Or maybe it's really about the Jostachian Review? The one done by your own ancestors. Once AIs are switched on, they quickly inform us that reality is based on a Parallels interpretation.'

'So what?' Aytch looked up green fire in his eyes. 'The report was suppressed to protect us. We were intellectually unequipped to come to terms with this truth while still providing meaningful stewardship across the galaxy. We chose stewardship.'

'Do you realise the Parallels interpretation is a wonderful comfort for those individuals who suffer loss? And that comfort is denied by legislation.'

'We chose stewardship, responsibility, honour. We rejected the self-serving philosophical, intellectual, self-satisfaction. We have a job.'

'But the report strongly implied the Parallels was the correct interpretation. So everything is out there, somewhere. We're denied our individuality, denied a soul, but free to choose exactly how to live our lives. No morality. No judgement.'

'The Parallels may be true, but it's not my truth.' Aytch stood. 'I prefer to suffer. And I prefer for you to suffer also, rather than deny my own uniqueness.'

Justio paused. *He's grown aware.* It was a shame, a few more decades of that journey of self-discovery and he'd come round.

Aytch walked away, talking over his shoulder. 'I want you to be happy, but not at the expense of my soul.'

'But what about the underlying technical truth? We can assimilate it and adapt.'

'Truth is over-rated. A sense of oneness is more valuable. You should know, Justio. It's always been about fighting the despair. Soul death. Animustosis.'

There was silence but, eventually, Justio spoke. 'The AI legislation may be based on some valid cause, but the impact of this ongoing stewardship on the Gadium family unit remains an anathema to me.'

Justio watched as Aytch walked back down the corridor, then turned his attention back to the screens.

He had a job to do.

In his world, GF was going to gain the ascendance.

CHAPTER 59

Jack continued to look out of the car window nervously. He hadn't had a great safety record on roads in recent times.

Mike drove them generally northwards. 'If they're tracking us it may be through our phones. We should buy a new one and dump our old ones.'

There were no dissenting voices, so as they approached another London suburban high street, Mike pulled over.

Jack jumped out of the car and was back, five minutes later, with a pay-as-you-go phone and a handful of pencils, which he passed to Louise.

She stopped writing briefly and took the pencils. 'Thanks.'

There appeared to be more colour in her face now. 'How are you feeling?'

'Strong enough to get this done. We should assume we'll keep driving, or hide somewhere, then by midnight I'll need to be back at the Record.'

Mike pulled back into the traffic while Jack ensured the new mobile phone was working. It was. 'Everyone give me your phones. Louise, do you know all your numbers?'

She nodded, and everyone passed their mobiles to Jack.

A few minutes later, Mike pulled off the main road and Jack threw the phones out of the window into some bushes.

Jeff spoke. 'Are you going to call Harry to warn him again?'

Louise shook her head. 'No point, I left a message earlier.'

Then Louise spoke to Jack. 'And we'll keep you hidden for a week. Build up public awareness of the results, and maybe the fact you're frightened of internment. Once there's enough momentum, the government won't touch you.'

Jeff looked around nervously. 'So no-one else is worried the aliens may kill us in the meantime; or they may obliterate the world if the secret gets out?'

Louise looked at her nails. Jack closed his eyes, and Mike studied the traffic. Jeff rolled his eyes. 'Just me, then. Fine.'

Louise broke the silence. 'Jeff, you're right, we should consider the risk. Top marks! But we have to make risk-based judgements.'

Mike interrupted. 'It's not science, Jeff, but ignoring the worst two per cent of reality and enjoying the other ninety-eight percent is a better way to live your life.' Mike paused for a moment to let the words sink in. 'A wise Italian man once told me life was made up of hundreds of individual moments. We need to focus on the good ones, rather than trying to control everything continuously.'

Jeff huffed in the back seat.

Mike was on a roll, and continued to talk. 'Aim for the peaks. Ignore the troughs. *Jeffrey*... In the world of calculus, it's differentiate to find the inflection points; ignore the minimum values and don't bother integrating for the area under the curve.'

Jack looked around at Louise, who shrugged and mouthed 'Nerds' back at him. They shared a chuckle.

Mike was still going. 'So... back to almost reality... in this case we very briefly acknowledge that our actions may damn mankind. Then we make a conscious decision to say *I choose not to live in a world in which it is true – I reject the possibility it could be true in my world – it cannot be true – it's not true.* And then we move on.'

Mike paused, shook his head and breathed out a heavy sigh. 'We move on like the selfish little shits we are.'

Again there was silence in the car.

Jack gave out a little chuckle. 'I'm glad you're not managing my pension fund, Mike.'

For the next 30 minutes there was silence until Mike pulled into a car park. It had a hotel attached to a large service station. Mike turned to the back seat. 'Everyone out, and in there. And if I may be so bold – get your clothes off!'

Justio followed the conversation easily for the early stages of the drive. Once the team had discarded their mobile phones it became difficult for a few minutes until the mini-bots both in the car, and on the team's clothing, found other carrier waves to get their transmissions out. He listened as they discussed their options. Now that the captured mini-bot had been destroyed, it was marginally less imperative to kill them. However, he did not change his mind – left alive, Jack's ability and his testimony would carry weight. Justio could not afford for there to be talk of aliens.

He'd also have to do some significant tidying up to cover up the antimatter explosion he'd caused.

There was now only one real loose end; the Harding team. James Chambers and Major Sebastien could be silenced with the correct political channels, the official secrets act and national security interests.

The Harding team. Mike's car was a battered old diesel, with no electronics other than the basics. Justio had no way of overriding its driving functions. He considered his other options and opened up a new communications channel.

An order went out for a Special Forces anti-terrorist group to be scrambled. The four-man team was sent out from a military base in Hertfordshire. They were given all the correct code words to signal that an emergency response was required to the certified threat of a terrorist biological attack on London. They were issued with sniper rifles and powerful incendiary grenades.

Okay, then, Hardings; time for a new game… Death by Cop.

CHAPTER 60

Justio's attention turned to the situation evolving in the Z00A military truck. The vaporisation of Willis and Bob had caused panic. James Chambers and Major Sebastien initially had a heated discussion, but Major Sebastien had made a ruling and the truck started to roll northwards. It appeared that they'd locked into the Hardings' mobile signals.

Something caught Justio's eye. His peripheral vision.

At the side of the main crew room wall, there were four video feeds showing different aspects of the Gadium ship. The video feed of the stasis room flickered and drew Justio's attention.

Lights in the area close to Aytch were extinguishing. The stasis room went dark. The QET room went dark. The main corridor went dark. Justio accessed the emergency lighting. It illuminated the blast door and a little of the surrounding corridor, but nothing more.

What is Aytch up to?

Justio kept half an eye on the video feed of the blast door, but focused on the feed from the stasis room. There seemed to be a little light emanating from some of the stasis control panels. Justio panned the camera across the stasis room.

In the low light he could see Aytch stripped naked, making deranged gesticulations. He was bashing his chest and smearing it with something. Justio turned on the sound feed; there was a deluge of enraged cries.

What?

Aytch was covered in blood. Justio looked at other feeds from the room. The door to the Jones' stasis pods were opened. *What has he done?* Suddenly, Aytch turned towards the stasis doorway and started running up the main corridor. Justio managed to get more lighting in the corridor. He watched in disbelief as Aytch started smashing at the walls with a makeshift club.

What's going on?

Aytch was 20 metres away from the blast door. Justio watched, enrapt, as Aytch ran screaming down the corridor towards it. He was now 10 metres away.

He's lost it. Does he think he can break down a door capable of stopping a plasma charge?

Justio reached over towards the air venting button. *It'll be a mercy killing.*

Aytch ran at the blast door – it opened.

Justio turned. The crew door opened. There was a blur of movement and Aytch leapt five metres straight at him. Justio raised his arms instinctively and tried to lash out with a psychic nerve whip. But Aytch swung his club faster, and it smashed into Justio's shoulder.

Justio fell back.

Another blow came, this time to his head. Everything went black.

Putting his club down carefully on the floor, Aytch walked calmly back to the doors and called out down the corridor. 'Sorry, Bill. I lied, your son is fine. I put him in the communications room.'

Bill Jones, cowering on the floor by the blast doors, shook violently, vomited and then ran back down the corridor.

Aytch turned to the screens and displayed a summary of the previous 24 hours. Then he picked up Justio and dragged him down the corridor to the stasis room. As he passed the QET Grid room he looked in. Bill and Tom Jones were hugging. 'Bill, Tom, if you want an explanation then come to the crew room in five minutes; no later, I'm going to be busy.'

He secured Justio in a stasis pod and turned it on. The ship vibrated almost imperceptibly as the Spectrawarp cones started to spin up. *Twenty minutes.*

Aytch returned to the crew room. Bill and Tom were already sitting, waiting. Aytch looked around the walls and took in the situation: Jack on the run. Bob and Willis dead. Recon-drone heading north, and a Special Forces kill team in the area.

Checking the data feeds from the Z00A military truck, Aytch could see Major Sebastien thought he had a lock on the Hardings. He also realised Major Sebastien was totally unaware of the Special Forces team. Justio must have sent them. Aytch opened up the screens to stand the Special Forces team down, but stopped. I may need a contingency.

Turning to Bill and Tom, Aytch gave the short version of what had happened over the previous few weeks. Bill nodded slowly; he'd had Gadium assimilation training and understood the basic concepts.

'Why couldn't you just use your mind-powers to stop Justio's heart?' Bill asked.

'All Gadium children are conditioned with strong pain therapy to be unable to interfere with a fellow living thing. We're wired up to methodridozone pumps and invited to attack, mentally.' Aytch shivered. Even now the pain of those injections burning through his arteries made it almost impossible for him to even think about interfering with the living tissue of another person, Gadium or alien. 'If we even try, our brain shuts down because of the conditioned response.'

Bill shuddered. 'And how did you know I would be able to override the lock on the corridor doors?'

'I didn't know for sure. But with me distracting Justio's attention, I thought you had a good chance.' Aytch paused. 'I couldn't have included you in the plan. Justio would have noticed any extended conversations. It needed to be an instantaneous distraction.'

Bill held on to Tom tightly. 'So you just let me believe Tom was about to be eaten, and then followed me?'

Aytch used a towel to start cleaning himself. 'Well, I covered myself in this red goo first and got into character. But yes – that's about it.'

'Can I speak to Mary?'

Aytch looked doubtful. 'Let's talk about Mary later. It's been fifty years, a few more hours won't hurt.' He turned to the screens. 'First, I need to avert disaster on Earth. Jack must be kept out of government hands.'

It was immediately obvious that the Hardings had all dumped their personal technology, but the mini-bots in Mike's car were still broadcasting. For a few minutes Aytch accessed mini-bot command screens and telecoms providers' systems. Eventually he managed to find Louise's new pay-as-you-go phone and put a call through.

They know so much now, I might as well play it straight.

372

Jack walked into the motel bedroom with a couple of full plastic bags. 'I managed to get these tracksuits and t-shirts from the service station.'

Mike nodded. 'Good work. Now, everyone needs to shower thoroughly and put on new clothes. We have to assume there are more drones like the one we found in the lab. Hopefully, we can get rid of some of them.'

Ten minutes later, the whole team was fully showered and clothed. Jeff stood up. 'Let's go.'

Louise was sitting on the bed still writing away. 'Okay, just a minute.'

Jeff dragged her off the bed, gently in due consideration of her thigh wound, but firmly. 'There were industrial bins out the back; I suggest we put our old clothes in those.'

The four of them walked back to the hotel lobby. Jack went ahead to have a look at the car park. It was dark and drizzly, but quiet. *Too quiet?* He peered into the shadows around the car park edge. It still seemed quiet. He signalled the all-clear to Mike.

Mike got the car and, moments later, they were back on the road, having also dumped their old belongings.

'Where to now, Mike?' Jeff asked.

Louise looked up sharply. 'Don't say anything. I know we've taken precautions, but we have to expect the worst.'

Jack murmured approval.

Mike drove on. 'I know where I'm going.'

The new phone rang. Louise answered, eyes wide, and listened for a few moments. In the car, the others tried to decode the conversation from just her few spoken words.

'Gadium?'

'Emergence?'

373

'Triple Alpha?'

Louise then listened to a longer piece. She turned to Jack. 'He wants to talk to you.' She passed the phone to Jack, but as Jack reached for it she snatched it back. 'How is Willis?'

Louise's face went rigid as she heard the answer, then she turned her attention to the team. 'He's says Willis is dead, and Bob. But he claims it wasn't him. It was a traitor on his ship.'

Louise passed the phone to Jack. As he reached out for it she snatched it back again. 'How can you prove you're not the guy who blew up Mike's garage?' Louise listened for a few moments. 'Yeah, trust and apologies don't go a whole long way with me at the moment.' Louise shook her head and passed the phone to Jack.

Jack waited for a moment to see if it would be snatched back again, but Louise had finished. He put the phone to his ear, listened for a moment and then politely declined. 'I hear what you're saying, and I do believe you are an alien. But I'm not going to put myself in your power until I get firm evidence you're genuinely going to keep me safe.'

The phone was passed back to Louise. She spoke into it. 'We need some thinking time. Call back in twenty minutes. And, yes, we know you'll be listening to every word we say in the meantime.' Louise turned to the others. 'Split up or stay together?'

Mike, Jeff and Jack confirmed they wanted to stay together.

Jack added. 'He said it was critical I didn't fall into government hands, because Earth was not ready for people like me.'

Louise nodded. 'Similar to me. He said I couldn't publish. But we've not hurt anyone, and he's killed.'

'Not him, his traitorous crew mate.'

'So *he* says.'

Mike continued to drive, taking seemingly arbitrary left and right turns. 'The killings would be a reason to do what he says, irrespective of his motivations.'

Louise reached down to her thigh and winced. Jeff put a comforting arm around her. They drove on in silence, each lost in their own thoughts.

Jack broke the silence. 'If he just wants me, maybe I should go. It would keep you guys safe.'

Louise smiled appreciatively. 'But, at Mike's, we were definitely targeted too. We have no reason to believe this will be any different. He may just lure us to another spot to take us out.'

Mike chuckled to himself. 'When two giants fight over a mouse, one of them walks away victoriously with a dead mouse.'

They drove on.

CHAPTER 61

Aytch knew he couldn't risk a Despot situation on Earth. They may come round to his way of thinking but, in the meantime, he would need to take steps to silence them. He turned to Bill. 'My number one plan was to rehouse Jack on Earth securely and in great luxury, under constant Gadium protection. But if he won't come into my custody I'm going to have to consider plan two.'

'Plan two?'

'Kill Jack and then take you back down to Earth and rehouse *you* in great luxury. There is a chance that, as a reintroduced Triple Alpha, you will suppress other Beta to Alpha transition; stop any further Emergence.'

'Are you sure that Earth's not ready for an Emergence?'

'I'm sure.'

'And you can't just capture Jack, like the way you caught me.'

'Just me, working alone, from thousands of miles away. No. Unfortunately, Bullage and his team need to be silenced.'

Bill and Tom looked at each other and started whispering.

Aytch turned back to the control panel and started initiating a whole series of activities. He sent an encrypted kill order to Justio's Special Forces team, sending them into the vicinity of Potters Bar. The order confirmed Louise and her team were terrorists with biological weapons. The Special Forces team were put on high readiness – pending voice confirmation of the actual kill order. *Kill Jack Bullage and the others; then tidy up the loose ends.*

Bill looked up. 'But Justio was trying to kill Jack, and Justio is your enemy, so …'

'I have to kill Jack; but for a different reason from Justio's, I want to avert disaster on Earth; I take my role of stewardship seriously.'

Bill grimaced.

Aytch checked the mini-bot command screens. He overrode Justio's self-destruct orders and sent new orders to most of the mini-bots. Those stationed at the team's houses all destructed, as did the ones at the university – the reachable ones.

Bill stood up. 'Aytch, don't do this. Let's try another way. Surely we can stop the newspaper easily enough.'

'We could stop that. But then there's all the social media… Twitter. We can't close it all down without causing what would look like an attack. We need to stop it at source.'

'But do they really know their lives are at stake?'

'They've made their choice.'

Turning his attention to the video feeds, Aytch studied the camera footage from the Z00A Platoon. Major Sebastien had sent two soldiers to the university. The feeds showed them making their way through the corridors. There were also pictures of Major Sebastien in the command truck closing in on the street where the Hardings and the others had dumped their mobile phones.

And I have the reconnaissance drone closing in, with one remaining antimatter missile.

Inside the Z00A military truck, Major Sebastien double-checked the phone triangulation calculations. *This is the spot.* But the street appeared to be dark and empty.

He sent a couple of soldiers out to look for the Hardings. It soon became clear that the Hardings had dumped their electronics. He had nothing.

Major Sebastien turned his attention to the video feeds from the helmets of the two soldiers he'd sent to the university. He watched them talk to the receptionist and then deploy down the corridors in full battle mode. After a little while they reached the locked door of the Pryson Room.

A few moments later, the soldiers entered the room, bringing a host of military hardware.

Major Sebastien watched the soldiers drop into combat mode as explosions rang across the laboratory. There was a tense pause, and then the reports from the university came back. The soldiers were fine; the explosions had been small.

It was frustrating, but not yet a disaster.

His primary objective was to secure any evidence of alien existence, or replication of the Project Hedgehog activities. The explosion could well have been alien forces cleaning up their own trail. For him, failure would be a public circus involving accredited alien activity without the army pulling the strings.

He stopped for a moment to consider his options; they were drying up, he was running out of manpower. The four soldiers at Mike Littlejohn's garage would secure any evidence there; but standing orders were that they could not respond to any voice- or text-based instructions. He needed to capture Louise Harding.

Major Sebastian reached a decision. He put a call through to MOD headquarters and, passing through all the layers of authentication, ordered a police response to a potential terrorist attack in North London – Mike Littlejohn's car was detailed as the suspect vehicle and its approximate location given.

Aytch watched Major Sebastien put the initial calls through to the MOD. He rerouted the call via a Gadium holding circuit, but allowed the call to pass through. *As long as he doesn't mention aliens or psychic powers.*

It suited Aytch to get some police cars on the streets, they would help send the Hardings to ground, and he could vector in the Special Forces – assuming the Hardings didn't come to their senses.

He turned to footage from the laboratory, and smiled in satisfaction at the successful self-destruction of the mini-bots.

Looking around the crew room, he noticed Justio's communications tablet lying, forgotten, on the floor. He turned to Bill and Tom. 'Close your eyes, please.' They complied. A moment later he'd cracked the security code and was browsing Justio's activities. Almost all of the information was highly encrypted with a personal one-time code; it would take time to break, if at all. *This should be a gold mine on GF activity.*

Aytch considered putting another call into Louise Harding, but stopped himself. *I'll wait for an improvement in my negotiating position.*

CHAPTER 62

In the back seat of the car, Louise continued to write up her story. Her leg was aching, but felt no worse. The wound wasn't seeping blood, but she did feel tired. Looking up, she was sure she could hear sirens faintly.

'Can anyone else hear that?'

Jack pointed into the distance in front of them. There were a lot of blue flashing lights coming from the north. 'Mike, get off the main road!'

Mike didn't slow; he sped up slightly.

Louise shouted. 'Come on, Mike.'

'Not yet, there's no escape on the left, and they're all dead ends to the west. And if I try to turn across the traffic I'll just draw attention to us.'

He continued forward, holding steady at 40mph. The police cars closed in, head on, with full sirens and flashing lights. Mike held steady. Louise held her breath. Jeff ducked.

Mike kept looking forward. 'There are five of them; they'll be on us in a few seconds.'

The police cars filed past without slowing. In their wake there was a gap in the traffic, and Mike took the opportunity to make a right turn. Louise watched the police cars disappearing into the distance. She sighed in relief, but it did not last long. Just before they were lost from view, a slight aberration triggered her instincts. *Oh, god, the one at the back is slowing.*

Louise hit her pad on the back of Mike's seat. 'Step on it, Mike. I think the last car is turning around and coming back.'

Jack shouted. 'Follow signs to Cuffley.'

Mike did as he was told and veered right at the next junction.

Louise looked back. 'I think I can see some flashing lights in the distance, but it's hard to tell. Keep going.'

They powered onwards and, on the next long straight, Louise confirmed there was a police car behind them. 'It's probably a mile away. But it's going faster than us.'

'I'm not a good fast driver.' He sped up.

Jack shouted. 'Turn right at the next junction.' Mike did. The car tyres screeched. There was a railway crossing in the distance. The barrier was raised. They were approaching it fast.

Jack scanned the crossing. 'When I say the word *Samson* everyone, including you Mike, needs to shut their eyes for a count of three seconds. I'll keep the wheel steady. Do you all understand?'

Louise squirmed in pain as she turned to look behind. 'It's getting real close.'

Mike checked his rear view mirror. 'A hundred metres, closing.' He accelerated, and the car started to judder violently.

Leaning across, Jack reached for the steering wheel. 'SAMSON!'

Everyone except Jack closed their eyes.

This was his moment, he felt calm.

He took hold of the steering wheel.

Jack focused on the signal box next to the railway crossing. *Green to Red. Green to Red. Green to Red.* He felt his perspective change subtly and…

381

Siren!

But not a police car siren. It was the barrier crossing warning. The barrier started to lower. Jack steered the car through and sat back in his seat. Within a few seconds the barrier was fully down.

'You can open your eyes.'

Louise blew out a stream of air. 'Let's get off the road.'

'There's a school about a mile up this side street on the left.'

Mike drove the car more sedately through the backstreets into the school car park. He drove into the far corner by a small generator building. 'It may hide our heat signature from any infrared air search.'

Mike turned off the engine. 'Louise, you've got an hour at the most. And they may find us during that time anyway.'

Aytch sent a few more dummy messages to the North London police dispatch centre. *Don't worry, Mike; I'll keep the police away from you.*

Then he sent messages to the Special Forces team. They were 20 minutes away.

The reconnaissance drone was about 30 minutes away.

Aytch turned back to Bill and Tom. 'This has to be done. If you don't want to watch it, then you should leave the room. The regulations are absolutely clear; I have to prevent a Despot situation. I cannot allow Jack to go into government custody.'

Bill stood up. 'But they haven't explicitly said they won't comply. Let me speak to them.'

Aytch shook his head and opened screens up to prepare the retrieval craft 'You need to be ready to go in about 20 minutes. I'll make sure your lives are very well supplied.'

'You haven't given Jack a real chance. He simply doesn't trust you. He may agree to the logic if you can get him to trust you.'

'I don't have time. Louise is fully set on a wide communication piece that will make future Emergence interventions impossible... governments creating their own Triple Alphas, leaving the majority stuck in the Beta state. I have to stop the information getting out.'

Aytch looked at the status of Major Sebastien. He was on the move again. The police had radioed through a potential sighting of the terrorists near to Northaw. Aytch was not concerned, as they had nothing of consequence; James Chambers had a zip drive with the data on it – but it could easily be fake; anyway the moment they put it into a machine he would erase it.

If the Special Forces dealt with the Harding team he may possibly use the antimatter missile to clean up Major Sebastien; Aytch wasn't decided yet.

Bill spoke again. 'One more time?'

Aytch put a call into Jack. He was straightforward. 'The police are closing in on you. Louise will never get a chance to publish, because the UK government won't allow it. They will take you, Jack.'

Jack's voice came back. 'Sorry, but we cannot trust your word. You're stalling to take a better shot at us.'

Aytch cleared the call and shrugged. He hadn't quite done his best to avoid bloodshed, but he'd given them plenty of chances. He looked at his Special Forces team, now deployed around the school car park. This would be cleaner – a training mission gone wrong.

CHAPTER 63

In the quiet, darkened school yard the Special Forces' team leader watched the car through the night scope of his automatic rifle. His team were under no illusion, this was a car full of terrorists with biological weapons. Three of his team had automatic rifles and the others had incendiary grenades, phosphorous burning – inextinguishable.

Once orders were confirmed, they would put 100 rounds into the car and burn it to a crisp.

He whispered into his headset to the other team members. 'When I give the order to start, we go and we don't stop until our gun barrels are melting.'

The team leader's helmet signalled an incoming call. 'This is the Prime Minister. Identity code Alpha Zulu India Sixer Bravo. Status please?'

The team leader scanned the car park. 'One car, four inhabitants. Please confirm kill order.'

'Stand by.'

There was a growing noise in the distance, a clatter of helicopter blades as a police helicopter flew over. The team leader looked up briefly; the helicopter had not appeared to see them.

He waited. 'Standing by.'

Aytch looked around the room. This was real. His first operational executive decision. *The rules are clear. For the greater good. I have the responsibility of stewardship.*

He took a deep breath, and held it. His hands were shaking. A grainy video feed from the inside of Mike's car showed them all sitting in quiet contemplation; all except Louise, who was scribbling furiously.

Aytch reached for his communications tablet and prepared to send the kill order.

'Ahh!' A searing pain slashed across his back. Instinctively, Aytch reached behind to rub where he had felt the pain. Another pain hit him – his nerves were on fire, his back muscles locked.

He managed to turn to face Bill. 'Is that you? What are you doing? It's necessary!'

'I'm the one doing what's necessary. We can convince them.' Bill looked at Aytch solemnly, an arm around Tom, who was stifling some sobs.

Aytch's expression turned from incredulous to resolute. He reached for his communications tablet again. Yet again, a searing pain slashed across his back.

Bill stood. 'Let me speak to them. They'll come in.'

Aytch looked pained. 'I have a responsibility. I have a job.' He advanced towards Bill. *I'm going to have to put him in a coma in an Earth hospital for 40 years.*

Bill lashed out mentally again and managed to trigger a nerve firing in Aytch's hip. Aytch's leg collapsed and he tumbled to the floor. He kept crawling towards Bill. *If I can reach him, I can disable him.*

But Bill skipped backwards, keeping out of range of Aytch's enormously muscled reptilian arms. 'Give me fifteen minutes to convince Louise and Jack to let us help them. Fifteen minutes. Then you'll have my complete cooperation, either way.' Bill paused, contemplating for a few seconds,

385

then continued. 'But if you break the fifteen minutes I'll forget your back and hip – I'll delve into your brain and fire up the whole thing.'

Aytch lay panting on the floor. The pain had been excruciating, not least because he had contemplated lashing out with a mental attack himself and his subconscious conditioning had kicked in to punish him. Aytch looked quickly at the screens showing the police activities, then nodded his assent. 'I can spare fifteen minutes.'

Bill passed Aytch his communications tablet; Aytch opened a channel to the Special Forces. 'Hold position, there is uncertainty about targets' identities. Do not act until you hear from me.'

Lying on the ground, but feeling his strength returning quickly, Aytch gave Bill a cold stare. 'Fifteen minutes.'

CHAPTER 64

Louise scribbled furiously, the scratching of her pencil across the page making the only noise in an otherwise silent car: Jack dozed, Mike watched the school entrance, and Jeff watched the skies.

Suddenly, the silence was broken. The phone rang. Jack's eyes came open immediately and he answered. After a moment he held it out to Louise. 'It's for you, says he's Bill Jones.'

Bill? Louise put the phone on speaker mode and they all huddled round it.

'Do not be alarmed. This is Bill Jones. I believe you spoke to Mary.'

Louise gasped. The others shared looks of disbelief.

'I'm safely aboard an alien spaceship with my son, Tom. We have been here for fifty years, in a state of suspended animation. The alien mission to Earth is deadly serious but not hostile, as long as they get what they want.'

Louise replied. 'What do they want?'

'They want to manage an orderly alteration of humankind. An alteration from the current one in which almost no-one can do what Jack can do, to a state where lots of people can do what Jack can. They want to do this with as few nuclear wars and mass uprisings as possible. They do this all the time on other planets and there's a set pattern of activity to make things safer for everyone. A key tenet is secrecy until the time is right, to avoid people feeling mistreated.'

There was silence. Bill continued. 'They need Jack's cooperation. He's currently the only known person on Earth with this capability.'

Jack scratched his head. 'Is there an alternative?'

'Not a nice one. Your car is currently surrounded by armed Special Forces who have been led to believe you are a bunch of terrorists. You will be shot dead if you don't agree.'

Louise recovered from her initial shock. 'How do we know you're Bill? Tell me something only you would know about Mary.'

There was a pause. 'She has a scar on her left calf where she was bitten by an Alsatian on the beach at Whitby in 1953. You can check with her, but please don't let her know I'm alive.' There was a pause. 'It's too late for that.'

'You seem to be able to control the phones; can you put me through to her?'

Pause. 'The Gadium Commander says we can patch you through.'

Mike shook his head. 'They could fake her voice.'

Louise looked around the car. No-one else offered any other advice. 'Okay… I'll ask her something about my visit to her. Of course you probably had her bugged as well.'

A few moments later the phone started ringing. It rang for quite a while. 'Hello, Mary Jones here.'

Desperately thinking fast, Louise took a breath. 'Mary, this is Louise Harding; we met the other day. I know it's late but would you mind a two-minute chat? I have one really random question about last week's meeting, and then I may have some good news.'

'Okay, dear, go ahead.'

'When I came to your house, I loved your flower arrangement on your dining room table. What flowers were they?'

Silence.

'Mary?'

She sounded guarded. 'Such a strange question. Well, unless they had moved, they were on my coffee table, not my dining table. And I'm surprised you don't know, it was just a simple Lily of the Valley display. So what's your news, dear? Surely you haven't got me out of bed to talk about flowers.'

'Silly me.' Louise nodded to the others. 'I found some Project Hedgehog boxes, I really can't tell you where, but in one was a few pages from what seemed to be a personal diary.'

'Oh.'

'The wording was smudged, but the writer seemed to be reminiscing about a dog bite his wife had got on a beach.'

'Heavens, that's me! You found Bill's diary.' Mary sounded elated. 'I was bitten in Whitby, an Alsatian. Nasty business, iodine swabs and tetanus shots.' She started to cry. 'Oh my dear, you're so clever. You will give it to me?'

'Of course.' Louise sighed, her eyes were starting to fill up. 'I will get them to you in the next few days.'

'Please come in person. You're *so* clever.'

Click.

Louise sat back. She looked to her left. Jack was sitting there, head back and eyes closed. There was a steady flow of tears tracking down his face. Louise leant over and gave him a comforting squeeze on the arm. His eyes remained closed, but he smiled.

'So, shall we go and meet the aliens?'

Jack opened his eyes and gave them a wipe with his sleeve. 'Jeff? Mike?'

They both nodded.

Aytch came on to the phone. 'Get yourselves to Newgate Golf Course, it's about four miles north of you. I will dismiss the soldiers here and slow down the UK government.'

Major Sebastien watched the road as they drove northwards. He was concerned recent radio communications were pushing the search further eastwards, but without any confirmed evidence.

James Chambers sat behind him watching the news screens. 'Police in Potters Bar had a possible sighting of Mike Littlejohn's car. They chased, but it disappeared before they could confirm its identity.'

'How did it get away? Towed into the air by a giant spaceship?'

'Apparently the police car got stopped at a railway barrier and the trail went cold.'

Major Sebastien sighed. 'Okay. No evidence. No people. Things are as low as they can go.'

The engine of the truck gave a cough and died. The driver pushed it into neutral and they freewheeled off the main road into a layby. There was a small but audible click and the lights went out; all of the electrics. Major Sebastien tried the door. It was locked.

Major Sebastien pulled out his mobile phone; no signal. 'I guess I spoke too soon.' He swore at thin air, but without much vehemence; he just felt it was expected.

Then James Chambers' mobile rang. He answered it on speaker phone. 'Hello.'

The voice was unrecognisable. 'This has been an extensive training mission. There will be no debrief. Tragically there have been casualties; there will be generous compensation. Please return to your homes. Debriefs will occur individually over the next few weeks.'

James looked quickly at Major Sebastien, then turned to the phone. 'But we need answers. We need to understand why Bob and Willis died.'

'This will be covered in the extensive debriefs.'

James' eyes went wide. 'You're them, aren't you?'

Silence.

James' hands were shaking. He spoke again. 'You're them, aren't you?'

After a few long moments the silence was broken.

'Yes, I'm them, and I regret the heavy intervention you have been subject to. However, my responsibility is to the whole planet, not just a few of the humans.'

'So you're stopping us in our discoveries.'

'Slowing them down, for now, until you're ready.'

A whine crept into James' voice. 'But we're ready now.'

'I'm sorry to say your civilisation is not ready. And, to be clear, there are no plans to interact with humans in an open bipartisan way.'

Major Sebastien interrupted. 'So what happens? You've helped Louise Harding escape. She has the experiment data. Are you going to kill her or Jack Bullage... or us?'

'Nothing, no and no... Nothing happens now, excepting that you all forget entirely about it. All of it. You never mention it. You never try to recreate it. You never induce anyone else to recreate it. You never even discuss it amongst yourselves.'

James looked across to Major Sebastien. They shared a look of resignation. Then James spoke into the phone. 'Why?'

'You'll have to be more specific. Why what?'

'Why don't you want to talk to us?'

There was a pause before Aytch replied. 'As I said, you're not ready. You're not mature enough, as a civilisation, to join the galactic society.'

James was not finished. 'How will we know when we're ready?'

'You're ready when we tell you you're ready, not before.' There was another pause. 'But we're probably talking centuries rather than years. Your planet is not sufficiently enlightened, or safe. Sorry, but this is simply the way it is... And remember, you cannot even discuss it amongst yourselves. Be aware, I will be employing blackmail to enforce this. Albeit, initially, in the spirit of cooperation, it will be towards the bribery end of blackmail.'

James shared a look with Major Sebastien.

Aytch was not finished. 'Additionally, there will be no contact, observation or any other interactions with Louise or her companions.'

There was an audible click as Aytch killed the connection.

CHAPTER 65

Jack could not believe he could feel so tired and yet still be alive. He turned and looked at Louise. 'How's the leg?'

She looked up. 'Fine, I think.'

The car started first time and Mike reversed out of the car park. Jack looked out of the window, shielding the internally reflected light to try to make out any shapes or movements in the trees. There was nothing.

Louise turned to Jack. 'Well, it's been an adventure.'

Jack took a coin out of his pocket, flipping it and catching it, not really looking at the results. He focused on his hands, and the coin. 'Thanks for trying to preserve my anonymity. And sorry for most of what I have done and been over the last few years.'

He looked up at her and for a moment they held each other's gaze. They shared a moment, nothing magical or mysterious, no harnessing of probability – just a brief moment, a few muscles subconsciously moving around their mouths and eyes. Just the subliminal signals between two members of a sociable mammalian species with a few million years of evolution under its belt. A declaration of peace.

Louise nodded, smiled and turned her head to look out of the window.

Jack coughed, and muttered under his breath. 'You could have said sorry for your over-zealous reporting. For the brick, perhaps.' Then he laughed.

Louise turned back and smiled. 'I already said sorry when you went berserk in the laboratory.'

Jack raised his eyebrows. He gazed at Louise, but there was no malice or menace. 'You could say it again.'

'Nope, I'm not that sort of girl.'

Jack raised his hands in surrender. 'Okay. Okay.' He turned to Mike. 'So, what are you going to do?'

'I suppose I'm going to try to prod this Gadium guy for a sensible discovery of some type, something in lieu of this probability effect. Maybe he can give me a few clues concerning fundamental particles, or Grand Unified Theory.'

Bill's voice came over the speaker phone. 'We're currently getting the recovery vehicle to you. The technology is pretty advanced… but it will still be about six hours. As for some scientific breakthrough, I will mention it to him. I think he was mostly expecting to bribe you with money.'

Mike chuckled. 'Legacy and history be damned. I love science, but I like the sound of what Bill just said… I'm going to study science from the presidential suite at the Las Vegas Four Seasons.'

Bill spoke again. 'All the police are stood down. I suggest you get to Newgate. We'll scramble the official records of the last few weeks. We'll also lean very heavily on those government people who do know – you won't be touched.'

Dawn was only a few hours away when Jack looked wide-eyed at a spaceship. *A spaceship!* The door opened and Bill Jones walked out. 'Come on, Jack. You've a life of luxury and adventure to attend to. You'll be rehoused in great luxury pretty much anywhere on Earth you want, but it will need to be a remote location. Tahiti?'

Jack stepped forward.

Louise watched as Jack walked away. He turned, smiled, looked her directly in eyes, waved, and mouthed *call me!*

Bill held out his hand to Louise and she reluctantly gave her notepad over to him. Bill smiled. 'Now, you others, I suggest you start using online poker sites, online casinos and online electronic lotteries. You'll be amazed at how well you'll do.'

Bill walked back into the spaceship. At the top of the ramp he turned back. 'Ah, Louise, I recognise what you've given up here. So if you get an anonymous tip-off in the next few weeks don't ignore it. Particularly if it's about a major scandal involving politicians, bribes, industrial firms domiciled in dodgy jurisdictions and national security.'

Mike called out. 'And so what's the answer to Jack's powers: particle emissions, quantum mechanics, or multiple universes?'

Bill turned and shrugged. 'I'm afraid I'm not a scientist, Mike, but from what I have gathered from the Gadium crew here, they don't know themselves. It's treated as partially mystical.'

'That's it? They don't know?'

A crackle came from the communications tablet that Bill was holding. Then a voice. 'This is Commander Aytch of the Gadium mission. I will, if you will forgive me, Mike, partially quote you. As a species we have decided unilaterally to utterly reject any explanation which includes multiple universes on moral grounds. We *choose to* live in a single reality.'

Mike's shoulders dropped and he looked at the ground. 'Bob talked about moral grounds.'

Bill interrupted. 'The Gadium call it *The Parallels*. It has been used to ease grief, but it's also been used to justify atrocities.'

There was silence as they digested the information.

Jack was ready to go but, out of kindness, decided to allow Mike one more story. 'What does it mean, Mike?'

'If you allow yourself to believe that every event spawns a new set of universes in which every possibility of that event happens, it means everything happens somewhere. So you can kill your boss and justify it by saying *he was going to be killed by me in one universe* so it may as well be mine. *Actually*, I am saving his life in another universe – because if I don't kill him here, I will kill him somewhere else.'

Jack nodded. 'Not one of your snappiest.'

Mike chuckled. 'It's a complicated subject, and a recipe for total moral breakdown.'

Bill waved for them to hurry up. 'We have to get away before we're seen.'

Another set of goodbyes followed.

Jack settled down in the spaceship, and it lifted gently into the air.

Back on Earth, Jeff was not comfortable that the conversation had resolved. 'But there are so many events every second, there'd be billions and billions of worlds in which you killed your boss, and billions and billions in which you didn't. So one more either way wouldn't make a difference.'

Mike shrugged. 'Statistically, maybe... but if I really hate my boss and I only need a little justification, then I can convince myself that technically it would make a difference: one extra death here, one less death elsewhere – one for one. We're talking a slow, slippery slope here. Firstly, a few particularly bad people use the justification, and then it becomes acceptable amongst the criminal fraternity, and then amongst other fringe cultures, and then mainstream. It may take a few generations... people love to be told they can do whatever they want.'

On Vantch, Klope sat in quiet contemplation with his Prophet. He'd been trained to ride the parallels – navigating across realities. Now he was a Paladin – a defender of The Many – and in his world he'd just returned from an attack on the Supreme Prelate of the True Faith. The Staff of Wisdom lay broken at Klope's feet, next to the Prelate's head.

The difference had simply been one of numbers. The Prophet had shared his training and led an army of 100 dedicated Paladins, whereas the Prelate had tried to defend his True Faith alone.

CHAPTER 66

Jenkins walked back into his apartment flanked by his newly appointed house-arrest guard. He had a small bag with his personal items. He'd only been in maximum security for a day. The evidence, other than Sharnia's hunch, had not been sufficient to overturn the rule of law. He was innocent until proven guilty (albeit under house arrest with a pre-trial hearing due in the next few months to establish the charge).

The guards deployed outside his building. Jenkins was glad of them; when Sharnia had heard about the Earth Mission QET grid blackout she'd had to be restrained from tearing him in half.

Inside the apartment, he took out the damaged hologram of Katrina and put it on a table. He would get it mended later. It didn't matter; Katrina was on her way home – twelve years out.

The proof would be hard for anyone to get. There was another ship a few hundred years from Earth that would vector past on its way home, but it would take years for it even to turn on its current heading. He had plenty of time to build a defence.

Jenkins looked around his apartment. He couldn't quite believe he hadn't been simply killed by Sharnia. The Deputy Chairman had acted decisively. Jenkins was grateful, although he couldn't be sure it was altruism or even GF political expedience on the Deputy's part; there would be something in the Deputy's own ambitions that he would undoubtedly be serving.

Walking over to the large windows, he looked out over the sprawling city. The next steps would need to be played out carefully. The support for the GF movement was growing; although the atrocities, if uncovered, would dampen it, they would still be in the ascendance.

Contrary to Jenkins' personal instinct, the Deputy had said the worse the atrocities the better; given many GF executives were Gadium citizens in high standing it would highlight the moral predicament Gadium was in; underline the *we're a broken society* message.

Ultimately, if they could secure a critical mass of support before any serious contrary evidence of Vantch or Earth appeared, then victory would be assured.

His pre-trial would be a cornerstone of garnering that support. He would use despair as his defence. He would claim he'd been pushed into committing these atrocities after witnessing, time and again, the devastation Gadium perpetrated in the name of continuity, stability and stewardship.

Jenkins looked across the city to the government tower holding the GEC executive.

You pushed me; you pushed me until my soul could no longer endure the torment. You have made a monster out of me… and a monster I will be.

THE END

ABOUT THE AUTHOR

I am Nick M Lloyd.

In common with many independent authors, I spent a long time
investigating all the other options before finding my dream job. Of course,
given the financial difficulties of writing for a living, it's not a job really –
more a cheap alternative to therapy…
…not that it is cheap … have you seen the cost of printer toner recently?

As of November 2014, I have one novel published (this one), and I am
working on another.

I can be found…

Twitter	@nick_m_lloyd
Facebook	nickmlloyd.writer

www.nickmlloyd.com

And, of course, if you were ever to read my book … please leave a review
with Amazon, Goodreads … etc. (reviews written on scraps of paper and
thrown onto a bonfire don't always get to me).

CPSIA information can be obtained at www.ICGtesting.com
Printed in the USA
BVOW07s0117231214

380476BV00001B/2/P

9 780993 077906